CW00816274

Albion

Albion

ANNA HOPE

FIG TREE
an imprint of
PENGUIN BOOKS

FIG TREE

UK | USA | Canada | Ireland | Australia
India | New Zealand | South Africa

Fig Tree is part of the Penguin Random House group of companies
whose addresses can be found at global.penguinrandomhouse.com

Penguin Random House UK,
One Embassy Gardens, 8 Viaduct Gardens, London SW11 7BW

penguin.co.uk

First published 2025

001

Extract on p. 96 from 'Ye Frog and Ye Crow' by Walter Crane, from
*The Baby's Opera: A Book of Old Rhymes with New Dresses and the Music by
the Earliest Masters* (London, George Routledge and Sons, Limited, 1877)

Map by Liane Payne

Set in 12/14.75 pt Dante MT Std
Typeset by Jouve (UK), Milton Keynes
Printed and bound in Great Britain by Clays Ltd, Elcograf S.p.A.

The authorized representative in the EEA is Penguin Random House Ireland,
Morrison Chambers, 32 Nassau Street, Dublin D02 YH68

A CIP catalogue record for this book is available from the British Library

HARDBACK ISBN: 978–0–241–69842–6
TRADE PAPERBACK ISBN: 978–0–241–69843–3

Penguin Random House is committed to a sustainable future
for our business, our readers and our planet. This book is made from
Forest Stewardship Council® certified paper.

There is nothing quite like the English country house anywhere else in the world.

Vita Sackville-West

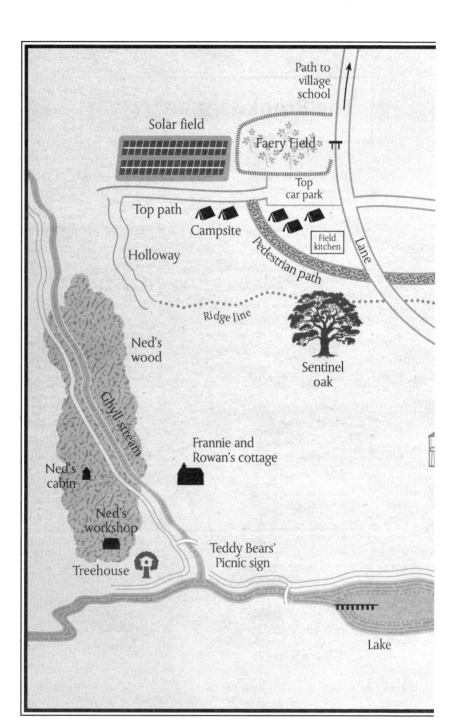

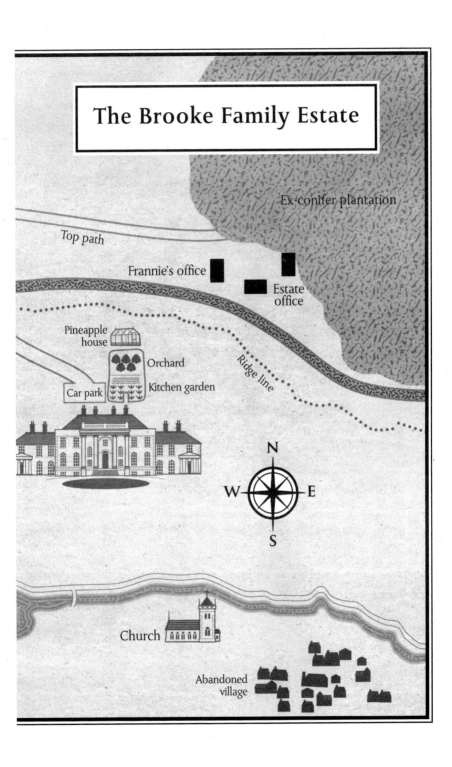

Day One

It is not yet dawn. Frannie lies in the dark of the bedroom, Rowan beside her in the bed. Something has woken her. Perhaps it was the wind changing direction, stirring the new leaves; perhaps it was Rowan, moving in her sleep. Her daughter who sleeps soundly now, breath steady and regular, arms flung out across the mattress, but who crossed the landing again last night, disturbed by a nightmare, tearful and afraid. Frannie checks the time on her phone – almost four. There will be no more sleep for her now, she is sure of that, so she slides out of bed and reaches for the pile of clothing she discarded late last night – jeans and an old hoodie.

Rowan does not stir as Frannie slips on her clothes, nor as she walks carefully across the floor, picking her way between the unpacked boxes, the suitcases, and the picture frames stacked against the wall. Then out onto the landing, closing the door gently behind her and walking downstairs, along the back corridor to the boot room, where she puts on her work jacket and beanie, finds her wellies in the darkness and pulls them on.

Outside, in the shadowed bulk of the house, it is cold, and Frannie's breath clouds before her in the still air. The sky is a navy blue, and a yellow moon hangs in the west. She takes the path through the kitchen garden, then opens the latch gate and passes out into the park. To the south, in the valley bottom, a low mist lies over the river and the lake it feeds, clinging to the tussocky grass at the water's edge. She hesitates, unsure which direction to take, then makes her way uphill, through the long grasses – their heads heavy with dew; clotted with dung and flowers and cuckoo spit, thick with thistle and dock and ragwort – her jeans damp now above the tops of her wellingtons, her breath deepening, arms swinging, heading west. She steps with care. It is May, and there are often birds nesting by the paths – woodlarks, skylarks – or there may be cows, sleeping; two females of her herd of Longhorns are close to calving, and it is not uncommon at this time of year to come across a mother and a newborn calf lying together in a patch of flattened grass.

The ground beneath her boots is hard. There was hardly any rain for the whole of April, and the earth rises and falls in deep ruts and furrows, churned by the pigs earlier in the year as they searched for plants and bugs in the rich clayey soil. For now, though, the pigs are on slightly higher ground; they often like to lie up against the trunks of the old oaks at the edge of Ned's wood. The acorns are most plentiful there in the autumn, and even now, in late spring, they can be found. She knows how they will be sleeping – humped together, in the companiable way they have, tucked into a depression in the earth.

She sends up a swift prayer for her own daughter to sleep on, undisturbed, as she climbs higher, towards the old oak that guards the ridge, the outline of its bole just coming into view above her, sagged and swagged with age. As she crests the hill, she stops to gather her breath. Below her the mist is rising, showing the curve of the river; moonlight lies silver on the water, and on the roof and chimneys of the house, which looks almost modest from here, tucked against the valley slope.

She leans her body against the trunk of the oak, feeling its gnarled bark through the fabric of her clothes. How old? Impossible to tell; the heartwood has been eaten by fungi and beetles and so there can be no counting of its rings, but it appears as an already thick-trunked tree in the portrait of her ancestor which hangs in the library – painted two hundred and forty years ago, when the house was built.

Her father used to say the tree was at least four hundred years old; that it watched over this valley when the iron forge was fed by the dammed river, by the Hammer Pond. That it was here when her ancestor built his house, erecting twenty bedrooms of Sussex sandstone, stone that was quarried from less than a mile from here, stone that had been deposited by the same river she can see below her now: millions of years of rock, laid down and down and down. That the tree saw the land pass from Brooke to Brooke, seven generations of them. And it is hers now – vertiginous thought – this house, this valley, this tree, this land; a thousand acres of it. They will lay her father in the earth in two days' time. It is still hard, somehow, to believe he is gone.

A movement, a small flicker to her right, and a herd of fallow deer emerges from behind a clump of thorn. They step lightly, almost silently. Frannie grows still, stiller, so as not to disturb them, makes her breath thin and light so it does not cloud the air, but they scent her, sense her, and look towards her as one. She knows they know her, know her shape, her intent, that their flight distance is less with her than with others, but still, after a few seconds of regarding each other in the almost-dark – deer and woman, woman and deer – the wild animals run.

Frannie watches, breath taken, and part of her is moving with them: heart flying, as they race further uphill towards the old forestry land. She longs to follow them, though knows she should turn back – she is far from her bed, and her daughter has not slept well lately; if Rowan wakes and finds herself alone, she will be distraught. But it is beautiful to be out here, to feel the cool air in her lungs – and how long has it been since she walked like this, alone? It has been hard, lately, to breathe properly. Hard to breathe deeply at all.

She turns, following the path of the deer, the house behind her, left to its slumber, as she crosses into the old conifer plantation. Here, as she moves amid a tangle of bramble and young birch, unseen animals scurry from her footsteps. The smells are different, the earth breathing out its scent of ramsons, of bluebell and leaf litter and the briny smell of the early bracken, waist-high and growing fast.

And then she pauses – because there is the song of a bird,

borne on the still air. There is no breeze, and it carries easily. At first she thinks it is a robin, or a blackbird, the first to sing every dawn, but it is still dark, and the song is stranger, more liquid than that. Her heart quickens as she listens: it is a nightingale. It must be. No other bird sings like this before the dawn. And so she moves forwards, the piercing song pulling her through the darkness towards it.

The bird is perched at the top of a blackthorn bush, just visible – a small brown shape against the sky: robin-sized. Frannie closes her eyes, breathing in, as the song carves the air into strange shapes. She knows how far the bird will have flown to sing here – thousands of miles from the west coast of Africa: the Sahara, Portugal, Spain, France; the dark water between there and here, where there is nowhere to stop and nowhere to rest, travelling at night, alone, the same route its ancestors have taken for millennia, since the ice melted and the earth grew warm. Thousands of miles to nest *here*, in her wood. She knows it will have chosen the hollow tangle of blackthorn for its safety from predators, from corvids and stoats and weasels. She knows too that she is woven with the story of this bird, for had she not cut down the conifers, had she not let the light into these acres, then these clumps of willow and thorn would not have grown. These refuges that now offer safety to a little brown bird – so endangered in this country that its local breeding sites can be counted on the fingers of her hands.

Frannie listens as it sings, and a low elation fills her as it pours its song into the sky. She does not know how long she stands for – time is suspended, and she is thinning, her senses widening. And although she knows their names, blackthorn, hawthorn, sallow, the clumps of thorn that surround her now are mythic in the moonlight, great humped creatures sleeping, ready to be roused. And she who minutes ago was a woman, a mother, a grieving daughter, is something other, something else – an animal, no more, no less.

And as the sky lightens and the sun begins to rise, the

nightingale is joined by others, by blackbird and robin, by chaffinch and chiffchaff and wren, by wood pigeon and crow and rook and jay, by all the birds, singing, sending their song into the thrumming dawn.

❧

Grace stands at the window, her hands against the heavy curtain, looking out. She finds it hard to sleep these mornings, with the dawn so early now, the light. It is this lightness that has woken her, along with the birds.

Three weeks since he died. Two days until they bury him. Four more days left in this house, and then – no more.

How many nights has she spent here? She tries to do the sums, fails, but it is thousands: she came here first almost fifty years ago, when she was twenty-one and terribly young, and now she is seventy and terribly old. Although she does not feel it, standing here in this lemon-coloured dawn.

How many mornings then, looking down at this view, at the parkland sloping to the lake, the glitter of the river that feeds it, the fresh green of the tops of the trees of Ned's wood. The squat Norman church in the valley below. Fifty years of mornings. The very first of them, the morning after Philip kissed her and claimed her, she stood at this same window. There was a mist rising from the fields below, and she could see the tents of the festival-goers, people moving around, just shapes from up here, blankets around their shoulders, as though survivors of a war, or an army waiting to go into battle. It could have been a hundred years ago, five hundred. Seven. And standing here, high up, twenty-one years old, dizzy with no sleep and the trace of Philip's lips on hers, Grace felt as though she had been plucked from the mud and the battle to the heights, to this eyrie, to this view.

What would she say to her now, if she could turn to the ghost of her twenty-one-year-old self beside her, standing here, looking out?

Run.

Turn around and run for your life.

Well. It is done. He is dead. And soon, in a very few days, she will leave this house and move across the park to Frannie's cottage: four more nights and she will be gone – to where the floorboards are wide and heated underfoot. Where the kitchen is modern and spacious and warm. The thought is so consoling she could sing. Never again will she have to brace herself against these uneven boards or suffer the indignities of the Edwardian plumbing. Never have to shiver through another winter in layers of woollens in ill-heated rooms. And never, ever will she have to endure the gaze of Philip's grandmother again.

Grace takes two steps back from the window. There she is, the woman herself, her husband on the other side of the glass: two charcoal portraits, sketched by Sargent in 1914. He in his captain's uniform, she with that beautiful early-twentieth-century hair all bundled and coiffed and tied with a band and the gaze that carries the irredeemable hauteur of the ruling class, that expression that has told Grace for the last fifty years, *I see you, I see your soft, suburban little heart. Never steely enough to deserve this view.*

What would she say, that woman in the portrait, if she were turned to face the park? Grace wishes she had lived to see its transformation – would love to have seen the look on her face: the parkland now with its rootling pigs and hardy little ponies and cows that like to shit right outside the portico; the knee-high grasses and the scruffy verges and all these rampant *weeds* left to their own devices.

Once – Grace forgets exactly when, but it was one of the many, many times when Philip was away, fucking one of his women in London – she took them down, both portraits, grandfather and grandmother, could no longer stand to be seen by them in her loneliness and misery, and stacked them in the drawing room behind the piano, their faces to the wall. Philip, on his return, and seeing their absence, became angrier than she had ever known him. Had she any idea how much they were *worth*? How much he *valued* them? They were *all he had*. She didn't say then that his actual grandmother, the real-life woman in the portrait, was still alive, in a nursing home just off the A24 – though mad now, calling for her lost husband, in his captain's uniform; smashed to pieces more than half a century before in northern France. Grace didn't say that, perhaps, if he valued her so deeply, this grandmother of his, he might visit her, take her flowers, console her in her wanderings, hold her hand? Instead she said nothing, she straightened her back, walked slowly down the shallow stairs, collected the portraits, and put them back into place. She never moved them again.

Trauma.

A word the generations below hers seem very fond of. She could speak of her own trauma. But she has kept her dignity. It is how she was raised.

And now here she is, with this lightness, this quickening, on this merry morning in May.

Is she allowed to feel merry?

Perhaps.

She lifts the latch on the window, swings it open and breathes in the morning air. She knows she must attempt to disguise it, this lightness, which is in danger of carrying her away – for it is unseemly, she knows, to feel so free on such a week as this.

She has said she will make the meal this evening, just herself and the children. Just a light supper. Something simple, served outside – the weather lately has been so unseasonably warm. So yes, salads from the hothouses, charcuterie from the estate. She will curate a lovely meal for her children before the weekend begins. Cover this feeling with busyness. Tether herself with tasks so she does not float away.

Rowan wakes, screaming.

She does not know, at first, that the scream is hers, there is only sound, and darkness. She sits up, heart racing, and she understands where she is, and where she is not; she is not at home in the cottage, nor in her bedroom. She is in the big house, where the shadows stretch into the black expanse beyond the edge of the bed. 'Mumma?' she says, reaching out, but her mother is not here.

'Mum?' she calls.

And then she sits up, and she shouts: 'Muummm!!!!'

Sounds come from the landing, the opening and closing of a door, footsteps moving closer. Light spills into the room, but it is not her mother who enters. 'What is it, Rowan?' says her grandmother. 'What on earth is wrong?'

'I had a bad dream.' She shivers. 'A nightmare. I was shouting and shouting for Mum, but she didn't come.'

'Goodness me.' Her grandmother switches on the overhead light and Rowan blinks. 'What a lot of fuss.'

Rowan's heart is banging; is she making a fuss? She didn't decide to scream – it just happened. 'Where's Mummy?' she says, her voice rising to a wail. 'Why did she leave me on my own?'

'I don't know. She's probably out, working. Now . . .' Her grandmother ties a knot in the belt of her dressing gown, then comes to sit on the edge of the bed. 'Why don't you tell me what your dream was about?'

Rowan screws up her face, remembering. 'Grandpa,' she says.

'What about him?'

'He was dead. But he was alive too. He was in his coffin, and he couldn't get out. And I was Grandpa, I was him and I was shouting. But then I was turning to liquid and there were flies in my mouth. And then I was awake and shouting too.'

'Gosh,' says Granny Grace. 'That doesn't sound very nice.'

'It wasn't.' She shakes her head. 'It really really wasn't.' She can still feel those flies – the terrible way they filled up her mouth.

'Well, it was just a dream. I'm sure your mother will come back soon. And I'm here, just down the hall, so why don't you snuggle down and try and get back to sleep?'

'No,' says Rowan, fiercely.

'Why not?'

'I'm scared.'

'Of what?'

'My dream. And the dark. And this house . . . It's spooky. I don't like it.'

'Ah well . . . I'm sure you'll *grow* to like it,' says Granny Grace. 'These things take time.'

'I'll *never* like it,' Rowan declares. 'I'll always hate it.'

'Gosh. How can you be so sure?'

'*You* don't like it,' says Rowan. 'And you've lived here for years and years.'

'Don't I? What makes you think that?'

'Because if you really liked it,' says Rowan slowly, 'then you wouldn't want *our* house.' Just then a thought comes to her, one so simple it's strange it hasn't occurred to her before. 'Can we have our house back?' she says. 'If you like this one still?'

'Ah . . .' Grace smooths out the duvet with her thin hands. 'I'm afraid not.'

'Why?'

'Oh . . . well . . . all sorts of reasons.'

'Like what?'

Her grandmother sighs, stands up and goes over to the window. 'I'm getting old. And I'll only get older. Soon I won't be able to manage all these silly stairs and all this space. Besides,' she says, opening the curtains, 'it's time for a change.'

'But –'

'Listen,' says Grace, as light floods the room. 'It's a lovely morning, I need to go out to the pineapple house and pick some salad. How about you come with me? Just pop a jersey over your 'jamas. School's not for ages yet. We can see if there are any ripe strawberries for breakfast.'

Rowan considers. She loves strawberries, especially the very early ones from the pineapple house, so small and sweet – they are almost her favourite fruit. But then she thinks of Grandpa Philip, of his body in the funeral home, how cold and dark and lonely it must be in there. And here is Granny Grace alive and warm, standing here talking about ripe strawberries in this morning light. 'Aren't you sad, Granny?' she says.

'Sad?' Grace comes back to where Rowan sits in the bed.

'About Grandpa being dead?'

'Of course I am, but he was very poorly, and in lots of pain. So, you might say, in one way, it's a relief.'

'What's a relief?'

'It's when we feel . . . that we can let something go. That it's the right thing to do.'

'But aren't you a *little* bit sad?'

'Oh I am,' Grace says. 'Very sad indeed. But one's outsides don't always look like one's insides, do they? That would be awfully messy for everyone, don't you think?'

This is exactly the sort of thought that Rowan likes thinking. The sort that can keep you company; one you can roll around in your mind for a good long while. 'It would be very . . . bloody,' she agrees, eventually.

'Yes,' says her grandmother, with a smile. 'Very bloody indeed.'

As Frannie emerges onto the park her phone buzzes. She pulls it from her pocket, reads a message from her mother.

Rowan is awake.

Fuck.

Is she okay? she types back.

She's fine. She was a little upset you weren't there. We are going to get dressed and go for a walk.

Then, the flashing ellipsis as her mother types again:

Take your time.

Frannie stares at her phone, disbelieving.

Are you sure?

Yes.

Thanks, she types. *I'll go to the office for a bit then. See you soon.*

As she takes the top track to the office buildings, she wonders how long she can get away with. How long her mother's rope is.

Her relationship with Grace has not been the easiest of late.

Her mother, who is claiming the cottage Frannie has lived in for the last decade. And when Frannie protested – suggested that the move might wait, perhaps, until her father was buried, until her daughter had got used to the idea of saying goodbye to the house she was born in, the only home she has ever known – her mother shook her head. *I have given fifty years of my life to that house. I will give it nothing more.*

So there has been nothing to do but comply, packing up the cottage in a matter of days, while overseeing the estate, planning the funeral, writing spreadsheet after spreadsheet, scrupulously cc'ing her siblings into emails and receiving only the most cursory of replies. From her brother – *Looks good Fran!* From her sister – *See you down there. We can discuss then.*

She is not a woman prone to loneliness, but lately, since her father died, she has felt its low black tug: it creeps, like the mould on the kitchen tiles. Loneliness and tiredness. An exhaustion so profound it will not let her sleep.

Frannie lets herself into her office, puts her beanie on her desk and goes into the little kitchen, switches on the kettle, swills out the coffee pot.

While the water boils, she brings out her phone, makes some brief notes.

Fallow deer

Cow calved??

Nightingale.

She feels again the low deep thrill of the encounter; there will be the official channels to inform, they'll want to come down, to verify, to listen and log – the first such bird recorded on this side of the River Medway for more than thirty years. She kicks herself for not getting out here sooner in the season – it is only she who walks those glades in the morning; the campers are all on the other side of the estate, as is Ned. The bird may well have been singing for days already – a week. And how much longer will he sing for? Three weeks? Four at the most, until he has called in his mate, who will arrive exhausted from her own epic, solitary journey; until she has found his song good and his territory sound.

Her first thought is to share this news with her father, because it means it has *worked* – the decision to clear those conifer forests eight years ago, her first great intervention in the management of the estate; still the costliest and riskiest and most brutal so far, clear-felling three hundred acres of conifers behind her family's home. The land looked like a battlefield that first winter, felled trees laid in rows like the bodies of the dead. And when the rain came and the forest floor turned to swamp and ooze, when the newly exposed earth ran down the side of the denuded valley and into the lake, filling it, clogging it, she doubted, and despaired. But her father never did. And when the snow retreated that first spring there came bracken, drinking in the sun, then birch, blackthorn, hawthorn, then oaks, their acorns planted by the jays, and the clumps of thorn billowed and blossomed and grew.

And now – this bird. This nightingale.

It worked, Pa. It worked.

She shakes freshly ground coffee into the pot, pours water, brings pot and mug back over to her desk, wakes her computer where a Word document fills the screen.

Pa – Eulogy.

The title is there but the rest is empty.

Nightingale?? she writes.

Restitution?

Return??

She flicks to her emails, sees one in her crowded inbox from Simon, sent half an hour ago.

Fran –

Sorry not to be there this morning. Have had to jump on a train to London. Sophie called and we thought it best to bring forward the meeting.
   Will fill you in later. Hope to be back before close of play today.

Anxiety blossoms in her chest but she resists the urge to call him immediately and demand he tell her what is happening.
   Okay, she types in response. *Will wait to hear.*
   Below Simon's is an email from her daughter's teacher. *Rowan yesterday* is the subject heading, sent just over an hour ago, at six a.m.

Good morning Francesca,

I just wanted to fill you in on Rowan in school yesterday. She seems a bit troubled by recent events. Particularly with regard to her grandfather's death. We all know how close she was to your father and how connected to natural processes you all are, but some of the language she has been using lately, relating to the process of human decomposition, is disturbing the other children.
   Rowan's not in any trouble. I just wanted to let you know.
   It would be great to chat this through when you have a moment. Some facts are just a little too much for the other children right now.

Beth.

Frannie plunges her coffee, pours, drinks, reads the email through again.
   It's true, Rowan has been asking a lot of questions lately, but

then their home has always been filled with charts showing how a dead oak harbours many more species than a live one, how many rare and endangered beetles and fungi need deadwood to live and thrive. And so when Rowan asked if the same was true of humans and Frannie realized she could not answer because she did not truly know, she put *human decomposition* into a search engine. She spared her daughter the images, but they learned together what happens to a body after a green burial.

Which is better? To mollify with euphemism, or to tell the truth? She takes a sip of coffee, presses Reply.

Dear Beth,

Thanks for getting in touch.

Let me be honest: I think a large part of the current suicidal trajectory of our so-called civilization is our incapacity to fully engage with the facts of death.

If Rowan is interested in the utterly natural process of decomposition and wishes to share this interest with her peers, then I fail to see where the problem lies.

I'm happy to discuss this further with you.

Yours,
Francesca Brooke

She hovers over Send, sees the face of Rowan's teacher: young and terribly earnest. Her first post – she moved out of London with her fiancé last year for a fresh start in Sussex, teaching in this tiny village school. Frannie goes back and removes the second sentence, reads it again, then deletes all but:

Thanks for getting in touch, Beth.
I'm happy to discuss this further with you,
Yours,
Francesca Brooke

Milo parks in the top car park and climbs out, lifting a slim rucksack onto his back. He'll drive down to the house later; for now, he wants the air. He picks up a woodchip-strewn path which leads along the edge of a camping field, past two shepherd's huts, several scattered yurts. You usually see fresh-faced campers around here, toing and froing with their luggage and stoves and chairs in wheelbarrows, or sitting on the bench outside the honesty shop clutching an organic ale. But today all is quiet. A small hand-painted sign hangs over the gate.

CLOSED UNTIL MONDAY

In the distance he can see the woman who runs the site, his sister's friend Wren, making her way over to the toilet block. She sees him, raises an arm in greeting. He waves back then lifts his vape from his pocket, taking a quick pull on it as he follows the path down.

All of it, he thinks, from the woodchip to the canvas yurts to the hand-painted signs, to the woman who runs it, is part of the same aesthetic beloved by his sister since her Newbury days: the antique market finds, the colourful blankets thrown across the futon beds. Fine – lovely even – if you're paying twenty-five quid a night to camp, or a couple of hundred to stay in a shepherd's hut. Fine if you're a country-starved city dweller with hippy-adjacent taste-buds; less so if you're used to a different level of luxury.

Still, people seem to love it: a yoga dome, a field kitchen with a one-dish seasonal menu. A wedding barn from which the vistas of Ashdown Forest to the south are astonishing, and which is booked up two years in advance. A honeymoon suite with a hot tub made from a whisky barrel. It seems that a rickety folksy aesthetic is what certain people want.

Not his people, it has to be said, but there you go.

A little further down the track and the house itself comes into view, glowing golden in this early-morning light. Now, this is an aesthetic he can get behind. Jesus, but it is beautiful; the two wings with their temple frontages, the columns on the Palladian central block based on those at the temple at Paestum, the whole concept inspired by the Temple of Apollo at Delos. Whatever may have occurred within its walls, the serenity and balance of that golden stone has never not made him catch his breath.

Does his sister know what exactly is hers now?

He suspects not. For as long as he can remember, Frannie has been completely uninterested in possessions of any kind, and he sees no reason that this should change, simply because she has inherited a rather large and rather magnificent one – one of the earliest and finest Greek Revival houses in the country still in private hands. On its walls, a small but significant art collection, including one of the last family portraits painted by Sir Joshua Reynolds before he grew blind and died. But his sister has little stomach for the past, does not know her Doric from her Ionic, her portico from her pilasters, and truly, he thinks, she does not care. Still, she has done well – marvellously well, in fact; credit where due and all that. She even made it onto the cover of *Country Life* last month: Philip, Frannie and Rowan, all of them posed by the sentinel oak, there amongst the snowdrops and the pigs and the thorn-scrub: Philip thin, almost drowning in his down jacket, Frannie in her customary beanie and work trousers, her sturdy boots. The shoot was accompanied by an article, an interview conducted a month before his father died, chunks of which Milo has committed to memory:

Francesca and Philip Brooke on Thinking Like an Oak

Both father and daughter in their own ways carry a very English strain of radicalism in their pasts: Philip, who came into his estate at the tragically premature age of eighteen, became notorious in the

Chelsea of the late 1960s and was the mastermind behind the now legendary free festival the Teddy Bears' Picnic, held in the grounds of his estate during the heatwave summer of 1976. A festival that brought him his beautiful wife, Grace, whom he married soon after and who has remained by his side ever since.

And Francesca, his daughter, a veteran of the road protest movement. Arrested as a teenager for trying to save the life of an oak tree in an ancient wood – what could be more truly English than that?

Here, at last, in their rewilded country estate, they come together to offer a vision of the future – the Albion Project – in harmony with the past.

He read it, then read it again. There was a lot he could have said about it, but instead he just sent his sister a message: *Congratulations Fran, what a beautiful piece.*

Down he goes now, the path steeper as it curves, until he reaches the old iron gate, where he lifts the latch and enters the orchard; he can take a shortcut through here to his sister's offices, avoiding the house – he is not quite ready for the house. Besides, he knows his best chance of catching Frannie, before her day takes her in a thousand different directions, is now.

To the left of him, inside the pineapple house, two shapes are moving behind the glass. He steps closer, peers through the foxed window, sees his mother and his niece, bent over the strawberry beds, picking fruit. They look thick as thieves. He remembers this; can, if called to, conjure a memory – memories – himself. The smell of his mother. Her closeness. The soft brush of her hair. For a moment he simply stands in the sunshine, caught by a pang so perfect, so familiar, yet so acute, so terrible in its completeness, that still, after all these years, it takes his breath away.

There she is – his mother: Eve and the serpent all at once.

He wonders if he can get past, head up the path without them seeing, but it is too late: Grace has seen him, is waving, and so he has no choice but to enter, tugging on his vape before pushing open the door, stepping inside to where the air suggests high summer, and heady musky green things push and tumble against the glass.

'Milo! Darling!' His mother moves towards him, offering her cheek to be kissed. The familiar scent: soap and Nivea. Warm skin.

'You look well, Ma,' he says. And it's true, he thinks, she does. She wears a baggy woollen jersey over a nightdress, and wellingtons. No make-up, of course. Never any make-up. Her hair worn as it always has been, parted in the centre, falling to her shoulders, light grey amongst the fair. Her beauty still startling somehow, undimmed by age or grief.

'What are you doing here so early?'

'Oh,' he says. 'I've got some stuff to discuss with Fran.'

'About your centre?'

'We're calling it a clinic now, but – yes.'

Grace regards him, her head on one side. 'You look well too,' she says. 'Although you've lost weight.'

'I've been fasting.'

'Fasting?'

'Intermittently.'

'Oh . . . ?'

'It's a thing. Helps with longevity. I don't eat until two p.m.'

'Gosh. Well, don't overdo it, will you? And don't forget we're all having supper tonight. Just the four of us. And Rowan, of course,' she says, turning to her granddaughter as Rowan approaches with her bowl. 'I'm going to cook.'

'Goodness yes,' he says. 'I wouldn't miss it. What's on the menu, boiled egg and soldiers?'

'Don't be sarcastic, Milo darling. It doesn't suit you.'

'Really? Are you sure?'

His mother shakes her head, looks down at Rowan. 'Uncle Milo thinks he's funny,' she says. 'But I think he's being rude. What do you think, Ro?'

'I like boiled egg and soldiers,' says Rowan.

'Who doesn't?' says Milo, turning to his niece.

So like his sister, this little girl: Frannie's wind-blown pollination of a child. Father never spoken of. There are few clues in her face – the Brooke genes have won out and his niece is the image of his sister; the same grey-eyed grave regard.

All this is yours, little girl. On it goes, down your line now, Frannie.

A trapdoor opens in his stomach. Is it right, he thinks, that a child whose parentage is unknown should stand to inherit over two hundred years of English history? One thousand acres of land?

'What are you picking?' he says.

'Strawberries,' says Rowan, gesturing to her bowl.

'Here.' Grace holds out her palm. 'We couldn't resist. Try.'

He pops one into his mouth. The berry tastes sharp, sour-sweet, like those boiled sweets he used to buy in paper bags from the tuck shop. 'Blimey,' he says. 'They're delicious. I can see why you've been gobbling them all up.'

'If you manage to find your sister,' his mother calls after him as he turns to leave, 'say we are on our way back to the house for breakfast.'

'Tell her we have a surprise,' says Rowan. 'Don't say about the strawberries though!'

Milo salutes, makes his way back out into the morning, the tang of the strawberry still in his mouth as he heads further up the path towards the estate offices – a suite of converted cow barns. Frannie is already at her desk, hunched over the screen. He knocks on the window, and she looks up, frowning, before beckoning him in.

'You looked deep in there,' he says.

'Just trying to get through some stuff before I get Ro ready for school.'

'I just saw her, down at the pineapple house with Grace.'

'That's good . . . Hang on, one sec, let me just send this.' Frannie turns back to the screen, typing furiously. While he waits, Milo unzips his rucksack, and slides out the folder containing the hard copy of the deck. The title page shows a sketch of a treehouse, a vine emerging, twining around a hazy human form, which leans against a railing, looking out. He is pleased with it; he gave the designer a couple of central images and she's created something great. He places the folder on the desk between them. 'You okay if I vape in here?'

'If you must,' says Frannie.

He pulls it from his pocket, walks over to the open window, where he takes a long tug, and blows the smoke outside.

'Okay.' She looks up from her computer, wheels her chair slightly away from her desk. 'I'm here. How are you doing, Milo?'

'I'm good,' he says, taking another swift drag then pocketing his vape. 'I think. Bearing up. Been working hard, which has been a distraction.'

'Yeah. Me too.'

'I figured.' He crosses back to the desk, pulls over a chair and sits opposite her. 'I've just come to nab you for a quick moment before the madness starts.'

'Before it *starts*? I mean – I'd say it started quite a while ago . . .'

'And to show you this,' he says, placing his hand on the folder.

'What's that?' Frannie eyes it with suspicion.

'It's the deck.'

'The deck for what?'

'C'mon,' he says. 'Really?'

'You'll have to help me out here . . .'

'Okay, Fran, it's the deck we've been showing to potential investors for The Clearing. I wanted you to see where our thinking's at.'

'*Our?*'

'Mine, and Luca's,' he says, lightly. 'He's flying in tomorrow.'

A flash of panic crosses her face. 'Milo, no,' she says. 'He can't. He's not invited.'

'Of course he's invited, Fran. It's Luca.'

'I assure you he's not. I have the guest list here. I sent it to you in a Google Doc along with the order of service for you to approve. I can bring it up for you if you like. It's just us, Milo, just close family. That was what Pa wanted. What he stipulated, in fact.'

'Okay, sis. Well, from what I remember, what Pa also stipulated, very clearly, on the morning after the treatment, was to have this clinic on his land. So, if Luca's investing, I think he's invited. He loved Pa, Pa loved him, and, as I just said, he's coming early to check things out . . . so . . . I can't look like I'm pissing around here, Fran. I need to have you across this before he arrives.'

She sits back in her chair, arms folded over her chest. 'You didn't tell me Luca was investing.'

'Did I need to?'

'It's a fairly big piece of information, Milo.'

'Fran,' he says, patiently, 'he thinks there's something special here. We should be biting his hand off. Have you any idea of the level of investment out there for this sector?'

'No. None.'

'It's insane. The patent scene is going *off*. It's a fucking gold rush . . .' He puts his hand on the deck, pushes it towards her. 'Don't you want to be part of the gold rush, Fran?'

'I'm not sure,' she says. 'Gold rushes didn't really have a great impact though, did they? On the indigenous population. Human or non-human.'

'Yeah,' he grins, 'but they built some good shit.'

'Like what?'

'Well, San Francisco? For a start?'

She doesn't smile.

'C'mon, Fran. It's a joke. Humour? Remember that?'

'Milo. Seriously. I don't have time.'

'For humour? Or for me?'

'I'm going to be really honest and say neither, right now.'

'Okay.' He arranges his face. 'I'm going to be very serious then. I can see you're busy, I can see you're stressed, but this is very, very important to me. Please,' he says. 'Just . . .' He pushes the deck further towards her. His sister gives an almost imperceptible sigh, looks down at the title page and reads aloud.

The Clearing

Humanity is at a bifurcation point. The Clearing is our offering.

Ensconced in fifteen acres of ancient woodland, on a rewilded family estate.

A place where Mother Nature welcomes you and invites you to heal.

A place to rise to the times we live in.

A place to reconnect.

Frannie looks up at her brother, an eyebrow raised. '*Bifurcation point? Offering?*'

'The text is a placeholder.' He waves his hand.

Frannie flicks to the second page, a photoshopped image of stage one of The Clearing: treehouses, walkways connecting them, people on the walkways, standing on the paths. 'It looks like the Teddy Bears' Picnic,' she says.

'Yeah. We gave some of the old photos to the designer. It's a major inspiration, culturally, aesthetically – why wouldn't we reference it, right?'

'I don't know, Milo. Maybe because I've spent the last decade working night and day to reverse the estate's associations with the past?'

'C'mon, Fran, it was iconic! Anyway, this is the Teddy Bear redux – there will be treehouses in the forest, each with its own turf roof, but luxury inside – no hippy crap, everything built to Passivhaus standards. The architect we're talking to just finished on this insane retreat in Costa Rica. We're thinking each client will have their own therapist, their own sitter. Their own chef. Their own masseuse. A five-to-one ratio.'

'What does that mean?'

'Staff to clients. Serious money for serious attention. But – here's the thing. You won't notice how luxe it all is because it's going to be so insanely . . . earthed. Think of it like Soho House on steroids, and then immediately erase that image from your brain because that is so much corporate horseshit compared to this.'

She flicks to the next page, one of a mocked-up treehouse interior, all muted greys and browns and greens. 'It looks a little . . . faceless. I mean, it looks like a hotel.'

'These people have to get a certain standard, or they won't pay.'

The next page is a picture of a large octagonal building, its turf roof covered in wildflowers. 'This is the healing centre' – he leans in – 'where the group ceremonies will take place.'

'The ceremonies?' She looks horrified.

'Ceremonies, treatments. We'll work on the language.'

'You make it sound like a cult.'

'It's not a cult, Fran.'

'And why is the building shaped like that?'

'Because it's built to the principles of sacred geometry.'

'Sacred geometry?'

'It's a thing.'

'In California, maybe.'

'In Sussex, actually. It means it aligns with certain principles – those that underpin the cosmos. Like the house.'

Frannie looks blank.

'The architect of the house? The references to the temple at Delos? Apollo? Seriously? You should know this, Fran. It's your house now.'

She doesn't rise to it, and he doesn't push, only stands, goes back over to the window, vaping while she flicks on, towards the final image, where the precise coordinates of the acres of The Clearing are mapped onto Google Earth.

'It'll have its own access road,' he says, 'leading out the other side of the estate. Ultra-low impact. You won't even know it's there.'

She frowns at the page. 'What about Ned?'

'Ned? I mean – we will credit him. He built the Teddy Bears' Picnic for fuck's sake. He's the originator. The OG. Exceptional. Massive. A massive part of it all.'

'No, I mean, what about his bus? It's parked right in the middle of the healing centre isn't it . . . ?' She points to the satellite image of the roof of a bus. 'If I'm reading those coordinates right.'

'For now,' he says, coming back to the desk, 'but buses have wheels. There's plenty of other places he can go.'

'That bus may have wheels, but they haven't moved for almost fifty years.'

'Okay,' he says, 'listen, that's phase two. We're thinking we can start the build here . . .' He points with the end of his vape. 'At the north-east corner of the wood, up by Faery Field.'

'And then? What happens when you want to build phase two?'

Milo frowns. 'Well . . . it's not Ned's land, is it?'

'Okay,' his sister sighs, closes the deck. 'Look, Milo, this feels . . . sticky. We need to commission a feasibility study before any of this gets going. That will take time. Perhaps for now, if you're in such a rush, you can think about situating this elsewhere.'

'What sort of elsewhere?'

'If Luca is so keen, then surely he can raise the cash for somewhere else? Ibiza? California? Why does it need to be here?'

'Fran.' He puts down his vape and takes a proper breath. 'It needs to be here because this was my home. And I want to build the brand on that sense of familial connection: organic, authentic, English. And it needs to be here too because it was here that I gave Pa the treatment. He was the seed –'

'I didn't realize he was seeding a company, Milo,' says Frannie.

'I thought he was our father, dying of cancer in his ancestral home.'

'C'mon, Fran,' he says. 'It helped him. The treatment. Didn't it?'

She gives a small non-committal sound. Could be yes, could be no. 'Look,' she says. 'It all sounds very impressive. And I can see how passionately you feel about it, but I guess I'm just struggling enough with what's on my plate right now. This sounds far more ambitious than I had imagined.'

'What are you thinking, sis?' he says. 'What's up? C'mon. Let me in.'

'Okay, Milo,' says Frannie. 'Shall I tell you what I'm thinking? I'm thinking we are two days away from our father's funeral and there's a shit ton of stuff still to get through. Not least that I haven't managed to write my eulogy yet. I'm thinking no one has offered to help with anything much at all. I'm thinking about where Simon is – I know he's got a meeting with the solicitor this morning to discuss inheritance tax, and I want to know what's being said, and why I wasn't invited. I'm thinking about the state of the house, how I haven't managed to unpack a single box or suitcase since everything was moved over from the cottage. I'm thinking about Rowan, wondering if she's okay with Mum, aware I'm going to have to leave in three minutes to run down the hill and chivvy her to get her ready for school, which she doesn't seem to be enjoying at the moment and for which I have no uniform clean. I'm thinking about whether there are enough of the only snack bars she likes, to give her one for school today, or whether I've run out because in amongst everything else I haven't done a grocery delivery because I've moved bloody house and haven't changed the address.'

'Okay, Fran. Okay.' He steps back. 'Do you need a hug?'

'No. Please. Spare me.' She begins to gather her things – car keys, phone, hat.

'Okay. How about this,' he says, coming to stand between her and the door. 'How about I send you a few pieces to read? There's a big interview Luca just did with *Forbes* – that's good for context – and a few other bits and pieces. Then I dedicate myself to helping you until the funeral, and you find time for a meeting with me and Luca while he's here.'

She sighs. 'Jesus. You're relentless. Okay. Send me the article. And when's he coming?'

'Tomorrow. Leaving Sunday.'

She shakes her head, picks up her phone, opens her diary. 'Tomorrow afternoon?'

'What time?

'Three?'

'Perfect.' He punches it into his phone, stows it in his back pocket. 'Now. Frannie. What do you need?'

'I need you to have asked me that two weeks ago. And then come along and done it.'

'I was in California two weeks ago. On a recce.'

'Of course you were.' She turns to her computer and brings up her emails. 'Okay. I just got this from the funeral home. They need the coffin by tomorrow midday. Ned doesn't know that yet, so can you go down and see him? Check on the coffin? Let him know?'

'The coffin?' he says.

'Yeah. Ned's weaving it. From willow.'

'I thought Pa wanted to go out on a pyre?'

'He did.'

'Well?'

'It was never going to happen.'

'Why not?'

'The A-road is too close.'

'Seriously?' He chuckles. 'What did he say to that?'

'*What's the point of having a thousand acres if you can't go out on a fucking pyre if you want to?*'

'Jesus,' he says, shaking his head. 'Pa.' He steps back, opens his arms wide. 'Come on, Fran, bring it in.'

She rolls her eyes. 'Okay. But none of your Californian crap.

I'd like a nice brisk English hug.' They come together, he just a little taller, tall enough to see the grey in the brown of her hair, feel the nub and nap of her ancient cashmere sweater. His sister, owner of a thousand acres. Winner of the lottery of life. Tense as fuck.

'You need to relax, Fran.'

'You need to stop telling me what I need.'

She moves to release herself, but he holds her tight, and speaks into her ear.

'Do you miss him?'

'Of course.'

'He died well, didn't he?'

'He did.'

'He wanted this, Frannie.' He pulls back, holds her at arm's length. 'You saw how much he wanted this, at the end.'

'Enough,' she says, pushing him away.

'Okay.' Milo lifts his arms to release her. 'I'm gone.'

And so he goes, dropping down towards the west side of the house, out onto the park.

It is the same route he has taken so many times before, and he is striding not running (he is in his forties after all, and wearing white trainers – sustainably sourced with Amazon rubber, but still) through grass and crusted dung. A route his feet know by heart, though so different now; the swimming pool is no more, the tennis court has been filled in.

How many times? How many trips down here to search out Ned? Sloughing off school, where he had no choice but to submit to the arcane rules for rules' sake:

No running in the halls.

No singing or whistling or running in the quad.

No long trousers until the age of thirteen.

Every exeat weekend, every first day of the holidays, after the obligatory car drive home, the stilted chat with his mother and father, he would rush upstairs to his room, where he would change from the hated uniform into jeans and a jersey before coming down here to where gentle lawlessness prevailed.

He reaches the stream, crosses it on the old wooden bridge, passing beneath the peeling painted sign that still hangs at the entrance to Ned's wood.

Teddy Bears' Picnic!

Pooh Bear with a spliff in his hand and sunglasses, Kanga bouncing, high as a kite, Tigger with eyes like the snake in *The Jungle Book*; all of it a gloriously stoned 1970s reference to the Hundred Acre Wood, which lies just a few miles from the edge of their land.

Usually, by the time you duck under the sign, you can hear the music: Hawkwind, Van Morrison, Dylan, blasting out from Ned's ancient vinyl deck. You can always guess Ned's mood by his song choice, can tell by the bend in the stream how he is feeling, but today all is quiet – only the occasional complaint of a chainsaw in the distance, the spray of birdsong, the rubber soles of his trainers scuffing the earth. Only the haze of blue-bells and the particular piercing green of the young leaves. Today the first sign of Ned is not music, but mess: the chassis of a truck propped up on bricks, a couple of uPVC windows resting against some plastic cartons, an oil drum on its side that has become an animal nesting site, though what sort of animal and how recently isn't clear. Engines, rolls of wire, a palimpsest of projects half abandoned, a thickening Hansel and Gretel trail of vehicle parts, leading to the clearing – to Ned's fire, to his home, a handsome old sixties school bus. And it is all, thinks Milo, despite its charm, despite the sun dappling the glade on this beautiful morning in late spring, you have to admit, a bit of a fucking state.

Ned is not by the fire this morning, nor sitting on the leather sofa beneath the sagging tarp. Milo climbs the steps and leans his head into the bus, but Ned is not there either, only the familiar smell of woodsmoke and sweat and old books and dope. A half-eaten pie sits on the range. The coffee pot is still warm.

Back out in the sun, Milo goes to the fire. There's a spliff balanced in the ashtray on the sofa seat. The chainsaw starts up again, deeper in the wood. Ned will be coppicing, he supposes, doing whatever it is that he does with chainsaws and trees. He should go and find him, give him Frannie's message, but there is time yet. He takes the spliff, bends on his haunches and lights it from an ember, lets smoke out in a thin slow curl, where it hangs in the air, then disperses gently in the hazy sun. The green taste of home, the same strain of pollen that Ned has been growing and dealing and sharing down here for as long as Milo can remember – this place they all gathered as kids; he and Isa and Jack, and Luca when he came to stay. Never Frannie though. Not his big sister. Not his older, moral, upright sister – even when she was a teenager, she was the same; she has never, for as long as he can remember, been one for drugs. Or losing control. Always been morally superior, or thinks she is. Ever since she was a child.

And he gets it, he does – he takes another deep, lovely drag – the way she might associate drugs with an aspect of their father, with the Teddy Bears' Picnic and the history of this land. But this is different – this is medicine, not drugs; ceremonies, not parties; healing, not hedonism. This is not an idea but a vision – one vouchsafed to him a year ago in a treatment centre in Amsterdam.

A five-day programme of psilocybin therapy. He was there because, three weeks before, after Sasha told him she was leaving, he had woken up in a toilet somewhere near Liverpool Street, a cleaner staring down at him in horror or terror or both. He was there because he had called Luca, desperate, and the next morning there was a ticket in his inbox from Luca's PA. A message from Luca: *I think you'll find that this will help.*

What he found there was nothing less than life-changing: a small group of fellow seekers. Three therapists. And five days in which the boneyard of his soul was reassembled. And in the final ceremony, when the crying and the purging and the foetal groaning were done, came the vision: The Clearing. His own treatment centre on the grounds of his family home. Helping men like himself. Boarding school survivors. Sex addicts. Drug addicts. Everything addicts. What is it Frannie is always banging on about? He pulls on the spliff. The *trophic cascade*? Sort out the top of the food chain. Bring the big predators back and the whole system realigns itself: the wolves eat the deer, the deer start behaving properly, the trees have a chance to grow. Everything benefits. The whole ecosystem starts to thrive.

Well, here's his version: you heal those at the top and the whole damn thing sorts itself out. Heal the leaders and you heal the world.

And yes, he started with his father, because where the fuck else was he going to start? Philip Ignatius Brooke. When the doctors told them the cancer had spread to his liver and gave him a month, Milo saw his lion of a father – a man who had never, as far as Milo knew, been afraid of anything in his life – was afraid to die.

And so he forwarded Philip the studies, the research papers, the astonishing results: *substantial and sustained decreases in depression and anxiety in patients with life-threatening cancer . . . increases in quality of life, life meaning and optimism, and decreases in death anxiety.* And eventually his father agreed. So he shooed his mother and sisters and the nurses away for the day and gave him the treatment: thirty milligrams of psilocybin tincture, sourced from a contact in the States. He gave his father the headphones, placed the eye mask on him, cued up the playlist, and sat beside him holding his thin hand for eight hours. And when Philip emerged, into the fading afternoon light of that winter day, it was like he was swimming up from the bottom of a deep beautiful sea, like he was free – reborn, just in time to die.

Milo, *Milomilomilo*, he said. It's all so beautiful. So magnificent and so strange.

He had never felt as close to his father as in that moment. And later that evening, their hands still clasped in each other's, Milo told his father his vision: painted it for him in the air of that winter afternoon.

Of course, his father said to him, gripping his hand: Of course you shall have it, darling Milo. I'll tell Francesca – it's yours.

Three weeks later, and he was gone.

Milo takes one last drag, blows the smoke out to the lattice of leaves, to the high blue sky over his head.

Jack moves through the water. He is wearing a T-shirt, jeans, waders that reach to his thighs. He steps slowly, carefully, the river moving around his calves. He carries an airgun. On his back a haversack, inside it a bag with a mixture of clay and sand, oasis foam, rope.

The new leaves are so green, the water reflecting on their undersides, filtering the morning sun above, that it is as though he is swimming in leaf-light. The river is low though – there has been hardly any rain since the old man died.

Jack is down here because the water voles are disappearing, something is killing them, mink are suspected. It is late in the season, though, for mink tracking and trapping; the females will have mated, be hungry for protein, for their kits.

He comes to the first of the small wooden rafts, floating where he moored it last week. The green foam block has been damaged; something has gnawed at it. He lifts it from the raft, sees it is peppered with animal prints. They could be mink, but there are so many other prints there it's hard to be sure.

He takes out a new foam block from his bag and bends, soaking it in the cool river water, watching it grow darker, letting it bubble, sit, soak.

His mother used to do this, when she did the flowers for the weddings and the funerals at the church, these same green blocks of foam. She would have the flowers laid out on the kitchen counter while she sank the foam into a sinkful of water. He liked to help her when he was small, handing her the stems as she named them:

Anemone,

    carnation,

        lily,

            delphinium,

                rose.

He loved being close to her in the warm kitchen of their house, the nicotine crackle of her voice, her fingernails painted pearly beige, the sweet cheap elegance of her rings. The smell of her: tobacco and hairspray and powdery make-up. Short hair, dyed blonde, wispy. Teeth that were a bit of a state.

It was a wet day when they buried his mother – November, and the Wealden mud was claggy. What name would she have given it? *Clodgy.* She knew all the old Sussex names for things; *bishy barnabee* for ladybird, *dumbledore* for bumblebee. Her people had lived here as far back as the Domesday Book, she used to say. They lived in the village at the bottom of the hill, the one they moved when they enclosed the park, only the church and ancient graves left now; thirty generations of Sussex peasants with thirty names for mud: clodgy, gawm, slab, pug, stodge. Some people inherit a thousand acres; he inherited thirty names for mud.

He kneels to the river, dips his cupped palm, pours water into a bowl, where he kneads sand and clay into a paste like butter icing, then lifts the block from the water, takes the mixture, smears it on top with a wetted spatula and smooths it off again.

A funny thing, grief. He took a bunch of early anemones up to her grave for her birthday last week. Just from Tesco, but he knows she would have been pleased.

He has no grief for Philip Brooke though. Something crooked in him. Something not straightened by the years of supposed atonement. If you hit him with a tuning fork, you would not like the sound.

Still, when Frannie asked him to help carry Philip's coffin, he agreed.

It's just going to be us – the funeral, she said. Just family, so it would be wonderful to have close people carrying the coffin too. It'll be you, Ned, Milo and Hari.

Hari? Isa's husband? Well, that'll be interesting, he thought.

Sure, he said. Of course.

He puts the block back on the raft and pushes it into the vegetation at the water's edge, startling a moorhen and her chicks from their nest, then tethers it with a rope, dressing it with twigs and leaves. This is where the mink will hunt, the females likely pregnant and ravenous for crayfish, but small enough to enter the burrows of the water voles in the banks. There are other rafts further down the river, and several of these have already been set with traps. If they're hunting down here, they may well already have been caught.

He wades on, almost silent, further downriver, finding his feet on the smooth rocks, careful not to disturb the thick clots of frogspawn clustered by the banks, treading through dappled light. The sun is on his shoulders, on his back. Clear water and sky now. Sun on the shallows, on the minnows darting from his tread.

As children they played in the river, but as they grew it became clogged and silted, shady with alder and willow, the sun only rarely shining on the water. When they were kids you could jump easily from bank to bank. Now, through Frannie's interventions, after ten years of widening, of allowing a stream that had been dammed for an old iron pond and was stagnant with agricultural run-off to meander in its ancient natural courses, sunlight and open water have come back. There are lampreys. Dabchicks. The crackle of damselfly wings.

You have to give Frannie her due. It's worked – her vision. And he has served it dutifully for the last ten years, staying on when his father was gone, overseeing the transition, learning, offering his thoughts, weaving himself in. He knows he is indispensable to her now.

He knows too that Frannie thinks this is it, that she's at the head of the curve, the breaking wave, this long slow wave of goodness rolling in. Beavers are next; whether or not they get the government green light, he knows she's going to go for it. She has been talking to someone down in Devon who's going to bring them up, release them under cover of darkness, let them do their thing. And he knows she wants to see her project join with others, they used to talk about it all the time, Frannie and her dad – a nature corridor all the way to the sea, like they can wash away all the pollution and the microplastics, bring the carbon back out of the air, make a future fit to live in. But he thinks she's wrong. It's too late. They've fucked it, humans. Everything is haywire. Everything in low-level havoc. You can feel it in the lack of rain; hardly anything for the whole of April. You can see it in the depth of this water. You can sense it amongst his mates in the pub, full of talk about Great Resets and Great Replacements, about New World Orders and vaccines and microchips. He's got mates that are preppers, that have garages full of tins and freezers full of roadkill and sacks full of pasta and cans of beans buried in the woods. People that read too much stuff online usually, but you don't need algorithms and YouTube wormholes to see that there's shit coming down the pike. This part of England would be carnage: a corridor between London and the sea. He's got mates living on the coast – they already have boatloads of refugees landing on the beach in summertime.

There's room for everyone on this ark.

That's what Philip said in that first meeting, when he and Frannie told them all what they had planned for the estate: *one thousand acres given over to ecosystem restoration.*

This ark. Like he was fucking Noah suddenly. But there's never room for everybody on an ark – you have to make choices. That's the point.

Anyway, he's leaving. Leaving all this; leaving this river. This estate that he has lived on all his life, where he was born and grew and worked and raised his two children and buried two parents; leaving this county, leaving this country. He is moving to Scotland. The Highlands. A new job. A new start. Hundreds of miles away from here. Charlie and the kids have left – she met someone online, moved to the West Country, posts pictures of her dog and the beaches and the kids in wetsuits. And he misses them, his kids, but they seem happy. Which is good. They deserve to be happy, and so does she.

He'll be overseeing a team. Have a cottage. A proper salary. This guy who he's going to work for in Scotland owns a hundred thousand acres, all ringed around with fences. He met him last month, one of those workshop days when Frannie had a party of people visiting, touring the estate. He was there listening intently to a talk Jack was giving, 'Transitioning from traditional game-keeping to land stewardship'. He hadn't come up with the title, that was pure Frannie, but afterwards the guy peeled away, sought Jack out over coffee. I can see what an asset you are, he said. You're exactly the sort of man I need. I'll pay you triple whatever you're on.

Seemed like a bit of a cunt. But a rich cunt, a billionaire cunt. Jack looked him up online after he made him the offer (sixty grand a year, pension, cottage, Land Rover). Head of a tech firm in Canada, loaded beyond the realms of sense.

A one-hundred-thousand-acres-of-Scottish-woodland-level cunt then: the sort who's going to build his bunker up there in the

Highlands and surround himself with electric fences and a version of life at the beginning of the last ice age: lynx, wolves, beavers, bears.

And who will be the unwanted visitors when the shit starts hitting the fan? The people trying to make it through the fences? What happens to them? Will he be patrolling with a different sort of firearm then?

Too much.

Too much of a thought for a beautiful morning like this.

There's no point in trying to get your head around it – if this is the way the wind is blowing, he is going to let it blow him as far away as possible from here, from trouble and pain and divorce and his past. From all of it. Onto high land. He has spent the last two weeks chucking stuff out and putting the rest in boxes, driving it to the storage unit on the edge of the nearest town. He just needs to tell Frannie. He's been putting it off for weeks.

He looks up, realizes where he is – by the big beech, its smooth trunk leaping out of the river like the prow of a ship, the boards of the old treehouse wrapped around it, the water reflected in flickering arcs on its trunk.

Who knows how many times he will see it again?

He clambers up the steep bank and climbs the spiral staircase leading to the den. It is a wildlife hide now, but when they were young it was just an old, abandoned treehouse, built by Ned for that festival they had, the Teddy Bears' Picnic. His mum and dad didn't go. They spoke about it with derision, disapproval; like all the locals, they looked down on these scruffy entitled hippies, incomers. He would have liked to have seen it though – there were fifty thousand people here in the end. They took all the fences down. The villagers still talk about it, say it was anarchy, shit in the hedgerows and piss in the streams, but that's not how Ned tells it. And Jack prefers to get his stories from the horse's mouth, from Ned: treehouse-builder, dealer, magician.

He sits back against the trunk of the beech, puts his hands down on the boards. They are warm to the touch.

Growing up they all knew this treehouse was a relic, that it belonged to the past, but they claimed it as their own, had their rope swing here. Other parts of the river, further down, the water used to be smelly, the ditches full of run-off from the fields, stagnant and low and covered in algal bloom in the summer months, but here was always deep and clean enough. They would all be down here in the summer, him and Milo and Isa; shorts and trainers and messy T-shirts, calves and wrists and ankles bramble-torn. Then, when they got older, they would come down to Ned's fire, raid his flight cases of records, listen to his tales. He'd play them music on vinyl and skin up and tell stories about the bands, educating them on the finer points of Hawkwind and Gong's back catalogues. Late-night extended monologues on the genius of Patti Smith. Even Milo didn't seem like such a dick when he was down at Ned's.

But it was always Isa, it seemed to Jack, of all of them, who loved this place most.

Her face on these boards beneath him, the first time they had sex. She was sixteen. He had a girlfriend already though. Hadn't told her. She didn't speak to him for two years after she found out. Stupid – the stuff you do when you're seventeen. He lost his best friend – she disappeared. Went off somewhere to school. It felt as though a light had gone out in his life and he knew he was to blame.

He remembers the first time he saw her again. It was early summer. He saw her in the village, walking past the pub, and stopped – couldn't believe it was her, like she had gone through a portal and come back beautiful. She ignored him. Just walked right past like she hadn't seen him.

He burned for her after that. Couldn't get her out of his head.

Then one day his mum gave him a message to deliver, a note for Grace.

He went up to the house to deliver it but Grace wasn't there. Isa was though, lying on the bench, smoking a cigarette. She had a book beside her, but she wasn't reading. She was wearing a hoodie and a pair of tracksuit bottoms despite the warmth of the day.

She sat up and looked at him. And he could feel his whole being tightening. As though she was a threat. And his throat was tight too when he spoke. Long time, he said.

Yeah.

I've got a message. For your mum.

The sun was bright, like a spotlight, like he was on stage, and she was watching in the cool dark. And she had all the power and all the shade. Sweat under his arms. On his upper lip. He shaded his eyes. What are you up to? he said.

Nothing much. You?

He shrugged. You want to come for a smoke?

And that was it. They set up camp down here, that summer, brought down mattresses and blankets, ate food from tins. It was hot and dry and there was no one to find them and it was like it was just theirs – the river, the wood.

The way she had of pulling her hair off her face, tying it high on her head, wrists flicking in impatience like it was annoying her. Dungarees. Trainers. Grey Adidas Gazelles – always. That blue trackie top she didn't take off that summer. Unless he took it off her.

They would go to parties sometimes, sound systems from Brighton and Worthing: take pills and stay up dancing, lose each other and find each other and in the mornings come back here to their tree and just lie, letting the green light ripple over their skin.

The things he remembers from that summer. Her intensity. Her strength. Her slightness. Her skin beneath his hands. The current she carried in her. How fucking her was like fighting her, until it wasn't anymore, until it resolved into something so deep and sweet and real that it, too, was almost too much.

40

Her anger: sometimes it felt like she was angry with everyone and everything. But most of all with her father – for leaving them all, disappearing to America for all that time, for the way he had always treated her mother; angry with her mother for letting him treat her like that, angry with Frannie for leaving her here to deal with all the weird dark shit alone.

Was he angry too then? Probably. Though he had less to be angry about back then; life was alright. His dad had the run of the place – had had it for thirty years – and he had respect from everyone. He taught Jack everything: how to act as beater for the pheasant shoot, then how to shoot himself, first with an airgun and then with a firearm. How to make a knife handle from a deer antler, how to butcher and skin and hang a deer.

But that hot dry summer when they came together, Isa's anger was an incendiary device that burned through everything, scorching the earth all around. Like the fires they would start up on the forest, his dad and his mates sometimes, with rags and tin cans of kerosene. Fists of deer grass, broom grass and sedge. Fires that laid waste to the bracken and gorse, and looked like the end of the world; leaving the charred skeletons of foxes, but then you'd go up there next spring and there'd be all sorts of new life, all sorts of flowers in the fires' wake. That was what she gave him. More life. Life in colours that he has not experienced since.

She went to university, and they tried to have an ordinary relationship, but if he ever tried to be with her away from the estate it didn't work, there were different eyes on them, telling them they didn't belong together, didn't fit.

So he got back with Charlie and Charlie was totally different. Ready for kids even then. She was pregnant at twenty and he was a dad at twenty-one. He started work at the estate alongside his dad. His mum was alive still, and she was brilliant with the kids. And that was life and it was good.

When Philip came back from America after all those years and started living at the estate again, he thought Isa would come down, but she stayed away. Or if she visited, it was fleeting, and she definitely didn't visit him. He heard about her; that she had become a teacher, was working in a school in South London, that she got married too – a teacher, like her. Had kids.

And then there was that meeting – the day that everything changed. He was there in the library, Frannie and Philip behind the big desk, the portrait on the wall behind them: Philip who had lived away for years, who had no clue of how this place functioned or how it was run; Frannie who had stayed here for all of six months, both of them standing there like they knew what the hell they were talking about, changing the way the estate had been run for more than two hundred years – when clearly neither of them had a clue.

Rewilding, they said.

Re-fucking-what? his dad said.

Jack was there in the bar of the Green Man that night, many of those who had been up at the house now crammed in for an impromptu meeting, alongside local farmers, landowners. There were all sorts of rumours flying about: they were going to bring wolves down here. Beavers. Lynx. The sheep would be decimated. The level of vitriol was insane. Led by his dad, they all decided en masse to hand in their notice, but if they were hoping to force a change of heart, it didn't work – the next day his father was given three months to vacate the gamekeeper's cottage he had lived in for all of Jack's life.

He remembered his mum, bereft, pleading with his dad to change his mind, and when he refused, packing everything away, in this terrible silence. They moved into a static caravan on one of the tenant farmers' fields, and watched while their cottage was done up and damp-proofed and rented out as a holiday let for two grand a week. His dad had a stroke not long after. His mum nursed him, then she got ill herself and died.

Isa was the only one of the family who came to his mum's funeral. Not even Grace. He only saw she was there when he pushed his dad out of the church – sat on her own in a pew at the back.

She came to find him that night. After the wine and the sandwiches in the pub. After Charlie had taken the kids home, Isa found him at Ned's fire. He looked up and she was there, standing a little way off, face pale in the firelight.

It's not right, she said. What Frannie did. Kicking your family out of your house. I don't condone it. I just need you to know that.

He stared up at her. He was a little drunk. Stoned. The pain in his chest was his grief and his heart and all that he could think was that she was here – that she was standing before him like this.

He nodded. He couldn't move. Then she came closer to him, closer to the fire, crouched a little way in front of him, staring at the flames. After a while of sitting like this, he reached out and put his hand on the nape of her neck. Held it there. He closed his eyes, felt the old current pass into him, still there, as strong as ever. Then she bent her head, twisted it, and turned back so he could see what was in her eyes.

They went without speaking to a place they could find blindfolded and they lay on these boards together, and when he came he cried, broke like a dam, and she held him and it was morning at some point, and cold, and she was there still, and he thought he had never been so grateful for anything in his life as her, still there, when he woke that morning. And he knew then that he loved her – that this feeling he had been holding for her all of his adult life was love. And it wasn't just some small thing that had happened when they were kids; it wasn't something he could leave in the past; it was alive, and it was real. And then she slid from him and was gone, and he was alone and that was three years ago now.

He gets to his feet, shoulders his bag and gun, and heads back down the steps, into the water. Mud-smoke drifts away from the soles of his waders – the water clouds briefly, then comes clear

43

again. A kingfisher dives ahead of him, slicing his field of vision with electric blue.

It's not like he's been thinking of her constantly for three years.

After Charlie left, he got out there, on the apps. Mostly he's not active, but when he is, he could be with a different woman every day. Sometimes he is. Sometimes another sort of current overtakes him; one, then another, then another. But after the first encounter or two it gets too much. He can feel the longing in them, all of them, in their own ways; everyone longing for something all the time. All these people wandering around with holes inside them, just longing for them to be filled by someone else. Something else. It didn't use to feel like that – like there was so much longing in the world.

So, no, it's not like he's been thinking of her for three years – but he's thinking of her now. Because he knows she will be here tonight.

And he's thinking – did Isa ever tell her husband?

He has only ever met him once, years ago, now. Bumped into him with Isa and their kids in the park in the village. Nice jumper. Sturdy shoes. Thin-framed glasses. That sort of guy.

This is Jack, Isa said to her husband. He works for my sister.

This is Hari, she said to Jack. He's my husband.

And Hari smiled and shook his hand in an absent sort of way, and all Jack could see was Isa that night in the wood. Hey, said Hari. Nice to meet you.

You too, said Jack.

I love your wife, he could have said.

We fucked. Three years ago.

And many, many times before that.

But the last time was three years ago. When you were already married. When you already had your kids.

We were in love with each other.

Or, I was in love with her.

Maybe I still am.

Does she scramble your brain the way she scrambles mine?

Hari looked kind. Like a teacher – like her. Like they belonged together in the world outside of the wood.

And just as he is thinking of her, he's also thinking how weak he is, how sentimental. Because it is in the past. And just because she came down here for a mercy fuck three years ago doesn't mean anything at all.

And just because he's going to have to carry this coffin with Hari doesn't mean it will be strange, or weird, or awkward. He can do it. It's only a day, an afternoon, a funeral – and then he will be gone, for high dry land. For a new chapter of his life.

The next raft has a trap on it, and he can see this one has something in it. It is a mink, brown nose pressed right up against the mesh. Big. Could be a male, but to Jack's eye she looks female – her sides swollen.

He doesn't like killing females, but he would rather kill a pregnant female than leave her pups to starve. He brings out his pellets and trap combs – two plywood combs Ned made for him. Leaves the mink in place for now. He checks the barrel of his gun is clear then loads, bends. He guides the mink to the top of the trap with the combs until its head is just below the mesh, then clamps it into position. The mink starts to scream. They know what's coming for them, that's the thing. And everything wants to live. You'd be surprised how much.

'Sorry,' he says.

He holds the muzzle a few centimetres from the head, away from the centre line of the skull, and releases the trigger. The mink convulses, kicks and then is still. He plucks a blade of grass from the bank and touches one of its black eyes, but there is no blink reflex – the animal is dead. He unloads his airgun, makes it safe, pulls on gloves and puts the mink into the sack.

❧

45

Frannie looks up and sees the birds – rooks and pigeons rising and falling in the still air – down by the water. What has disturbed them? A shot, most likely. Jack is down there, she knows, and if he is shooting that means mink, and mink mean a shitshow she doesn't have time for right now.

Outside the window the day is advancing, still and warm. Two brimstone butterflies wheel up in jerky flight – batting their acid-bright wings against the blue air.

She blinks back to her screen.

Luca Gugioni: The Wealth Whisperer on Keeping it Simple

As he launches Clarity – his new VC fund for psychedelic start-ups – the notoriously private fund manager lets us into his converted Ibizan finca.

'Profit for profit's sake is over,' says Gugioni. 'The future is a beautiful place.'

The article is accompanied by a series of photographs, the first of which is of Luca, taken from the middle distance, sitting on a low wall beside the gnarled trunk of an ancient fig tree.

After public school and university in England, Gugioni, son of an Italian father and an English mother, joined Primobanca, working on the investment side. He transitioned quickly to Horizon Capital, where he cut his teeth as an analyst investing across credit, private equity and real estate, before setting up his own fund in the late noughties, where he swiftly built his reputation on his capacity to scent and invest in the next big thing.

He has always been a contrarian, the kind who nets incredible returns for a devoted clan of Ultra High Net Worth Limited Partners. He's a man who lives in the future, and when he sends us the weather report from there, we believe him. But the new psychedelic revolution, he tells us – poolside in Ibiza – is going to be bigger than anything we have seen before.

'We know that VCs like to lend to the disruptors, but the psychedelic market is something else. Clearly, it's going to transform conventional medicine: the trials that are happening right now are showing incredible results for treatment-resistant depression, pain, and mental health. But there's this whole other visionary dimension to the psychedelic experience: these compounds have the potential to guide us to make the step change we need as a species. I believe we will look back on these decades, these multiple crises that engulf us, from a wiser, saner perspective in the years to come.'

Over a simple lunch on the terrace, soundtracked by goat-bells in the distance, Gugioni speaks frankly about his own experience of psychedelic transformation. 'After the first ceremony, I took a good hard look in the mirror,' he says. 'I started taking measures to wind down my previous fund and bought this place.'

'This place', as he refers to it with characteristic understatement, is an exquisite finca in the Ibizan hills.

Frannie flicks through the photo gallery: Luca on the stone terrace, Luca by the saltwater pool, the meditation room, the salon with its mid-century design, the firepit, all of it speaking of that stratum of frictionless wealth where the world is smoothed of its edges like a pebble worn and warmed by sun and sand.

Gugioni is putting his money where his mouth is, having made over twenty deals in the ten months since his fund was launched last year. He's not giving us exact details but he's happy to share that it's the largest fund yet raised for psychedelic investment.

'Clarity is all about finding and funding the best and most exciting start-ups in this sector,' he says. 'These compounds are only going to continue to move into the mainstream.'

He points to the fact that more and more companies are going public on Nasdaq, and that collectively they are worth more than $5 billion.

As a closing question, we ask him for his vision statement. He pauses, smiles,

'Nothing less than a revolution of the soul. The optimizing of the human experience,' he says. 'We are so much more beautiful than we can imagine.'

The last photo is of Luca, staring down the lens of the camera, haloed in the apricot light of an Ibizan afternoon. Frannie sits back, minimizes the window on the laptop.

Fucking Luca.

She can feel it beginning already, the way that his presence – even the threat of his presence – has always had the ability to destabilize her own. The particular brand of disquiet that her brother's oldest friend has evoked in her ever since she first met him – how long ago? Since he first came home for the holidays with Milo. She was eighteen, so he would have been no more than fifteen, but she remembers feeling it even then; the way he had of looking, the way you knew he was rating you. Fuckable. Not fuckable. The way she knew she always fell somewhere just on the wrong side of the line. The way she hated that she cared.

She lifts her phone, checks for messages from Isa. She wants her sister here. Isa has always been able to puncture Luca's power – take the piss.

Hey Isa, she types. *Do you have an ETA yet? Really looking forward to seeing you.*

The ellipsis flashes and she stares at the screen, waiting for her sister's reply.

. . .

Then the three dots disappear.

Isa? she writes. *You there?*

From outside comes the sound of tyres on gravel; she looks up, sees Simon's car. He climbs out, wearing a wool coat and suit in place of his usual gilet and cords.

'You look smart,' she says accusingly, as he comes into the office. 'I always worry when I see you in that suit.'

He shoots her a small smile, shrugging off his coat, hanging it on the hook by the door. 'How's everything here?'

'Fine. I mean. No. Not fine. Stressful.' She drums her fingers on the desk. 'Except, I almost forgot – I heard a nightingale up in the glades this morning.'

'That's fantastic, Fran! Is there anyone we need to inform?'

'Just the ornithology trust for now.'

'I'll do that. Let's hope he finds a mate – establishes a breeding site.'

How grateful she is for him, she thinks, as he moves to take his seat at the desk before her. His geniality. His enthusiasm. She feels the taut edges of her responsibility slacken a tiny amount, and then remembers where he has been. 'How was London then?'

'Interesting,' he says.

'That sounds ominous.'

'Look, Fran.' His eyes find hers. 'I know how much you've got going on here. I'm wondering if we should keep this conversation till after the funeral.'

'Come on, Simon. Why did Sophie call you in? There must be some news.'

'Okay,' he sighs. 'Well, first things first. The survey you requested on the house has come through. It's not pretty reading, I'm afraid. We knew it wouldn't be great, but it's worse than we thought.'

'In what respect?'

'You name it. Philip essentially left the house to its own devices for fifty years. It has suffered greatly as a result. And then, inheritance tax – we've had the valuation back.'

She nods, jaw clenched. 'Go on.'

'The house is valued at around twenty million. The Reynolds and the Sargent portraits of your great-grandparents have

49

come in rather higher than we expected too. All in all it leaves an inheritance tax bill of around twelve million. Clearly that's an astronomical amount and not one that can easily be found.'

'You said there would be a way around it . . .'

Simon's face contracts. 'I'm sorry, Fran, I'm not sure I did. I believe I said I *hoped* very much there would be. But that hope, I'm afraid, is far slimmer than I anticipated. Here.' Simon reaches into his briefcase and pulls out a set of notes. 'These are the qualifying conditions for heritage property status. The assets must be buildings, estates or parklands of outstanding historical or architectural interest,' he reads, 'land of outstanding natural beauty or scientific interest, including special areas for the conservation of wildlife, plants and trees, and objects with national scientific, historic or artistic interest.'

'Well,' she says, relief surging in her, 'that sounds good, no? It looks as though we may qualify on all counts.'

'Indeed.' He nods. 'The fact that the house was designed by such a significant architect, the art collection. And above all, of course, what you've done here in the last ten years; it all adds up to a compelling case.'

'What will it mean? If we are granted status?'

'Tax exemption. The twelve million waived. Although you must agree to abide by what are called "undertakings" to preserve the property and allow reasonable access to it.'

'And what are the terms?'

'All very civilized. Under the radar. Not at all like the Trust. You won't have people tramping through here with screaming kids looking for the loos. Members of the public need to make an appointment to view the house or the art.'

'I can tell there's a but coming, Simon.'

'It's not a but, it's an and . . .'

'Whatever it is, just give it to me.'

'Well . . . they were kind enough to say they will make it a priority, but as the valuation is so complex, it's going to be many months before we have any clear picture. And just to manage expectations – there is only one other house in Sussex which has qualified in the last twenty years.'

'I see. Shit.' She feels immediately nauseous, presses herself against the desk. 'Go on. What else? I know there's more.'

'The part I didn't understand,' he says gently, 'and I should have been more diligent in my research, and I'm really terribly sorry to say, is that even if we manage to secure the heritage property status, we still have an awful lot of the estate which lies outside of that.'

'Such as . . . ?'

'The cottages. These offices. The renovated barns. All of it was work that was done before I came on board and I'm afraid none of it qualifies for either agricultural or business relief. The valuation has come in on that and it adds up to about three million. So we need to find around one-point-five million to cover the tax on that.'

'You're joking,' she says, her heart pounding.

'I'm not, I'm afraid.'

'So – you're telling me that all the good work and all that money we spent renovating the barns and the cottages has led to this?'

'Not entirely, but – yes.'

'Jesus Christ.'

'I'm truly sorry, Fran.'

'Okay,' she says, as a wild panic rises in her, 'so we pull the house down. Get the cherry-pickers in. Do what we did to the forestry land. Raze it to the ground. Plant blackthorn and hawthorn instead. I've always hated the bloody house. Rowan will be happy. I'll be happy. Grace doesn't care . . .'

Simon gives her a faint smile. 'I think we are financially better off with a house that's architecturally important and needs a good deal of repair, and an estate that is in great shape, than any sort of alternative, however tempting that may be.'

'So, what are our options? What does Sophie say? What's your advice?'

'Okay.' He sits back and steeples his forefingers under his chin. 'Option one – and assuming we secure the exemption for heritage property – we sell a parcel of land plus cottages. Your own – soon to be your mother's – cottage is by far the best candidate; sympathetically renovated, three bedrooms, it has its own large garden and access. It should be worth close to one million.'

'Seriously?'

'Easily.'

'Impossible. Mum would never forgive me. She's all but moved in already.'

'That's what I imagined you'd say. So, option two – we keep the buildings, and we raise the funds elsewhere.'

'Ideas?'

'Here's a rather extreme one . . . and it's just a thought experiment . . .'

'Go on.'

'Stay with me here . . . we sell the Reynolds.'

'The Reynolds? Have you lost your mind?'

'I hope you don't mind, but I spoke to an old school friend who works at Sotheby's just to get a ballpark figure. He knows the painting well, he spoke of its provenance – one of the last family portraits Reynolds completed – and the significance of the date, 1789. He seemed very keen to come and take a look. He confirmed it would likely fetch between six and eight million.'

'Right,' says Frannie. 'I see. Well. That's an awful lot of money, isn't it?'

'It is,' he says. 'And it would go a very long way towards covering the tax if we don't qualify, and giving us an exceptional cushion if we do; it'll allow the estate to wash its own face for many years to come. They've got a big sale coming up, apparently. He said if we dealt with him, he would do everything to make sure that it didn't go into a private collection somewhere overseas.'

'But surely,' says Frannie, 'if we sold the Reynolds, the sale would invalidate the heritage property status of the estate?'

'I don't think so. The house is architecturally important enough on its own to qualify.'

'Okay,' she says. 'Well. Thought experiment over. Thank you, but no. Never. It would be a dereliction of duty.'

'To whom?'

'To my ancestors. To all the Brookes who went before. To my father. He doesn't even have a grave to turn in yet.'

'Of course,' says Simon, leaning forward, 'but the combination of your father's past financial negligence and – I'm going to be very honest here – his stubbornness in refusing to contemplate the possibility of his own death until it was too late, means you are going to have to make some tough decisions, Fran, if you want to keep this place in private hands. If he'd have made the house out to you seven years ago and moved into the cottage we wouldn't have to face a penny of this.'

'There must be another option.'

'Well . . . you tell me. You mentioned that Milo is interested in developing a parcel of land. For a clinic of some sort? Psilocybin, no?'

'Yes. He is.'

'Has he made you an offer? Anything formal?'

'No. He wants Ned's wood. He's not about to be making any offers though. He thinks the land should be his.'

Simon's face changes, becomes sharper. 'Now why would he think that?'

'He believes that Philip promised it to him. After he gave him the psilocybin treatment. And he did – in a way. At least, he said that he could have land on the estate. He didn't say where.'

'There was certainly nothing in the will.'

'No, I know. But Milo is convinced.'

'Well, I'm afraid whatever Milo thinks is immaterial at this point. What matters to the estate, and what should matter to you, is how much he's going to offer us to build here.'

'Luca's on board,' she says gingerly. 'As an investor.'

'Luca Gugioni? Seriously?'

'He's flying in tomorrow.'

'That's good news, Fran!'

'Is it? I suppose so. But even if we were to do a deal with Luca and Milo,' says Frannie, 'then Ned would be displaced. I have to say that makes me very uncomfortable.'

'Well, back to the difficult decisions, Fran. I'm afraid you can't move here without displacing someone. If the estate were a chessboard you'd be in check. Not yet checkmate but we must move very, very carefully indeed.'

'Go on then.'

'Well . . . first things first – you cannot *give* Milo any parcel of land. As your estate manager I won't allow it.' He sits back in his chair. 'The estate needs investment. But if we can get Luca Gugioni in a room with us and hold our nerve, then we can try and reach a decent deal which everyone is happy with.'

'Here.' She picks up the folder from her desk and hands it to Simon. 'Milo dropped off the proposal this morning. Have a look.'

Simon takes the booklet, flicks through it. 'They clearly know what they're doing,' he says when he has reached the final page. 'And they've obviously spent a lot of time and energy on it. I have to say it's pretty impressive.'

'I'm really not sure.'

'Of what?'

'Well. Psilocybin? Mushrooms? I've spent the whole of my adult life trying to distance myself from my father's past predilections. And I'm now being asked to consider hosting something on the grounds that, to me, just speaks of that past. Drugs have no place here. Not anymore.'

'I admit I'm no expert, but isn't this different? I read an article in the *Economist* recently; they were citing some rather impressive research. Milo and Luca are obviously wanting to attract some serious clientele. And there's no doubt that Philip benefited from whatever it was Milo gave him. He seemed more peaceful than I'd ever known him, at the end.'

'I know. You're right. It's just . . . Luca.'

'What about him?'

'I'm not sure he's sound.'

'Morally, or financially?'

'Either. Both. I just read a piece on him,' she says. 'The fund looks legitimate, but it feels . . . unstable. I mean, most of these compounds aren't even legal yet. This is high-risk, surely?'

'I get it. And it's a sector I have no experience of, but if the big money is sniffing at our gates, then don't you think we should at least let it in to take a look?' He slides the folder back towards her. 'Ultimately this is your decision, Fran. I can only advise. Take some time – don't negotiate with Milo and Luca alone, okay? Milo is inevitably going to try to apply whatever leverage he has, I imagine. As you said, he's going to want to make you feel guilty. You have to keep in mind that this is *yours*. You father gave it to you. All of it. And that's a huge responsibility and a huge burden – I get that – but it's also a huge freedom, in so far as you don't need to listen to anyone. Except me, of course.' He smiles. 'But really, not even me. But I'm here for you, Fran.'

'I know.'

'Except . . . not for the next few days. I'm going away.'

'Oh God. I forgot. How unbelievably selfish of you.'

'I know. I'm sorry. It's just my wife. She thinks we're having an affair.'

'Seriously?' Frannie feels herself flush.

'No – I'm joking, of course not. But she did say she'll divorce me if I don't spend a few days with her for her birthday without Wi-Fi. Norfolk apparently.' He grimaces. 'Off-grid. It sounds absolutely terrifying.'

'I'm so sorry, Simon. Please apologize to her from me. Can I send her anything? A hamper? Flowers? Wine?'

'No! You don't need anything more on your to-do list. Just – stay steady while I'm away. Concentrate on the funeral, not on this. We'll talk through everything when I'm back, okay?'

'Okay.'

'Good. That's the Fran I know. Right.' He moves to take his coat. 'Just to be abundantly clear, when I say I'm away from Wi-Fi I mean it. Stay strong. And I'll see you on the other side.'

Frannie follows him out onto the gravel, where she sees Jack, walking up the hill towards her. It must be almost three. Time for their daily meeting; half an hour every weekday before Rowan comes home from school. He never fails. He's never late. Simon and Jack – these two men her mainstays for the past decade. One at home in the world of figures and forms, the other who knows these acres like no one else. She waves Simon into his car then turns to Jack. 'Shall we walk? I could do with the air.'

'Sure,' he says. And they set off, side by side, making their way out onto the park. 'I saw there was a shot,' she says. 'Did you find any mink?'

'Yeah. One female. Pregnant.'

'Shit.'

'I'm on it. Don't worry.'

'Everything else okay?'

'Yes. When do you want the deer out of the freezer? It'll need time to thaw before we put it in the pit.'

'Tomorrow morning?'

'Cool,' he says. He looks restless, she thinks, doesn't seem able to meet her gaze.

'Everything okay, Jack?'

'Yeah. I'd like to make a time. To talk to you.'

'We're talking now.'

'I know. It's . . . it's fairly important. There might be a better time, although it probably needs to be soon. I mean. It does.'

'Well,' she grimaces, 'I've just been told that I might have to sell the family silver. Nothing you can tell me can be as bad as that. Go on. Do your worst.'

'I've had an offer of a job.'

'What sort of a job?'

'A similar one to here. But bigger.'

'And?' She searches his face.

'I've been thinking about it.'

'And what have you been thinking?'

'I've decided to accept.'

'*What?* Where?'

'Scotland. Glasnevin.'

'*Glasnevin?* Joe Dahlberg's estate?'

'Yes.'

'You're kidding.'

'I'm sorry, Frannie, no. I'm not.'

She can remember it – taking him into the library, introducing him to Jack. Joe Dahlberg, the tech guy. The lynx guy. The wolf guy.

'No, seriously. Hang on. He *headhunted* you? Under my roof? You can't leave, Jack.' Panic again, scrabbling for purchase inside her. 'How much is he offering you? I'll match it.'

'You just told me you're struggling.'

'I don't care, Jack. I'll find it.'

'It's not just the money.'

'What then?'

'It's the right time. For me to get away.'

'The *right time?* I'm sorry, Jack, but it's the beginning of May. How is that possibly the right time?'

'For *me.* The right time for me. I've been here my whole life, Fran.'

'And what's wrong with that?'

'Nothing. I just – I have to get out at some point. It might as well be now. I'm going to be forty next year.'

'When? When are you leaving?'

'Sunday. He wants me to start straight away.'

'You're kidding.'

'I'm sorry. I'm not.'

'That's preposterous. You need to give notice.'

'Actually, I don't, I've never had a proper contract.'

'That can't be true.'

'I've never officially been on the payroll.'

'How the hell?'

'Philip used to pay me and my dad from a separate account.'

'Does Simon know?'

'Yeah. Of course.'

'Fucking hell. I'll sort it. I'll do it now. I'm so sorry –'

'I won't change my mind. He needs me, Fran.'

'*I need you.* You think I don't need you? Everyone needs every-one at the beginning of May. The mink will run wild. The voles will die. The whole balance of the river will tip.'

'I'm sorry, Fran,' he says again. 'But I have to do this. You'll be okay. You'll find someone else.'

'Who? Who can I possibly find who knows this place like you do?'

He says nothing, and she sees there is no use in her saying more.

'Okay,' she says.

She can do this. Pull herself in. Not leak. Not show emotion. She has been doing it for years. She has been doing it since she was thirteen years old.

'Okay.' She nods. 'Okay.'

❧

Rowan walks down the hill from school in the wake of Wren. The lane is shaded and cool, and it is pleasant after the warm, stuffy classroom, which smelt of the other children and the guinea pigs they keep in a cage in the corner. Ahead of her, fur-ther down the lane, Wren's back has the busy twitchy look of

58

someone who wants to be hurrying, but Rowan hates hurrying anywhere. Especially after school.

Wren is Rowan's mum's friend from Newbury, when they lived in a bender in an oak tree, trying to stop it being chopped down. A bender is a sort of a dome house made of willow and tarps. After that Wren lived in Portugal for years and years but now she's come back to England, to help Frannie with the campsite and the cooking. She's a really good cook. She had her own restaurant in Portugal, and her own land, but she sold them both and moved back here. There's going to be no water there soon, is what Wren told Rowan's mum. It's time for a change. And Wren's okay, she's quite nice really, but it means that Rowan has to walk back from school with her now, and not with her mum, like she used to. No one has really explained why. It's another thing that's changed since Grandpa Philip died.

Rowan takes a switch of grass from the bank beside her, shredding the seeds from the head of the stalk. There's a rhyme they all say at school: *Here's the tree in win-ter, here's the tree in sum-mer, here's a bunch of flow-ers and here's the April show-ers*, and when it gets to the April showers bit, they throw the seeds all over each other's heads. She does it now, saying the rhyme under her breath, and wonders if she should run up to Wren and throw the seeds on her, but Wren is a long way ahead now, and anyway, she doesn't really seem the sort of person that would like it, so Rowan just scatters them all over the path instead.

What Rowan really wants, if she can't be with her mum, is to be alone. To release her thoughts, which have been cooped up in her head all day in the classroom. She would like, for instance, to think about her dream, which has kept coming back to her in pieces all day. And about Grandpa Philip's body in the fridge in the funeral home. She knows the men came to the graveyard today, to dig the hole that he will be buried in. She knows how important it is that they dig it just four feet deep, not six, because it's a green burial and they need to make sure that the beetles and the flies can get to him more easily and speed up the process of decomposition. She'd like to go and check on the hole with her mum, to make sure they've lifted the earth out carefully so it can be put back with all the fungal filaments intact.

She would like to think about Jemima, who was mean to her this afternoon in break, who put her hand in front of her mouth and whispered about her to Olivia, saying that Rowan is weird – just because she decided to start drawing a decomposition chart in open learning. Part of her felt angry, so angry she wanted to pull Jemima's hair so it ripped out of her head, but the other part of her thought that she *does* feel weird a lot, so maybe it makes sense that other people think that too. But do other people feel like they are normal? This is what she can't understand. It reminds her of what Granny Grace said about people's insides and outsides: that their insides don't look like their outsides, and that's a good thing. But is it? And maybe Rowan's outsides *do* look like her insides, and that's why people know she's weird?

Ahead of her, on the shady lane, Wren turns around and calls, 'Come on, Rowan, let's get you home!' She says it in the way grown-ups say things when they really mean something else – when their insides don't match their outsides.

'Coming,' says Rowan.

They climb over the stile that leads to Faery Field, then take the woodchip path down towards the park. There's a lot of sky up here; the hollows are hollower, and the dips are more dippy and the thorn bushes are bent from the wind that's windier. There is the faint coconut smell of the yellow gorse flowers; the sweeping shadows of the clouds.

Below them, spread across the valley, is the estate, and all the other fields: Hilly Field, Brambly Field, Coopers Field, Rowan learned their old names last summer with Ned and now she holds them all like a jigsaw that fits together in her head. When it came to Faery Field, she asked Ned if there really were fairies there. He frowned and said faery was different from fairy, that fairy was something in books and tame and pretty, whereas faery was real and strong and something you needed to be careful about. And because he said that bit about being careful, she believed him.

There is a book in the library, a book so old it was Granny Grace's when she was a little girl, and there's writing in it from Granny Grace's grandma. So that's Rowan's great-great-grandma, and *she* got given it when *she* was seven, in 1906. And the book is set just near here, in a Sussex field. In the book there are pictures; there's one where the two children meet Puck on Midsummer's Day, and his face is all squashed and strange and he looks a bit like a goblin or a monster. Puck asks the children for a knife and carves out a piece of turf – and then he says it's *taking seizin . . . by Right of Oak, Ash, and Thorn.* And when the children have taken the clod of earth from him, when they have taken seizin, that's when all the good, exciting things start happening, when Puck shows the children all sorts of things that happened on their land that they didn't know about before, like Roman legions and stuff like that.

And even though Ned said faeries are not in books, when Rowan showed the book to Ned last summer and pointed at the picture of Puck and said *is that actually a faery not a fairy*, he said *hmmm . . .* in a way that meant *perhaps*. And then she asked Ned if he knew what taking seizin was and he said, Taking seizin is when you cut a clod of land and hand it over to someone and it means your land, and all the creatures in it, belongs to them now.

She wasn't surprised he knew because Ned knows everything about old things. Before he died, Grandpa Philip said to her: *You could do worse than apprentice yourself to Ned.*

'Rowan,' calls Wren. 'Come *on!*'

So she runs after Wren, down the path through the campsite, to the gate that leads to the orchard, into the kitchen garden, past beds of rosemary with their purple flowers busy with bees. When they reach the pineapple on its stone column, Wren stops. 'I just need to pick some things from the pineapple house for tomorrow,' she says. 'Do you want to help?'

Rowan considers. She lifts the toe of her right foot and places it behind her left calf to help her think. 'I think I'll just go and find my mum,' she says.

Wren looks relieved. 'Are you going to be okay from here? Your mum's working in the library, she said to find her there.'

Rowan nods. 'I'll be fine.'

As she watches Wren go into the hothouse she thinks of her mum, sitting at the desk in the library. If it was before, when they lived in the cottage, before Grandpa Philip got ill, she and her mum would have walked home together from school and sat and talked and eaten peanut butter and jam on toast in the kitchen where all of Rowan's drawings were on the wall. After she'd had a snack, she would have played in the garden, where her bug hotel was that she made on an insect day with Grandpa Philip last spring, and the swing that her mum brought back from the tree at Newbury hung from the rowan tree at the bottom of the garden. Her mum used to tell her how, when she was pregnant, when her contractions were coming, when she was walking and walking around that garden waiting for her baby to come, she used to stop at the rowan tree and catch her breath. It was in the spring and the blossoms were creamy white, her mum said, and just when the contractions were at their strongest, she hung on to the trunk of that rowan tree, and the rowan tree held her up, and that's when she knew Rowan was going to be her child's name.

What if I had been born a boy? she asked her mum once.

You'd still have been my Rowan, said her mum.

But she can't go back to the cottage because it is not theirs anymore, it's Granny Grace's, and so is the silver birch and the rowan tree and the garden.

And she doesn't want to go back to the big house, where she

knows her mum is waiting and working in the library, because everything has been turned upside down since Grandpa Philip died, and it's a terrible feeling, anger and sadness all mixed up; she doesn't know who she is angry with more, Granny Grace for making them move, or her mum for agreeing, or Grandpa Philip for dying and making all the changes happen, and she doesn't know what she is sad about more, not seeing him ever again or not being able to go home ever again.

And she doesn't want to be inside at all – it's such a lovely day. So she turns and walks in the other direction, over towards Ned's wood. Instead of going down, the quickest way, past the cottage, where she could be easily seen by her mother in the library, she runs uphill again, cutting in near the top of the wood where the trees are deepest, and small shafts of sunlight pierce the dark green.

As soon as she is in the wood, she feels a bit better. She follows the path of the ghyll down towards Ned's clearing, letting the hot sharp feelings inside her unfurl into the green of the trees and the sounds of the water. The bracken is already waist-high. Soon, she knows, it will be as high as her head, and then, by the middle of the summer, it will be higher than her mother's head, then higher than Grandpa Philip's head, and he was one of the tallest people anyone had ever met.

Just then, a terrible whining pierces the afternoon: a chainsaw, quite close, drowning the birdsong and the river. She feels suddenly afraid, because why would anyone be cutting down trees in Ned's wood? She follows the river path until she comes out at a small clearing, where a man is standing at a worktable and the sweet smell of fresh-cut wood fills the air. At first, she is confused, because it's Ned she sees, with the chainsaw and visor and gloves, Ned who is bringing the saw down onto the tree, making it scream as chips of wood spit and spray all over the ground. She puts her hands over her ears. By the side of the track there are more felled trees, most of them made into piles of posts. When he has sliced through the wood, and everything is suddenly, ringingly quiet, Ned pulls up his visor and spots her. 'Rowan?' He looks worried. 'What are you doing here, Ro love?'

'I wanted to come this way down to the bus and say hello . . . but you're here instead.'

Ned puts down the chainsaw carefully.

'What are you doing?' she says. 'Are you building something?'

He is quiet as he takes off his visor and gloves. 'Give me a minute,' he says. 'I'll just have a tidy-up.'

While he stacks the new-cut logs, she has a closer look: four posts set in the ground. Some sort of winch system. 'What is it?' she says again. 'What are you building?'

'Let's go down to the bus and have a cuppa, shall we?' he says. 'It's time for a break. I've got some biscuits for a change.'

So they head back down the track to his clearing. He walks slowly, with his stick, and she is filled with the urge to go around him, her legs are twitching with the need to run, but she knows that would be unkind, so she follows him slowly, instead. She remembers what it was like when he had his accident – how she went to visit him in the hospital with her mum, his legs all trussed and held up high to help them heal. When they get to the bus Ned turns to her and his face is serious. 'Now then,' he says. 'First things first . . . does your mum know you're down here?'

'No.'

'I think I'd better tell her, don't you?'

He brings his phone out of his pocket and calls Frannie. As he is talking to her mum Rowan wanders over to his workshop. This is her favourite thing about Ned's – this old wooden dresser which is full of all his bottles and jars. She knows what's in most of them now. The really purple one, almost black, is bilberry tincture; it makes you see in the dark. The ruby-bright one is elderberry. She helped him harvest them in the late summer; he showed her how to pluck the berries off the stalks, gently so the skins didn't burst. When they were all plucked, he made a big pot of elderberries on the stove and put honey in from the bees and echinacea, and made this tonic. Whenever she has a cold, he gives her a big dose of it. *That should do the trick*, he says. And it always does.

'Your mum says you can stay for a cuppa,' says Ned, as he stows his phone and makes his way towards her. 'Or would you rather have something fizzy? I've got some dandelion and burdock.'

'That please.'

He goes over to one of the glass demijohns, uncorks the lid, gets a mug, and pours out a glass. 'Rich Tea or Hobnobs?' he says, as he hands it to her.

She rolls her eyes because it's such a daft question. 'Hobnobs please.'

He fetches the biscuits and she drinks the fizzy, earthy liquid. It still has soggy dandelion petals at the bottom, but it is delicious.

'Your mum sounded a bit stressed,' says Ned. 'How's she doing?'

Rowan shrugs. 'She's busy.'

'She's got a lot on her shoulders.'

When he says this, she has an image in her head of her mum, standing underneath that big house, lifting it up like a weight-lifter. It's almost funny, but she doesn't laugh. 'She didn't use to have.'

Ned looks at her.

'Will you tell me what you're building now?' she says.

'Listen,' says Ned. 'I don't much like secrets. Particularly grown-ups asking kids to keep them. But if I tell you one, can I ask you to keep it? Not for long. Just for a couple of days?'

'Alright,' she says. 'Can I have another biscuit then?'

'Course. But I'm not bribing you. You have to give your word – biscuit or no biscuit.'

'I give my word,' she says, reaching for the packet, rifling out two more.

65

'I am building a cabin,' says Ned. 'Up there at the top of the wood.'

'What sort of a cabin?'

'One to live in.'

'But, what about your bus? Don't you want to live there anymore?'

He shakes his head. 'It's damp. No good for my leg. Not after the accident. And it's covered in black mould. I need something solid, drier, on higher ground.'

'But you've always lived in your bus,' she says, her voice rising. 'That's your home.'

She can't imagine Ned not being here. This clearing *is* Ned. He is in all these bottles and jars. In all his things. 'Why can't you just make the bus better?' she says. 'Or build your cabin here? Why does everything have to change?' She can feel the hot feeling rising again, burning, pushing against her, wanting to come out as tears.

'Not everything,' he says. 'But some things do. What's up, miss?' he says. 'I can see something's wrong.'

'Why does Granny Grace have to take our house? She's got *her* house. Why does she need ours?'

'You've got a new house now,' says Ned. 'It'll be all yours one day, that house.'

'I hate that house,' says Rowan. 'It gives me nightmares.'

'What sort?'

'Last night, I dreamt I was Grandpa Philip . . . I was in the coffin . . . and I couldn't get out, and everything was turning to liquid. I was trying to bash against the lid, but I couldn't because I didn't have proper arms or hands anymore.'

Ned listens then after a moment he gets his stick and hauls himself up to stand. 'Come and have a look at this,' he says, and he leads the way round the back of the workshop to where a wicker basket lies on the table.

Rowan knows immediately what it is. She doesn't need to ask.

'How did you make it?' she says, running her hands over the plaited lid. It makes her feel shivery.

'Not so tricky really, I just put in the uprights, then wove the willow through. The lid was the hardest,' he says.

'Can I see inside?'

'Course.' He lifts the lid. Inside is a rough fabric lining. Light-coloured. It smells clean and earthy at the same time. 'So, you see,' Ned says gently, 'it's not so scary really.'

She thinks of her grandpa's body, of how long it will take the beetles to find their way through the weave of this willow and burrow into him, of his insides leaking out, of the ways in which this clean fabric will get all stained and green and black before it turns into the soil itself. 'But where will he be?' she says. 'When he is in here? Will he be in his body? Feeling it all turn to mush?' His body that has been his home for all his life. No longer his.

'No,' says Ned, 'he won't be there.'

He sounds so sure about it.

'Where will he *be* then?' She looks up pleadingly at Ned. 'Where is he now? Is he in himself, in the funeral home? In the fridge? Is he cold? Where has he gone if he's not there?'

'I don't know, is the truth. But I know he won't be there.'

She reaches out again, feeling the woven willow beneath her hands.

'It's insect day tomorrow,' she says, in a small voice.

'What happens then?'

'There's no school. And me and Grandpa find bugs and draw them for our phenology book.'

'Ah.' Ned smiles. 'That sounds good.'

'But it's *not* good.' Her cheeks are hot now – tears feel close. 'Because now I can't do insect day properly. Because Grandpa Philip's dead. And Mum's too busy. And everything's wrong.'

'Tell you what,' says Ned slowly, 'I know I'm not your grandpa, but how about tomorrow you find some bugs and come and show me? I'd love to see the book too. I'll be working in the morning, but you come down here in the afternoon and find me and we'll have some biscuits and chat.'

She takes a last look at the coffin, then up at Ned. She remembers her grandpa's words: *You could do worse than apprentice yourself to Ned.*

'Alright,' she says. 'Yes, please.'

'There you go,' says Ned. 'Come on now, let's get you home.'

Isa walks slowly, finding her way by the light of the torch on her phone. There is no moon, and the sky is cloudy. She parked by the gates, so as not to disturb the house's occupants with her headlights, just in case they are already asleep.

At least like this, in the darkness, with the estate shut, she isn't assailed by the usual triggers. The honesty shop with its local ales and its organic eggs for campers. The shepherd's huts. The yurts. The caravan serving lattes to middle-aged white people while they sit on haybales and chatter about their Pilates teachers and their dogs. A theme park for solvent fifty-somethings. All of it about as wild as a fucking printed tea towel.

She moves past the shape of a cow, sleeping by one of the oaks. Funny, how close they come to the house nowadays. Her phone buzzes in her hand. A text from Hari. She squints at the screen.

Did you get apples at Tesco? Also, where is Rani's PE kit?

Her husband: the only person she knows who puts commas in texts.

He will be moving around the kitchen, preparing for the morning; the gentle methodical way he has of doing everything, pushing his glasses back onto his nose with his right knuckle. The kids always prefer it when he makes their snacks. He will smuggle in Indian sweets, bought on Sunday afternoons in Tooting after visiting his mum, their orange stickiness wrapped in kitchen roll.

They did a couples' course once, a few years ago, when things were really bad. They were both asked to speak about their love language.

Hari smiled – mine's food, he said, with that particular brand of eagerness and self-confidence; the demeanour of a beloved first child who meets the world knowing he will be loved in return.

What's your love language, Isa? the therapist said, turning to her.

She felt herself colour then. I . . . don't know, she stammered.

Hari, said the therapist. What's Isa's love language?

She doesn't really remember what he said. Something nice, she is sure, in the end, but she remembers more the puzzlement on his face as he searched for words. The several beats before he spoke.

She feels a twist in her stomach. When was the last time she was down here? Just before Philip died. She ran away then. She could do it again. She could turn around. Drive somewhere. Be alone. Check into a hotel; somewhere anonymous, halfway to the coast. Just sit and stare at the wall of a Premier Inn. Dinner is over now. And she is very, very late.

She didn't mean to be; for once, she meant to be here on time. Seven o'clock, as Grace's many texts had iterated. She left London just after the end of the school day, but then, sitting in traffic in Croydon, she lifted her phone and checked her emails, scrolled, saw one whose subject line and sender made her catch her breath, made her pull off the A23 and into the car park of IKEA. She opened the email, read it. Sat immobile for several minutes, as shoppers passed her with trollies loaded with bookcases and beds and lamps and Swedish snacks.

A message came from Frannie.

Do you have an ETA yet? Really looking forward to seeing you.

By then, she was already formulating her lie, her alibi, so she couldn't reply. Instead, she got out of the car and walked down the filthy pavement to a garage, where she bought a packet of tobacco and some papers. While she was walking back her screen flashed and her phone vibrated with a call from her mother.

Then, twenty minutes later, another. A voicemail which she did not listen to. Another text from Frannie: *Where are you? Mum's worried! We are about to eat.*

Then – forty minutes after that: *Isa, are you coming? What's going on?*

In the course of the two hours she sat in that car park, she read the email seven times, and smoked three cigarettes, and when she started the car, when the car park was emptying, she drove differently – carefully – as though she were carrying a bomb in her boot.

She heads for the back entrance now, the old servants' quarters, where the door is always unlocked. The particular smell of the corridor assails her, old carpet and damp. Confinement. A special sort of sticky despair. She takes small shallow breaths, careful not to inhale too deeply.

At the bottom of the stairs, she pauses, turns, heads to the kitchen where she stops at the door. Her sister is sitting in a pool of light, hunched over her laptop, her forehead resting on her right fist. An open bottle of wine stands on the counter before her. Her sister looks up. 'Isa!' Frannie stands. 'You're here.'

Isa moves to her sister, and they embrace. She buries her head in Frannie's shoulder.

'Where *were* you?' Frannie pulls back. 'Mum was trying to get in touch. She got worried. We all did.'

'I'm sorry.' She slides her eyes from her sister's gaze. 'A kid pulled a knife on another kid.'

'Shit. Was anyone hurt?'

'Not this time. But, you know, there's a process to go through: witness statements, police. It all takes time. You can't use your phone in there.'

Liar. Liar.

'No. Of course. I'm sorry. That sounds awful.'

'S'okay.' Isa takes a deep breath. 'What are you up to?'

'Oh,' says Frannie, 'just trying to understand how I'm so neck-deep in the utter shit.'

'What do you mean?'

Frannie waves her hand. 'It can wait.'

Isa feels a sharp pang of concern for her sister. She looks exhausted. 'I'm sorry, Fran.'

'What for?'

'That I haven't been more helpful.'

'Well. You're here now.'

Isa reaches for the wine. Turns the label towards her. Lets out a low whistle.

'I know,' says Frannie. 'I thought I deserved it. You want some?'

Isa nods. 'Though I'm not sure I deserve it quite so much.'

'Don't be silly.' Frannie fetches a glass and pours out a large measure. 'Sounds like you've had quite a day.'

Isa slides onto a stool, opposite her sister, lifts, drinks. 'Wow.'

'Yeah, right? We've got two cases of this to get through. Pa chose it.'

'Of course he did. How's Mum?'

Frannie gives a small shrug. 'She seems good. Surprisingly so. I can't work out if she's in denial or liberated or . . . what. She's moving into the cottage next week.'

'And how's that for you?'

'Honestly? Not great.' Frannie sighs. 'But no one is pulling any knives. It's just a two-hundred-and-forty-year-old relic with a damp problem and a massive hole in the finances.'

'What hole?' Isa takes another sip of her wine. 'I thought you'd turned the ship around.'

'Inheritance tax. Pa was always so reluctant to plan properly for his death. I think he thought he was incapable of dying somehow . . . The bill is astronomical and the loophole I was hoping for is far slimmer than I imagined. We may well still qualify but there are no guarantees. And Milo –' She cuts herself off, shaking her head.

'What about him?'

'He's intent. Desperate to corner me. To get me to sign off the plans for the centre he wants to build. Luca's coming tomorrow, apparently. He wants to invest.'

'Happy days.'

'Yeah. Milo seems to think this is a funeral-cum-business-meeting. Anyway,' says Frannie, 'you don't need to know all this. It's just the last thing I need right now.'

'Is there an issue though?' Isa says. 'I thought Pa had made it clear Milo's thing should go ahead.'

'He did. But they never discussed exactly where. Milo's insisting on Ned's wood.'

'Seriously?'

'And Simon's suggesting that Milo will have to pay for the land.'

'But what about Ned?'

'Exactly.'

'So what are you going to do?'

'I don't know. It's a double bind. A triple one. It seems to have been what Pa wanted. What Milo so desperately wants.' Frannie spreads out her hands. 'And of course, it's not Ned's land, ultimately – it's ours.'

'Really? How long has he been there? Fifty years? How long do you have to be somewhere to have the right to stay? What about that guy on Hampstead Heath?'

'So, you're saying he's got squatters' rights?' Frannie laughs, looks back at her sister. 'You're serious?'

'I'm not joking, no.'

'Isa. Please. I really don't want to fight. Not tonight. Not this week. Is that possible, do you think? Is that okay?'

On the table between them, Isa's phone buzzes. Hari. She lets it ring, then presses Decline.

'Everything alright at home?' says Frannie.

'Yeah.' She shrugs. 'Fine.'

Frannie searches her face. 'I've missed you, Isa,' she says.

'I know. I've missed you too.' Isa puts her hands on the counter, turns them palm-ways up, slides them over to her sister. Frannie puts her own palms on top, they hold each other, place forehead against forehead. This gesture, or something like it, has been how they find each other again – how they short-circuit – since they were children. Their secret signal. Sister to sister: *I'm here.*

'How come you left,' says Frannie softly. 'That night? When you came to see Pa? I thought you were staying, I'd made food for us – I was waiting here in the kitchen for you, but when I came to find you, you were gone.'

'I'm sorry,' says Isa, extracting herself.

'It's okay,' says Frannie. 'I just – I could have done with the company, you know?'

'Sure. I get it.' Isa thinks of the tobacco in the bottom of her bag. Of the petrol station. Of the email.

'Fran?' she says.

'What?' Frannie's eyes are mild, the pupils large, open.

'I've got something to tell you. It's about the funeral.'

'Oh?'

'I wrote to New York. After I last saw Pa.'

'New York?'

Isa nods. 'To the address of the apartment that Pa and Natasha used to live in. I had no idea if she was still there. It was just a note to say he didn't have long to live.'

'Why on earth would you want to do that?'

'I thought Natasha deserved to know. I mean – I would want to. Wouldn't you? I'd want to know if someone I had been in love with, and lived with, was dying?'

She looks back up at Frannie. There are two high spots of red on her sister's cheeks.

'Probably, yes. Go on.'

'I didn't hear anything back for a while. Then a reply came via

73

email about three weeks ago. I mean – I had put my email address in the letter . . . so.'

'From Natasha?'

Isa shakes her head. 'From her daughter. She told me that she no longer lived in the apartment, but the current resident had passed the letter on. I told her that Pa had died. And she replied, saying that Natasha was dead too. A year ago, of breast cancer.'

Frannie lets out her breath, and in it, Isa feels her sister's relief: a frayed end tied up.

'Her daughter – Clara, that's her name – said she was very sorry to hear of Pa's death. That she remembered him from when she was very small, that she felt . . . connected to him. That she had been planning a trip to the UK this summer, for research, and she wondered if she might combine it with a visit to the house. To the funeral.'

'Research? For what?'

'Graduate studies, I think. A PhD.'

'And?'

'And I said . . . I was sure that would be okay.'

She watches it land, watches Frannie absorb it – her face register disbelief.

'Honestly, Fran, I didn't think she'd come. I just thought it was the right thing. And it was before you said the funeral would be just us.'

'You thought it *the right thing*? Are you kidding me, Isa?'

'Think about it,' Isa says. 'When was Pa in the States? He came back – what, almost twenty years ago? And he lived there for how long? Seven years? But Natasha was young, wasn't she, when she was with Pa? Really young. So she must have been fairly young when she died. And to have a daughter studying for a PhD already – surely she can only be mid-twenties. Late twenties at most. In which case the dates add up.'

'What *dates*, Isa?' Frannie is combative now, her arms crossed over her chest.

74

'C'mon, Fran. Surely it's obvious? She's the right age to be his daughter.'

Frannie shakes her head.

'So . . .' says Isa. 'This young woman wants to come to the funeral of a man who it seems likely is her father. Are we going to tell her she's not welcome?' She drains the wine in her glass, reaches for the bottle. 'I mean,' she says, her voice rising, 'Pa was a shit. Let's be honest and clear. And the measure of his capacity to shit on Mum and the rest of us again and again was unparalleled. However wonderful your relationship might have become, Frannie, you can't forget that. And we've all done a lovely job of papering over the cracks since he came back, but surely, this is a time for gathering in, for clearing.'

'I'm all for honesty, but this is his *funeral*.'

'So?'

'*So*? So this isn't the time for inviting people who may or may not be Pa's daughter into the fold.'

'Well, I'm not sure I agree with that.'

'Isa . . .' Frannie's voice is low. 'I have been working on this funeral for weeks. I have hardly slept. And that's on top of packing up my home and moving here so that Mum gets her wish to leave this house. Rowan's distress. Simon telling me this morning that the estate is up to its neck in it. And Jack's leaving on Sunday – leaving me in the lurch. I have to find a replacement for him next week or I'm royally scuppered, but there's really no one who can do what he has done – for me, for this place – for the last ten years, and you're sitting here, having hardly replied to a single email, telling me that you think this funeral should be a *clearing*. Can you hear yourself? Seriously?'

Isa feels herself sliding, as though the chair were slippery. Or is it the wine, starting to take effect?

'And what the hell is Mum going to say to this?' Frannie continues. 'Did you even think about her?'

Isa pulls her gaze back to her sister. 'Why is Jack leaving?'

'What?'

'You said Jack's leaving. Why?'

'He's got another job.'

Isa laughs. 'That's not possible. He'd never leave.'

'I can assure you it is. He's moving to Scotland. He came to tell me earlier today. He gave me a weekend's notice, which was nice of him.'

'Scotland? What on earth is he going to do there?'

'The same thing he does here. They're rewilding a hundred thousand acres. The tech billionaire Joe Dahlberg. They're getting crazy grants from the Scottish government. Salary. House. The whole bit.'

There is a roaring now, at the edge of thought. A dark beating.

Frannie looks back to her lists, speaking still, but from further away now, much further away. 'Anyway. I have to find someone else. Or we'll be in trouble; there are mink killing voles out there. It was colossally shitty timing.'

Isa turns back to her sister. And everything about her now enrages her.

'Shitty *timing*?'

Frannie's head snaps up. Isa sees the shock in her sister's eyes.

'Are you seriously bringing up timing in relation to Jack?'

'What do you mean?'

'Wasn't it you who booted his mum and dad from their house when Jeannie was ill? I mean, it's interesting isn't it – that manoeuvre, getting rid of them and renovating their cottage. Renting it out. It seems to be coming back to you, no?'

'I didn't know his mother was ill.' Frannie puts up her hands. 'And it wasn't a *manoeuvre*, Isa, it was a tied cottage that came with his dad's job, which he resigned from in no uncertain terms. Jesus, Isa, are you seriously bringing this up now?'

'It was you who mentioned timing.'

'Okay, you know what?' Frannie scrabbles her lists together, tucks them inside their plastic folder, closes her computer. 'This is not a time to discharge your emotional load all over the place. I'm barely holding things together in here. If you want to let off steam, why don't you go for a walk?'

'Woah. Okay. So you're in charge, Frannie? And as this is your house now, you're in charge of everyone's emotions too? Are you telling us how we are allowed to *feel*? What we're allowed to express inside these walls?'

'Isa, that's not what I meant at all.'

'Really? Well, it sounded very much like it.' Isa stands, drains the second glass. 'Just because everything here has always been easy for you.' Her hands in fists now. The kitchen tilting around her.

'Easy?' says Frannie. 'What on *earth* do you mean?'

The door from the garden opens; Isa looks towards it, sees her brother standing there.

'Hey, Isa,' Milo says. 'What's up, sis? You okay?'

Isa pulls her jacket from the back of the stool. 'Frannie was just telling me how I'm supposed to feel about Pa's funeral. And how I'm supposed to behave.' She shrugs on her jacket, zips it. 'And now this is all hers, I suppose it's – you know . . . up to her.'

Frannie is shaking her head.

Milo comes further into the kitchen towards them. 'What's really going on?'

'What's *really going on*,' says Frannie, 'is that Isa has written to the States, found out Natasha has died, and invited the grown-up child of Pa's former lover to fly over for the funeral. When does she arrive, Isa?'

'Tomorrow,' says Isa. 'She gets into Gatwick in the morning.'

'Fantastic,' says Frannie. 'There we go. I can't wait.'

Milo looks between his sisters. 'Seriously?'

'Seriously,' says Frannie. 'And since our conversation here is getting nowhere fast, and since Isa can't possibly conceive of anyone having any feelings about this other than herself, I'm going to take myself to bed. I need to get up at dawn.'

'What time's dawn?' says Milo. 'I'll help you.'

'Five thirty.'

'Ah. Okay. Well, maybe I'll see you at six?'

'Whenever, Milo. Whatever works for you. Sleep well, both of you.' At the door she turns. 'Can we meet, please? In the morning? With Mum? We need to go over all of this. Funeral plans too, but we need to give her this news.'

'Sure,' Milo says. 'When?'

'Eight thirty. In the library.'

Isa is silent, her arms braced across her chest. She nods once as Frannie leaves the room.

'So . . .' Milo turns to Isa. 'What the fuck?'

Isa pours herself a third glass of wine. 'You want one? I can open another bottle if you like?'

'No.'

'It's good.'

'I'm sure it is,' he says. 'I haven't had a drink for over a year though.' He takes his vape from his back pocket, tugs on it.

'Shit. Sorry. I forgot. How's that working out?'

'Really well, actually.'

'Good for you.'

'You want to tell me what's happening, sis?'

Isa reaches for her bag, scrabbles inside, pulls out the tobacco, papers, starts to roll herself a cigarette.

'When did you start smoking again?' says her brother.

'When did you stop?'

He puts down his vape, grins. 'Go on,' he says. 'Pass it over.'

She finishes rolling and throws him the packet, then she goes over to the range, bends to the flame.

'So,' says Milo, when she returns, reaching for Isa's cigarette to light his own. 'Go on. Tell me. Natasha's daughter is our half-sister? What the actual fuck?'

'Think about it.' Isa says. 'When was Pa in the States? The dates make sense.'

'I met her once,' says Milo, pulling hungrily on his cigarette. 'In London.'

'Who?'

'Natasha.'

'You're kidding.'

'I'm not.'

'You never told me.'

Milo turns and taps ash into the sink. 'None of us spoke much, did we, back then?'

'I guess not . . . So . . . go on – what happened? What was she like?'

Milo shrugs. 'It was pretty awkward, as far as I can remember . . . Luca and I had the keys for the flat, and we were planning a fucked-up weekend – I mean, we were teenagers. And we walked in and Dad and his girlfriend were there. I think they might even have been in bed.'

'Oh God.'

'Yeah . . . I mean, I think they came out of one of the bedrooms. And he introduced me to Natasha, told me he was selling the flat, that he was over in London to put it on the market, that he was going to be buying a place in New York. He must have asked me how I was doing. I don't really remember. It was all pretty excruciating, as I said. And I was probably drunk.'

'Fucking hell.'

'We got out of there fairly quickly. I think we must have stayed somewhere else.'

'Well – what was she like?'

'Natasha?' Milo shrugs. 'I don't know. She seemed very young. Sort of Pa's type I guess. Long brown hair. Beautiful. English rose-y. Though American, obviously. And edgier than Mum for sure. She was something in the art world, wasn't she?'

Isa nods.

'And yeah, just . . . very young.'

79

'Fuck,' says Isa. 'Okay. Well. Here we are then – I think Clara must be their kid.'

'Really? Must she?'

'It would be weird if she weren't.'

'Would it? Did she give any hint in her letter that she was? And why hasn't she made more of a fuss up to now. If she is, I mean. Surely?'

'She'll be here tomorrow. We can ask her then.'

Milo regards her for a moment, frowning. 'Do you think she wants something?'

'Who?'

'Whatsername?'

'Clara?'

'Yeah.'

'What do you mean?'

'Well. Flying all this way. I think she probably wants something. If she's Pa's.'

'Do you mean – if she's Pa's, she'll be venal? Or, if she's Pa's, she'll hope she's entitled to some money?'

'The latter. Both. But she won't be entitled. To anything. Will she?'

'I don't know.'

'Well – would she be? Do you think she's entitled to any of it? And what about the flat? I mean, that must have fetched millions. He bought a place in Manhattan, right? Who the hell inherited that? Why the fuck haven't we thought about this till now?'

'I have no idea, Milo, but can't this person just want to come and pay her respects? To her dead father? Does she have to have a motive other than that?'

'Everyone has a motive, Isa. What's yours?'

'What do you mean?'

'Why do it? Why write to Natasha?'

Isa frowns. 'I don't know. I suppose . . . I felt she ought to know.'

'Really? What else? Sure you didn't want to cause a bit of trouble? Stir the pot?'

'Why would I want to do that?'

'Because you love drama?'

'Fuck off.'

He opens his hands. 'Tell me I'm wrong.'

'Fuck off, Milo.'

'You need to get off the drama train, sis.'

'Are you kidding me? You're standing here and preaching to me about drama, Mr Solipsism? Frannie says she hasn't been able to get you out of her hair all day. Banging on about your clinic.'

Milo doesn't respond. One of his very special silences. The ones that communicate that, whatever may have occurred in the past – whatever manner of colossal fuck-up he may have been – now, having ingested whatever purgative it was last week, he is *far more spiritual than you.* 'That's not drama,' he says, taking a long last drag then grinding out his cigarette. 'That's healing.'

'Ah, yes. Go on,' she says. 'Give it to me. Give me your plans for saving the world.'

'You really want to know?'

'Yes, I really want to know.'

'Okay . . . well, I believe that if you heal the leaders, you heal the world,' says Milo. 'If we get it right, then people will be coming here to have their souls blown. We can birth a new ruling class right here.'

'Jesus Christ,' she says.

'What?'

'*Birth a new ruling class?* It sounds like the psychedelic eugenics programme. What about structural inequality? Have you stopped to consider that? Or do the one per cent stay the one per cent, just with the culturally appropriated psychedelics thrown in?'

'They're not culturally appropriated, sis. This isn't ayahuasca, or mescaline, this is psilocybin. Mushrooms. They grow every-where. Besides, we source them from the lab.'

'Whatever, Milo. You know what I mean.'

'No, I don't think I do. I'm planning something so *benign* here. And all I'm getting is pushback.'

'*Benign?*' says Isa. 'Really?'

'Connection with nature, Isa? The natural world?'

'You're saying that the natural world is essentially benign?'

'I'm saying connection with the natural world is a good thing, yes. Are you contesting that?'

'Even the fascists loved nature, Milo. Especially them.'

'Okay, Isa.' He puts his hands up in mock defeat. 'I can see you're sad.'

'I'm not sad,' she says. 'I'm angry.'

'Whatever – maybe you need to get sad then. Maybe you need to address some of your unprocessed grief instead of projecting it onto me.'

'Oh, okay, I get it. So you're saying my conception of the ini-quities of structural inequality is my unprocessed grief talking? Nice. I like it, Milo. Very cool. So – what? When I've done my psychedelic therapy, I'll be okay with the massive shitshow that is the one per cent? What did they give you in that clinic in Holland? Are you actually completely fucking *insane?*'

Isa stands up, throws her cigarette end into the sink, pours cold water on it, drains her glass and places it back on the counter, then walks across the kitchen, hauls open the door and steps outside.

She moves quickly, out onto the park, walking fast over the rutted earth, and then she is running, her breath high and fast, through the heavy rising dew, which is making her jeans cling to her calves, until she is close to Ned's wood. She crosses the stream on the old wooden bridge, makes her way along the path until she reaches the treehouse. She stands, looking up, catching her breath.

She calls out. His name, small at first.

But there is no one there. Only the bulk of the tree and the dark boards above her. Only the cold relentless sound of the river.

She calls again – a call from the place inside her that has been making that call, shaping it inside her, silently, for years.

Then again.

Silence.

She sinks to her knees in the new bracken, the green turned blue in the moonlight – the night sounds all around her, and the low yellow light of the slowly rising moon.

Day Two

Ned lies in the small glow cast by the solar fairy lights around his bed. Redbluegreenorange – blink on blink off. Blink on. Blink off.

Beneath the blankets he tries to stretch. These first few moments of the day are always full of a certain sort of despair: his leg is bad, has been so all winter. The accident happened at the beginning of the autumn, the quad bike slipped in mud and fell on top of him. Leg broken in seven places. The end of an era. He saw a physio for weeks in the hospital and he's supposed to do exercises every morning, but it's too chilly still to do them properly, and anyway, there's not enough space in the bus. So, he relies on a different sort of medication to ease him into the day.

He hauls himself up to sitting. From here, he can just about reach to open the belly of the stove and chuck another log on the embers – then, leaning, take the old coffee pot, tip the grounds into the heaving bowl on the side of the sink, spoon in fresh coffee, fill the water and pop it back on the hotplate. Then he reaches for his baccy tin and tray and lies back on his pillows, gathering his breath.

He balances the tray on his chest, reading glasses always left there from the night before, pulls out his papers and starts to assemble a joint while the coffee brews: the finest bud, grown himself, six feet from where he's sitting, five plants, all along the back window of the bus where they get the best of the light.

The coffee fizzes and sizzles, as he licks the spliff, seals it, twists the top, places it with care on the tray then pours the coffee into his mug, swirls some condensed milk into it: sugar and milk in one. Seven minutes, the ritual takes, from start to finish. He lights the spliff, sips the coffee, reaches behind him and cracks the window wide. Pain relief, mood relief, Prozac and Ibuprofen in one. Who needs the pharmacy when you have the pharmacopoeia?

He smokes, he sips. Outside, the birds have settled into their morning chatter. They had their rampage on at dawn though, broke through his dreams. Peak testosterone for the little fellas now.

When he feels the spliff has started to work and he can stretch a little, he taps off the cherry and tucks it behind his ear. He rubs his right leg . . . his left, reaches for his jeans, pulls them on, then brings his woollen jersey over his T-shirt. He has worn the same clothes since he was fifteen: Levi's and a navy fisherman's guernsey. When the jeans wear out, every three years or so, he ventures into Tunbridge Wells and buys another pair.

He pushes his feet into his boots and, going gently, coffee in one hand, holding on to the rail, makes his way down the three steps into the glade, where his blackthorn stick waits for him in the little porch. The morning is overcast, the gentle patter of rain on young oak leaves. Still, he loves it – how he will miss this when he lies in his grave. May again, Beltane – the Bright Time – how he loves it best.

He walks over to a patch of nettles and pisses with difficulty. Harder and harder these days; his flow only a mild spatter, hardly enough to make the leaves bend. Aim all off. Always that lingering feeling that you haven't quite emptied yourself. Always the straining to get the last drops out. Every day now is a measure of some sort of loss.

He zips himself up, takes a sip of his coffee.

He is understanding something, at this late stage of the game: the human being ages not gradually but in stages. You have a setback, an accident or so on, and after a certain age, you never recover properly from it. *Shifting baseline syndrome*. They talk about that a lot, up at the house, and he knows what they mean: he can still remember the nights filled with moths, can remember his grandfather speaking about the shoals of herring miles wide. The vast oyster beds that made the waters round these islands gin-clear. Lapwings and swallows filling the skies. The basic idea is this: you get used to a scarcity. You think that's what it always was. You cannot measure the losses you cannot see.

But he's aware of his own shifting baseline. How it's plummeting. How he needs to level the curve somehow. It has become clear, lately, that he needs to take some sort of action; that the way in which he has lived so far will no longer do.

His bus is damp. The woods here are wet. The river that makes them so rises just a few miles west of here, a tributary which becomes the Medway, cutting across Kent, before reaching Rochester, spilling out into the Swale and then meeting the sea. He started life at one end of this river, and now he's ending it at another: born in Chatham to a young mother in '48, just after the war. His father a tinker, tailor, soldier, sailor, rich man, poor man, beggarman, thief (pick one – his mother would never say), but soon after he was born she got another husband and another kid and made a family which didn't have room for him in it, and so he was taken in by his grandmother, Mary Lamb. Lived in her back bedroom by the Chatham docks: the arse end of England.

And here he is now, all these years later, living at the rise of a tributary of the Medway, in wet woodland, in a damp bus. Seventy-six, with no savings, no insurance, no children and no pets; nothing but what he has always had – his hands. His only life insurance policy is beginning to be built five hundred metres further into the wood, in a part of the estate where no one goes but him. Higher ground than here. He managed to keep it quiet too, until Rowan came to find him yesterday. He'd known it was bound to happen sooner or later. He would have preferred a little later, but there you go.

He's building it with help from a lad from the village. Good kid. Smart kid. Kid who's turning up every day to help him get the basic structure laid. You don't need planning if you're not building foundations. He has sketched no plans; he carries them in his head. Just a little cabin, three rooms. A deck. But built beautifully – built to last: lifted up on stakes so he won't be underwater if the river bursts its banks. Not far from the access track, which is close to the A-road in case an ambulance needs to come by. He has to think of such things now – he was lying under that bike for hours before they found him. He can't risk that again.

Nobody gets out of here alive – and over there, lying on a workbench beneath his lean-to, is the proof: Philip's coffin, seven feet of woven willow.

He harvested the willow in the winter, down by the lake, when he could see Philip was only going one way. Stripped it of its bark, boiled it, then dried it out by the stove in the bus and stacked it into bushels. When Philip finally went, three weeks ago, he told Frannie he would make the coffin.

Do you know what you're doing, though? she asked him.

If you can make a fence, he said to her, you can make a coffin.

And it was true: a simple ply base, then drill holes for uprights, uprights in, soak the willow to make it pliable, then weave.

Besides, he said, my great-grandmother was a weaver.

His great-grandmother, Dot Lamb, was a basket maker. He thought of her while he wove – twelve kids and thirty grandkids. She was a singer, a keeper of old songs; had songs that were hundreds of years old, had songs about Waterloo. Songs that would make the hairs on the back of your neck stand up. She didn't so much sing as growl.

It was tough work though, the weaving – surprisingly so; tough enough anyway, with the pain in his leg where they put the pins in, and the ache in his hip and the arthritis in his winter joints. He makes his way over to the workshop, passes his hands over the coffin. He is pleased with his handiwork, the tight plaiting along the edge of the lid. It would have been easier to weave a gentle arc, a rounded line, but Philip was all edges. All angles. And as

Ned worked, as he wove those angles and those edges, he thought of the man who was to go into it: Philip Brooke. How he first met him down at the UFO Club in London in '67. One of Pink Floyd's first gigs; both of them high as kites.

Ned had come to London a couple of years before, had fallen into the scene, a bit of dealing, mostly odd jobs for the bands, fixing anything that needed fixing, building stages, lighting rigs. He quickly got a reputation as the sort of bloke you wanted around; he had left school at fourteen, barely able to read, but with the skills he has lived by ever since: carpentry, joinery, an eye for detail that is all his own. His grandfather had taught him on the weekends. He was a good man – had been a sapper in the First World War, Home Guard for the Second. As Ned grew, he understood that he was lucky – so many of his friends were beaten by their fathers and grandfathers. A dark spell lay over England then. So many unexploded bombs in men's hearts. So many of those men brutalized by war.

When he hears it talked of now, people seem to think that by the end of the sixties everyone was at it, getting high, hanging out on the King's Road, but as far as Ned remembers, most of England was still in its potting shed – it was a small coterie of nutters, a ragbag of assorted aristos, musicians, art school kids and hustlers moving between Chelsea, the UFO Club and the Roundhouse, that kicked the whole thing off.

Philip was posh, but then they all were, or most of them anyway, most of those who were into getting high. Ned himself was a novelty: the way he spoke, the way he dressed; they all wanted a part of whatever he was carrying – drugs yes, but something else. Something inside. He was free, he supposed, unfettered by class or place, in a way they were not. He was English, but his England was no green and pleasant land. He had spent his childhood truanting, exploring wastelands, bombsites, ugly places, in-between places, but they were places that held him – held whatever wild current was running through him, however it needed to be expressed; those places let him run and fight and shoot and fuck, when the time came for that too. They brought him up, those places, far more than any human ever did.

After a while Philip would come to Ned for his drugs. He was the sort of man who always wanted more, a man of unbridled appetites: hash, acid, booze, girls. Each time Ned saw him there was a different woman on his arm. The height of him; Philip seemed to embody something essential about the ruling class: something not quite cruel, but not quite kind. You could see it at twenty paces. Entitlement. Still, he was alright with Ned. He had money, and would pay well for whatever Ned was selling – was never stingy, not like some of the toffs on the scene, never mean.

In the early seventies Ned started doing trips overland to India, Afghanistan, Pakistan, crossing umpteen borders with kilos of hash. But he always loved to come back to England when the land was greening: Maytime.

It was May when he first came here, to this clearing in a Sussex wood. He had just bought the bus, driven it back over-land from India. Inside it were seven kilos of hashish, hidden in seventy Afghan dresses and fifty sheepskin coats that smelt of goat piss. He was walking up and down the King's Road trying to find a shop that would sell the dresses for him when he bumped into Philip on the street and sold him a lump of hash he had in his pocket. Philip looked harassed – no girl with him for once – raking his hand through his long fair hair as he told Ned he was having a party at his place in the country and needed help with structures. He had a group of idiots on the job who needed sorting out. Did Ned know of anyone – cash, about six weeks' work? He quoted a figure that was generous by any-body's estimate.

I know of me, said Ned, and set off for Sussex that afternoon.

He drove down here and parked up in the wood. Right here. This very spot. He remembers the way it struck him – the green of it, after India, after London, the way it almost hurt you it was that lovely, that perfect.

That first night Philip invited him up to the big house, sat him down at the desk in the library beneath the portrait of his ancestors and all the old maps on the walls, with a bottle of whisky and some hash. The doors were flung open onto the terrace and the moths were thick around the low lamps while Philip revealed more of himself to Ned during the course of that evening than in all the years since. They sank the best part of that bottle of whisky and Philip told him about how much he loved this place, how he had spent his early childhood here in a sort of enchantment; he could tell Ned about the best spots to find thrushes' eggs in the springtime and edible mushrooms in the autumn. How as a boy he would row over to the island in the middle of the lake, camp there in the summer; he had needed nothing and no one. How he used to meticulously record the natural world – he got the books down from the shelves and showed Ned sketches he had done as a boy, year after year of beautiful, detailed drawings.

As the night wore on and the whisky bottle emptied, Philip told him of the death of his parents – eleven years ago, killed in a car crash driving from London to the house. He had been away at school. He told Ned how he had hardly been here in the decade since the estate became his. How this party, this weekend, was a chance to change that, to fill the place with enchantment again, with the wonder of childhood: to make it his own.

He sketched out his plans in the back of one of those childhood notebooks: treehouses, walkways between them, a stage by the oak in the park – his vision for a wild, wonder-filled party to end them all.

What they did in those weeks in this wood remains the great work of Ned's life: the treehouse village they built, the stage – Philip had been to Glastonbury, had seen the pyramid they had there, wanted something similar here but Ned persuaded him it should be something else – simpler, just using the great old oak as the backdrop.

Originally the festival was ticketed, but when the freaks started pouring down from London in their thousands, it was decided the festival had to be free.

The *Teddy Bears' Picnic.*

There are books that devote chapters to it. *Britain's Woodstock,* they call it.

There are people that come down here and seek him out in this glade even now – earnest young writers, podcasters, musos. They all want to know the same thing: *What was it really like?*

He always tells the truth: *It was fucking magic.*

That summer: the heat, as though England had become a taut drumskin. It was in the air and in the soil and in the trees, a sense that anything might happen, that the course of human history might be changed, that you might dip your palm into the stream of time and anoint yourself with it; that here in this crucible of green, a different England from the one of war and violence and empire could be born. An England forged in the soul, around the campfires of an English wood by all the beautiful wild mad children of her shores. And he was right here, in this very glade, right at the centre of it all, orchestrating the madness from the back of his bus. Once the festival got under way and his work on the structures was done, he set out his wares on blankets in the clearing: the dresses and the sheepskin coats at the front, in the back the LSD. He was supplying the whole place with the cleanest acid straight from the Welsh hills. He was turning on half of the youth of southern England.

The girls all went mad for the dresses. It was a particularly lovely haul he brought back that summer. He sold most of them in two days flat. On the third day a young woman came to the stall. She was quiet, looked straight, just in a pair of jeans and a simple top, not like the girls who were bare-breasted, or painted and rolling around. Her hair hung in sheets to her waist, and the face it framed was like a flower.

The young woman lifted one of the last dresses from Ned's blanket. A yellow one, with sleeves like bells, its black velvet bodice all covered over with mirrors. And it was strange, because this yellow dress was, to him, the loveliest of all, and yet here it was, left till almost last. How much is it? she asked shyly. When he told her she flinched and went to put it back. Try it, he said. Go on. You want to go in my bus? I'll guard the door. As the young woman climbed the three steps into his bus, and he shuffled so his back was to the door, Ned had a sense of something about to occur, a shiver of expectation, a plucking on the threads of his fate. After a moment there came a soft knocking behind him, and he turned, stepped away, gave her space to emerge. That moment – he still doesn't really have words, even fifty years later, for that moment. For the way she looked, stepping out into the dappled sun, for the way the dress fit her, the way it seemed to catch and amplify an inner light, as well as the sunlight that was sharding through the leaves as she turned this way and that. You can have it, he said, when he could speak. It's yours. You'll be needing something to go with it. Here. He pulled out his envelope – LSD. You had it before? She shook her head. I just got the train down from Barnes yesterday, she said. Someone gave me a flyer in the street, and I thought – why not? Well, he said gently. This'll take you a long way from Barnes, if you let it. He smiled. If you're going to have it then now would be the time. He opened his pocketknife, dipped it into the envelope, and brought a microdot out upon the knife's tip. This is the best and cleanest you'll ever get. She licked her finger, dabbed the tiny grey dot onto her tongue. Is that a lot? He smiled. Enough, I'd say. She looked suddenly afraid. Am I going to be alright? Oh yes, he said. I should think you'll be just fine. I'll keep an eye out for you, if you like. Then – wait – he said. What's your name? You haven't told me your name.

Grace, she said.

Grace.

He lost her not long after, of course he did, but he knew better than to look for someone at a place like that, there must have been forty, fifty thousand people there by then.

But he saw her again in the dawn. And she was dancing in his dress at the front of the stage. It had rained, just before the sun rose, a sharp shower, and she was whirling and whirling – bare feet churning the earth to mud. The sun rose higher, the music stopped, and there was silence, but she was still dancing, still whirling, the heavy skirt ballooning around her, sleeves like bells, hands stretched to the sky. And as Ned stood with his back against a tree and watched her, a refrain from one of his great-grandmother's songs came to him:

> *O! there is sweet music on yonder green hill, O!*
> *And you shall be a dancer, a dancer in yellow,*
> *All in yellow, all in yellow.*

As she slowly, slowly came to rest.

He began to walk through the crowd towards her – there was the song of a blackbird high in the tree – but then, when he was almost upon her, he halted.

Her eyes were closed, her face upturned to the sky – that beautiful face offered to life just as a flower offers itself to the morning sun and rain. And who was he to put himself between a flower and the sun? So he stopped – a short distance from her. And then something else, someone else: a figure striding through the crowd and the crowd parting for him.

And Ned watched as Philip made his way towards the girl in the yellow dress. Watched the way he walked, the way his footsteps met the earth: heavy, certain. He watched as Philip stood before her. He saw Philip's hand reach out to touch her cheek, and then both hands on either side of her face. It was clear he was entranced, and why wouldn't he be? Ned was too far to hear, but from where he stood, it looked as though no words were exchanged – only a kiss. And so, Ned watched as Philip claimed her, that morning of mist and birdsong; that girl with a face like a flower in the rain; for this land and all upon it was his.

And he who had hesitated, he who might have reached her first, was no longer the agent of his own destiny; he was pulled into a different story, cast in a different role, a courtier, a bystander, a watcher. His life lived in the wake of a kiss that was, and a kiss that never was. A flower that would bloom now on the other side of a wall.

He finishes his coffee, chucks his grounds on a nearby patch of bramble.

He is getting sentimental. It's a worrisome habit, the older he gets. He knows, doesn't he, how it would have gone? He was never good with girls, not in the way they wanted him to be, there were too many of them and they were all too lovely and they liked him, and he liked them and so he could never have stayed faithful to one.

But in this way, he has been faithful. Has taken care. He has kept this fire going, a fire Grace has always come to, in times of need. For nigh on fifty years he has seen the flower grow paler and wilt. Not enough water, not enough sun.

He knows there have been many cruelties – too many to count. Grace never told him, not really, but he could imagine.

But Philip, that strange, angular, visionary bastard, was always alright with Ned. He never once spoke of Ned moving his bus on, or paying any rent. They understood each other from a distance, he and Philip – live and let live.

And it is this glade that has let Ned live. Some of it has been innate, some taught, some he has learned. He coppices the wood for fuel. Seasons the logs under the roof of the workshop. Takes his water for washing and cooking from the river, has rigged up a filter system with a hose and tap for the rest. He used to run his stereo from a diesel generator; now he has a decent solar panel donated by Frannie that does for all his needs. For more than forty years he watched the wildlife thin – the birdsong falter and grow quiet, the woods populated only by dopey pheasants, fattened for the shoot. And then, in the last decade, under Frannie's watch, he has seen and heard and felt it thicken. The little grebe back down by the river. The cuckoo and the turtle dove and the lark returning; the sounds of his childhood once again patterning the spring air.

He plays his role in the new estate; delivers the baskets of logs to the campers down from London with their wide eyes and ready smiles, all of them looking for an experience. He knows they like him: the wild man of the wood. And they might hear the chattering of a nightjar, or see a herd of Exmoors in the dusk, but they don't get it, not really, not with their Rioja and their firepits and their pizza ovens. Neither do the family; like they are strange, detuned instruments, the lot of them. They cannot feel the harmonics of the wood.

Small things, things you would not want to speak about to others, lest they laugh at you or lock you up: the way the wind speaks through the branches, each its own melody – ash, beech, hornbeam, oak. But it is not what they're selling out there in the park. Not what you're going to get paying two hundred quid for a night in a shepherd's hut with a basket of ready-seasoned firewood delivered to your door. And you don't need a thousand acres to experience it; he has been an apprentice to the wild all his life. But here's the thing: you can't buy it, not even a little bit; neither can you rent it for a night. And here's another thing: it's full of fucking ghosts. It was there in the bombsites where he grew up, in the mounds of tumbled bricks. You'd be out there, playing, late at night in the gloaming, and you'd feel it. A certain sort of quiet would descend. A certain sort of hush. And you knew you weren't alone. But it has been here, in this wood, that he has felt it most: things without explanation, sounds without reason. A woman calling for her husband, blown to bits in a field in France. The husband stumbling in the dark, trying to reach his home. Men and women and children, arm in arm, dancing together, flattening the earth floor of a barn, a thousand years of dancers, centuries of them; layer upon layer of ghosts.

He knows he will join them soon; in three years, in five years, ten at most.

For now, though, he needs to get this coffin up to the house and bury the man who will go inside it. Then he can focus on the rest. On finishing the unfinished business of his life. He's going to build his cabin, like the poem – have some bean rows, and a hive for the honeybees. Live out his life in the bee-loud glade.

He's going to get old and sit on the deck. Watch the light change through the trees. Love the world a little longer. Finish his unfinished business before he goes.

✥

It's insect day, and Rowan is making her way downstairs.

She has decided she will go ahead: she'll find some bugs, put them in the field microscope, then make her drawings and take them to Ned to show him, as he suggested. She just needs to be brave enough to get the phenology book first.

She hesitates when she reaches the bottom of the stairs; to her right is the door to the library, slightly ajar. She steels herself, pushes it gently and steps inside. The curtains are open, but the sun has not reached round here yet, and the room is shaded and chill. She takes a couple of steps over the threshold; this is the room that Grandpa Philip died in, and she hasn't been in here since. There was always someone with him in those last weeks – her mum, or Granny Grace, or the men and women who came and washed him and gave him medicines, with their rustly plastic aprons and gloves – but now the room is quiet, so quiet it is like the furniture is listening to itself. She steps a little further inside. It smells like it always used to – like wood and old books and corners – not like medicines anymore, or the sour smell of Grandpa's body in the bed.

Still, even if he has gone, everything here reminds her of Grandpa Philip; the books on the shelves and the things on the desk and the huge portrait of Oliver Brooke over there on the wall behind the desk. In the painting Oliver Brooke is standing at the back and he's actual life-size, and in the front are his wife and his son, and the oak tree they are all standing against in the picture is the exact same oak in the park, the same tree that her mother and her grandfather stood against for the photograph for the magazine – the photo they made Rowan come and stand in too. A *recreation*, that's what they called it – a *recreation of the Reynolds*. Joshua Reynolds is the man who painted the picture. He was a very famous painter. The photo, which went on the cover of a magazine, is here too, in a silver frame on the table. In the photo it's her mum who is standing though, and Grandpa Philip who is sitting, and Rowan who is the child, and where in the painting everything is neat and tidy, in the photograph everything is wild and thistly, and the oak tree is old and gnarled and hollow and all around them the grasses are long and there's a large sow lying not far from Rowan's feet.

It was an accident that Rowan ended up in the photo; she was coming home from school and there were loads of people there, people with cameras and people holding big silver foil things that reflected the sun, and when they saw her, they all called to her to persuade her to be in the photograph, even though she didn't want to. Come on, Ro-Ro, Grandpa Philip said, it's history we're making here.

It was February and he could hardly stand up. Do it for me, Ro-Ro, he said. Please.

His voice was all whistly. Like something had poked holes in it.

She remembers her mum got down on her knees, so she was the same height as Rowan, which she only ever does when she really wants something.

Do it for Grandpa, her mother said. Please.

So she did it, because she loved her grandpa. But she didn't like it. They didn't ask her to smile, which was good, because she never smiles in photographs. When the magazine arrived with the picture of them all on the cover, her mum took it out of the envelope at the breakfast table and her cheeks went a bit red, then she took Rowan by the hand and went straight in to show Grandpa Philip.

He was really nearly dead by then, his hands on the top of the covers were all thin and gnarled and yellow like chicken's feet and his face was yellow too. Rowan climbed on the bed and Grandpa Philip put his arm around her and he cried.

There we all are, he said. Get it framed, will you, Fran?

There's another photograph in a frame on the table. There's an oak tree in the background of this one too; it's of her mother at Newbury. In it her mother's face is painted, but not to look like a tiger or a butterfly or anything, just covered in blue paint. When Rowan asked why she had blue paint, her mother said it was because they wanted to make themselves look like warriors. Her mother has leaves in her hair and a ring in her nose. She has a man in a yellow jacket on either side of her, and standing behind her is another man, with a chainsaw.

This picture of her mother before she was born has always made Rowan feel funny – her mother looks so fierce and so does the man with the chainsaw; he looks like he is about to chop her in half. Imagine if they had cut her in half? Then she would have been dead and would never have met Rowan's dad and Rowan would never have been born.

Her dad.

Whenever she thinks about her dad, she's not really thinking about a man, more a big sort of hole where a person should be. And she knows if she thinks about her dad for too long she can tumble into the big black hole, and anyway, she has forgotten to do the thing she came in here for, which was to get the phenology book for insect day, so she goes over to the other side of the desk and opens the drawer where Grandpa Philip kept it. It is in there, along with two chocolate bars, a Dairy Milk and a Milky Way.

Her heart beats a bit faster when she sees the chocolate, because it's like he's giving it to her like he used to; passing it to her when her mum wasn't there, because Frannie would never let her eat it because of sugar and palm oil, but her grandpa always said, *Bugger the posh chocolate. This is the real stuff, Ro-Ro.*

She brings out the chocolate and the phenology book, then opens the Dairy Milk and breaks off a square. And sitting here, the sweet secret taste of his chocolate flooding her mouth, looking out over the desk and the windows and the park beyond, with the Reynolds picture behind her, she feels close to him again. Because her grandpa loved this desk. He loved all the things that had belonged to Oliver Brooke, like the globe, which is huge and held in a wooden frame. Sometimes she would come in here and he would say, *Spin the globe, Ro-Ro, go on – see where you end up.*

Behind the globe, on the far side of the desk, is a wide, deep box, made of wood, and on the lid is a painting of a ship. She pulls it towards her and traces the outline of the boat; three tall masts with their sails. Beneath the ship is one word: *Albion*. Albion is the name of her mother's project because Albion is in the past and in the Albion Project they are bringing back all the species that are longing to return.

She knows what's in this box, she's seen them before, but she was never allowed to touch them unless she was with Grandpa Philip, so she's never opened the box by herself. She flips the catch and lifts the lid and the sight makes her catch her breath, because inside are hundreds or thousands of small white shells. They are not the sort of shells you find on the beach in Cuckmere or in Brighton, nor like the collection she had somewhere in her old room, shells which lose their shine when they are far away from the water; these are white-white even though they are old. She lifts a palmful, lets them sieve back into the box. They make a satisfying metally clacking sound.

Once, when she asked Grandpa Philip where they came from, he spun the globe and showed her, his hand on the bottom half of the sphere: the South Indian Ocean, he said. *Cowries* – each one held a creature inside it, imagine that! He showed her a drawing of a dark grey snaily mollusc in an old nature book. Over two hundred years old, he said, wonderingly, and yet they look like new.

She plunges her hands inside the shells again, and this time she lifts her palms out more slowly, letting them tumble through her fingers. They make her feel excited – make saliva mix with the chocolate in her mouth.

She wants to keep them. Just for a bit.

Would he have let her, if she had asked him?

He might.

He could be like that. Suddenly kind and exciting. Sometimes he would give you things. Unexpected things.

She closes the box, makes sure the catch is safe and nothing is going to spill, then she lifts it into her backpack, puts the chocolate on top, checks that the zip is secure and pulls it onto her back. Then she carries the phenology book and walks down the hall and out into the morning sun.

'Hello,' says a voice behind her.

Rowan turns. Her aunty, Isa, is sitting on a bench, smoking a cigarette. 'Hey, Rowan,' she says, raising her hand.

'Oh hello,' Rowan says. 'Are Rani and Seb here?'

'No. They're in school today. They're coming tomorrow with their dad . . . how come you're not in school?'

Rowan shifts her backpack. 'Because it's an insect day.'

'Inset,' says Isabella.

'What?'

'Don't worry,' says her aunt. 'Insect is much better. What happens on insect day then?'

'Me and Grandpa find bugs and draw them for our book.'

'Is that what you've got there?' Her aunt points with her cigarette.

'Yes.'

'Can I see?'

Rowan considers. She doesn't really want to talk to anyone, she wants to find a good, private place to eat the rest of the chocolate and take out the shells and play with them for a bit, undisturbed.

'Come on,' says Isa. 'I haven't seen you for ages. Come and keep me company for a bit.'

'Alright.' Rowan does as she asks and joins her on the bench and passes the book to her aunt.

'What's phenology then?' says Isa, putting the cigarette on the ground and opening the book.

'It's citizen science,' says Rowan. 'If everyone notices what they see and records it then we know what's happening when. Everything's getting earlier,' she says, as Isa slowly turns the pages. 'Like budburst. Trees' leaves. Flowers. And sometimes the bugs are coming out at the wrong time; blue tit chicks hatch later than the caterpillars they need to feed on . . . the whole web of life is getting tangled. So we need to pay more attention to the threads.'

This is something that her mum says a lot. But Isa doesn't seem to notice, she is staring at a picture of a hazel catkin that Grandpa Philip drew in February. Her aunt's finger traces the dangling out-line of the catkin, then she turns the page to a picture Rowan did of a brimstone butterfly in watercolours, two brown spots on its yellow-green wings.

'Grandpa Philip loved those,' says Rowan. 'He said they were the herald of spring.'

Isa nods. 'And these?' she says, pointing to the next page, a drawing by Philip of the adders that came out of their winter sleep to sun themselves at the bottom of the ha-ha in the weeks before he died.

Rowan remembers that: how delighted he was to see them, like old friends.

'He managed to walk as far as the ha-ha to see them,' she says. 'After that he was mostly in his bed.'

The last picture is double-faced – two chiffchaffs, one that Grandpa Philip did, and Rowan's one beside. She's quite proud of her picture – she even managed to do shading. Grandpa Philip's is a bit shaky though.

'It was just before he died,' says Rowan. 'Like a week or something. He was really happy he got to hear the chiffchaff come back.'

'Where had it been?' says Isa.

'In Africa,' says Rowan, surprised her aunt should ask. 'Though some chiffchaffs stay in England for the winter now. Cos everything's getting warmer.'

Isa grows very quiet and still then. A drop of water lands on the page. Isa rubs it with her sleeve and smudges the lines of Rowan's drawing. 'Fuck,' she says. 'Sorry. I'm really sorry, Rowan.'

Rowan looks up at her aunt. 'It's alright,' she says, quietly. 'It's not that bad.' She doesn't know quite what her aunt is sorry for, whether it's the swearing or the crying. Or maybe she's sorry that things are getting warmer and it's not Rowan's fault. She doesn't know what else to say. She could ask Isa for money for her swear box; she gets a pound for a fuck word, but she decides against it, and besides, Isa's crying is making her feel itchy, which is a sure sign she needs to move. 'Do you want to borrow it?' she says, getting to her feet. 'For a bit? The book? You can give it back to me later. Or tomorrow. I've just . . . got some things to do.'

'Sure,' says her aunt. 'I'd like that. Thank you, Rowan.'

Rowan stands with relief, glad to escape, skirting the side of the house, standing in the cool shadows of the colonnade. She looks out over the park, wondering where she can go. Not back inside. Not anywhere too close to the house, where people might see her. She'd like to go home, to her bedroom in the cottage, its roof just visible from here – just sit on her old bed and tip the shells out there – but she knows she can't, and so the best closest hiding place is the old oak; there's a den in there she made last summer, but she hasn't been back there yet this spring.

She climbs down the stone steps and sets off up the hill towards the oak. When she reaches the great old tree she crawls inside through the hole, which is not much bigger than her. Once inside the space is cosy though, there's leaf litter on the ground, and an old cushion and a nice blanket that's a bit damp but not wet and still good to sit on. She always feels calm inside when she's in here, because the inside of the tree is always the same temperature; even on the hottest days it's cool.

She lifts the Albion box out of her rucksack and the bars of chocolate, and she's just about to eat another piece of Dairy Milk when there's a sound of footsteps outside. She pops her head out and sees someone walking slowly towards her – Jack, with a dead deer on his back. The sun is behind him, and the deer's head is in shadow, so he looks like a creature that is half man and half deer: a man turning into a deer, or a deer turning into a man.

He hasn't seen her yet, and if it were anyone else she might hide again, but because it's Jack and because she wants to see the deer, she calls out to him and waves.

'Hey, Rowan,' he says, 'you're up early.'

'I'm just doing some stuff,' says Rowan.

'Nice. Well, I won't disturb you, I'm looking for your mum. Have you seen her?'

'She went up to the office after breakfast,' says Rowan. She clambers back out of the hole and comes to stand beside Jack in the morning sun. 'Why are you carrying that deer?'

'We're going to cook it tomorrow, for Philip. For your grandpa. I've been digging a pit.'

'Where?'

'Over by the wood.' He turns and points.

'Can I see?'

'I can't take you just now, but you're welcome to check it out.'

He shifts the deer on his back, and Rowan can see the place where the bullet went into the side of its body: a perfectly round hole crusted with red rime.

'Did you shoot it?'

Jack nods. 'A few days ago. It's been hanging in the cold store. But the cold store is very cold. It needs to thaw a little before we start to cook it, so I'm bringing it up to the house to put it on the slab in the cold room.'

'Like Grandpa Philip,' says Rowan.

'In what way?'

'He's in a cold store so his body doesn't stink. Because if he wasn't, all the bacteria would multiply and he might explode. He has to be kept just above freezing. And then he'll come out and we will bury him.'

'Right,' Jack says. 'Well, almost exactly like that then, yes. I'm going to bury this guy in a pit to cook him.'

'Can I touch it?' says Rowan.

'Sure.'

She reaches out and puts her finger to the bullet hole, with its rind of crusted red; the place where life became death. It makes her shiver. She can't work out if the shiver is good or bad – excitement or disgust. Maybe both. 'What's it like,' she says, 'to shoot something?' She looks up into Jack's face. 'What's it like to make something dead?'

Jack frowns, and a deep line comes between his eyebrows. He takes a long time to think about this and while he is thinking she watches him. Watches the way the breath comes in and out of his chest. She understands he is taking his time because it's a big question and he is taking it seriously. And this makes her heart hurt in a good way, and an aching way too, and she can't really say why.

'It's . . . strange,' he says. 'Before I pull the trigger, I'm not thinking – I'm just concentrating on getting the shot; hitting the animal in the right place so it doesn't suffer. And then, just after I shoot, I can feel almost happy and excited. But then afterwards I often feel quite sad. And I don't like it very much.'

'And did you cut it up, with your knife?'

'I did, yes.'

'And what's that like?'

'I quite like it. Seeing all the different parts of the animal. It sort of feels like . . . honouring it, somehow.'

Rowan nods, because she understands exactly what he means to say, and that makes her happy somehow, even though what he is talking about is quite sad. And then, with a fierce sort of tug she remembers – last night she heard her mum saying something to Uncle Milo over dinner, about Jack leaving. About him going to Scotland – something she forgot about completely when she woke up and was thinking about insect day. 'Are you leaving, Jack?' she says. 'Mum said you were.'

'Ah,' he says. 'Yes. I am.'

'Why?' she says, her voice rising. 'Why do you have to go?'

'I've got another job,' he says, 'that's going to pay me a lot more money. And it felt like time for a change.'

She doesn't know what to say to this. She would like to say that she hates change. That she would like to stop it all. To go back to before Grandpa Philip died and everything was still in its right place. And that Jack's only making all of this worse by leaving, because he is part of it all here, and without him nothing will be the same. But she can't say any of this and so she says nothing, just stands there feeling hot and sad and cross.

'Well,' says Jack. 'I'd better get this fella into the fridge. I'll see you later, Rowan.'

She watches him walk away, then she goes back into the cool darkness of the tree and fumbles with the catch on the box and stares again at the shells before plunging her hands inside.

She does it over and over again, until all of her thoughts are still.

Grace is outside, walking the shaded lane; the holloway that marks the eastern edge of Ned's wood, where the wildflowers grow in profusion on the steep banks.

She has said she will gather the flowers for Philip's coffin herself – no florist, no hothouse blooms, just a simple arrangement, and so she is out here this early morning to see what is in bloom. There are buttery primroses in flower still, in the relative coolness of the lane; higher on the banks lie cow parsley, cowslip, cuckoo flower. Bluebells in their great fleshy clusters stand at the edge of the wood.

Of all the thousand acres of the estate, this holloway has always been her favourite place. When they were first together, she and Philip, those heady days after the Teddy Bears' Picnic, he walked her all over his land – *beating the bounds*, he called it.

He told her of the accident that had killed both his parents and led to his inheriting the estate. How he rarely came down here, that he lived in London mostly, where he had a flat in Chelsea on the river, but he had done it all – the Teddy Bears' Picnic – for the love of this place, and now she – Grace – was here, he could love it properly again. How their meeting was meant, how they must marry, and live in this enchantment forever. When he spoke, his hands wheeled around him, carving the air. She remembers how it felt to be close to him; it was not comforting, nor pleasurable even – her internal compass unable to gain purchase, its needle spinning round and round. It was an encounter with life on a scale she had never imagined: the height of him, his huge head with its mane of hair, the vastness of the estate, the house. But when they reached this holloway, his voice lowered, and he spoke differently. He told her it used to be a Roman lane, that their legions had marched through the great forest of Anderida here, called to this part of England for the rich iron ore that ran like blood through the sandstone beneath their feet. That his own father had told him that, later, when the iron industry came, building the charcoal furnaces that dotted these hills, forging the rivets and weapons of empire, the ironmakers would roll their cannonballs down this holloway to test their strength. That then it was a drovers' track – connecting the village in the valley bottom to the market in the town several miles away, at the top of the hill. That the village had gone now, had been gone for hundreds of years, all that remained of it the old Norman church. He would show her the beautiful church where his ancestors were buried. The church where they must marry.

Philip felt like a different creature here in this sunken lane, his voice hushed, his electric energy tempered by something stranger, something mysterious. And even now, Grace thinks, fifty years later, there is something of mystery here – as though Puck might appear from that bank of primrose and cuckoo flower, or pop his head from behind this cowslip and wink. Just like in the Kipling book – the one she inherited from her grandmother – *Puck of Pook's Hill*. She loved that book immoderately when she was a child, read it to her own children in turn; could get lost in those Arthur Rackham illustrations even then, Puck beneath a thorn bush in an English meadow, young girls in smocks with flowers in their hair and their bare slender feet on the earth. Poor old Kipling – so unfashionable these days, for good reasons, she supposes, but still. There remains, for her, some deep sense of wonder, in those stories and those pictures, something about a way of seeing that has been lost. Or perhaps it is not lost. Perhaps it is still here, a breath away, a petal away: here with the primroses and the bluebell; the stitchwort starring the clumps of grass.

Grace emerges from the end of the lane into the morning light of the park. The house below her now: that great golden, terrible house, the sagged bole of the old oak beside her. The place she first set eyes on her husband, or he set eyes on her.

Strange, the pathways that led her to this land: if she had not gone out that Saturday afternoon in Barnes, if she had not bumped into the young man on the high street with a flyer:

The Teddy Bears' Picnic
Three days of mayhem and magic in a Sussex wood

If she had not tucked the flyer into the back pocket of her jeans, then gone home and told her mother she was going camping, persuaded a friend to come too. She was twenty-one years old, shy, diffident, happier reading than talking, had never done anything so spontaneous in her life. Two nice middle-class girls, just finished secretarial college, taking the train from Victoria with a tent her friend had borrowed from her brother, a huge unwieldy thing, more suitable for scout camp than a music festival. She was wearing jeans, a top she had crocheted herself. It was hot – the endless high summer of that year – and the view from the train was all yellow stubbled fields.

Why had she done it? Why had she got on that train?

Because she had started, at the age of twenty-one, to feel old – as though the brief bright vista of life beyond her Barnes bedroom window had sped past while she was looking the other way, and no one had told her she must leap through it somehow if she wished to escape.

The train to Sussex was full of young people, the warm air heavy with the smoke of sweet-smelling joints, the conductor tutting and shaking his head but the luggage piled so high in the corridor that he couldn't squeeze through. Someone passed her a joint and she took a drag – her very first. They caught a lift from the small station down to the festival site, were dropped off in the dusk at the edge of the wood, where there were people everywhere, walkways between the trees joining exquisite treehouses together. Figures clustered around small campfires; people dressed like wizards, like elves. It was like moving through the looking glass, or passing through the wardrobe: all of her childhood fantasies come to life, Narnia and Middle-earth and Wonderland all rolled into one.

She lost her friend to a hippy boy in the first few hours and so was left to wander the festival alone: a spectator – happy to watch, but not to partake. She did not truly venture down the rabbit hole until the final night, when a man with the kindest eyes she had ever seen gave her a dress which said *Wear Me*. Gave her a crystal which said *Eat me*.

And she did.

And it was just here, by this old oak, that she met the dawn, dancing by the stage, laughing and laughing because life had revealed itself to her – as though underneath it all, the streets with their houses and the men in their suits and the golf club dinners and their hands on your knee was some great cosmic joke, a deep clear crystal river running beneath all the human chatter. And before the dawn it rained, a sharp heavy downpour, a respite from the heat that had pounded England for weeks – and still she did not move from the front of the stage, her bare feet in mud now, understanding that this was what she was put on the earth to do – to dance like this, to be free – everything so far beyond her and so terribly beautifully close. And then, when the sun rose, there was mist, and the music stopped – a huge silence. She opened her eyes, saw a great, tall man before her who reached out and touched her with his fingertips, and when his lips were on hers it was as though he had drawn something out of her, something essential, dormant until now. He took her hand and led her through the fray, through the crowd, which melted before them as they moved across the dawn park, the mist around their ankles, and there was a high ringing somewhere as of fairy bells as they approached the house, this great golden house, with its pillars and pilasters and stone steps and temple frontage, and she looked at him, confused. It's mine, he said, and he swept his hand around the park, the stages, the wood, the crowds of people in the dawn mist, as though he were wizard and laird and conjuror all at once. And it felt to her, that summer morning, as though Philip was Gawain and Arthur and Aslan and she was Guinevere and Lucy and Alice, as she followed him up the wide shallow stairs, past the portraits on the wall, their pale faces floating above dark clothes, as Philip led her by the hand into the bedroom and lifted her onto the bed. And as he lifted her she saw her feet were caked in mud, and she laughed and laughed at her filthy feet as they lay side by side on the bed, while the tapestries moved all around them, the embroidery alive with heavy, laden vines and stags, and the mirrors of her dress caught the light, sent it all around that bedroom as he kissed her on her brow and on her neck and she lay quite still and let him, like an offering, or a sacrifice.

She knows now what was lying in wait for the young woman laid out on the bed. The young woman who beat the bounds with Philip, full of hope. The young woman who married him on a day in early autumn in the old Norman church at the bottom of the hill. Simply put, she had been safe, and now was not.

Philip's initial enchantment with her and with his home was brief – there were bright patches, when he would show himself to be kind, or attentive, but they became fewer and fewer. She knew he expected her to be pregnant within weeks, and when the weeks became months, he left for London, for longer and longer periods. She began to understand that he had never lived here properly, did not know how to live in the country, was utterly ill-equipped for a life in this house so haunted by his past. As the autumn turned and winter claimed the house and the estate, she was left alone. The house, so golden in the summer sun, was something quite different in the wintertime; there were only two rooms that were habitable, and those barely. She wore layers of clothes indoors. Buckets caught the drips from the leaking roof. Animals scurried in the walls – louder at night.

There was a housekeeper, a gardener, an estate manager. There was food, of a kind, presented three times a day, but there was nothing for clothes or days out or books or magazines or face creams or cinema trips or hairdressers or biscuits. There was no car. No friends. A small television mostly kept in a cupboard. A radio.

Philip would return, relatively often – she would never know when. He would bring gifts, seem to be kind, attempt to kindle her smile, take her to bed, try to be good and live with her again, but all too soon he would grow fractious and angry and petulant, blame her for every petty thing and leave.

Or he would drive down – again without warning – set up camp and throw a party that would last for days. There would be others with him, women often. The women would look at her curiously or pityingly or brazenly. She would look away, unable to meet whatever was in their gaze.

She became thin, dangerously so. She haunted the library, would ask for a fire to be lit there and sit, still bundled into coats, reading.

Looking back, it seems extraordinary that she put up with it, but she had been brought up to believe that marriage was sacrosanct. And as the full catastrophe of her marriage revealed itself, the full catastrophe of her upbringing, which had fitted her for nothing but the desire for fantasy and the acceptance of subjugation and pain, also became clear. It was as though she had gone through the looking glass, down the rabbit hole, through the wardrobe – only to be left there, cast under some sort of spell.

Finally her children came – conceived between Philip's affairs. Frannie first, two years after their marriage, desperate to walk, to talk. Milo, when he came several years later, was different: he needed her as much as she needed him, and all the dammed-up love in her she poured onto her son. He clung to her, they clung to each other – as though each was the ship and the shipwreck all at once. And Isa – if Frannie was her challenge and Milo her love, then Isa was her double.

Her children tethered her to life. Philip's absences were less stark or painful with three children in the house – until, when their son was eight, Philip informed her that Milo was being sent away to school.

Nothing in her life had prepared her for the loss of her son. Who, from that first exeat weekend, would no longer touch her, or accept her love; he whose touch had been the simplest, the most easeful of her life. He was a changeling boy. His face pale and his smile forced. His laughter, the stream of which had filled the house, disappeared – it would surface again years later, when he was an adolescent, a different kind of humour then, sarcastic, cutting, and she knew he had been harmed in that school, harmed in ways he had no words for. And she knew she could not protect him from this harm, that it was his birthright, his inheritance.

Still, though, it was a life of sorts, a family of sorts: her daughters in the house, her son there in the holidays. Philip away more often than not. And so it went until, in his early fifties, Philip left her for a young woman in America. She felt no pain, only relief that there would be an ocean between them.

She did not divorce him – why not? Perhaps because she knew he would leave her with nothing, perhaps because she was like the prisoner in the experiment who grows to know and love her captor – by then, the estate, for all its horrors, was all she knew. And there was always Ned. He would return from wherever he had spent the winter, and she would see the smoke rising, or hear the distant music from the wood, and she would know he was back in residence. She would find her way down to his glade, take off the coats and cardigans that had swaddled her all winter, and there, at Ned's fire, warmth would enter her bones. He would chide her for her paleness, her thinness, feed her – give her tinctures and make her sit by the fire while he told her stories of where he had been and what he had seen.

Then one day Philip came back. Just like that, just as he always had – without warning, without telephoning ahead. He took a taxi from the airport one early morning, dropped his bags in the hall. Came to find her, where she slept in the tapestried bed. Leant over her. When she opened her eyes and saw him there she screamed.

And so he moved back home. And they lived together, at first bitterly, and then, over time, less so. She could not love him though, never let him touch her again. She presumes he found ways to meet his needs, but they lived in an unspoken agreement: he would not trouble her physically; she would not trouble him with questions about his life beyond the boundaries of the park.

And then Frannie returned, taking up residence in the cottage down by the lake. Grace thought her eldest daughter would leave again quickly, but she stayed in place all that winter; Grace would see her walking in all weathers – a strange sad figure, beating her own solitary bounds. She could see her daughter was broken and lost, but did not know how to reach her, so did not truly try. It was Philip who reached her: Philip and Frannie who found each other that spring. Philip who began to walk with his eldest daughter around the estate.

She began to see wonder return to her husband, in the years before he died, as though the wish he had held as a young man was finally granted. It was there in his delight in the natural world, counting swifts and tallying them, collecting dung beetles in jars. Studying insects through the microscope with his granddaughter.

It was there in him too the day that Milo gave him the treatment: the wonder in his eyes. He caught her by the arm that evening, when all their children had melted away and she was tucking him in for the night – his skin yellow with jaundice from his dying liver, the cancer everywhere, his jaw clenched, speaking through the pain.

I fear, he said, that I have been a bad husband to you. A terrible one in fact. That you did not deserve me. That your life would have been far happier if you had married someone else.

She stood frozen in the act of smoothing the pillow beneath his head, the claw of his hand on her arm.

Will you forgive me, Grace? I am asking you to forgive me, please.

The fury she felt – as though in the moment of his asking forgiveness he had trapped her once again. She stood very still, imagining taking the pillow from behind his head, smothering him, staring down at his wild blue eyes, his panicked flailing hands. She wondered how many seconds it would take until the breath was gone. Then she took his hand from her arm and placed it under the covers, which she smoothed over him. Of course, she said. Of course I will.

And so what, then, of grief?

She has grieved her husband for years. Since they were first married.

She has no more grief left in her, only this new space inside her – a space whose contours she does not yet fully know. She knows only that somewhere in her a small flame burns, a small thin flame she cannot name, for fear the breath of naming it would be enough to snuff it out.

She turns away from the tree, from the ghost of herself in a yellow dress, her arms raised to the sky, and crosses the park to the orchard where the trees are blossom-laden, white and pink. Beneath them stand the wild hives that Ned built, and the morning air is already sonorous with bees.

As soon as Jack rounds the side of the house he sees Isa, sitting on the old stone bench, reading a book. There is no going around her. And so he calls out softly.

She looks up. Her face is raw, gouged with feeling. He can see she has been crying. She looks ambushed, and he is immediately anguished: he should not be here, intruding on her grief. 'Sorry,' he says, 'I'm really sorry. I didn't mean to disturb you.'

She closes the book. 'It's okay.'

'Are you alright? Do you need anything?'

She looks older. Sadder. Maybe thinner. But she is the same.

'No.' She puts the book gently down onto the bench beside her. 'I was just looking at some of Dad's drawings. Ones he did with Rowan.'

'Oh, yeah,' he says. 'They're pretty good, some of them.'

'You've seen them?'

'Some.'

Isa pushes the heels of her hands into her eyes. 'I'm okay,' she says, more to herself than to him. 'How are you, Jack?'

'I'm fine. Good, yeah.'

'Who's your friend?'

'Oh.' He puts the deer down on the ground between them. 'He's going in a pit tomorrow morning to be cooked.'

'That looks like some heavy symbolism right there.'

'Symbolic of what?'

'I don't know. The end of innocence?'

'Whose innocence?'

'Just . . . innocence.'

'Yeah. Maybe.' Then, because he can't think of anything else to say he says, 'I'm sorry. About your dad.'

'It's okay. Death happens, apparently,' she says, gesturing to the deer. 'I'm sure your mate can attest to that. Are you coming to the funeral?'

He shifts his weight. 'Frannie asked me to help carry the coffin, so –'

'Oh. Okay. Right.' She frowns.

Did she know this, he wonders? He feels embarrassed somehow. He wants to say, *It's okay – don't worry – I don't want to. It's just that Frannie asked me. I can say no.*

She reaches into her back pocket and brings out cigarette papers, tobacco. Offers them to him wordlessly – an outstretched hand, an eyebrow raised.

He shakes his head. 'Gave up years ago.'

'Yeah. Me too.' She laughs. 'I bought them on the way here yesterday. Something about this place just makes me want to smoke the shit out of myself.'

He watches her slim fingers as she rolls her cigarette. His heart is fast, but heavy. This exact spot. This was where she was. Reading on a bench.

Twenty years.

Half a life.

He finds it hard, standing here, to think of what exactly has filled that life, filled the space between then and now. In one way it feels inevitable that she is here. In another it is shocking, like the universe is playing a trick.

Isa brings out her lighter, lifts the flame to her cigarette.

'How's London?' he says.

'Oh. You know.'

'Not really, no.'

'Well . . . teaching's pretty intense. The kids are full on. Good, though. They made me head of year.'

'Congratulations.'

'Thanks. Although I think it's a bit like being made second mate on the *Titanic*.'

'Sorry – I'm not sure what you mean.'

'They're decimating the education system. Haven't you noticed?'

'Not particularly. I mean, it was always shit.'

She looks irritated. He wonders what he was supposed to say. Something clever. The sort of thing her mates would say. Or maybe he was supposed to tell her how great she is for working in a school like that. She must have people telling her that all the time.

'Well, I won't keep you,' he says. 'Do you know where Frannie is?'

'No. But she'll be here soon. We're due to have a family meeting this morning. Pa's long-lost daughter has turned up from the States.'

'Sorry,' says Jack. 'You've lost me.'

'Don't worry. It's not important. I mean it is, it's important, but . . .' She won't look at him. 'Frannie told me you're leaving,' she says. 'For Scotland?'

'Yeah. I'm going on Sunday.'

'That's a long way away, isn't it?'

'I guess so.'

'What about your kids?'

'They're in Devon with Charlie. Anyway, they're big now.'

'I guess they are. How old?'

'Sixteen. Eighteen. What about yours?'

'Twelve. Eight.'

They didn't talk about her kids, he thinks, when she was here after his mum died. When they were together down at the tree-house. He can picture her body, the skin beneath the clothes. He knows the placement of the moles on her torso. The shape of her nipple, the way it felt when it was in his mouth, against the tip of his tongue.

'How's Charlie?' Isa says.

'Good. Yeah. She loves it there. By the coast.'

'That's good.'

'Look,' he says, 'I've got to get this deer inside.'

But he doesn't move, and neither does she. The air between them has thickened somehow.

'You're going to work for that tech guy,' she says, eventually.

He nods.

'Have you met him?'

'Sure. I met him here.'

'Here?'

'He was here for one of Frannie's workshops. She holds them for landowners who are interested in rewilding. There's a lot of them about.'

'I didn't know she hosted people like that.'

'Like what?'

She shrugs. 'I read some stuff about him. An article. A while ago. I mean, what is it? Can you tell me? These big-swinging corporate dicks and their predator fetish?'

He is silent.

'And it's a lot, isn't it?' she says. 'A hundred thousand acres. I mean – is that ever okay?'

'Sorry, I'm not sure what you mean.'

'Well, on one level it's just plain wrong, isn't it? One hundred thousand acres?'

'Worse than a thousand?'

'A hundred times worse.'

'Really? I think that depends.'

'On what?'

'On what you want to do with it.'

'So that's where we are now? Anyone that expresses an interest in beavers and wolves has the moral slate wiped clean?'

'I didn't say that.'

'You sort of did.'

'I don't think so. I just said I was going to work for him.'

'And it's a lot to manage, isn't it? A big jump up.'

And he can see now, where this is heading. She wants to hurt him. She is going to hurt him. 'What do you mean?'

She shrugs.

'You mean you don't know if I'm up to it?'

'I didn't say that.'

He laughs. 'You'll forgive me, Isa, if I don't come to you for career advice, since you have no idea what it is that I do, or what I'm capable of.'

'It's just . . . disappointing.'

'Oh really? Okay. I disappoint you, do I? Wow,' he shakes his head. 'It's fucking remarkable.'

'What is?'

'How I can not see you for three years and disappoint you within three minutes.'

She goes to speak but he raises his hand, stopping her. 'Listen, I've got to get this deer inside, can you let Frannie know I have it? And that I was looking for her? And that the pit is ready? Tell her I'll light the fire in the morning and put the deer in early. Please.'

He bends down and hauls the deer onto his back.

In the pantry he puts the deer on the side slab to thaw.

As he does so, he considers its body: the places where he cut into it with his knife. Where he lifted the innards away from the bones. He wonders if this is how he appears to her, to Isa. Wandering around with his insides out. Ready to be flayed. Astonishing, still, the pain she can cause him. She's lethal. She can slice him at ten paces. You think it's a paper cut, and you see it's a flesh wound. And then you see you're bleeding out.

He pushes against the slab, holds himself up, feeling the cold marble beneath his palms. He feels suddenly, completely bleak, as though everything that was good in him and in the future has drained away.

He closes his eyes, and waits for it to pass.

At least it's over now. The waiting, the wondering if she felt the same. In amongst the pain is a sort of freedom. A sort of relief. Perhaps, now, he can move again – perhaps he can feel something new.

❧

Perhaps, thinks Frannie, taking a swig of coffee, she could start the eulogy with this, her father's desk. She could write about the desk itself: a solid, stolid rectangle of mahogany, its writing surface leather-tooled – two hundred and forty years old, commissioned by her ancestor Oliver Brooke, he whose portrait hangs behind her on the wall. A desk which was the last redoubt of her father's – even when he was well past the point of no return, when his bed had been set up down here in the library so he could avoid walking up the stairs, when the cancer was everywhere and he had mere weeks left to live, she would still catch him sitting here, staring out: at his walls of books, at the park beyond the glass of the French doors, his binoculars beside him, almost too heavy to hold.

She leans to her laptop, brings up her Word doc.

Desk?? she types. *Ancestry?*

Continuity?

The cursor blinks, expectantly. She deletes her words. Too distant. Too sober. She needs to be more simple, more direct.

Pa, she writes . . . *Who he was to me?*

She knows what her siblings will expect her to say tomorrow, when she stands at the rostrum in the church, has felt it in the tenor of every interaction she has had with them in the last twenty-four hours: Isa's surly rage with her last night, Milo's lobbying, both exhausting, both in their own ways versions of old, entrenched dynamics.

Why must it be so? Why must Isa be so angry? *It's not fair,* she longs to say. *It's not okay for you to speak to me like that.* But it has always been so, hasn't it? Isa's pain somehow more painful than anyone else's; Milo too, always in conversation with the wounds of his childhood. And she, Frannie, must play her role, the one that was assigned to her so early on: to not complain, to get on with it.

Has anyone ever stopped to ask her, after all these years, whether she has her own nightmares in this house?

What did Isa say last night? *Just because everything here has always been easy for you.*

Perhaps she could shock them all. Get up there tomorrow in the church and speak of her own wounds. She could tell them all about the time when she was thirteen, and her father threw a party. Something he did periodically, but during this particular gathering she woke in the night because the music below her window was so loud; went out to the corridor and made her way down to the bathroom, opened the door and turned on the light. In there, pressed up against the sink with his back to her, was her father. She could tell it was him from his height, and the length of his hair. Between her father and the sink was a woman, the woman's legs were wrapped around her father's waist, and one of her father's hands was on one of the woman's breasts. She remembers the paleness of his buttocks, the way they moved rhythmically. He didn't turn around, didn't even stop moving, just hissed at her, where she stood frozen in the doorway.

Whoever you are, just . . . fuck off.

So, her father didn't see her, but the woman did, and Frannie can conjure the horror on her face even now – her lipsticked mouth hanging open, slack with shock. She did as she was told, switched off the light and swiftly closed the door and went back to her bedroom, where, desperate to pee but too terrified to move, she stayed all night, huddled in a hot tight ball, until the music stopped and the dawn broke.

She never told a soul. Or – that's not quite true. She tried to tell her mother, but as she stumbled to find the words to describe what she had seen, she saw her mother's face discompose to reveal an inchoate distress; a sight far more awful than her father's buttocks or the slack jaw of the woman on the sink. And so Frannie ceased speaking, looked away, and when she looked back her mother was herself again. And in that moment, she understood all she needed to know of the horror of her parents' marriage, and the pain beneath the elegance of her mother's façade. And she knew too, that Grace would never meet her in her own confusion and pain, or lift it from her – that it was her job to manage it herself. And so she learned from her mother how to parcel the unthinkable away.

And she said nothing; certainly not to her little sister, who was five years old at the time, nor her brother, away at school. Instead, she grew around the sickening fact of her father's nature – after that party she didn't have the expectation that he would be otherwise; not accepting the truth of it would only have slowed her down.

Is it any wonder, though, that she doesn't want drugs on her land?

And should she have to explain this to Milo? So desperate to claim his portion of the estate, now she has cleansed it, finally, of its toxic inheritance: of the drugs and the parties and the debauchery her father pursued with such relentless energy? And should she have to explain herself to Isa? To say that she too has had her nightmares, here in this house, would never have chosen to live here. She got out and away as fast as she could. Hasn't kept a room here since she was a teenager (not so her siblings, both of whom have kept their teenaged bedrooms just as they are). Should she have to explain why it was she ran away to Newbury; why, later, after university, she took jobs in far-flung places, never wishing to return – how she only came back because, in the course of a week in her mid-thirties, her life fell off a cliff. A contract ran out and was not renewed for lack of funds. A brief, painful relationship ended at the same time as she discovered she was five weeks pregnant – she flew back to the UK and miscarried on the plane. She never told a soul.

Should she tell them how she found herself, finally after seventeen years, and at the age of thirty-five, with nowhere to go but home. How she moved back to the estate, to a tiny damp cottage by the river, with a rowan tree in the garden, stunned by grief and loss. How strange it was to be once again in the orbit of her parents, living together again for the first time in years. They invited her up to the house, Philip plied her with wine and whisky in the library and asked her what she planned to do. Grace came down to the cottage one day. Do you want to talk about what happened? she asked. Just life, Frannie shrugged, because it was too late then, for any kind of intimacy, and anyway, her mother had proved herself incapable of that long ago.

Would Milo and Isa have the patience to hear how she spent a winter walking the estate, coming to know the land she had grown up in: the conifer plantation a breeding ground for pheasant, feed hoppers every several paces, eerie, hung about by death. Field after field rented out for oilseed rape. How she began to understand the land was sick – as sad and bereft as her own heart. How it was chance, fate, call it what you will, that she read the *State of Nature* report that spring, that she went to an open day at a re-wilded estate, forty minutes west, where she sat in a cow barn while an energetic, vital husband-and-wife team spoke of how they had turned their struggling dairy farm – the same Wealden clay of her family's estate – into a refuge for the natural world.

How she closed her eyes and saw the oak tree she had lived in at Newbury. How she felt twenty years of time concertina – and understood what she had to do.

It was not arrogance that made her do it. It was the understanding that she must – that if she did not do it then no one would.

And the project grew between them, her and Philip, rooting them both in ways they could never have foreseen. And as long as they were both looking forward at the long future, there was no need to ever look back.

But it was not *easy*, Isa, and nor was it inevitable.

Her fingers start to fly over the keys, and Frannie writes steadily for several minutes, frowning intently at the screen, until the door opens, and Milo's head appears around it. 'Hey, sis,' he calls softly.

Frannie looks up, unable to smother a small sound of exasperation.

'I came down early to help.' His tone is emollient.

'Thanks,' she says. 'But I really need a little time to write this.'

'What's that?'

'The eulogy.'

'You haven't written it yet?'

'I'm writing it now. Finally.'

'You're cutting it fine.'

'Clearly, yes.'

'Okay. I'll leave you to it – but listen,' he says, 'is there anything you need from me today? I mean it – other than the meeting, I'm free all morning till Luca turns up.'

'Just to please leave me alone for fifteen minutes to write this.'

'Okay.' He holds up his hands. 'Nothing practical then?'

The morning light is slanting onto her brother's face. He looks, it seems to her, profoundly rested. She wonders irritably how many hours' sleep he had last night. She takes a swig of coffee. 'Well . . . there is something that occurred to me.' She saves her document, pushes away her computer. 'This is probably not the right time for this, but . . .'

'Name it. I'm here for it, Fran. Anything I can do.'

'Okay. If you really have time to spare this morning, maybe after the family meeting, you could make a start on clearing out your room?'

'My room?' He gives a small laugh.

'Yes.'

'My *bed*room?'

'Yes.'

'Okay. I mean. Sure. Is it a problem though?'

'Not a problem exactly. But it can't stay like that for another twenty years – the rooms will be needed.'

'For what?'

'For accommodation. In the future. For students – that sort of thing.'

'Really? That sounds pretty vague.'

'Does it? I just thought it might be good, while you're here. You and Isa.'

'So you'll be asking her too?'

'Of course.'

Milo grows quiet. 'So, it's no longer my bedroom? Is that what you're saying?'

'Well . . . yes, I suppose I am.'

'Okay, wow.' He blows air out from his cheeks. 'I mean. That's pretty harsh. Kicking me out of my room on Dad's funeral weekend.'

'It would be if you lived here, Milo. Or if you were eighteen. Or sixteen. Or twelve. But you have your own home. The room is a museum to your teenage self. Same with Isa's. It's sort of creepy.'

'I don't though,' he says.

'Don't what?'

'Have a home. My flat is rented. I've hardly been there in the last year.'

'Okay, fine. Listen.' She puts her hand up. 'Don't bother. It's really not a big deal.'

'It sounds like it is.'

'I promise you it's not. It's fine. I'm just . . . I'm surprised.'

'Okay,' he says. 'Just, give me a moment. I'm feeling pretty triggered here.' He pulls out a chair and sits down. She flicks a look at the time on her phone – she does not want him to sit down, she wants him to stand up and walk over to the door and leave her alone. But her brother does not stand up. Instead he puts his hands flat on his thighs, closes his eyes and takes a big, measured breath. Just having to watch him breathe like that is making her feel more stressed.

'Can we revisit this conversation?' he says eventually. 'After the funeral?'

'Sure. Of course. Let's do that.'

He nods. 'Okay, thanks. Appreciated.'

She pulls her laptop close, reawakens the document, but it's useless, her thread is broken.

'So . . .' Her brother hasn't moved. 'Can we briefly talk about the meeting with Luca? I just want to be sure we're all facing the same direction.'

'Jesus, Milo.' She gives a quick sharp sigh, saves the document, flips her laptop shut and pushes it away. 'Okay, I'm just going to say this because you're asking, and because Luca's coming . . .'

'Go on.'

'I spoke to Simon yesterday. And he's given me rather a stark picture of the finances.'

'What sort of a picture? What do you mean?'

'It's complex. Despite appearances and colossal amounts of hard work, we are still just about breaking even. We have no cushion, which would be fine, perfectly normal, as you know, but the issue is inheritance tax: because Pa lived here until his death, we are liable for a huge amount, unless we qualify for heritage property status. And even then, we are short.'

'By how much?'

'Probably around one to two million.'

'Okay,' says her brother with a shrug.

'It's a lot of money, Milo.'

'Of course. In some ways. In other ways, not at all.'

'Yes, to some people I can see that it would be loose change.'

'Listen, Fran, we can always ask Luca to loan to the estate. Bring him in, that's all I'm asking. This is a great opportunity for him to weave into what we're doing here.'

'*We?*'

'What?'

'You said *we*. What *we're* doing here.'

'You. I meant you, Fran. Jesus. Relax. We're on the same side here.'

'Okay, well – no. That's not happening. I don't want him weaving anything. I've run this place successfully for ten years. I don't need Luca.'

'But you do. You've just told me you need someone with some cash. Listen, sis, let's wait till Luca comes – he's much better on the detail of this, but we can really scale up the brand you've started here, create multiple revenue streams. He's already got some great ideas.'

'No!' She slaps her hands down on the desk. 'No. No one's *scaling* anything. No one's optimizing anything. No one's trading on the name of the project. Let's not spend any more time on this. We've got other priorities this morning – I'm just saying, Simon was very clear.'

'And what did he say?'

She takes a deep breath. 'His advice is that you and Luca buy the acres for The Clearing. Fifteen acres plus planning and the right to develop.'

'I see,' says Milo. 'This is what Simon says, is it?'

'Yes.'

'And Simon's running the show, is he?'

'Simon has been the estate manager for the last several years, yes. You know this, Milo. And he's done a bloody good job.'

'Are you serious?'

'Yes,' she says. 'It's pretty Faustian, I admit, but it's either that or make Mum pay a million pounds for my old cottage, and I'm imagining neither of us wants to ask her to do that.'

'You are! You're serious! There are a thousand ways to solve this, Frannie – and you've jumped straight to this? Disinheriting me? You saw Dad after the treatment. He *told* you what he wanted. We were sitting on the bed together, Frannie. *Holding his hands.* Do you remember? Or has that slipped your mind too?'

She remembers: that evening when she came back into the house with her mother, the strange stillness that seemed to hang over everything, Philip tear-rinsed and beatific in his bed – the sense that something had, indeed, occurred.

'He did,' she accedes, 'yes. But there was no mention of Ned's wood. Did you mention the wood to Pa? That day?'

'I didn't have to. It was so strongly in my heart. In my vision.'

'Well, I'm sorry, Milo, but visions are not legal documents.'

'I actually cannot believe what I'm hearing here. You're telling me things are really that bad?'

'They could be if I don't act strategically.'

'Ah, okay. Okay. *Strategy?* Is that where we are? Forgive me for thinking we were in the same family.'

'We are in the same family, Milo.'

'Jesus Christ, Fran. It's like that game when we were kids. Simon says. *Simon says put your hands on your head . . . Simon says disinherit your brother.*'

'Milo. Listen. I really don't want to hurt you. Or undermine you, or your vision. And as I said, it wouldn't be my choice to be speaking about this today; if anyone has forced the issue here it's you. Just to be clear, if the estate goes under there will be nothing. No visions. No land. No house. No nothing. I'm not disinheriting you. How can I? You haven't inherited anything.'

'Wow. Okay, Frannie. *Wow.*'

'Milo, please. This isn't what I want. Do you think I want this?'

'I don't know, Frannie.' He looks down at his hands, then: 'Okay,' he says, 'well I really wouldn't bring this up otherwise, but I have to say it. *Do you remember?* Do you even *remember* that winter when you were living in the cottage?'

'Of course I remember.'

'You were lost, Fran. You were stagnating.'

'Milo – stop it.'

'No.' He holds up his finger to silence her. 'You were lost, Fran, and you didn't know where to turn. I came down, we talked, and I *showed you the way.*'

'Hardly.'

'Oh, *hardly?* You're recasting history now? I remember it like it was yesterday. We sat up all night. We drank wine –'

'Milo –'

'No. Listen to me. We drank wine, and you told me how lost you felt.'

'I'm not sure I said that . . .'

'You said *lost*, Frannie. And you were. And I said to you – *You should do something here. On the estate.* The next morning, I woke up and you were still in bed, because you were so sad you couldn't get up, and I wrote it on a piece of paper. I wrote it on a piece of fucking paper, Fran. I left it for you to find.' He is standing right in front of her now, the cords on either side of his throat pulsing. '*You.*' He jabs his finger in the air towards her. '*Should. Do. Something. Here.* That's what I *wrote*, Frannie. That's what I left propped up by the kettle so you would find it. And after that you did. You did do something. You did something fantastic, as I always knew you would, you could. But it was *my fucking idea.* The truth is that you owe me, Fran. I'm not paying you for my *birthright – you owe me*, not the other way around . . . you know what your trouble is, sis?'

'What's that?'

'You pretend to be so moral. So straight. But you *love* the limelight. You want it all for yourself.'

'Is that right?'

'Yeah, it's right. That article. Seriously? The cover of *Country* fucking *Life*? Where was the acknowledgement, Fran?'

'I should have acknowledged you. It was wrong.'

'Too right it was wrong. And you should have apologized a long time ago. *I am part of this story too.*'

'What's happening here?'

Frannie turns, sees their mother is at the door. 'Nothing,' she says.

'No,' says Milo. 'No, Frannie. I'm not having that – it's not nothing, Mum. It's very much something.'

'I can see you're quarrelling,' says Grace. 'Whatever it is you're quarrelling about, I don't want to know. Not today. I'm sure you'll understand.'

Frannie is breathing hard. She cannot quite fathom it, it is as though someone, something, has rowed them both – she and her brother – out onto a cold dark sea. She manages a nod to her mother.

'Good,' says Grace. 'Milo?'

Milo nods, though his face is mutinous.

'So,' says Grace. 'I'm here for a meeting, yes?'

'Yes.' Frannie opens her computer again. Her face is hot. She can feel her tears close, feel the strangeness of this: she is not someone who cries. She has not cried yet.

'It's lovely out there,' her mother is saying. 'There's apple blossom, and then I thought we could have columbine. They're just coming out. And celandine. There are ox-eye daisies. Cow parsley. I'll use the willow whips to make the frame later today and then weave into that in the morning.'

Frannie glances gratefully towards her mother. 'Thanks, Mum,' she says. 'That sounds perfect.'

Grace nods. A fleeting look passes from mother to daughter: *Gather yourself.*

'The deer should be brought up from the cold store,' Frannie says.

'It's here already,' says Isa. 'I just saw Jack.'

Frannie looks up. Her sister is here now too, sitting at the table, a copy of their mother, with her long hair. Her neat frame. But whereas their mother is straight-backed against the vicissitudes of fate, her sister is slumped, her face flushed. She looks as though she has been crying.

'He said he would put it in on the side to thaw a little. And the pit is ready. He's going to light the fire early in the morning.'

'Okay,' says Frannie, 'that's good. Wren has the rest of the catering in hand. The ceremony will be at three and we can eat at four . . . the weather looks beautiful for tomorrow, so we've decided on a range of small plates to go with the venison. In terms of the ceremony – it's everything that Pa requested. I sent you all a Google Doc with the details for you to okay.' She looks up at her siblings. 'I don't think either of you have read it though. Shall I just go through it now?'

'Sure,' says Isa. 'That would be great, thanks.'

'So,' Frannie breathes, 'I'll start with the Order of Service.

Rani's going to sing the coffin into the church – the John Dowland that Pa requested. Is that still okay, Isa?'

'Of course. She's been practising for weeks. It's beautiful. She'll do a beautiful job.'

'Okay.' She gives a swift nod. 'Great. Then, coffin bearers, we have Milo, Ned, Jack and Hari. Hari's okay with that, Isa?'

Isa nods. 'Yes. Although only four people? Is that enough? I mean, Pa was pretty huge.'

'I've talked to the funeral director about this and four is fine, apparently. Philip weighs about nine stone.'

'Fuck.'

'Yes,' says Frannie. 'He lost an enormous amount of weight in the last three weeks.'

When you stayed away, Isa.

When you hardly answered my texts or returned my calls.

'So,' says Frannie, looking back to the screen. 'The vicar will say a few words, and then it will be you, Milo, to speak first; the Richard Jefferies extract that Pa loved. Did you get it? It was in an attachment I sent.'

'I'll find it,' Milo says icily. 'I suggested it, after all.'

'Great,' says Frannie, her face pulsing. She longs to go outside, or to the bathroom, to splash her cheeks with water. 'Then it will be me to speak, and Mum, I know you said you'd read the Edward Thomas poem he asked for, is that still okay?'

'Of course.'

'What about you, Isa?' says Milo, turning to his sister.

'I've decided not to say anything,' she says.

'Really?'

'Yes.'

'Don't you think you'll regret it,' says Milo, 'if you don't?'

'I don't know. Why? Do you?'

'I just think this is your last chance to say goodbye.'

'I came down. I saw him before he died. We said goodbye. It was private. This feels . . . performative.'

134

'Jesus Christ,' says Milo.

'What?'

'It's a funeral, Isa. What are we supposed to do? Perform the whole thing in silence? Do the mime version?'

'Milo,' says Grace. 'If Isa doesn't want to speak then she doesn't have to. We don't all have to say what we feel in words.'

Frannie watches her mother's hand land for a moment on Isa's, until Isa pulls her own away, and places it into her lap.

'Okay, Isa,' says Frannie. 'If you change your mind, even in the church, you're welcome to speak.'

'I won't,' says Isa, 'but thanks.'

'So, you'll see from the doc, the guest list is just us. This was what Pa wanted. It was always going to be the choice between a huge funeral and a small one. For lunch it's just us plus families, then Ned. Oh . . . and Luca.'

'What about Jack?' says Isa.

'Jack's carrying the coffin, as I said.'

'Yes, but what about the meal?'

'Well, he's not family, is he? Besides, he's not really my favourite person at the moment.'

'So,' says Isa, 'he's family enough to kill and butcher a deer, dig a pit to cook it in, and carry Pa's coffin, but not to be invited to the meal?'

'I'm sure he's got a lot to do,' says Frannie, 'getting ready to leave.'

Grace looks up. 'What? Jack's leaving?'

'On Sunday. For Scotland.'

'Goodness . . . that's a blow.'

'Yes, it is.'

'But darling,' says Grace. 'You must invite him. He's carrying the coffin. He must be at the meal.'

Frannie brings her bottom lip between her teeth. 'Fine,' she says. 'Jack's invited to the meal. Isa, when is your family coming?'

'Not until tomorrow, late morning. Hari's driving down. He reckons they'll be here by eleven thirty.'

'Okay. I've put Rani in the room beside yours and Hari's. And Seb is on the other side.'

'Luca will need a room,' says Milo.

'No,' says Frannie. 'No way.'

'What do you mean, *no way*? C'mon, Frannie. Seriously? How many spare rooms do we have? I think probably about seventeen at the last count. Or are you counting my room? And Isa's? Are they spare now too? In which case it's more.'

'Darling Luca!' says Grace. 'I'm so glad.'

'Alright,' says Frannie, typing again. 'I'll put him in the blue room. Please. Enough.'

'Anyone else?' says Milo, sending a look to Isa. 'I think we're leaving someone out.'

'Isa?' says Frannie. 'Do you want to tell Mum?'

'Sure,' says Isa, 'but could you close your computer now please, Frannie? It's disconcerting. I feel like we're in a work meeting.'

Frannie closes her laptop and looks up as Isa draws breath.

'There's something we need to tell you, Mum. There's someone coming to the funeral. Natasha's daughter . . . she's flying in today.'

Grace's hand flies to her heart. 'And why on earth is Natasha's daughter coming?'

'I wrote to her,' says Isa. 'To Natasha I mean. To tell her Pa was dying. I thought she ought to know.'

'Why would you do that?'

'I . . . well . . .' Isa shakes her head. 'It seems that Natasha died a year ago . . . but her daughter replied. She wants to be here. To pay her respects.'

'We think she's his, Mum,' says Frannie. 'Dad's daughter. The dates sort of . . . add up.'

Grace brings her hands into her lap. The thumb of her right hand goes to her wedding ring, and she begins to turn it round and round. 'How old is she? This young woman?'

'We don't know, exactly, but we think somewhere in her mid-twenties. She's studying for a PhD. She said she'd like to come for a research trip . . .'

'And what did you say?' says Grace. 'In reply?'

'I said she'd be welcome.'

'*Welcome?*'

'I'm sorry, Mum,' says Isa, miserably. 'I didn't know the funeral was so small. I thought it was going to be very different.'

'I see.' Grace stands.

She turns, her back to Milo and Isa; only Frannie can see the expression on her mother's face – a version of a look she saw once when she was a child – a terrible chasm of distress. 'Well,' she says, briskly. 'I think we're all done here, don't you?'

Grace walks under the sharded light of the cupola, out through the high doors, to the front of the house, where she stands at the top of the steps, and wonders where there is to go.

She tries to remember how she felt, walking out here this morning, the sense of lightness, of promise – but it is as though it happened to a different person.

And she is walking without thinking, almost running now, across the park, over the stream, the old wooden bridge, beneath the sign, but she is unsteady, and as she enters the wood she stumbles on a tree root – puts out her hands to break her fall, landing heavily, scratching herself on bramble and thorn.

For a long while she does not move, only curls around herself on the dusty earth, her breathing heavy and raw, while above her, the birds carry on, their alarm calls returned to song, untroubled by her falling.

She could just cease, she thinks, and all of this would continue, would be none the worse for her passing. But she knows she will not die. Not today. That she is hurt, but not badly, and that soon she will have to get up, will have to find her way to her feet and use them to enter her life again.

And then someone is there. 'Grace – Gracey? Did you take a tumble, Gracey? Can you get up?'

'I'm alright,' she manages. 'I think.'

'If you get onto your front,' says Ned, 'then I can help you up.'

She moves with difficulty onto her hands and knees. He holds out a hand, the other balanced on his stick, reaches for her, pulling her to her feet. They hold each other – both shaky, as they gain their balance – in a strange wayward sort of dance. 'Look at us,' she says. 'We're old, Ned. We can hardly stand.'

'You've bust your lip, Graceylove.' He takes out his hanky and gently dabs her lip.

He takes her arm, and they move slowly; he guides her over the roots, along the path to the clearing, where he helps her to the sofa. 'You sit there, Graceylove, I'll make us some tea.'

Her teeth are chattering. 'I'm cold,' she says, and when she has said it she realizes how terribly true it is.

'Wait here.' Ned's hand is on her shoulder, and then he has gone, into his bus. He returns carrying blankets, begins to wrap them around her, knotting them at her chest, swaddling her in their heavy wool, and they smell of animals, of deep comforting animal life. A memory rises, unbidden. 'You did this for Milo,' she says. 'When he tried to die.'

'Yes,' says Ned. 'I did.'

He moves around her, and she remembers that terrible morning, seeing Milo prone on Ned's bed. The awful greyish-white of his skin. The way that nothing was the same after that: every phone call an alarm call. The chattering in her teeth moves into her body and she is shaking now, despite the blankets' warmth.

Ned goes over to the water and fills the old kettle, then hangs it on its tripod. The flames lick its tarnished black bottom as the fire jumps into life. 'Are you hurt?' he says, as he comes back to where she sits. 'Apart from your lip?'

'I don't know,' she says. 'I can't tell. I don't think so.'

'We'll get you warm for now. Take a proper look at you later.'

Slowly, as the warmth returns to her body, she finds she is able to speak. 'He had another child,' she says.

She knows she must now understand everything in the light of this new knowledge, this new injury: her husband fathered another child. And she knows it is not a new injury, not really, it is the old one made visible, its last stagnancies brought to the light.

'I was looking for flowers,' she says. 'For the coffin. I felt light. Complete. I thought he couldn't hurt me anymore. And now it's as though he's reached out and pulled me down, back into his murk again. I honestly don't care about a child. It's not that . . . It's that all that time, and all of those years in which I took him back . . . he was still lying.

'I've lived my life in a poisoned place. I've drunk from a poisoned well. I won't do it, Ned. Tomorrow. I won't stand there and honour him. He was a bastard. He sowed nothing but misery. Let his bastard child bury him.'

Her body is moving involuntarily now, rocking, forward and back. Ned is still for a moment, taking this in, then he puts down the log he is holding and comes and stands behind her, holding his arm across her chest, pinning her. 'Now,' he says. 'You breathe. Breathe deep, Grace. Come on. Breathe into my hands.'

She does as he commands, fists like claws on her lap. Her feet in the brown earth. The shaking is shuddering now, and then the shuddering gives way too and there is quiet. A lone bird singing high in a tree.

'Do you remember,' she says to him, to where he stands, behind her, 'when we met? It was here. Just here. By this fire.'

'Yes.'

'I was so young.'

'You were.'

'You gave me that dress. The yellow one.'

It is easier, she thinks, to speak like this. Not looking at him, only feeling his arms on her, across her, around her. The familiar scent of him: woodsmoke and tobacco and wool.

'It's funny, you know,' she says. 'I thought I had made a friend, when I met you that night. But I couldn't find you after that – I never saw you again that weekend.'

'No,' he says.

'Then last week I was packing up my clothes for the move to the cottage, and I found it – the dress. It was at the back of the wardrobe. It's beautiful still. I took great care of it. It's as lovely as the day you gave it to me.'

'Well,' he says. 'Fancy that.'

'You know the strangest thing?'

'What?'

'I have never worn it again. From that day to this.'

His arms are still there, still holding her.

'I put it on the bed,' she says. 'And I stared at it. Yellow. It's such a hopeful colour, don't you think?'

'I do.'

'You've always lived in colour, haven't you, Ned?' She twists to look at him now. 'You used to send me postcards – do you remember? When you were away. In the winter. I always hated it when you went away. But I loved to imagine you in those places. Living your life in colour.'

She stands and takes a couple of steps towards the fire. 'Let's go, Ned,' she says to the flames. 'Let's get away from here.'

'Where?'

'I don't know – there are so many places to go, aren't there? The desert.' She turns to him. 'You always told me about the desert. Rajasthan. Jaipur. Jaisalmer. Why didn't you take me with you? All those times? All those winters I was here alone? All those winters I was cold?'

He smiles. 'Oh, Gracey,' he says. 'You know I couldn't have done that.'

'The postcards you sent. I would stare at them for hours. Imagine you there. The colours. The light. Come with me to India, Ned.'

Ned laughs, shakes his head.

'Look at me, Gracey.' He lifts his stick towards her. 'I can hardly walk.'

'You can get on a plane. I'll help you.'

And she can feel it rise in her, the thought of it: *escape*. Of a heat so fierce it burns away the last of the cold in her bones. It is not so stupid, not really, not so far-fetched. 'Why not?' she says. 'When did Philip ever really care for what I thought? What I did? I should have run away years ago. Let's do it now, Ned. We can take a flight, tomorrow – tonight. Leave them to it – all of them. I want to see colour, Ned. I want to feel heat on my skin. I want to be warm.'

'Oh, Gracey,' he says.

She watches as he moves his stick around, as he manoeuvres himself around the sofa, as he walks towards her. And she sees his difficulty, the stiffness in him. It pierces her suddenly – the pain he must have been in after his accident, how bad the breaks were. How has she not taken more care of this? Of him? Of Ned – dear Ned? What was she doing while he recovered from his accident? Tending to her dying husband. Washing his traitorous body. Wiping his faithless mouth.

Ned looks at her. 'I know how hard it's been. I do, Graceylove. I've seen it from the start.'

'Then why didn't you do something? Back then?'

'I was scared, I suppose. I don't know what I could have done, anyway. You were married, this was his land. I just – tried to take care. Now . . . you listen to me. I'll be there tomorrow. I'm always here, aren't I?'

'Yes,' she says. 'You are.'

'Well then.'

Ned moves towards her, and she lifts her face to him. She brings her hands from beneath the blankets, reaches for his. Feels his callused thumb, passes the tip of her own thumb over his knuckles. 'Ned,' she says, softly. 'Ned.'

He does not reply, they only stay like this, facing one another, hand in hand. How few, she thinks, are the times that they have touched. Almost fifty years since she met him, in this glade, in this wood. He touches her gently. He touches her as he touches everything: his hands make things steady; they make things beautiful.

She closes her eyes, breathing in the scent of him. And then he gives a small sort of sigh, and he lifts his hand away, placing it on the top of her head.

'No,' she hisses, twisting from him. 'Don't *mother* me, Ned – I'm not a child. Look at me. Do you think I'm not serious? I want to leave this place. I have never, not in all my life, done anything that was unexpected. Apart from marrying him.'

The kettle is whistling. He goes to it, lifts it, and makes his way to his workshop. She watches his back as he lifts mason jars from his shelves, making tea.

'Here.' He comes back towards her, holding out a mug. 'Hawthorn,' he says. 'For the heart. Bit of elderberry honey in there. Do you good.'

She takes it as he moves back to fetch his own, then they both sit on his old leather sofa. They grow quiet. She sips the hot sweet tea.

'Gracey,' he says. 'Listen to me. We need to lay him in the ground. If we don't lay him, he will roam around here. I tell you.'

'Roam?'

'If we don't bury him. If we don't throw earth on him, then he will wander. And no one wants that. You don't want that. There are ghosts enough round here. He was a restless soul. He needs to be put to rest. Then you can be free. That coffin,' he nods towards the workshop, 'I spent a lot of time on that coffin. And I promise you, when that coffin goes into the earth, the poison goes with it.'

'What do you mean?'

'I wove it in with the willow – we put this coffin in the earth and it's over. You say there was a poisoned well – I believe you are right, there was. But now the water will run clear.'

'Oh, Ned,' she says, shaking her head.

'You think I'm joking,' he says in a low voice. 'But you listen to me now. You need to be there. You need to witness it. You need to throw earth on him. And you need to bless him. You don't bless him, you'll have another ghost here. And that's not what you want.'

'I'm not blessing him, Ned. That bastard. Never. No.'

'I'm telling you, Gracey, you must. You bless him and it stops with him. All the poison. The earth takes it. You just look for me. You start to feel shaky, and you find my eyes. I'll stand where you can see . . . you find my eyes and I'll hold you up.'

※

The day lengthens, early afternoon. A young woman sits in the back of a taxi, which makes its way along the top road, past the school. The young woman landed in this country less than two hours ago. She is wearing slim trousers, a black T-shirt, a long navy coat. Sober clothes for a scholar. For a scholar attending a funeral.

Clara is very still. It is how she has always been; a still sort of person, the better to take in what surrounds her. In times of anxiety, stress or excitement, she becomes a receiving machine: a watcher, a noter, a gatherer of evidence. So far it has served her well.

She cracks the window halfway and the cool air pours in. The hedges on either side of the lane are thick with white flowers and the air is alive with birds and it looks almost laughably lovely, looks in fact like a dream of England – all white and blossomy, as though it's getting ready to marry itself.

She is not greatly travelled, has never visited Europe, has only taken a flight a couple of times: to the Caribbean once, to Canada for a conference last year. And so it was still a thrill to her to take off from JFK, watch the lights of the island of Manhattan rear high and then grow smaller through her window, as they banked over the ocean and headed east. It was dark then, for the rest of the flight.

She stayed awake, working in the fierce little overhead light, while others slept, and when the cabin crew started passing out breakfast, and pulling up window blinds, she was astonished to see it was morning, the sunlight hitting the blue water – and soon she would be in England. They descended through cottony clouds, the dark reflection of the plane on the fields below. To the right was the coast and along it a string of towns, each with its own jutting pier reaching into the sea. They banked steeply and flew north, the white cliffs below, as the friendly, talkative pilot told them they were flying over Eastbourne, passing over the Downs, and she saw them stretching beneath, a raised ribbon of green hills: the spine of a sleeping dragon. And then field upon field all edged by large-crowned trees: Sussex. And then they were down, and she was blinking in the grey light of the arrivals hall.

The border control officer had his shirt rolled up, sleeves of tattoos on his arms. He asked her who she was visiting and for how long.

Friends, she told him. Until Monday.

It's a long way to come for the weekend.

It's a research trip. I have to get back. I'm giving a paper at a conference next week.

And what is it you do?

I'm studying for a PhD.

In what?

The Long Eighteenth Century, she said. And Cultures of Taste.

He studied her. Looked her up and down. A version of a gaze

she knows well. A version of a gaze she has been receiving from certain men in uniform her whole life.

Have a nice trip, Clara, he said, eventually, as he stamped her passport and handed it back.

She had no hold luggage, and so in a matter of minutes was standing outside on grimy tarmac waiting for an Uber. And now here she is, thirty minutes later, turning off the main road onto the lane which leads to the house. And although she has imagined it already, has sat in front of her laptop and clicked onto Google Maps and dropped the little yellow man onto this very road – through the village, past the pub with the battered sign for the Green Man and its two benches outside, past the school to the top of the lane to the sign which reads *PRIVATE LAND – ROAMING ANIMALS*, beyond which her Street View cannot reach – what she hadn't done was calculate the journey time from Gatwick airport to the house. And so, it is now – the car nosing its way down the narrow lane – that she finds herself surprised; she knows from her map haunting that soon the gates will appear, and there will be nowhere to hide and this whole crazy idea is going to be very much a reality.

The taxi turns, she catches sight of a lake, a flash of water in the distance. Waist-high grasses dotted with wildflowers. She takes a breath, inhaling the cool, birdsong-thick air, trying to calm the adrenaline spiking in her blood, tells herself to be still, stiller, stillest. But – too soon – she is here far too soon, she should have left herself more time to acclimatize, should have booked a room nearby – in the village perhaps, walked the area, got the measure of the place without having to face the family first. Perhaps it is not too late for that. She leans forward, about to tell the driver to turn around, but they are through the gates already, their tyres pressing gravel, a great golden house ahead, and her stomach plummets, because she is here now – Philip's house – and she knows that there is no turning back.

She unties the scarf at her neck, ties it again.

'Alright, miss?' The driver pulls on the parking brake, idles the engine.

'Yes, thanks. Have you got a card machine?'

He reaches into the glovebox and comes out with a little device. Twists around, so she can tap her phone to the screen. He jerks his head towards the house. 'Are they expecting you?' He looks sceptical.

'Yes,' she says. 'They are.'

She climbs out and the taxi reverses, turns, heads away back up the lane, and she is standing alone with only the beat of her heart for company. Her first thought is how quiet it is; there are a few cars parked, an old Honda, a Tesla, a battered-looking Land Rover, but there are no people, not that she can see. Ahead of her is the rear of the house: three storeys of sandstone, the lowest part of the lowest window higher than the height of her head. There is also no obvious door. A thickness hangs in the air, a haziness, it is milky almost, heavy with pollen and with insects. It even tastes green.

As she stands there, a woman emerges from a back door of the house. The woman takes out a packet of tobacco from the pocket of her trousers and begins to roll herself a cigarette. She has not looked this way, and so Clara has a moment to gather herself, to observe: the woman looks to be somewhere in her late thirties. Her hair is lightish and messy and piled on top of her head. She is wearing jeans, a hoodie, battered sneakers, and carries an air of preoccupation. She is not Francesca, instigator of the Albion Project and inheritor of the estate, because Clara has watched the short video – the one on the website where Francesca explains the project – several times by now. Francesca is taller, rangier, older, looks much more like her father, who appears with her in the promotional video – side by side, faces shining with purpose. This woman is slighter, younger – still, though, the family resemblance is there; this then, surely, is Isabella, writer of emails, inviter to funerals. Youngest child.

Clara picks up her bag and walks over the gravel towards her. The woman looks up at the sound of her footsteps. 'Shit,' she says. 'You gave me a fright. I didn't see you there.'

'Sorry.' Clara comes to a stop a little way from her. She grips her bag. 'I didn't mean to scare you.'

'S'alright,' says the woman. 'I'm easily scared.' She lifts her cigarette, takes a drag, lets out smoke, regarding Clara with what feels like bemusement. 'I'm really sorry,' she says, 'but the estate is closed today. There's a funeral this weekend. There's no public access till next week.'

'I know.' Clara makes her voice as calm as she can. 'I came for the funeral.'

'Are you sure?' The woman frowns. 'Sorry. I know that's a silly thing to say, it's just – it's really just family this weekend.'

'Philip Brooke?'

'Right.' The woman puts her head on one side. 'That's my father.'

'Then I think you invited me.'

The woman's face is all confusion.

'I'm Clara.'

'*Clara?*'

'Yes.'

'You're Clara! Jesus. I'm so sorry.' The woman thrusts out the hand that isn't holding a cigarette. 'I'm Isa,' she says. 'We emailed. It's lovely to meet you, Clara.'

Clara reaches out and they shake. 'I'm sorry about your father. About Philip.'

'Thanks. I mean. We weren't close, but – thanks.'

'Sure. I guess that's harder sometimes.'

'Is it?' The woman flicks her a look. 'I suppose.' She takes another drag on her cigarette. 'How was your flight?'

'Fine. Thanks.'

'You must be tired.'

'A little,' Clara admits. 'Yes.'

Isa takes a last drag on her cigarette, then rubs it out against the wall, where small red sparks bloom against the sandstone. She tucks it into a hole in the brick, where there already seems to be a small collection of butts. 'Okay,' she says. 'Well, what would you like to do? I could give you a tour, or . . . I can show you to your room if you like. I know where you've been put. And then you can have a walk, or rest. Sleep. Whatever.'

'Sure. My room would be great. Thanks.'

The woman leads the way into a long narrow corridor with rooms on either side. The corridor is dark, and there is a powerful, pervasive smell of damp. The carpet underfoot is stained and rucked. 'Servants' quarters,' says Isa. 'I should probably take you round the front for the full experience . . . but you're welcome to explore, just . . . go anywhere,' she says, with a careless wave of the hand. 'Feel free.'

At the end of the corridor is a window, and through it Clara can see a deep green vista. Her eyes follow the rolling contours of the land to a sort of ledge where it falls away – the ha-ha. Beyond the ha-ha there is water – the lake she saw from the cab, an island dotted with trees, and then the vista continues, giving an unobstructed view for two, perhaps three miles to the south, where hills rise: green upon green upon green.

'You okay?' says Isa.

Clara turns, sees Isa is already mounting the stairs. 'It's quite a view.'

'Ah.' Isa sounds apologetic. 'Yes. It is, I'm afraid.'

Clara follows her up shallow narrow carpeted stairs to a long corridor of a landing, where Isa opens the door to a large room with a small double bed. Isa steps inside and stands in the middle of the floor, looking sceptically around. 'It looks like the bed hasn't been made up yet, but I'll come and do it for you later this afternoon. Unless you need to sleep now?'

Clara shakes her head. 'I'm fine, thanks. Later is good.'

'I hope you'll be okay in here. There's no bathroom I'm afraid. It's back out on the landing, down on the right.'

'That's cool.' She places her bag on the carpet beside her.

'And no Wi-Fi, from what I remember . . . it doesn't reach to this side of the house.'

'That's fine . . .' she says. 'Really. All good.'

'Great. Well, I'll be downstairs. Just . . . come down whenever you're ready. There's coffee. Tea. I can get you some lunch – a snack – whatever you need. I'll try and rustle up some of the others to say hi. They're all around somewhere. They're all just – we've got a lot to get through before tomorrow.'

'Sure. I mean – I can imagine. Of course.' Clara gives a small smile.

Isa turns to leave but Clara speaks again. 'Thank you,' she says. 'For writing, I mean. And for saying it was okay for me to come. I realize this is a difficult time for you all.'

'Oh,' says Isa. 'Not at all. Thank you for coming,' she says, 'all this way. I want you to know that you're welcome here.'

'And . . . are the rest of your family okay?' says Clara. 'With me being here, I mean? I know I only heard back from you . . . so . . .'

'Honestly?' says Isa.

'Please.'

'I think they're going to be very happy to meet you.' Isa gives a quick smile, then takes her leave, shutting the door behind her. Clara exhales. She turns slowly, taking in the room. It is high-ceilinged, but drab; spots of mould pattern the coving. The same ancient creamy-beige carpet as downstairs, the same pervasive smell of damp, though slightly less intense in here. It is not at all what she imagined. What did she imagine then? Not this sense of decay – as though the soul of the house is tired. She goes over to the washbasin, one of those 1970s avocado ones, on which lies a hard sliver of soap that looks like it hasn't been changed in fifteen years. She splashes her face with her cupped hands and dries herself on the thin hand towel hanging by the sink, then brings her bag onto the bed and starts to unpack. Washbag. Laptop. A small selection of clothes: T-shirts, underwear, socks, another pair of trousers.

She feels a sort of seasickness; the sensation of the plane is in her body still, a low whooshing, as though part of her is still moving across the Atlantic. Seven hours to cross an ocean – it feels unseemly somehow. She pulls out her phone, checks the screen. Two p.m., so – what? Nine a.m. in New York. Hardly any battery life left. She searches in the front pocket of her bag for her charger – but it isn't there. Fuck. She must have left it on the plane.

There's barely any signal, but when she clicks onto her emails, she manages to pull them up. The most recent is from her supervisor, sent half an hour ago in response to a hurried mail that Clara sent her just before she boarded the plane at JFK, telling her she wouldn't be able to make the supervision meeting this morning.

Hey Clara,

Sorry to hear that you're ill. I really think it will be a shame to miss this one. I think it's important you don't lose any more ground. Let's try for Zoom? Sending you a link now.

Clara hesitates, then types back.

So sorry. Just feeling too ill for that. Will get back in touch as soon as I am feeling better.

She presses Send, tosses the phone onto the unmade bed beside her, lies back and stares up at the coving.

What she could have written:

So sorry. I haven't done any work for the last three weeks. I've got seven thousand unwritten words. I got completely sidetracked by something else. I'm actually not ill at all. I'm in England. In Sussex. For the funeral of my mother's ex-lover.

What else she could have written:

So sorry. You're a power-hungry narcissist who treats me like an unpaid research assistant.

What else she could have written:

So sorry. I'm losing faith in the P h fucking D.

She closes her eyes. Should she try to sleep? She is exhausted, but full of jittery energy. Even if she could sleep, she should stay up, surely, until later, and then she will at least be somewhat in sync with herself? She snaps her eyes open and sits up, slides off the bed and goes over to the window.

Her room is at the front of the house, and through the glass she can see the same view she saw from the window downstairs, although it is, if that is possible, even more magnificent from up here. The window is an old, single-paned sash, its corners dusty with cobwebs and long-dead flies. She pulls it open in a series of small jerks. The afternoon air is welcome, the room immediately less stale.

To her right, where the sun is, is a treeline, a wood which stretches as far as she can see. Above it she can see some sort of bird of prey, hovering on an updraught. Everything has a golden-green beauty to it, and all of it, extraordinarily, is quite uninterrupted by any human form. She has never seen anything like it in her life.

She walks back out onto the landing, where she takes the opposite direction, turning left and following the corridor until it opens onto a wide gallery, with more rooms leading off it, from where she descends slowly, grazing her hand along the banister rail. The hall below is sparsely furnished, laid in large square chequerboard tiles, and so there is nothing to detract from the main event – the cupola, a semicircle of glass four panes high, reaching up to twenty feet or so above her head. It is at once preposterous and remarkably lovely: light upon light upon light. The architect knew what he was doing – standing here, warming herself in an amber pool of sun, there seems to be nothing above her head but sky.

Noises reach her from deeper in the house, from what must be the kitchen, the sound of plates, of chatter. The family. She turns away – there will be time enough to face them later. A door is ajar to her right, she pushes it open softly and steps inside a large room, walled with books. Above the desk hangs a life-size portrait of three people, their faces luminous in the sombre light. She moves slowly through the room towards them.

A pricking in her fingertips. A strange metallic taste fills her mouth.

There he is – the man himself, with his wife and son. Oliver Brooke, painted in the Grand Manner, full-size, full-height, his eyeline almost level with her own. The signature visible on the bottom right-hand corner of the canvas: *Sir Joshua Reynolds, 1789.*

The season in the painting is spring, and the oak leaves are fresh and new. The family group forms a pyramid shape; stable, secure. The poses of the mother and the son echo each other: the side of the mother's dress the left-hand side of the pyramid, the sloping back of the boy's coat the right. The father's head the apex, the father who stands – straight on, staring out, chin slightly raised. All the foreground, the bottom of that stable pyramid, is taken up with the fabric of the mother's dress; with the sunlight falling and splaying onto the pink silk tumble of her skirt. The mother's head is crowned by a hair arrangement which stands a good foot and a half higher than her brow, framing the pale oval of her face. Her hair is almost the same brown as the trunk of the oak, as though the silk of the skirt and the oak leaves and the woman's high, high hair, the green of the band which holds it, and the green of the spring leaves above her head, were all part of the same moral universe: stability, security, strength, renewal. And behind, stretching as far as the eye can see: the park, the land itself – that which confers this stability, security, strength. The very same view she has from her bedroom now.

She stares back, her heartbeat low and fast. She didn't expect to be face to face with them all so soon.

There are sudden sounds in the hall behind her. Voices. Footsteps. She crosses quickly over to the double doors, twists the handle and steps out onto a stone terrace. Ahead of her a colonnade of stone columns stretches. She moves quickly from pillar to pillar, until she reaches the edge of the terrace, where there are no windows, no doors and she cannot be seen. She stops to catch her breath, checks behind her, but whoever was in the hall has not followed her out here. She is aware of the clench of her fists, of her jaw, her body full of the feeling of transgression, of the fear of being found out.

Why? Isa said she could go anywhere she liked, didn't she?

Feel free, she had said, with that careless hand. But it is the sort of thing people say, Clara knows, the sort of invitation they extend, when they have never really felt anything but.

The sound of a bamboo pipe being played.

Milo sits upright, eyes lowered, back against the wall, as a woman's voice starts to intone.

Lower your gaze . . . become aware of your body sitting here. Aware of the movement of the breath . . . open to receive it.

This voice usually does the trick: fifteen minutes every day; steady, reassuring, calm.

With the outbreath releasing unnecessary tension . . . unnecessary holding . . .

But his stomach is tight today, and so is his chest.

Soften the eyes . . .

Sensing the shoulders falling away from the neck . . .

Soften the hands . . . feel the sensations that are there; tingling, burning . . .

His hands *are* burning. Really fucking burning. His fingertips are tingling. The tip of his tongue.

Soften again . . .

Soften the chest . . .

The region of the heart . . .

Let the breath enter . . . leave . . . helping you contact and connect with the feelings and sensations in the area of the heart . . .

His heart feels angry.

That's the thing.

Letting go of whatever wants to be released . . .

What he can see though – projected onto his eyelids – what really wants to be released is the cork in that bottle of wine downstairs. It was standing on the table in the library all the way through that family meeting.

Pommard 2005. A great year for Burgundy.

It'll be a fucking great wine. Course it will. Philip chose it.

Jesus, Pa.

You old fucker.

You had one last surprise in store, didn't you?

He opens his eyes, and checks the time on his phone. Two p.m.: a perfectly respectable hour for a drink. And who would blame him? This weekend, of all weekends? His family, of all families? This house, of all houses?

He could just go downstairs now and have a little glass. Take the edge off.

He lifts his vape, takes a pull.

It's not like he's an alcoholic. Not exactly. No one has ever said that to him. Not in so many words. Not even his therapist, and she was ruthless.

He's just someone who has medicated with drink.

In the past.

So it's fine.

He presses Pause on his phone, stands up and heads to the door. But when he reaches it, his hand on the handle, he stops, because he knows full well it would be better, really, if he didn't. He knows full well what happens next: the next drink happens next.

And then the next.

And then the next.

And he might be able to stop, and he might not.

And that might be okay, and it might not.

And if he bumps into anyone and looks like he's on for drinking wine at two p.m., then Frannie may well find him another job to do.

Better to stay up here, out of the way. So he heads back, takes another tug on the vape, crosses his legs in front of him, and with his back against the wall again he presses Play.

With the outbreath, releasing . . . letting go of whatever wants to be released . . .

Receiving the breath deep in the torso . . . releasing any tension or tightness . . .

Widening the field of the body to this whole field of sensation . . .

Letting go . . .

But what if he doesn't want to let go?

What if he can't release?

He's sitting here, trying to breathe. Trying to do everything in his power not to be triggered, not to be small Milo, scared Milo, bitter Milo.

If his therapist were here, he knows what she'd be saying.

She'd be saying – that's little Milo. That's little abandoned Milo who wants the wine.

His therapist would say – see, that's the child in you who never got enough

love,

support,

praise,

attention,

time,
basic care.
(You fill in the gaps.)
Which left you feeling,
bereft,
traumatized,
abandoned.
And then there's also the big Milo, the adult Milo, who understands that all humans are
fallible,
traumatized,
lonely,
scared,
to be forgiven.
And you can choose, Milo. You can *choose*. But for Jesus fuck's *sake*, come *on*. What is it about this family? His own needs neglected, relegated. Again, and again and again.

His sister's face, in the library, sitting behind his father's desk, beneath the portrait of Oliver Brooke. Her desk now, he supposes, like everything else. (How quickly, how smoothly she has assumed the mantle of inheritance.) Her *condescension*. Speaking to him like he's a child. And she's the parent.

Maybe you could make a start on clearing out your room?

A museum to your teenage self.

He snaps open his eyes. It's true – the room is as he left it when he last lived here. When? Twenty-five years ago. But what, exactly, is the problem with that? What does Frannie care?

Twenty bedrooms, only three of which, by his count, are being used – and his mother will be moving to the cottage.

It's a power play, pure and simple.

It's outrageous, is what it is.

Letting go . . .

Feeling the earth beneath you – the air around you . . .

Jesus, this woman's voice is really starting to fuck him off.

He hits Pause on the phone.

A thought occurs to him, and he goes over to the wardrobe – opens it, sees them still there, on the back of the top shelf, a stack of magazines. He takes them down, brings them over to the bed and fans them out: *Loaded, Nuts, FHM.*

He flicks through them – Jesus, the girls in the photos look so unbelievably young. So innocent actually. Poignant, almost. After the sort of thing that came later. If only he could return to a time when his sexual imagination was satisfied by smiling, inviting, healthy-looking young women with their smiling, inviting, healthy-looking breasts.

Sadly, those days are done.

Any residual relief he may have got from porn has been well and truly torpedoed by his steely-eyed therapist.

A therapist he started to see after the first trip to Amsterdam.

In the integration circle at the end, when he had wept for the first time since he was a child, for the first time since he had been sent away to school, the serious Dutch facilitator (lovely guy, little humour, lots of heart) touched him on the arm. You did really well here, Milo, he said, in that earnest Dutch way he had – but remember, this is just the beginning. We always recommend you find a therapist to integrate more fully. Take your time, start to talk it out.

And so he started therapy with a grey-haired woman in Queen's Park. He told her what had happened, what memories had come back to him, in that treatment centre in Amsterdam: sharded, lethal memories, each with the capacity to pierce him, like shattered panes of glass. He told her how he remembered being eight, his first day at prep school. Standing on the stone steps in socks and shorts. His new and uncomfortable shoes. The shiny S-shaped clip of the belt that was holding his shorts up.

All of the noise around him.

He told her how he remembered his father standing over him. Huge and terrifying, shaking his hand, saying goodbye.

He told her he was looking for his mother.

His beautiful gentle mother who was not there.

Where was she?

She was in the car – he couldn't see her face. Why couldn't he see her face?

He told her how he remembered being in bed, that first night, and the dormitory captain, a boy of eleven, explaining that the belt with the shiny S-shaped clip, of which he had been so proud when he put it on that morning at home, would be used to beat anyone who made a sound.

How he pissed the bed in terror and lay in it all night, too frightened to move.

How every day and night that followed that terrible first, he thought that he would be rescued. By his beautiful gentle mother.

By his father.

By his big sister Frannie who had always been there, and now was not. Where was she? Still living at home, in the house he loved, with the mother he loved, with the little sister he loved. While he was here, left in this place without love. And as the nights became weeks and it was clear no one was coming to get him, he became obsessed with a central driving question: why had he been sent away when his sister was not?

And he became convinced there must be something in him, some inherent evil that had been seen, sniffed out.

He told his therapist how his eight-year-old mind had alighted on the answer – at night, when he had nightmares, which he often did, he used to creep across the landing to his mother's room, his mother's bed. And they would sleep together, and sleep well. But, then one night, or very early morning, Philip arrived at the house, came up the stairs to claim his bed, saw Milo lying beside his mother, and pulled him up and out with such violence and ferocity that Milo knew he and Grace must have done something dreadfully wrong.

He spoke of how, during those terrible nights after he was first sent away, the only rational explanation he could come up with was that he had been banished for the crime of sharing his mother's bed.

He told her the abuse he suffered at school was not terrible, not in the great scheme of things – more a bleak inevitable coda to the misery of the place.

What is *the great scheme of things?* his therapist asked him.

You know, he said to her. A relative scale.

Who makes up the relative scale? she said. Seriously? Can you tell me? Who? Suffering is suffering, his therapist told him. No matter who it happens to.

He knows now, through his therapy, that he was not sent away because he was bad, or unloved, or unwanted. Nor because his father found him, one morning, sharing a bed with his mother. He knows that the truth was much less dramatic than that: that the chief reason he was sent away was because *it was what was done.* His name had been down for that prep school – the same his father went to, and his grandfather before that – from the day that he was born a boy.

It is somehow worse, thinking of it like that: not even a conscious decision. No real causal thread. All that misery, all those years of torture, and all because it was simply *what one did.*

As the sessions went on, his therapist asked him about his sexuality, his relationships with women, about his ability to form lasting relationships.

Lasting relationships? he said, and laughed.

And he told her about how he had treated women, all his life.

The things he had done. How often, especially when he and his fellow brokers were hiring girls, it was like a game, a stupid game – like one of the games at school, how low could you go?

That was the culture, he said to his therapist, and she nodded. We were in finance.

I see, she said. And finance in this context is shorthand for . . . what?

And it wasn't just us, he said. Still . . . maybe I went too far.

How far? asked his therapist.

Hmm. Well, he said.

Go on, she said.

And so, he told her the worst thing of all.

He told how once, when things were really bad, he had paid an awful lot of money to hurt someone quite badly. How she had submitted to it, and taken the cash, and how he had felt when they finished: this quietness inside his head, the sort of quietness he had been searching for all his life.

How sometimes, after that, he had wondered if he was the devil. How not long after, when the noise in his head started up again, he had started to think seriously about ending his life.

The therapist listened to all of this. He had expected her to judge him, in that severe way she had. Instead, she told him that she was not surprised – that he was a person *so alienated from the feminine that he could enact the most desperate things upon women.*

You were rejected very badly by your mother, she said, when you were sent away to school. And damaged very badly.

And so you chose to reject women in turn.

Your personality has been organized around survival, not love.

Thanks, Mum.

Whatever.

The long and short of it is he just can't get off to porn anymore, even the most depraved.

He's managed to get some relief a few times recently, while thinking about his therapist kneeling in front of him. It's pretty twisted. But mostly his sexual imagination has been empty – a void. Like the rest of his life.

He told her how, after he had hurt that woman, he came home. Came back here. He'd had the crazy thought that he needed to tell his mother what he had done, but when it came to it, he couldn't. So instead, he drank himself stupid, took a bottle of pills and a bottle of his father's whisky, and tried to take the boat out into the middle of the lake to the island.

He laughed as he told her what a disaster it had been. How shambolic. How he had collapsed on the jetty trying to untie the boat and woken covered in his own vomit and shit. How Ned had found him, cleaned him up, wrapped him in blankets and taken him back to his bus.

Why on earth is it funny? his therapist said.

I mean . . . it's a *little* bit funny, he replied. Don't you think?

But she didn't seem to think it was funny at all.

There will be a space for humour in his Clearing. For The Clearing, he will hire people who know how to speak to men like him. Men who get bored easily. Who have spent their lives seeking sensation. Therapists who know not to be dull or earnest – that's the thing about psychedelics. They are not worthy, or boring, or dull.

Fuck, but he needs this break. He's been treading water for far too long, looking for his out.

Jesus Christ, all he wants is to take this trauma and do some fucking *good*.

Fifteen acres. *Fifteen acres out of a thousand, Frannie.*

Time was it would all have been his, every last leaf on every last tree. Primo-fucking-geniture. Not to have to bend and flatter and cajole his worthy sister, who owes him – he whose idea all this was in the first place.

He who kick-started this whole thing.

Alright – he may not have said *you need to rewild the shit out of this place*, but it was after that night that he came here to stay with her that Frannie kicked into gear. Not long after, she called him, told her his plan, and he congratulated her.

He was *purely fucking happy for her.*

More fool him.

He gathers up the magazines, takes them over to the bin and dumps them inside.

There you go, Frannie. I've made a start.

He goes over to the window, pulling on his vape.

A person is standing at the very edge of the terrace, looking out. They are wearing a cap, a long coat. From up here it's impossible to tell if the person is a man or a woman, old or young, but there is something about them, something compelling about the way they are standing.

They look like they don't quite fit in.

Certainly, at the very least, they are more interesting, more intriguing, than anything that is happening in here, in his childhood bedroom. In his fucking head.

The speckled stone of the steps beneath Clara's feet is split by the pink and white of myriad daisies, their faces turned to the sun that shines in a sky – clear, now, but for a few high clouds. To the right and the left of her, huge ornamental stone urns spill with rosemary and lavender; beyond them the grass is bright with wildflowers. Everything has a scruffy overgrown quality, everywhere a sense of humming, buzzing life, the gentle fizz of birdsong, swallows dipping around her head.

She starts to walk, taking the stone pathway between the wildflower meadows, passing an old stone fountain: two entwined cherubs above a bowl in which a small amount of rainwater stands. There is a tearing sound to her right, and she turns to see a large animal moving towards her through the high grass. Its massive head is down and swaying, huge, rounded horns on either side. It looks like a bull – maybe an angry one. Should she run? But if she runs, then will it chase? She knows nothing about animals really, has no idea what to do. And so she freezes. 'Oh shit,' she breathes, as the animal advances.

'Hey!'

Someone is shouting.

'Hey!'

She turns, shielding her eyes from the sun. A man is standing at the top of the steps, waving his arm. 'Are you okay?' he calls.

'Is this animal about to eat me?'

The man jogs his way down the stone steps towards her.

'I shouldn't think so,' he says, as he draws near.

The animal lifts its head, but does not move closer; it tears at the grass, switches its tail and lets out a great steaming pile of shit.

'Jesus, I thought that was it,' she says. 'Gored to death by a bull.'

The man laughs. 'That would have been a terrible shame,' he says, 'but I promise you, they're females and not aggressive at all.'

'Because they're females?'

'No. Because they're Longhorns, I believe.'

It's true, she thinks, its horns are enormous. 'Aggressive or not,' she says, 'they look like they could do some serious damage with those.'

'They're terribly docile, I believe. Chosen so that the walkers won't be disturbed. This place is usually crawling with them. Walkers, that is. Not cows. Though cows too. Not that I'm any sort of authority on the subject. We have reached the beginning and the end of my knowledge of bovines.' The man gives a small bow.

She takes him in; one of the family, surely. He looks a lot like Philip – less tall, but with the same angularity. Milo, then. Second child. Only son.

He smiles at her, a vague, self-deprecating smile. He is dressed simply, a shirt and jeans. The outline of a weighty vape in the pocket of his shirt. Not preppy, but preppy-adjacent. His eyes are mild, a light greenish-blue, but with the suggestion of something other, something wayward in their depths. A similar quality, she thinks, to his sister Isabella.

'I don't think you should be here though,' he says. 'I'm pretty

163

sure the estate is closed today.' He thrusts his hands in his pockets, rocks a little on his heels. 'Are you just here for a walk or . . . ?'

'Yes. Not just. I mean – I've been wanting to see this place for a while.'

'Really? How so?'

'I'm studying for a doctorate.'

'In . . . ?'

'The Long Eighteenth Century and Cultures of Taste.'

'Blimey,' he says, taking a step backwards, pulling out his vape. 'I didn't expect you to say that.'

'What did you expect me to say?'

'Oh, I don't know – perhaps, *where can I find the loo? Or, is there anywhere I can buy a coffee? What time is the next bus to Tunbridge Wells?* That's the kind of thing most people ask when they're walking round the grounds.' He grins.

'Well,' she says, 'a coffee could be great.'

'I'm sure it can be arranged.'

'It's fine,' she says. 'I'm okay for now.'

'So.' He tugs on the vape, blowing the smoke behind him. 'Tell me . . . the Long Eighteenth Century?'

'Mmhmm?'

'Was it any longer than the other centuries?'

'No.' She gives a small laugh. 'It means that scholars draw a line. So, we might start in the 1680s, say, and end in the 1820s' – she holds her fingers in the air – 'and examine the way in which cultural mores live between those dates: ideas of taste. Of manners. Of decency. Money. Architecture. Literature. Art.'

'Ah. I see. Well, if you're interested in the culture of taste then you'll know about garden design. Landscaping?'

'A little, yeah.'

'Humphry Repton?'

'Of course,' she says. 'He's pretty foundational. It's hard to get around him.'

'Well,' he lowers his voice, his back to the house, gesturing to the grounds before them, 'we think he had a hand in the gardens here. We can't be totally sure, but his signature is everywhere. The ha-ha. The vista . . .'

'The trick of the picturesque?' she says. 'The lack of anything human to strain the eye?'

'Exactly! Though he was rather brutal in his aesthetic. Moved a village out of the way because it interrupted the view.'

Clara says nothing, only watches Milo's face, which is displaying a sort of baffled, rueful bemusement.

'And I'm not sure what old Humphry would have made of the most recent iteration of the estate . . . I'm not sure this level of cowshit fitted in with the aesthetic ideal.' He grimaces slightly, then spins on his heel towards the house, opens his hands as though greeting an old friend. 'Now this,' he says, 'is something else.'

She nods her assent.

'Go on then,' he says, 'a scholar's first impressions?'

'Sure, okay.' She crosses her arms over her chest. 'Well . . . it's big, but not huge, but it's been made to look huge – the way the columns taper and create a sense of height. The temple fronts on the wings. It's a trick. A *trompe-l'œil*.'

'Yes! Precisely!' He sounds delighted. 'You know,' he says, 'I grew up here, I have never not known it, it's part of me, but it still blows me away when I really stand and consider it.'

'How so?'

'Well, the audacity of it all. The architect was a kid; twenty-seven or so, twenty-eight – not much older than you, I guess?'

'Yeah,' she says. 'Not much.'

'So it's 1788, he's travelled to Greece, seen the temples there, and he decides to make something similar here from Sussex sandstone. The stone was quarried from nearby, but the design is taken from the Temple of Apollo in Delos.'

'Right.'

'He finishes this house in 1789, decides England isn't radical enough for him – there's a revolution in France, the US is kicking off. So, he goes to the States where his career ignites: he becomes friends with Jefferson, goes on to design the portico of the White House. He brings Greek Revival architecture to the States. Those Founding Fathers couldn't get enough, right?'

'I guess not.'

'Wild, no? And it all begins here, in a Sussex valley. This young man, this twenty-something architect, exports Arcadia to the New World.'

'*Exports Arcadia*,' she says. 'That's a good one, can I keep it? I'm sure I can make use of it somewhere.'

'Of course,' he says, with a little bow. 'It's yours.'

He takes another pull at the vape, grinning at her through the smoke.

He is obviously enjoying himself. And he is not unpleasant, even if she has met his type before, felt this same mixture of humour and arrogance and diffidence peculiar to a certain type of privilege, a certain type of man.

'But I guess,' she says, slowly, 'in the States, when it comes to the big buildings, the Greek Revival is a style that's associated with democracy. Federalism. Civic consciousness . . . Whereas here . . . in this valley, on this land, or on a plantation, say, it's anything but.'

He turns to her, an eyebrow raised. 'Go on.'

'Well, it's interesting, isn't it?' she continues. 'How in the case of buildings like this, something that was radical and audacious and kind of crazy at the time, as you say – this bringing of Greek temples to the British countryside – is made, with the passing of years, into something which seems permanent, even inevitable.'

'Say more?'

'Well . . . it's like the shop window for a way of seeing the world, an ideology: symmetry, order, rationality. Abstract ideas finding material form.' She gestures to the house. 'And this ideology, in turn, once it is set in stone, naturalizes a way of being.'

He is fully facing her now, the amusement and indulgence gone. She has his full attention, she knows.

'So this house feels like it's been here forever, but two hundred and forty years? Not that long, in the scheme of things. Not compared to a tree, say, not compared to a redwood or a yew –'

'You sound like my sister –'

'But its very sense of permanence obscures. Or makes something seem natural that isn't. Or, at least, might be questioned.'

'Like what?'

'Patriarchy. Privilege. Hierarchy. Ownership of land.'

'A-ha,' says Milo. 'I see.'

Close by, the cow gives a low grunt and turns around, showing its hindquarters, which are covered with grass seeds and flowers and crusted dung. It lifts its tail. They watch as another thick stream of shit lands in the grass.

'Well, the patriarchy has been well and truly shat on here,' says Milo, chuckling.

'Is that so?'

'Have you met my older sister? The owner of the estate?'

'No.'

'You should. You'd love her. She's all about exploding hierarchies. Giving up top-down processes. Doing away with the controlling hand. But of course, the irony is, she's a fucking control freak of the highest order. Oops. Sorry. Did I just say that?' He winks, grins again, and out comes the vape. She supposes he imagines it's endearing. He's tugging on his pacifier, clearly waiting for a response. Something to signal complicity – naughty kids together.

'I'm imagining,' says Clara mildly, 'that to get a project of this scale working this well, you've got to intervene pretty radically at the start.'

'Oh gosh, yes. Absolutely. That's true. That's exactly right. And

I spoke out of turn: Frannie has done great things.' He steps back. 'Woah,' he says. 'What the hell are you doing here anyway? I haven't had such a good conversation in months. Have you just teleported in from another dimension?'

She laughs. 'Not really. Well, sort of. I came from New York, this morning.'

'And that's where you're from?'

'Yeah.'

'And what's your heritage?'

'My heritage?'

'Originally, I mean.'

'Originally? I was born in a hospital in Queens.'

'Sure. I'm sorry. Jesus.' He slaps his palm to his forehead. 'That was crass of me.'

'My father was from St Kitts,' she says.

A buzzing from his jeans. He lifts his phone, checks the screen, then: 'Excuse me,' he says, lifting his index finger, 'I have to take this.'

He steps away, turning to look up the hill as he takes the call. 'Mate!' He squints in the direction of the house. 'Okay. Sure,' he says. 'Put it in the top car park. You know where it is? The satnav takes you there – it's the one the campers use. I'll be there in ten.' He stows his phone, looks back at Clara. 'Listen, I'm sorry to cut this off but I've got to go. It was really great to meet you.' He puts out his hand and they shake. 'Do you know your way out? Are you staying nearby?'

'I hope so.'

'In the village?'

'In the house.'

'This house?' He frowns. 'I don't think so. It's closed. My father's funeral is tomorrow.'

'I'm pretty sure I'm staying at the house. I have a room. I just came from there.'

'The big house?'

'Yes.'

'Hang on – sorry. I'm just catching up with myself here – you said you came in from New York? So you're . . . Natasha's daughter?'

She nods.

'*You're* the girl!' He lifts his palm and crashes it against his forehead. 'Fuck. Well. Jesus. Welcome! So you'll be here for the weekend?'

'Yep.'

'And does this mean I get to see you again? We get to speak again?'

'I think it's probably likely, yes.'

'Okay, well – that is really bloody lovely news. Clara? Right?'

'That's right.'

'Okay, well, I'll say goodbye, Clara. For now. See you later, I guess?'

She lifts her hand, stands in the sunshine, as he jogs away from her, up the hill.

❧

Frannie's phone buzzes with a text from Milo:

Luca in top car park. Meet there in 10?

She texts back, *Sure* – is putting the phone in her pocket when it buzzes again.

Guess what? I met Clara. She's not our sister.

How do you know?

You'll see.

She waits, but there is nothing more from him, so she stows her phone, goes quickly into the small bathroom at the side of her office, where she splashes water onto her face then regards herself sceptically in the mirror. For now, she thinks, Clara can wait. Her hair is a mess. Her clothes too – she has been wearing the same hoodie and jeans for days.

Fucking Luca. That way he has of looking – it was there in

those photographs; the way he stared straight down the lens, sitting on his bone-white terrace in the sun.

What will he see when he looks at her?

In the unkind light of the overhead bulb, she looks closer at the dark circles under her eyes, the rash of spots on her chin. She traces them with her fingertip, she sees them every morning but has not stopped to think about them. What has caused them? Stress? Lack of sleep? She has no make-up up here, at the office, to cover them. And anyway – fuck it. Fuck Luca. She's not here to make herself attractive to him. This is her land. Her home. He can take her as she comes. She goes back into the office and tucks her hair beneath her old beanie, then heads out, taking the shortcut up the steepest part of the hill.

Why – *why* should she have to deal with him, this weekend of all weekends?

She knows why – because Milo is still, after all these years, in thrall to him, still punch-drunk with the need to be seen by him, to be acknowledged, to be loved; whatever particular personal charisma Luca may carry, he has cast a spell over Milo for almost thirty years. But to invite him here, this weekend – to suggest he will have a say in the running of the project, however small the acreage – it's too much. She won't have it. She understands she will do almost anything not to have him here, on her project. Leveraging her integrity. Trading on her family name.

And yet she is walking so fast she is almost jogging, already almost halfway there, her breath coming in quick rasps. She makes herself slow down – if she's ten minutes late then he can wait. She knows, though, the true cause of the cortisol raging in her blood: the last time she saw Luca – Philip's seventieth birthday. Milo had persuaded Philip to open the house up for a party – a marquee on the lawn. *Like the old days* – she remembers that's what they all kept saying, that night, as they got drunker and drunker. *Just like the old days. Isn't it?*

Personally, she was no fan of the old days, but she smiled and laughed and drank with the best of them, that night. It was Philip's party, but she also had something to celebrate: she had managed to secure funding for the next round of the project. Her memories are hazy after a certain point; it was hot, she hadn't eaten much, and she was drunk quickly on the champagne. The house was full of all sorts of people, there was a cohort from the village too; just before midnight Philip had driven up to the Green Man, roared to the last-orders crowd in the tiny pub that he was seventy that day, and told everyone to come down to the house.

They had the sound system set up in the hall, lights were strung in the cupola, and the music was good, some DJ friend Milo had gone to school with. She remembers what she was wearing: a long burnt-orange silk dress with a slash at the side. She had bought it in Brighton to wear to a friend's wedding, a year or so before – had been shopping on a rare outing with Isa, who had lifted it from the rail.

This one.

No way.

Trust me.

And she had been right.

Anyway, it was a good dress, a great dress, and it was summer, and her skin was tanned, and she was swimming every day in the lake, so her arms were muscled, and she felt good, like her body suited her for once. She had a sense of emerging – that she had shrugged off the sadness that had hung about her, that things were moving, finally. She had been back at the estate for three years, and she was thirty-eight years old. At a certain point she went into the library for a break from the dancing. Luca and Milo were there already, racking up lines on the leather-tooled top of the desk. She told them off, saying what the hell did they think they were doing, that leather was over two hundred years old, and Philip would kill them, but the two men just laughed, telling her to shut up – offering her the note so she could go first.

She was never, ever one for drugs, but for whatever reason, that night, she took the note and bent to the desk. She remembers how genuinely delighted they seemed that she had taken the coke, like she had crossed over and joined them somewhere they had been living for a long while. And in a sense, she supposes, she had.

They were talking, all of them, animatedly, for hours, although about what she has no recollection. She remembers the way that Luca listened, that he asked questions, and seemed genuinely interested in what she had to say in reply. At a certain point a particular tune came on and Milo jumped up. He went back out to dance and she and Luca were left alone. She remembers standing, making to follow Milo, but Luca remained seated.

The room was spinning a little, and she thought how odd it was that he could be so still. How his gaze could be so steady and relentless somehow.

Come here, he said to her.

What?

Just – come here.

She took a couple of paces towards him, close enough so he could touch her. But he didn't touch her. He just carried on sitting there, looking.

I've always been fascinated by you, he said. Did you know that?

She shook her head.

You keep yourself so upright. So straight.

Do I?

Yeah, he said. You know you do. He leant forward, caught her wrist, circled it with his left forefinger and thumb. But you know what I've always wondered?

She shook her head slowly.

I've always wondered how you fuck.

She didn't reply. But she could feel her body respond immediately, her nipples hard against the thin silk of her dress.

He stood then; their faces were inches away from each other.

He walked her slowly backwards towards the desk, pushed her against it.

She remembers the sounds of the party in the rest of the house, the beat coming from the hall. The low-lit room. His breath on her neck, as he pulled up her dress. Can I do this? he said, his hands on her thighs.

She nodded. He moved her knickers to the side and slid three fingers inside her. The things I could do to you, he said, into her ear.

She said nothing, but she was almost coming, just like that, with his fingers inside her. He moved them, slowly, and touched her where she was most swollen, pressing the heel of his thumb hard against her.

Tell me you want me, he said.

I want you.

Here. On this desk.

Here, on this desk.

He unbuttoned himself then and pushed himself inside her. She came within seconds – as did he, his head pressed hard against her chest.

She went back out to the party, feeling horribly drunk as soon as she met the evening air, although she had been unaware of it before.

When she woke, later that morning, she felt sullied, hungover, but with a low-slung backbeat of – what? Triumph? She knew she had done it, in part, for her teenage self. The girl who had always felt unbeautiful – compared to her mother, her sister – who had always felt less.

They are there already when she arrives, standing together by the cars, deep in conversation, their voices low but animated, both with their backs to her. Frannie slows her pace, steadies her breath as she takes him in.

He is tanned. His dark hair cropped shorter than in the photographs. Jeans and a blue T-shirt. A simple bracelet where a watch might be.

She is sweating, after her walk, in her hoodie and hat. She pulls off her beanie, shoves it into the back pocket of her jeans, thinks of losing her hoodie, but can't remember what she has underneath it – it could be any number of vests or T-shirts of questionable cleanliness, plucked from the washing basket in the early-morning dark, and now bound to have damp patches on the armpits. She plays it safe and leaves it on.

They turn to her as she approaches across the gravel.

'Hey,' says Luca, holding out his arms.

She leans in, and they kiss lightly on both cheeks. He smells of something fresh and clean. 'It's great to see you, Frannie. How are you doing?' His hand is on her shoulder, his gaze level with hers.

She steps back a pace, passes her hands over her hair, tells herself to breathe. 'I'm fine,' she says. 'Good.'

'Milo says you're holding this whole funeral thing together.'

'Does he?' She flicks a look to her brother, who looks – what? Certainly less aggravated than the last time she saw him.

'You know you are, Fran.' Milo inclines his head.

'Well . . . thanks.' She pulls the ends of the sleeves of her jersey over her thumbs, then releases them.

What are you, Frannie? Fifteen?

Everything seems very bright up here, at the top of the hill, where there are few trees, and little shade. The blue of Luca's T-shirt. The rampant pink of the ragged robin in the flowerbeds. The whitish-gold of the sandstone gravel beneath her feet.

'Did you fly in this morning?' she says, making herself turn back to Luca.

'Yesterday. I spent the night at Wallingford.'

'Wallingford?'

'Henry Marmon's place. You know he bought the biodynamic vineyard near Rye?'

'Oh shit,' says Milo. 'Yeah. How is it?'

'Next-level, mate – beautiful property – and I know you don't like the heavy stuff, but this natural wine is Ribena. Barely ten per cent. Glou-glou. He's got a Pet Nat that'll blow your mind. I bought a couple of cases for you all.' He turns to Frannie. 'He'd love to reconnect. Sends his love to you all. Sends his condolences. He's doing great things over there – right up your street I imagine. You should check it out.'

'Thanks,' she says. 'I might.'

'Listen, Frannie,' says Luca, 'I've said this many times to Milo, but I am just so sorry – I still can't believe he's gone. The last time I saw him he was – what – turning seventy? I went with him up to the pub – he was roaring at everyone to come down here and dance. Do not go gentle, eh? What a fucking legend.'

She can feel her body react to his words – the low-level chaos of attraction and repulsion, of magnetic fields gone awry. 'He was pretty gentle,' she says finally, 'in his final years. Surprisingly so, but . . . yeah.'

Luca nods, still that same steady gaze. 'How's Grace doing?'

'She's okay. Bearing up.'

'I got my assistant to get her a little gift. It'll be beautiful. She's got incredible taste.'

'That's kind.'

'It's nothing. Look,' says Luca, 'I'm just going to jump straight in here. I hope that's okay? I know you're a busy woman.'

She inclines her head.

'I understand from Milo that the legal and financial picture isn't as clear as it might be, but I just want to let you know, from our side, speaking for Clarity and our investors – our enthusiasm is undimmed. It's a beautiful afternoon – let's just explore some ideas together. We might yet find a way forward that works for all of us.'

She turns to Milo, tries to gauge his expression.

'I don't want any conflict this weekend, sis,' says Milo. 'I know you've got a lot on your shoulders. So, while Luca's here, let's just dream into it – we can home in on the financial side of things when the funeral's done.'

'Okay.' She nods. 'That sounds sane. Shall we walk then? It's just – time is at a premium this weekend, as I'm sure you'll understand.'

'Let's do it.' Luca clasps his hands, rubs them together, and she leads them out onto the upper path, which passes along the bottom of the solar field, where sheep tear at the grass beneath the panels. Half of the field is fenced off, and here the spaces between the panels are thick with tall grasses, bright with wildflowers, busy with butterflies and bees. 'Wow,' says Luca, slowing to take it in. 'That's beautiful. So the sheep do the mowing for you?'

'Yes,' she says. 'But we rope off certain areas and rotate their grazing so we can maximize the biodiversity, let the wildflowers come through.'

Luca brings out his phone and takes a photo. 'I love it,' he says. 'It's like Constable meets Tesla . . .' He pockets his phone as they start to walk again. 'So how many acres are given over to solar?'

Milo is walking slightly ahead, but Luca hangs back, falling into step beside Frannie.

'Five for now, although we're looking to expand.'

'And what sort of power are you getting from it?'

'Decent. I mean, it offsets the electrical consumption of the estate – all the businesses here are run on it. We want to run the village on solar by the end of the decade.'

'Nice.' He nods. 'And how many businesses have you got?'

'It varies, year to year, but usually comes in around twenty. They're all microbusinesses and it's a patchwork, as you can imagine, but we're making it work . . .' She is aware of the admixture of pride and defensiveness as she speaks. 'There's the issue of inheritance tax,' she says, lightly, 'as you probably know . . . but we've got a very strong case for heritage property status. The estate will be washing its own face soon enough.'

A little further along they reach the gate which marks the boundary of Ned's wood – here they pick up the path which leads alongside the stream, where sunlight falls in dappled shards onto the mossy banks of the steep-sided ghyll. Once they are amongst the trees the temperature drops by several degrees, and Frannie feels immediately easier now they are away from the bold sun.

'So these trees are pretty old, right?' says Luca.

'Yes. They are designated ancient woodland, which means they've been undisturbed for over four hundred years. But really we think this wood would have looked like this right back to the last ice age; we have all sorts of rare mosses here, liverworts, ferns, all relics of ancient ecosystems – more like Cornwall and Wales than the south-east. Ned coppices here – if he didn't, then we'd have a closed-canopy, climax vegetation. There would be no bluebells, not much life on the forest floor.'

'Yeah,' says Luca, 'these bluebells are insane. I don't think I've ever seen so many in my life. And what are those?' he says, pointing to where white flowers carpet the ground. 'They're stunning.'

'Wood anemone,' says Frannie. 'They only really flourish in ancient woods.'

She looks ahead, sees Milo has disappeared, around a bend in the stream.

'Look, Fran,' says Luca, 'just to fill you in, I had my team set up some little focus groups last week, just a temperature check for potential investors. We got all sorts of people in there. The great news is that people love what you're doing here. It's the cachet of the brand that you've been building – the Albion Project. It's got such wide appeal: a dream of England before it all went to shit, right? And a future in which it could be transformed. It played so well with everyone.'

'Well, thanks,' says Frannie. 'But I've never thought much about branding. I'm just doing what feels right for the land.'

'Of course,' he says. 'That's what makes it so powerful. You're the real deal, Frannie.'

They reach a clearing, a series of humped mossy mounds,

where birch logs are strewn in an informal round. The stream carves a semicircle here, and Milo stands waiting in the centre, an air of expectancy to him. 'Am I right in thinking,' says Luca, 'forgive me, Frannie – but since we're here – Milo, if in any way our plans come to fruition, that this would be about where we would start phase one?'

Milo nods. 'About here,' he says, 'yeah.'

'Okay,' says Luca. 'Then, can we just . . . pause for a moment?' He sits on a birch log, pulls off his trainers and socks, puts his feet onto a thickly mossed log. 'Wow,' he says.

Milo sits on a tree stump nearby and does the same. 'C'mon, Fran.' He grins. 'Don't you want to feel the earth?'

'I'm fine,' she says. 'Really. You two go ahead.' She checks her phone. 'I've literally got ten minutes. And then I need to get back to the house.'

'Okay.' Luca's hand is on his heart. 'I'm going to say this, even though I promised not to – because it's just too beautiful here to stay silent. I'm going to tell you why I think Milo's right, why we should build a treatment centre right here in this wood.'

She crosses her arms over her chest, her skin prickling with the queasy sense she has walked into an ambush. 'Go on.'

'People like me and Milo,' says Luca, 'we've seen it all. We've climbed every mountain they told us we should. We've been taught from school onwards to look for the next peak, and the next, but no one ever taught us to breathe the air – to take in the view. And all the time, there's this great big gaping hole in us that's desperate to be filled. So we try to fill it . . . with all sorts of shit. At least I did. I know you did too, mate,' he says to Milo.

Milo nods ruefully.

'Personally speaking,' says Luca, 'my life has changed radically in the last few years. I have sought out sacraments from all over the world, but you know what I've understood? That beneath it all is a simple longing.'

'And what's that?' says Frannie.

'To belong. To connect with the earth.' Luca gestures to the moss beneath his feet. 'Now you know as well as I do we could create this clinic in Mexico, we could do it in Ibiza – we could do it on a private island in West Cork . . . but it's here that's calling us. This is not just some piece of land, not some country-house hotel that the family have long since left – we've all stayed in places like that. They're soulless. Faceless.

'Milo's been talking to me about this for months, Frannie, but it wasn't until he sent me that *Country Life* piece that something dropped. What you said in that interview, Frannie, moved me deeply: that your ancestor came by this land seven generations before – that you do everything for seven generations hence. That you think with your acorn brain, that you want to be a good ancestor, to think like an oak. I mean, I *love that*. I'd heard it before, of course, but I'd always understood it as a Native American concept. You brought it home. I mean, who doesn't want to learn to think like an oak?'

There is the drilling of a woodpecker, sounding out its territory in a nearby tree. The rushing sound of the stream. The sun on her back.

'Look . . . all I'm saying is – the world is pretty fucked right now, but underneath it we're all the same, aren't we? If we can weave your thinking with our thinking – if we can utilize that sense of deep-rootedness – then I think we can offer something unique. And if we can get the right sort of people here – well, who the hell knows where we'll end up. Somewhere very beautiful, I think.'

'That's it,' says Milo. 'That's exactly it.'

'And who exactly are the *right sort of people*?' she says.

'We'll get them all here, Fran,' says Milo. 'Fund managers, thought leaders. MPs. *Presidents*. This place – The Clearing – will be so stealth you'll have no idea what's hit you until you're out there in the world changing it for the better. It's like taking the malware out of the hard drive and replacing it with love.'

Frannie laughs, shaking her head. 'Please,' she says.

'And we can all make an awful lot of money in the process,' says Luca. 'We found the brand here – right here – the original, the authentic, and then we can move into the compounds. The patents. Expand from a deeply rooted base.'

'This is major, Fran,' says Milo. 'I'm telling you. In every single way you can imagine: spiritually, financially, ethically. It's the shit.'

'Look, I appreciate your ambition, gentlemen, and I can see that you're both sincere, but isn't this all a little . . .'

'What?'

'Bombastic? It all sounds insanely hubristic.'

Luca smiles. 'I think the thing you're missing here, Frannie,' he says softly, 'is the potential for humanity.'

'Oh, right. Of course,' Frannie snaps. 'Forgive me. The potential for *humanity*? It's only humanity we're concerned with here? Only the humans we want to help? When I talk about thinking like an oak, I mean it; that's what I'm interested in – not the CEOs, I'm afraid, not the fund managers or the *thought leaders*, whoever the hell they are. Not the scaling or the branding or the *optimization of the human experience*. Shall I tell you what thinking like an oak means, to me? I lived in one for three months. I can tell you a little if you like?'

'Please do,' says Luca.

She moves across the glade, to where a wide-trunked oak abuts the stream, its roots splayed along the bank, its crown rising fifty feet or more above her head. 'This tree,' she says. 'It's what – a hundred years old? Maybe a little less. It's only just coming into maturity. It'll spend another few hundred years in the prime of life, producing millions of acorns – acorns which give food to badgers and squirrels and deer – and then when it starts to die, in the act of its dying, it will give *so much life*. Birds and bats will live in the hollows of its bark. It will drop its limbs, which will rot and give home to thousands of species of insect. They *give*,' she says. 'That's what oaks do: they support more life than any other tree, and they transform carbon into oxygen, the most selfless, the most necessary act on the planet today. They don't think about the bottom line, or winning, or scaling. They give away. They *share*.'

'They share, do they, Fran?' says Milo, lightly. 'I mean, I'm all for sharing. Aren't you?'

'Okay.' She is exhausted suddenly, her body drained. 'Look. I'm late. I'm supposed to be back at the kitchen to meet with Wren. So I'm going to round this up now. Why don't I just – leave you two here to take it all in.'

'Sure,' says Luca, putting his hands up in supplication. 'Whatever you want, Fran. You're the boss.'

They stay seated as she turns, walking swiftly away, picking up the stream path to head deeper into the wood, heading downhill, taking the shortest route back to the house. She pulls her sweater off over her head and ties it around her waist, glad of the cool relief of the air on her skin, pulling the same air down into her lungs.

The sound of hammering reaches her. At first, she thinks it is another woodpecker, but it is too slow and steady for that. She rounds a bend in the river and finds herself in another clearing, smaller than the first, but no less lovely. There are four posts set in the ground, some sort of winch system, a worktable, chainsaws. By the side of the track there are felled trees – piles of posts, two-by-four timber. A sawmill.

Her first reaction is confusion, then white-hot fury – because the only sane explanation for what she can see is that her brother has started work down here without telling her. She calls out in anger, and a face appears around the post, a young lad of nineteen or so.

'Can you tell me what the hell is happening here?' says Frannie.

'Sorry?'

'I said. What. Is. *Happening?* What are you building? Is this Milo? Are you working for my brother?'

'It's Ned,' he says. 'I mean, I'm working for him. Helping him out.'

'*Ned?*'

'He's building a cabin.'

'I can see that. Who told him he could?'

The boy looks confused. 'This is his wood.'

'No it bloody isn't,' says Frannie. 'It's *my* wood.'

The lad frowns.

'Where the hell is he??' says Frannie.

'Screwfix. He went to get some hinges.'

'I see. Well, you can stop whatever Ned has told you to do this afternoon. And you can leave. Right now.'

She stands watching, breath high and fast, as he gathers his things.

When he has gone, she walks around the site. Whatever Ned is building, for whatever purpose, he has been working on it for quite a while, and it is clearly built to last.

It doesn't make sense. His deceit. She thought more of him than this.

She feels an immense sense of constriction at her temples, a pressure in her head. These men. All these fucking *men*. The moment she turns her back they are all there, waiting – all just waiting for their moment. All clamouring to take their chunks from her – to lay their claim to their portion of her land.

When Clara wakes it is dark, and for a moment, in the thick, insulated quiet, she has no idea where she is. Then she remembers – England. Philip's house. She reaches for her phone, but the screen is blank. The battery has died. Shit. She came up here earlier to lie down after her walk and must have fallen asleep on the bed, fully dressed. The house sits silent around her. The window is still open from earlier, and cool night air spills into the room. She lies on her back, staring up at the ceiling, savouring the quiet – it is like wearing noise-cancelling headphones: no sounds of the city, no sirens or cars or distant trains. No chatter outside her window, or slang from the taxi drivers grabbing coffee at two a.m.

She turns on the bedside light and sits up in bed. She has no idea how long she slept for, but it's clear it's late. She will have missed dinner, missed the opportunity to meet the rest of the family, and they must think her rude. And she is ravenous now, hasn't really eaten a thing since boarding the flight what must be twenty-four hours ago. She thinks with longing of the Dominican bodega below her apartment, the cat curled into the chair in the corner, the tables in summertime which spill out onto the street. If it were the middle of the night in New York she could go downstairs, pick up arroz con habichuelas, or mashed plantain, bring it back up the two flights to her bedroom, sit at her desk and work into the night.

She is filled with the need to call her mother, to tell her she is here, in Philip's house, describe it to her in all its strangeness and beauty, and – quicker than thought, her phone is in her hand. But she cannot call her mother because her mother is dead. So often, still, she gets caught like this: the vertiginous feeling of aloneness that grips her in these moments has not eased, not really, has grown less sharp, less dizzying, but still has the power to snatch her breath.

Inside the front pocket of her phone case is a small strip of photographs. One of those photobooth ones, taken twenty-five years ago, before the world went digital. She slides it out and lays it on the bed before her. It is of her mother and her father, the only one she has of them both together. Her mother liked to tell her the story of this photograph and Clara liked to hear it: they had gone to Coney Island for the day when Natasha did not yet know she was pregnant – rode on the rollercoasters and ate ice cream. Her mother is wearing an oversized man's white shirt, and is staring into the camera, and her father's face is sort of pressed into her mother's chest so you can only really see his right cheek and that is a little blurred. They had only been together for a month, and it would only be another couple of months before he died. Clara knows what the blurred man in the picture never would: that she was busy forming herself deep in her mother's womb all that long day, while her parents rode on the roller-coaster and crowded into the photobooth and splashed in the sea. Still – whether he ever knew of her life or not, they are here, together, a family.

Her mother stares out at her, now, across twenty-five years and from beyond her death. Her languid, laughing eyes, the way her lips curled up at the edges like her mouth had no choice but to smile. Natasha was a person with a gift for living; she didn't so much make decisions or steer as let life erupt in her, around her, through her. Her mother would always accuse her of being too serious, when Clara fretted over the mark she got on a term paper or exam. *Your generation*, she would say, shaking her head.

She places the photo strip against the lamp and goes to the window. The moon is low and hanging in the sky, below it she sees the outlines of tall trees, the darkness of the wood beyond the park. It is quiet out there, but a restless sort of quiet, the small whisper of a breeze. The plaintive call of an occasional owl. She moves to the door, opens it, and looks down the corridor; there's no sign of anyone, but a small tray lies on the carpet before her. She brings it back inside the room, where, by the light of the lamp she sees an assortment of cheese, some bread, some hummus, several small, beautiful-looking tomatoes. A glass of wine. A little note beside the plate. *Thought you must be sleeping. There's some food here for you. Isa.* She places the tray on the desk and eats hungrily, gratefully. The wine is good and welcome, a deep, earthy red; as she sips it she feels it flush through her, warming her, and when she has finished she is a little restored.

She pulls her laptop towards her and brings up the documents she was working on during the flight: her own loose notes, then PDFs of archival material, page after page of crabbed eighteenth-century handwriting – correspondence, ledgers, letters. Three weeks' work. Three weeks since she received the letter and replied to Isabella. Three weeks since she put Philip's name into a search engine and came up with the Albion Project – since she clicked a link on its website to a photograph of a family standing against the trunk of an ancient oak. Since she saw the emaciated frame of a man she had once known – not well, but who had walked through her young life and marked it indelibly – his daughter and granddaughter posed around him. She recognized the way they were standing – their bodies forming a triangle, the tree in the background – but at first, she could not say from where. She read the article in which father and daughter spoke movingly of their commitment to the natural world, to the generations to come. In which their shared radicalism was celebrated – in which they spoke of working for the future in harmony with the past. And then it surfaced: a buried memory, a book that Philip had left in the apartment, one she had loved to look at when she was a child. She went to the shelves and found it, turned the pages until she reached the picture she remembered: a family posed against the trunk of an oak on a beautiful spring day.

Oliver Brooke and Family, 1789. Sir Joshua Reynolds.

And so three weeks ago, on a misty morning in Brooklyn, she opened her laptop and she tugged on the end of a thread. A thread which led her deep into the archives. The story laid out before her now, the one she has been swimming in for the last few weeks, is a story that touches her own life, and reaches back in time to stories far more compelling than the paper she is due to write on research methods for her PhD. A story that has shaken her so profoundly that she felt she had no choice but to follow the thread back across the Atlantic, to the home of Oliver Brooke himself, and the heart of the family of a man her mother once loved.

She booked the flight on her credit card, late one night last week, two beers down and a little drunk, averting her eyes from the screen and the eyewatering cost to her wallet, to the planet – the insanity of all that carbon for a single weekend. The fact that she couldn't stay longer, make a proper trip of it. The fact that she should have stayed at home, preparing for a paper at a conference she had been lucky to get and for which she was nowhere near ready. Even despite all that, she felt – what? Not guided – not that – but sure. Now she is here though, she understands she has no real idea of what happens next.

What the hell was she thinking? How is she supposed to insert herself into this narrative? What was she hoping to achieve that wouldn't better have been served by a letter, or a long email? A piece of writing rinsed of emotion. Direct. Clear. Who does she think she is to come here now, this weekend of all weekends? To disrupt this family, who have gathered here, after all, for their father's *funeral*? To upend her own schedule, to jeopardize her PhD? What would her mother say if she could call her tonight? If her batteryless phone could reach across the divide and call her mother up?

Hey, honey, she'd say. *C'mon. Are you sure you want to do this?*

I don't know, Mom. I don't know what this *is.*

She thinks of the picture downstairs, of Oliver Brooke with his imperious gaze. Surely no one will be around now, and she can spend some time looking back at him, meeting that gaze, undisturbed. She gets up from the desk, pulls on a sweater and makes her way to the door, following the same route as yesterday, moving as quietly as she can along the dark corridor until she reaches the main landing, where the doors to all the bedrooms are shut. Behind one of them, she hears a child cry out in their sleep. She goes down the shallow staircase in the half-light, moving swiftly, ghost steps, crossing the chill of the hall tiles, then pushing open the tall library door. The curtains hanging from the windows onto the terrace are undrawn and moonlight lies across the furniture, the books, the high-backed chairs arranged before their low table. She holds her hands out in front of her, so she does not trip as she walks towards the desk, where she rests her hands for a moment on the dark polished wood. Her fingertips touch the edges of the leather, so carefully inset into its surface, and her heart quickens. What letters were written from this desk? What deals were struck from this place of deep peace – this quiet green corner of the English countryside?

She gropes for the cord of a desk lamp and switches on the light. The family float above her – too close, from here, to see properly, so she takes two paces back.

Oliver Brooke and Family, 1789.

Her blood pounds in her ears.

1789, year of revolution, of upending, of unravelling, and yet this family stares out across the centuries, their bloodline undisturbed, their souls unperturbed, the very image of harmony, of natural order, of everything in its right place.

She knows she is in this man's debt – caught so deeply in a web of implication that it is hard to untangle where she stands. Perhaps, she thinks, it was simply for this she came, to stand here in this library, before this desk, to face him, to feel this firestorm of emotion – and in doing so to come face to face with the knotted truths of her own implication in unimaginable harm.

From behind her comes the sound of the door opening, and Clara, heart racing, wheels round to see a woman standing in the doorway, a mug in her hand, clutching a laptop under her arm. 'Oh,' says the woman. 'Gosh. Sorry. I didn't mean to disturb you.'

'It's okay,' Clara manages. Her body is electric with cortisol.

The woman crosses the room towards her, and reaches out a hand. 'Frannie,' she says.

'I'm Clara.' She meets the woman's hand, which is large and rough-palmed. There is something hawkish about her – the profile, the height. An intensity to her. The light of the low lamp pools in the hollows of her face; she looks tired.

'I'm so sorry I haven't met you yet,' says Frannie, putting coffee and laptop down on the desk. 'I fed my daughter early, then I'm

187

afraid I fell asleep putting her to bed, and I woke up in a bit of a panic just now . . .'

'I missed dinner too,' Clara says. 'I guess I slept. Isabella left me a tray.'

'Ah,' says Frannie. 'Well. That was kind of her . . . and is your room okay? The guest rooms are in a bit of a state I'm afraid. But then so is the rest of the house.'

'It's fine,' Clara says, backing away. 'Really . . . Listen, I can see you're busy. Hopefully we can meet tomorrow – I'll leave you to your work.'

'It's not really work. I mean, sort of – I'm trying to write my father's eulogy.' Frannie gives a ragged sigh. 'Look . . . I'm going to have a whisky. Do you want to join me?'

'Okay,' says Clara. 'Sure.'

Frannie goes over to a cabinet set on a table by a wall of books. She lifts glasses, pours a couple of generous measures out and brings them over to the low table, where she puts them down. 'Have a seat,' she says, pulling out one of the chairs and gesturing to the other. And so they sit. Behind Frannie is the desk, and behind that the painting, all of it held in the chiaroscuro effect cast by the low lamp; beyond which the room stretches, darkly.

Clara takes a small sip of her whisky, feels Frannie's gaze rake her. She sits still, stiller, waiting for Frannie to speak.

'I'm just going to come out and say it,' says Frannie eventually.

'Please do . . .'

'There was a lot of concern, when we heard you were coming, that you were Philip's daughter.'

'Of course . . . well . . .' Clara says, gesturing to herself. 'As you can see – I'm not.'

'No,' says Frannie. 'And I hope you don't mind me saying what a relief it has been to us all. For my mother especially – I think she would have found the idea of another child very hard to bear.'

'I understand,' Clara says.

188

'But I want to say how welcome you are. Not because you aren't his – but . . .' Frannie's face is lighter. 'Did you know him? Philip? Do you remember him at all?'

'A little.' Clara cradles the glass in her palms. 'My mother and Philip were no longer properly together when I was born, but he was around still. I think their relationship had changed. The way my mom told it, they had become more . . . platonic – I guess they had both moved on. But they remained friends even after I was born. And Philip stayed on in New York for quite a while, as you know.' She takes another sip of her whisky. 'I remember . . . how tall he was. Although I guess that's kind of an obvious thing to say.'

'Well he certainly was that.' Frannie smiles. 'He always seemed huge to me too when I was small. He died in here,' she says. 'His bed was just about . . . there.' She gestures with her glass to the dark space between the table and the bookshelf. 'It was easier for him to be here, once he could no longer manage the stairs.'

'He was lucky. To die at home.'

'Yes. He was . . . I know your mother died recently too,' says Frannie gently.

'A year ago,' Clara says. 'She was in a hospice at the end. They were kind, but it was hard.'

'I'm sure,' says Frannie. 'I am afraid I know nothing of her, other than her name, and the fact that she was obviously very dear to my father . . . Tell me about her. What did she do?'

'She was a gallerist. Downtown. At first she rented a little place in the East Village, and then when she and Philip were first together, Philip gave her the money to buy something bigger and set herself up.'

Frannie nods.

'I carry a deep sense of gratitude to him for that. All sorts of things became possible in the wake of that generosity that wouldn't have been easy or even likely otherwise.'

'Like what?'

'I mean, my mother was not someone who had anything much really, and Philip gave her something which changed her life – and so mine. She sold the gallery eventually and so had means for the first time in her life. It meant I was able to go to college. I'm studying for a doctorate now.'

Frannie nods. She does not look displeased. 'He was a complicated man, but he was certainly capable of real generosity, when he wished to be.'

'It's funny,' says Clara. 'Since he died, I've realized he gave me something else too.'

'What was that?' Frannie leans towards her.

'I've been reflecting on how he might have shaped my life unconsciously. On how I'd never really considered why I'm studying the eighteenth century for my PhD.'

She grows silent again, and she knows it is her imagination – the strangeness of this scene, of this midnight intimacy with a woman she has just met – but something in the room around them feels tensile, listening.

'And who was your father?' says Frannie.

'He was a photographer. He was born in St Kitts, in the Caribbean. And he came to live in the Bronx when he was ten or so, in the late 1970s.' She takes another sip of her whisky. 'He was part of an uptown scene – kids whose creativity emerged from nothing, and they would go downtown, hang out at these DIY clubs. And he took photographs of the scene. And then, I guess, he realized he was talented, and others did too. He started getting shows. But he was – not super well in other ways. He died when he was thirty-three, just before I was born. I never knew him. But I carry his name. My mom wanted me to have it when he died.'

'I'm sorry,' says Frannie.

'It's okay. It's a long time ago.'

'What was his name?'

Clara sips her whisky, lets it burn her throat. 'Nelson,' she says. 'Allan Nelson.'

It feels strange to speak his name here, in this room. This room so thick with other fathers. Generations of them.

'So you're Clara Nelson?'

'Yes.'

'It's funny for me, you know,' says Frannie. 'Hearing you talk. That whole period of my father being away in America – the time he spent with your mother, which must have been very important to him – I have no idea about. After he sold the London flat, I didn't speak to him for many years. Which is hypocritical perhaps, because I knew he was never faithful to my mother – America or not. But after he moved to the States, I cut him off. And even when he came back home and started living here again it took me a long time to want to spend any time in his company. In some ways, I suppose all of this, the first years of the project, dreaming it into being together, was our movement towards repair.'

Frannie gestures with her whisky glass to one of the framed photographs on the table before her, and Clara leans over and picks it up: an image that is well known to her now – Frannie and Philip and Rowan, by the oak. 'I read that article,' Clara says, 'This is the photo, right? The one they used for the cover?'

'Yep.'

'And it's the same pose as the portrait? The Reynolds?' Clara gestures to where the painting hangs on the wall.

'Well spotted.' Frannie gives a small laugh. 'They suggested we replicate it for the shoot.'

'Philip left a book,' says Clara. 'Of Reynolds portraits, in our apartment. When I was a kid I used to imagine myself into it. I used to think that was how people dressed. In England, in like, 2005: frock coats and pink silk. Hair like that.'

Frannie smiles. 'That's very sweet.'

'I guess.' Clara bridles, something in the word – *sweet* – but Frannie doesn't seem to notice. Clara places the photograph carefully back on the table, then turns her gaze to the painting on the wall. 'Do you know much about him?' she says, with a lightness she does not feel. 'Oliver Brooke?'

'Not really.' Frannie twists a little in her chair, looking up at him. 'Not enough, I'm sure. He was in trade, as they say in this country, when they're trying to be mean. Not a proper aristocrat. There was no hereditary title.'

'Do you know what sort of trade?'

'Not really,' say Frannie. 'At least, I'm not absolutely sure . . . Marine insurance was the main thing, I believe. Beyond that it's all a bit hazy. I'm sure I wouldn't have liked his politics. He looks very pleased with himself, doesn't he?'

'Yes,' agrees Clara, 'he does.'

She thinks of the documents upstairs. Is it now? Should she speak now? Perhaps she should; right now – here, in this low light – get it over with, get it out?

She looks back up at Oliver Brooke, then pulls her eyes away. No – not yet. Instead, she lets her eyes rest back on the photographs on the table before them. 'Is this you?' she asks, leaning in and lifting the one closest: a young woman, hair matted and wild, standing in the dawn mist, flanked by two men in white hard hats and neon-yellow jackets. Her face is painted blue, mouth stretched in a silent scream.

'Yes.' Frannie sips her whisky and grimaces. 'That's Newbury.'

'Are they arresting you?'

'I'm afraid they are.'

'What for?'

'Aggravated trespass. For trying to protect an oak tree. It had been my home for three months. They chopped it down in front of my eyes about five minutes after this photo was taken.'

'How old were you?'

'Very young. Very impressionable. Still a teenager.'

'You look like some kind of warrior. Fierce.' Clara places the photograph back on the table. 'You talked about Newbury in the article,' she says, 'but I wasn't totally sure what it was.'

'It was a protest site in the mid-nineties.' Frannie leans forward. 'The government had a huge road-building programme. They wanted to build a bypass through ancient woodland, to cut ten minutes off the journey through the town. There were a thousand of us living there, protecting ten thousand trees. Swearing they would clear them over our dead bodies. And at the time, it felt like that might be what it would take.'

'And that time was part of why you did all this? The rewilding? The Albion Project?'

'Well . . .' says Frannie. 'The reasons were many, but I understood something recently . . . perhaps I've needed hindsight to come to know it, but that oak tree – the one that was my home – had asked something of me, in the moment of its felling. And I took decades to find my reply.'

'That's beautiful.'

'It's true. Those months changed my life, in ways I'm still coming to understand . . . Although,' she says ruefully, 'it seems almost quaint now.'

'What do you mean?'

'Well, the desire to simply protect trees. Now we are in the age of extinction. Ecosystem collapse. The stakes have rather ramped up, haven't they, since then?'

'Yes,' says Clara. 'They have.'

'I think about it a lot,' says Frannie. 'Intergenerational justice. What you'll see in your lifetime. What my daughter will see. How fortunate, relatively, I've been. I think now I'm a mother the stakes feel especially acute.'

'How old is your daughter?'

'Seven. Rowan's seven . . .' She stops, her face momentarily unguarded, and Clara sees fear there, and pain, until Frannie counters, her chin raised. 'I want her to know that I tried. That the world she inherits may be a little kinder for the work we did here.' She takes a draught of her whisky. 'I want her to shelter in the shade of the oaks I planted. And her children and her children's children. And I want to be able to speak of love for land in a way that's generative. That's not politicized. That's beyond politics, in fact.'

'Is anything ever beyond politics?' says Clara softly. 'I mean, particularly when it comes to land?'

'Oh God, yes! I think it can be. I think it *must*. Worms. Nematodes. Soil. Mycelium. They each have their own agency. It's our hubris to think we can impose our human narratives on them.

'You know,' says Frannie, 'when I'm scared – and I'm often scared nowadays – I go outside in the very early morning, and I stand and listen. I think of them all: those creatures beneath the soil and above it, all going about their lives, most of them with no idea of us, crashing about above. And I feel easier. Our human dramas, our human foibles – they don't care. If I can make their soil better, richer, stronger, then I will have done a good thing, I think, with my life.' Frannie drains her drink. 'Rant over, sorry. Do you want another? I wouldn't usually, but it's been a hell of a day.'

'I'm good, thanks.' Clara watches Frannie as she rises, makes her way over to the decanter, pours herself another healthy measure.

'And the other children?' says Clara.

'What do you mean?' Frannie turns back to her.

'Well, your daughter for instance . . . Rowan is one child, right, in a thousand acres of land. On this rich, healthy soil. What about the other children? The kids in the cities? I mean, how far away is London? Forty miles? How many kids live there?'

'I'm doing it for them too!' Frannie sounds astonished she should be questioned. 'Of course I am! Every fraction of carbon sequestered means less in the air. Every clean mile of river is a victory. And we're thinking huge-scale here. Did you know of Philip's vision? At the end of his life? The wildlife corridor? Here – come and see.' Frannie moves to where a framed map hangs on the wall, and Clara rises to join her as she switches on a low light which illuminates the foot of Britain – the counties of West Sussex, East

Sussex, Kent, the English Channel, woods and hills and ancient burial mounds and small towns, and Clara thinks of the view from the plane, those high white cliffs of England, the rippling, ridged spine of the Downs.

'Here's where we are,' Frannie points, 'on the border of the Ashdown Forest, you can see the house, the extent of the estate.' She circles the area with her whisky glass. 'You see how small the project is really – even a thousand acres – but the idea is to link up with like-minded landowners across Sussex to the sea, to create a nature recovery corridor a hundred miles wide, one of the largest schemes in the UK. Philip threw everything into it in his final months. He loved to think of wildlife, travelling through this landscape unimpeded. Not interrupted by walls, or fences or wire, or by us humans.'

'And the fences?' says Clara. 'And the walls? What will happen to them?'

'I think he'd have liked to tear them down!' Frannie turns to her, her face shining. 'But seriously – the idea is massive, radical: imagine no barbed wire, only GPS collars. If Philip had his way, there would be no barriers to the wild. He loved to think that we could intervene, and then leave the wild world to its own devices.'

'You make him sound like God.'

'Ha,' says Frannie. 'Yes, he could seem that way, sometimes. But really, the point of it – the very *ethos* of rewilding – is to give up hierarchy. If we get this nature corridor right it has the potential to be a sort of de-enclosure, recreating a commons of the non-human.'

'While retaining ownership of the land?'

'Well . . . yes. But in deep collaboration – this is a shared vision: landowners, gardeners, councils, schools and national parks. Communities coming together. If it comes off, it will be a huge part of his legacy. It'll give us massive gains in biodiversity, massive amounts of carbon locked away from future generations.'

'Well,' says Clara. 'You say you want to live beyond politics. But I think you could be a good politician.'

Frannie winces. 'Thanks, I think. Well, who knows. Maybe one day. Actually, no.' She gives a diffident shrug. 'I can't really do people. I'd rather be with the non-human – the more-than-human – any day of the week. I'll just stay here, doing what I'm doing for as long as I can, and hoping it spreads out from here.'

Frannie falls silent, absorbed again in the map, in the power of her vision. And it is now, Clara knows, that she must speak – before tiredness overtakes them both, before this intimacy is broken.

'I've been doing some digging,' she says.

'Digging?' says Frannie, turning to her with a small smile.

'Not literal,' Clara says. 'Not soil. In the archives I mean.'

'Oh?'

She takes a deep breath. 'I'd known for a long time that I had benefited financially from the gift that Philip gave to my mother, but until I got the email from Isabella, telling me of his death, I'd never really questioned the origins of that money. And so . . . I started researching. And I ended up in kind of a . . . deep dive.'

Frannie frowns, a wariness to her now.

'And I'm wondering,' says Clara, 'if you want to hear about it?'

'When? Now?'

'Now could be good.' Her heart is pounding. 'I mean. If you're willing.'

'Sure,' says Frannie. 'Of course.' But the energy has drained from her face, from her voice, and what was open and eager in her has shut down. She looks exhausted as she moves away from the wall, from the map, from her vision of the future, towards her laptop on the desk.

'Actually,' Frannie says, 'just now's not great for me. It's almost one in the morning, and I still have this eulogy to write. But let's find a time while you're here. Let's definitely do that. I'd love to hear what you've uncovered.'

Frannie's tone has changed. Perfectly genial, perfectly polite, and yet Clara is left in no doubt that she is being dismissed. Ushered away from the centre of operations, from the seat of power. For this is how power operates, she knows – it invites you in, lets you look around, and then, when your time is up, it shows you the door.

Clara places her whisky glass down on the table. 'Sure,' she says. 'No problem. I'll leave you to your writing.'

'Thank you,' says Frannie. 'It's good to have you here, Clara. And I look forward to talking more.'

Clara walks to the door, where she turns, sees Frannie is already sitting at the desk, pulling the lid of her computer up, her ancestors above her, their faces and her own face, pale in the light of the laptop screen.

Day Three

Isa is awash, in her childhood bedroom, sitting in her childhood bed, with the familiar, queasy feeling of amends needing to be made. Apologies given. Scenes replayed to understand how they can have ended so badly. She knows she has been cruel and stupid: the way she spoke to Frannie and Milo when she arrived, the way she spoke to Jack yesterday morning. It is almost as though, when she is here, at home, within the park, she cannot be otherwise; that as soon as she enters the gates, the shadow of this house falls upon her and she turns into someone she would not like to cross the road to meet. Or perhaps, she thinks, it is that she is always this person, this stupid cruel person, and this place only reveals it – it is the rest of her life that is a lie.

She brings her knees up beneath the duvet. Outside, the sky is a thinning grey. A sole bird starts to sing.

It doesn't happen away from here, though, does it? This cruelty? This stupidity? People like her, she has friends, she can name her friends – they themselves are good caring people; they are teachers and doctors and social workers and fellow mothers and fathers. She does good things: she teaches, and she believes in the humanities as a force for empathy and good; she cares about the kids in her classes and gives extra tuition for free to the talented ones. She takes them to visit art exhibitions and theatres and sometimes pays with her own money. She loves her own children immeasurably. She tries to encourage their talents but not over-burden them with expectation – tries, in fact, to be the sort of parent that she never had herself: present, engaged, interested. She gives regularly to several charities from her bank account. She loves her husband, in her way.

Her way.

What's your love language, Isa?

Her husband, who is exactly the sort of man her father was not: safe, normal, kind. And if sometimes she may feel bored or trapped, she knows that this is because of her damaged childhood, a sign she is equating love with drama. With too much feeling. An equation she has spent many years trying to undo.

Outside the window the bird sings on, melodious and clear. What is it? A blackbird? A wren? A thrush? Frannie would know; their father would have known what bird is singing first, to call in the dawn, on this day he goes into the ground. This funeral at which she has said she will not speak, where she will sit in silence while Milo and Grace give their readings, while Frannie gives her eulogy. She knows what they all think: that this silence is churlish, immature, and perhaps they are right, perhaps it is. Because of course she could find something to say – something good – that's what you're supposed to do, right? Think about the good. Find it, name it. But she does not think she can speak without telling the truth, and today is not about the truth, it is about a version of the past that people can bear.

Perhaps the truth is that they all had different fathers: she did not really know Philip as an adult. Not like Frannie, who worked with him closely for a decade before he died. Not like Milo, who seems to have reconciled and forgiven him after his trip to Amsterdam. But she doesn't buy it. Not really. It's as though they both need their father to be part of their narratives of personal redemption – the relentless, performative optimism of their personal brands: Frannie rewilding the world; Milo with his crazed plans. If she were going to say anything today, she would like to speak of *her* father. She would like to say that *her* father was a difficult, damaged and damaging man – a narcissist who used the world and the people within it as the backdrop for his appetites, who left them all with scant contact for the best part of a decade while he lived in the States with a woman half his age; a man with whom she never forged any relationship of worth and from whom she remained estranged.

The light in the room is a little stronger now; she can see the outline of the sink in the corner, the chest of drawers, the bookshelves with the spines of her childhood books. All of it the same strange admixture of familiar and unfamiliar: a house in which she never felt at home.

It was not, thinks Isa, that the seven years Philip was away were so different from the ones that went before; her father was often absent then too, and it was clear their parents were desperately unsuited and unhappy, but Frannie was at home, Milo was there in the holidays, Jack was always present in the cottage beside Ned's wood. And if Frannie did not play with them in the same way, was always that bit older, more serious, she was always there, still, steady and kind. Until Philip left, and Frannie went away.

To Isa, hovering on the edge of adolescence, there were two abandonments in one, but only one felt brutal. And she knows that Frannie had every right to leave when she did, but when she went, the buffer of a shared childhood world disappeared; Milo was away at school and Isa was left alone with Grace. She was lonely, but more than that, it felt to her as though she had been left to absorb all the strangeness of the house and the unhappiness of her mother into her body; all the dark air filling up her lungs and coating her hair.

She never invited anyone here after school. The park was neglected, far too vast for a skeleton staff; only the spooky conifer forest was maintained for the income of the shoot – full of pheasants feeding themselves for death.

She would write to Frannie, long lonely emails on the dial-up modem whirring into the night.

Please come home. Please, Fran, you have to help me get out of here. Please.

She received only sporadic, distracted replies.

And so, rather than sit alone or across from her haunted

mother, Isa began to go down to Jack's family's cottage to eat. It was warm there, and welcoming – it smelt of Jeannie's cigarettes and dogs and bread. And Jack was there, and it was easy to be with him; it was always easy to be with him, until everything changed between them – until, when she was sixteen, they had sex. And she knew it was supposed to be awkward, perfunctory, disappointing, but it was none of those things.

But then she found out he had a girlfriend, a girl in the village. Charlie.

She can feel it now, still, at the age of thirty-eight – how it felt in her body, the desolation of it. The ground giving way beneath her. How stupid she had been to trust him. How he had betrayed her, but also their shared childhood; how everything that was good and fine in that childhood felt broken and polluted now.

And so she begged her mother to let her go away to school, and her father agreed, sending money from the States for a boarding school in Surrey. At school, although she was far from happy, she learned to mask her unhappiness with the trappings of young womanhood, things that had never occurred to her as being important before. She learned about hair straighteners and make-up, learned she was beautiful and that this was a complicated weapon with many moving parts she had to learn to use, to keep clean and shiny and ready for action. She accepted invitations to friends' houses, and to holidays abroad. She had sex with lots of boys and a few men and most of it was terrible and some of it was not, but for two years she managed to hardly come home, until the summer after her exams when she found herself back here.

It was the year after Milo had tried to kill himself. Grace had turned into a ghost of a ghost, haunting the remnants of her life.

She remembers the feel of returning to the estate, those summer weeks stretching before her, the constriction in the house and in her heart: all the dark air filling her up again, Milo gone again, Frannie away – Frannie always away. Until Jack came to find her. It was Jack who saved her, Jack who held the keys to release her back into the green. She felt more real that summer than she has ever felt since; everything since has been an approximation of that feeling. Nothing with any other man. Nothing with Hari. Never close to that intensity.

She believed they could live here together, on the estate. Make a life. And it was a ridiculous dream perhaps, but it felt as real – more real – than anything ever had. And then her father came home. (Why then? She has never really known.) She remembers coming up from the wood, seeing his suitcase in the hall. He was sitting at the desk in the library like an apparition, beneath the portrait of Oliver Brooke. He looked at her as though he didn't know her. And she remembered she had been a child when he left.

You look just like your mother, he said. He looked shocked, confused. Old.

And so, when Philip came back, when as far as Isa could see he repented and came home only when he was too old and too broken to do anything but, she went and fled in her turn.

She knows she broke Jack's heart then. But they didn't make sense in the world beyond, and now, with her father in residence, that was where she had to live. It was a place which was less beautiful and less wild, but was sane and clear, and in time, she found it operated by rules that she could understand: it was a place where people worked hard and got married and had kids and didn't live in treehouses. Where they saved for deposits for two-bedroom terraces in battered parts of East London and saved up again for side return extensions and voted Labour and believed in the NHS and sent their kids to state schools as an article of faith and cared about civic responsibility and the welfare state. And she realized that the world beyond was a place where she could live. She trained as a teacher and met Hari and got married. And she loved her husband – but she knows now that she loved him more for what he was not than for what he was: he was not a liar and he was not her father and he was not Jack.

And then, when Jeannie died, when Rani was nine and Seb was five, she drove down here for her funeral and she betrayed her husband with Jack. And even though, in the treehouse, in the wood, what happened felt natural and right, she knows by the rules of the world outside it was a travesty: she spent the night with her childhood love while Hari was with their children, reading Seb a bedtime story. Getting up early to make lunch and drive them to breakfast club. She remembers driving home to London, how much she smelt of Jack, of sex. How she called in sick to work and went to bed and lay down and curled around herself and wept for Jeannie and for Jack and for home and for herself and for the past.

She knows that Hari senses something, that for the three years since that betrayal things have been different. And she knows too that the lava of her is beginning to geyser up to the surface, more and more often lately, scorching their family life. She knows she has to do something, knows how selfish it is to hang on to Hari while hurting him in this way; but her husband is safe, and her life before him was full of danger, and she does not know how to be a grown-up without him.

And in Isa's self-imposed exile, Frannie returned, and the great narrative of redemption began. And she was forced to watch from the sidelines while Frannie and Philip – serial abandoners both – rooted into the soil of home, transforming it, while she who had loved it so deeply found herself on the outside looking in. She knows full well this facile redemptive arc – Philip and Frannie as the bringers of the light – is the story that will prevail today. That this whole narrative, this whole funeral, in fact, is a form of familial gaslighting.

Whatever – she will remain silent. About all of it. Because she does not want to lie. And in her lack of lying, she will feel on the outside, as she always does, away from the inner circle of mutual deceit.

And yet.

She keeps thinking about the last time she saw her father: six weeks ago, three weeks before he died, the evening after he had the psilocybin treatment. Milo had called her, said Philip was asking for her, so she took the afternoon off work and drove down. She arrived when it was already getting dark, and her brother met her in the hall.

He's waiting for you, Isa. He'll be so glad you're here. Frannie's longing to see you too. We'll wait in the kitchen. Come and find us when you're done.

She went into the library alone. It was cold and she kept her coat on. Her father was lying in bed; from a distance he looked piteous, shrunken, marooned in the vastness of his inheritance. He was thin, shockingly so, and his skin was a terrible, creeping yellow, but his eyes were a deep, lucid blue. He held out his hand above the blankets and she took it.

Isa, he said. I've just had the most magnificent experience of my life.

She had no idea what to say and so she said nothing, standing there in the room with her father's thin hand in hers.

And I understood I need to tell you that I love you. That I am proud of you. And that I hope you know that. My beautiful girl.

She stayed in there with him as long as she could bear, but it felt appalling somehow; a stilted play in which she didn't know her next line, for which no one had handed her the script. She could not tell him that she loved him too. And besides – what was she supposed, at this catastrophically late stage in the game, to do with her father's love?

After a while, he fell asleep, and she slipped away. She did not go to find Frannie – Frannie who had so often left her alone. Instead, she opened the doors and stepped out onto the terrace. It was freezing outside, still as still, with a hard frost already on the ground. Her breath streamed into the air before her. She walked quickly away from the house, from her sleeping father, from her brother and sister, waiting in the kitchen, from her mother, wherever she was, and drove back up to London, carrying this gift of her father's love like a golem on the seat beside her. Every so often she would remember it was there, and feel it, a shrunken twisted thing; something that had grown in the dark and never known the light. She left the golem in the car when she arrived back in London, locked it in there, went and stood in her kitchen, where she drank the best part of a bottle of wine standing up, then walked heavy-footed up the stairs and curled into the bed she shared with Hari.

How was it? he said to her.

I don't know. Weird.

What did he want to say to you?

That he loved me.

Oh, said Hari. That's good. He put his hand on her back. After a while, she turned away, but stayed awake, staring at the wall, thinking of the twisted creature out there in the cold in the car, as she felt her husband claimed by sleep.

But what if? What if during these last ten years the water ran clearer? What if the project cleansed him of his sins? She knows that Frannie believes that in the last act of her father's life he atoned and made repair. That his redemption was not facile, but earned and true, makes Isa ache: for the father she never had, the man who might have been behind the persona all this time, the grandfather who drew hazel catkins and chiffchaffs and blackcaps with such sensitivity and care. She aches for the fact that her own children never shared that with him, that they do not possess Rowan's ease with the natural world, her sure-footed tread; she moves like a creature that understands she is a part of it, and it a part of her. Her own children walk differently, her daughter's thin shoulders already hunched into the posture of technological adolescence – the swiftness of her fingertips over the keys of her phone. She would like to throw her daughter's phone away, bring her here so that she starts to understand this green world, but she is an urban teenager, anxious outdoors in a thousand ways, scared of spiders, chary of bugs. And why is that? Because she, Isa, their mother, has been in flight from this place for years.

Outside her window the blackbird, or the wren, or the robin, has been joined by other birds. Was it always this loud, or is this another thing that Frannie has done – turn up the volume on the dawn chorus? She goes to the window and pulls up the sash, a moment's hesitation, and then she is up and out, sitting on the flat roof of the storey below.

She thinks of Clara, sleeping elsewhere in the house. Of Milo's question to her on Thursday night: *Why did you do it, sis? Why write to Natasha?*

The answer, she knows, is that she does not truly know.

Perhaps because we were all in danger of forgetting who he was. What he was.

Still, she did not expect her to come.

Despite the thrumming birdsong the morning air is still, and she can see a lazy scarf of smoke in the distance, making its presence felt above the mist that is hanging over the river and the lake. She remembers what Jack said: that he would place the deer on the coals at daybreak. So the smoke is his. The signal of his whereabouts.

She makes her way down – the old way, the way her feet know, all the old footholds still there – and lands on the gravel, then sets off, carving a path through the waist-high grasses, heading towards the signal of the smoke. It is chilly and she is wearing only joggers, only a T-shirt, her feet bare, but it is beautiful to walk like this in the early light, to see the dull-bright colours of the wildflowers dot the grass, to feel the coiled-up promise of the dawn.

As she nears the fire, she sees him kneeling on the ground, the deer lying on the coals before him. He is packing the earth around it, covering it up. He lifts his head as she approaches. 'Oh,' he says. 'Hey.'

She wraps her arms around her against the chill. 'I'm sorry,' she says.

'What for?'

'For yesterday. The way I was.'

'How were you?'

'The things I said. About your new job. I didn't mean them.'

'Oh? What did you mean then?'

'I meant . . . I don't know – it's just, it's none of my business. And I'm sorry.'

He squints in the smoke, regarding her for a long moment, then he turns his attention back to the fire, to the deer, to packing the earth. 'Okay, Isa. Well. Thanks for that.'

'And I wanted to say . . . can't we just be friends?'

'Was I not being friendly?' he says. 'Yesterday?'

'No. It's not you. You were fine. It's me.'

'So maybe you need to have this conversation with yourself.'

'I've been having this conversation with myself for years.'

The deer is covered now. All the earth is over it. He sits back on his haunches. 'Okay, Isa,' he says, brushing the dirt from his hands and getting to his feet. 'Sure. We can be friends.'

'Please then – can we walk?'

'You want to walk with me?'

'Yes.'

'Where to?'

'Anywhere. Away from here. Away from the house.'

'You've got nothing on your feet,' he says.

She looks down, and her bare feet in the wet grass are surprising, pale, like the white bare roots of plants.

'Aren't you cold?'

She shrugs. 'Not really.'

'Do you want my jacket?'

'I'm fine.'

'Here,' he says, shrugging off his jacket and holding it towards her.

She takes it from him – his old Belstaff – wraps it around her. It's warm. It smells of him: of the animal that he is. His smell has not changed. 'I always liked this jacket,' she says.

He frowns a little, as though the comment were unseemly somehow, then turns and sets off, walking quickly, and she falls into step slightly behind him, following where he leads, where he presses the long dew-soaked grasses down with his boots. The morning is growing lighter, growing warmer, and the grasses are smoking in the early sun. Rabbits lope between tangled thickets of thorn.

After a while he stops, turns back to her. 'Are your feet alright?'

'I like it.'

'Your trousers are soaked.' He sounds cross.

'It's okay. Really. I'm warm now. Thanks.'

They walk on for quite a long time without speaking at all, and she thinks that she would like to carry on walking like this, just like this, walking without speaking, her bare feet on the damp earth, wrapped in his scent, heading to the river, to the wood.

'The water's low,' Jack says, when they reach the bridge. 'There's been hardly any rain for weeks.'

They stand quietly as the water passes them – dark green, silver-rippled. The treehouse is close – just over the bridge, and around the bend in the river. 'I forget,' she says. 'What the birds are like here.'

'Yeah,' he says.

'Why are you going, Jack?'

'Why? . . . Because it's time.'

She stares at his profile in the mist: the tiny pulse of a blue-green vein beneath his eye, the pale skin of his cheek, of his neck.

'Aren't you going to miss it?'

'Maybe. But I'm way overdue finding out.'

'It just feels like everything's changing.'

'Really? When was the last time you came down here, Isa?'

'I came to see Philip. Just before he died.'

'And before that?'

'I don't know. Last summer?'

She can hear her voice, this crust on top of her, saying stuff.

She would rather say nothing than this crust of speech that does not say what she wants at all.

'Yeah, well, things are going to seem like they're changing pretty fast if you only visit once a year. You know what it feels like to me? Like nothing ever really changes round here.'

'I'm sorry.'

'Don't be sorry,' he says. 'I'm just telling you how I feel.'

'I'm glad. I want to know how you feel.'

He frowns again. 'Are your kids not here yet then?'

'Not yet. They're arriving late morning.'

'With your husband?'

'Yes.'

'Well.' He looks at his watch. 'It's been nice to catch up. But I'd better get on.'

'Just. Not yet. Please, Jack. Listen to me. I have to say this. I have to say this to you. They will be here soon, and it will all begin again.'

'What? Who?'

'My family. And my life.'

He looks at her.

'I wanted to see you,' she says, 'so much. So many times.'

'So why didn't you?'

'You know why,' she says. 'Why do you think I stayed away? Why do you think I couldn't come down here? It wasn't safe.'

'Isa,' he says. 'Don't do this. You're only doing this because I'm going.'

'I just need to know.'

'What?'

'That you think of me too. That you think about us too. That you remember. What it was like.'

'I remember,' he says. 'I remember all of it. What was it like for you, Isa? I never asked you. You never told me. What was being with me like for you?'

'Like home,' she says. 'Like coming home.' The sun is starting to break the mist now, lighting the tops of the trees. Flaming gold on the new green. The sight of this green does something to her: a green fuse in it, lighting a green fire inside her. 'I want to come home,' she says. 'I want to come back home.'

He looks at her, as if trying to fathom her. 'Did you ever tell your husband?' he says. 'About us? That time? After my mum died?'

'No,' she says. 'Did you tell your wife?'

'It's not really an equivalent question.'

'Why not?'

'Because I'm no longer with my wife.'

'No, but you were then.'

'Fair enough.'

'So, did you?' she says. 'Tell her?'

'I didn't,' he says. 'No.'

'Why not?'

He reaches out then, cupping her chin. His thumb lightly grazes her cheek. She lifts her own palm and presses his hand onto her face. She can see the pulse in his neck, the pinkness at his throat, the raised skin.

'Isa,' he says, and his voice is low and grainy. 'You're married. You've got your kids. You've got your life.'

'It's my life that's killing me.' She presses harder, pushing his hand against her skin. 'I'm drowning, Jack. Please. I'm telling you. I can't breathe.'

'Then you need to do something about it, Isa. You do. Something that doesn't involve trying to make me stay here and wait for something that's never going to come.'

'What if I told you I would change it all?'

'You won't though, will you?' He takes his hand away, lets his arm drop by his side. Coldness rushes into the space between them.

She imagines some violence, imagines tearing into the vein at his throat, filling the cold space with warm blood, butting her head against him – anything, anything to bridge this gulf between them. She reaches out but he sidesteps, her nails grazing against the skin of his wrist as he moves away.

'I'm going, Isa. That's it. That's all there is to say. I have to go now. I have to find your sister. Frannie needs my help today. I'm sure she needs yours too.'

'Sure . . .' she says, and her bitterness rises like bile. 'Frannie needs our help,' she repeats dully. 'Have you never wondered how it is she manages the high-wire trick of holding the moral high ground while suiting only herself?'

'What do you mean?'

'She wasn't even going to invite you to the lunch. You know that? I had to persuade her you were worthy of a seat at the table.'

'Well, thanks.' His face is pale. 'That's really kind of you, Isa. Thank you for letting me know.' He shakes his head. 'Jesus,' he says. He is silent, then: 'You know what, Isa. Maybe today is not about you. Or me. Not about what you want or what you feel or what you think you might need. Maybe it's not even about Frannie. Maybe it's about your dad. Maybe today is about laying Philip to rest.'

'My father was a fucker.'

'You don't mean that.'

'Don't I? You know it's true. Don't you remember?'

'I remember, yes. But it's in the past, Isa. Now's the time to let it go. And if you can't let it go, get help. Just – get it together. Okay? Whatever you think this is. Whatever this was is over. Is in the past. It's done.'

Her teeth start to chatter.

'You look cold. You need to get back. You need to get into the house. Get warm.'

She shakes her head, hands in fists. 'You're a coward, Jack Kyd,' she says.

'Wow,' he says softly. '*I'm* the coward? Seriously?' He gives a small whistle. 'Seriously, Isabella Brooke?'

The sound of his boots, walking away. She looks down at her

feet on the earth. They no longer look like roots. They look shrunken, a dead person's feet. Or stranger – like the golem. Like she is the golem. With her white feet and her clumsiness, lurching around and longing for love.

Closed to her. Her childhood closed. The roads back to innocence shattered, and all of the bridges blown.

***

'Mum?' says Rowan, from the kitchen table.

'Mm?' says her mother, from over by the counter.

'What time is it?'

'It's . . . hang on . . .' Frannie checks her phone. 'It's almost eight o'clock.'

'Will Grandpa be out of the fridge yet? In the funeral home? Will they have put him in the coffin?'

'I suppose he'll have to be, soon,' says Frannie. 'They'll put him in the coffin and bring him to the house for ten. So perhaps . . . yes. Now, what would you like for breakfast, Ro? Toast?'

'How long was he left for before he went into the fridge?'

'We sat with him all night, in the library,' says Frannie, going over to the bread bin, 'before the funeral directors came. So about ten hours I think.'

'So he would have definitely gone into rigor mortis by then. Rigor mortis starts four hours after death.'

'Ah, well then, yes. Most likely. Listen, sweetheart, would you like Marmite on toast? Peanut butter? Jam? Peanut butter and jam?'

'Can I just show you this?' Rowan is adding to her chart. It's a big drawing – an illustrated timeline of decomposition. 'Do you think Rani and Seb know about decomposition?' she says.

'I shouldn't think so,' says Frannie, putting a slice of bread into the toaster. 'Not as much as you, anyway. Listen, I've got lots and lots to do but I'd really like you to eat some breakfast, so . . . what do you want on this toast, Ro?'

Just then her mum's phone buzzes and she snatches it up.

'Oh,' she says to the person on the other end. 'Oh fuck. Well, shall we substitute the mustard leaves then? There are plenty of those.'

Rowan selects a green felt-tip.

B

L

O

A

T, she writes, in capital letters. She starts to colour in the B in greeny-blue. Bloat is the second stage of death. If Grandpa Philip is out of the fridge already, then this will be beginning by now.

'Okay,' says Frannie, into her phone. 'Thanks, Wren. See you soon.' She looks at Rowan as though surprised she's still sitting there. 'Or an egg?' she says. 'Do you want an egg on toast? Poached?'

'Marmite,' says Rowan. 'On toast. And you said a word for the swear box. But can I just show you what I'm doing, Mum?'

'Hang on,' says Frannie, going over to the toaster, taking out the bread.

Just then Uncle Milo's friend Luca comes into the kitchen. He doesn't see Rowan, but he says good morning to her mum, and he goes to the counter. He has some green powder in a jar. 'Have you got any oat milk?' he says.

'I shouldn't think so,' says her mum.

'Any plant milk at all?'

'Unlikely,' her mother says, without looking at him. 'We drink raw cow's milk. Our tenants run a micro dairy.'

'Cow's milk?' says Luca. 'Seriously?'

'The calves stay with the mothers,' says Frannie. 'It's cruelty-free. And delicious. You should try it.'

Rowan starts to colour in the L.

'I'll just use water,' says Luca. 'It's fine.' He goes over to the tap where he shakes the green powder into a glass and swirls it round, then he brings it over to the table where Rowan is sitting. 'Oh,' he says. 'Hello. I didn't see you there. Who are you then?'

'Rowan,' says Rowan.

Luca pulls out a chair and sits at the table opposite her. 'What do they call you then? Rowan? Ro?'

'Ro,' says Rowan. 'Mostly.'

Her mum gives this strange click in the back of her throat. She puts the toast down in front of Rowan with a glass of juice, then she opens her computer and starts typing away, fast.

Rowan finishes the L and starts on the O. She chooses a mix of green and red for this and it turns a weird kind of orange which is actually quite good.

'Ro,' says her mum, looking up from her computer. 'Are you going to eat that toast?'

'Yes,' she says. 'I'm just finishing this.'

'What are you up to, Rowan?' says Luca.

'I'm making a decomposition timeline.'

'Wow. That sounds epic. Can I see?'

'I've just got to Bloat,' she says. 'That's the second stage. I did the first stage already.'

'What happens in Bloat?'

'Foam with blood leaks from the mouth and nose.'

'Blimey,' says Luca. 'That sounds serious.'

She can't tell if he's joking or not. She finishes the O and starts on the A. 'Then the body turns from green to red.'

'Then what happens?'

'The nails and the teeth fall out.'

He takes a sip of his green drink and grimaces.

'Then, about a month after that, the body turns to liquid.'

'Ouch.'

Her mum lifts her head from her computer again. 'Look, Rowan,' she says sharply, 'we are all busy here. We all have jobs to do today. Can you be helpful?'

Rowan feels hot then, can feel her cheeks burning and her

hands prickling. 'I'm not *not* being helpful,' she says. 'I'm just making my chart.'

Her mum's phone goes again. She snatches it up and walks over to the window and starts to talk about food while pacing up and down.

Rowan looks up and sees Luca is making a face. He rolls his eyes towards her mum, like *bo-ring*. And it is funny, but she doesn't know whether she should smile or laugh or cry.

'Right,' says her mum when she has finished the call, 'I have to go. Come on, Ro, let's go and find Aunty Isa. Or do you want to watch something? You could watch a film, if you like?'

'I can stay here,' says Rowan. 'And finish this.' She lifts her red pen.

'No,' says her mum.

'Why not?'

'Just. No. Let's go and find Isa.'

'I can hang with her,' says Luca.

'That won't be necessary, thanks. Rowan doesn't know you. So.'

Rowan looks up. There is something jumping and uncomfortable in the air between the grown-ups. It makes her feel strange.

Then she remembers the shells: the shell box. It was too late to go and fetch them in last night after supper. And as soon as she thinks of them, her fingers start twitching, wanting to feel their cool hard whiteness tumbling through her hands. To cool the heat inside her and inside the room. And she needs to check on them to make sure they are alright, to make sure no animal or creature came and scratched the box in the night. 'Okay,' she says, slowly, putting the cap back on her felt-tip. 'I'll go and find Aunty Isa.'

'Thanks, Ro.' Her mum looks relieved. She comes over and puts her hand on the back of her head. 'Good girl. I'll see you back here in a little while, okay? I won't be long.'

Rowan makes her way out through the kitchen door and cuts around the side of the house.

Good girl. Is she a good girl?

She's not sure she's such a good girl. She has lots and lots of thoughts that aren't good. Every day. All the time. She just lied to her mother, for instance. She has no intention of seeing Aunty Isa at all. Would her mother think she was good if she told her she had taken the shell box? And that right now it might be getting damp and spoiled from the morning dew?

When she reaches the tree she climbs inside, finds the box and checks it all over. It looks fine, nothing has happened to it in the night. She drags the box out into the morning sun where she opens it and plunges her hands greedily into the clacketing mass of shells. She lifts a palmful, lets them sieve back through her fingers. She does it again and again and when her fingers have had their fill of the feeling, she sits with her back against the trunk and takes out just one of the shells and examines it in her palm. One side is rounded, and the other is more flat. The flatter side has an opening that looks like teeth.

Footsteps interrupt her, light and fast – someone coming up the hill towards her. It's too late to hide the shells properly again, so Rowan puts the shell back in the box, hurriedly closes it, and slides it behind her, between her bottom and the trunk of the tree.

'Hello,' says Rowan, to the person, who is standing above her now, blocking out the sun.

'Oh!' says the person. 'Hi. Sorry. I didn't see you there.'

There are drips coming off the person's skin and her clothes are sort of stuck to her body. The person has very short hair. So short it's almost not there at all.

'I'm Clara,' says the person.

'I'm Rowan,' says Rowan.

'Frannie's daughter?'

'Yes.'

'Nice to meet you, Rowan.'

'You too.'

There is water dripping off her shorts and running top. Small drops of water stand out on her skin, and she is shivering a bit so the drops are shivering too.

'Are you the one who came from America?'

'Yep.'

'Who's not Grandpa's daughter cos you're black?'

'Yeah,' the woman laughs. 'That's me.'

Rowan squints. 'You're not really black though.'

'No?'

'You're much more brown than black.'

'Yeah. Well, I guess I am. My mum was white. Or pink. Or peach or – whatever.'

Water is plopping onto the ground. Clara's trainers look soaked.

'You're really wet,' says Rowan.

'Yeah,' says Clara, shivering a bit more. 'I went for a run and then I went for a swim, but I didn't have a costume, or a towel.'

'I've got a blanket,' says Rowan. 'In my den. You can borrow it if you like.'

'Sure,' says Clara. 'Thanks. That would be great.'

Rowan goes inside the tree and takes out her old blanket. 'It's a bit mucky,' she says, 'but it's nice and warm.' She shakes it out and most of the twigs come off, and Clara doesn't seem to mind, because she wraps herself in it quite tightly.

'Thanks, Rowan,' she says. 'That's really kind. I was getting kind of cold there.'

'You're welcome,' she says.

'Hey – can I sit down with you?'

'Sure.'

'So . . . what are you up to?' Clara says, when she has sat facing Rowan, a little way away.

Rowan shrugs. 'Everyone's busy, so I came out here to play.'

'It's a good spot,' says Clara. 'Is the tree hollow?'

'Yes.'

'Nice. I bet it's a great place to hide.'

'It is.' Rowan squints at her in the sunlight; the light and the water drops are making it look like there are glinting jewels in Clara's hair. 'Can I touch your head?'

'Um . . . sure,' says Clara. 'I guess.'

Rowan reaches up and pats Clara's scalp. 'It's nice,' she says. 'It feels like wool. When wool goes bobbly on a jumper.'

'Thanks, I think. I mean – have you even met a black person before?'

Rowan considers. 'There was one last summer who came to help with the soil assessment. He was from Sussex University. He was called Frank. He was really nice.'

'The soil assessment? That sounds serious.'

'It is. Everything depends on the soil. All of life. There are hundreds of millions of life forms in a teacup of soil.'

'Wow. That's a lot of life. So . . . any black people here other than Frank? Are there none in your school?'

'There's one girl, in year five.'

'Any working on the estate?'

'No. I don't think so.'

'Jesus,' says Clara.

'I get twenty pence for a Jesus from my mum.'

'Twenty pence for a Jesus?'

'In the swear box.'

'Ah.'

'I get a pound for a fuck word. Fifty p for a shit. Once Mum said four fucks in a row, so I got four pounds.'

'Jesus,' Clara says, laughing. 'What happened then?'

'One of the ponies died, giving birth. We found her on the way to school. The foal was dead too. It was stuck half out of her.'

'Oh. Wow. Okay. Not so funny then. I'm sorry.'

Rowan shrugs. 'That's another twenty pence, by the way. Two Jesuses is forty p.'

Clara laughs. 'You drive a hard bargain. Well, I guess I'll have to give you what I owe you later. You might have to help me though, I'm not sure I've got the hang of the money around here.'

'How come?'

'I've never been to England before.'

'So why did you come?'

'Oh, because I wanted to say goodbye to your grandpa. And because I'm really interested in English history.'

'Me too.'

'Yeah? That's cool. Is that why you're playing with that box?'

Rowan can feel herself grow hot. 'What box?'

'The one behind your back.'

Rowan looks back up at Clara's face.

'I saw it when you went into the tree,' she says. 'It looks beautiful. Can I see? I won't tell a soul. I promise.'

'Alright,' says Rowan, and she shuffles the box out into the sunshine between them.

Clara pulls the box over towards her. 'Wow,' she says, 'it's heavy.'

'I carried it all on my own,' says Rowan proudly.

Rowan watches as Clara traces the picture of the ship with her fingertip, but when she reaches the word *Albion* in its tiny writing she stops.

'That's Albion,' says Rowan. 'The name of the project.'

Clara looks up and it's like the weather inside her has changed. 'Is this box why your mother gave it that name then?'

'It was Grandpa Philip,' says Rowan, because she knows this story – she has heard her mother tell it many times. 'They didn't know what name to give the project, and he was sitting at the desk, and he saw the box and said it to Mum, and she thought it was perfect.'

'And why do you think your mum thought it was a perfect name?'

'Because . . .' Rowan has heard her mum say this too, she used to speak about it with Grandpa, they both loved to talk about it. 'Albion is England in the past. England with all the old creatures, the pine martens and the water voles and the beavers, and people were kind to each other in Albion and there were giants. And it's in the past but it could be the future too. And it's not true either, but it could be if you believe enough and work hard enough to make it better, to make the world better and England better again.'

Clara is listening very hard. Even after Rowan has finished speaking, she is still silent, and serious-looking, as though she is listening to the silence, or still trying to understand. And Rowan wonders if she hasn't explained it properly – it seems very important to explain it properly. 'It's like a story,' says Rowan. 'A good story about England. Not a bad one. Lots of people tell bad stories about England. And this one could be true if we work hard enough and believe enough.'

Then, because Clara has still not replied, she says, 'Does that make sense?' Which is something her mum says to her sometimes.

'Yes,' says Clara. 'It does. Thanks for sharing that with me.'

But it's like Clara is saying one thing and thinking another – like the thinking part of her is not really here anymore. It's like when grown-ups bring out their phones and disappear, even though they're still sitting right in front of you.

Then Clara seems to come back into herself again. 'Can I open it?' she says.

'If you like.'

Clara opens it, and for a long time she says nothing, she just sits there staring down at the mass of white shells. 'They're cowries,' says Rowan. 'Money cowries.'

Clara looks back up. 'How'd you know that, Rowan?'

'Grandpa Philip told me. He liked to put his hands inside the box sometimes . . . You can try it if you like,' she says. 'It feels nice.'

Clara looks unsure.

'It's alright,' says Rowan, encouragingly. 'That's why I brought them out here. Because it feels so nice to touch them.'

Slowly, slowly, Clara puts her hand inside the shells.

'See?' says Rowan. 'Each one was a creature's home. An animal lived inside the shell.'

But Clara's face looks sort of grey and strange, and Rowan is filled then with the feeling that something is wrong, and she is part of the thing that is wrong but because she doesn't know what it is then she doesn't know how to fix it or make it better. Clara looks up again. 'And do you know why they were called money cowries?'

Rowan shakes her head.

Clara stares at her for a long moment and it's like there's something in the air between them, like it felt last summer in the orchard, just before the bees began to swarm.

'Ro! Rowan!' Frannie is calling from the house. 'Your cousins are here! Ro-Ro. Where are you?'

'I have to go,' says Rowan, standing up, brushing herself down, grateful to be able to move away.

Clara's hands are still in the shells.

'Can I take the box back?' says Rowan.

'Maybe you can lend it to me for a bit?'

'I don't think I should . . .'

'Ro! Where are you?'

'I'll put it back for you,' says Clara. 'Where'd it come from?'

'The library. On the desk. Beside the globe.'

Clara nods. 'I'll put it back, later today. I promise.'

And because her mum is calling, and because she really wants to get away, Rowan says okay, and then she turns, and she runs back towards the house.

❧

Ned's fingers flicker through his vinyl and selects an album.

It can only be Floyd.

This day of all days. He slides the record from the sleeve, places it onto the deck, hovers the needle, lets it fall – the last track on side one. The warm crackle fills the wood, followed by that soaring female vocal.

'The Great Gig in the Sky'.

He cranks it up, way up.

He goes over to the water butt, splashes water on his chest, his face, and soaps his armpits. Dries off. Checks himself in the mirror.

The mirror is small, and he can only see part of himself at a time. Nonetheless, he doesn't mind what he sees. As he shaves, he tries to quell the feeling rising inside him. It's a wrong sort of day, he knows, for hope to rise in a man, but he can't help it: the way she was with him, down here, yesterday. He hasn't been able to get it from his mind. What she said about the dress; that she has kept it, that she has it still.

He is old, he knows, but like an old tree, he can still put out his leaves, however gnarled the trunk or shrunken the canopy – still the leaves come every spring, still they say, there is hope, there is life, there is more to come yet.

He pulls on his shirt, and it feels crisp, good against his skin. The shirt is a belter, one of those treasures you find every so often, hidden in the rails at the Salvation Army in Tunbridge Wells, made for him: beautiful heavy cotton, with a thin blue stripe in it.

Just then there is a movement at the edge of the glade. He turns and sees Jack standing on the other side of the fire.

Jack is dressed and ready, wearing what looks to be a very expensive blue suit.

'That's a very nice whistle,' says Ned.

'Is it too much? They sent me a bit of cash. A sweetener. I thought . . . why not.'

'Nah. You look great, lad. You look fucking great.'

'You too,' says Jack.

'Got time for a spliff?' says Ned.

'Always.'

'Go and put the other side of the record on then and sit down. You want a shot of something? There's some hawthorn vodka on the side there. Bring it over.'

Ned makes his way over to a chair by the fire, gathers the necessaries from the tray on the table, while Jack goes to turn over the record, then carries over the vodka, two glasses. Pours the yellow-orange liquid out. 'What are we drinking to?' says Jack, as they touch glasses.

'Philip,' says Ned. 'The old bastard.' They raise their glasses, throw back their shots. 'I first met him at a Floyd gig. The UFO. Did I ever tell you?'

'You did, Ned. Plenty of times.'

'I was doing the door. I remember arguing with him. He was sure he should be getting in for free . . . said he was mates with the band . . .'

'And you told him he could fuck off back to Chelsea.'

'That's it. That's exactly what I told him.' Ned chuckles. 'I've run out of stories, you see. I'm just recycling now.'

'You've been recycling for thirty years.'

'Alright lad, just because you're leaving doesn't mean you can be rude. Come on, pour us another of those.' Jack obliges, takes his glass over to a nearby stump, sits down.

Ned takes Jack in, in that new suit. The light in the glade that's pouring down on him. 'You're a great-looking lad, Jack. Did anyone ever tell you that?'

'Maybe,' Jack says. 'Once or twice.'

Ned smiles. 'You really going then?'

'Yeah.'

'Tomorrow, is it?'

Jack nods. 'Flight's in the afternoon.'

Ned twists, licks the papers, lights the spliff. Takes a couple of meditative drags. 'Where do you fly to?'

'Inverness. Then drive. I've got a car waiting. They've got a Landy for me.'

Ned nods. 'You going to be okay up there?'

'Yeah. Why?'

'It's a long way from anything that looks like home.'

'That's the point.'

'Is it?'

'Yeah,' says Jack. 'It is.'

Ned takes another drag. 'You won't be lonely?'

'Don't suppose so, no.'

'What about your kids?'

'They're okay. They can come and see me.'

'It's a long way.'

'So's Devon. Didn't stop Charlie taking them there.'

'True enough.'

The sun strikes the ground.

'What about her?' Ned says softly.

'Who?'

'You know who.'

Jack shrugs.

'You seen her then? Since she's been back?'

'Yeah. Couple of times.'

'She doing okay?'

'Hard to tell . . .'

'Her husband here?'

'He will be by now.'

'And her kids?'

'I expect so.'

'Be careful with yourself, lad.'

'I'm always careful with myself, Ned.'

Something about Jack. About this lad in this suit, this afternoon, twists his heart. 'You deserve happiness, lad,' he says.

'What's that?'

'I said you deserve to be happy.'

'Do I?'

'You do. Come on. Come and get this: this is happiness encased in a few Rizla papers over here . . .'

Jack crosses to where Ned sits and takes the spliff. 'Doesn't everyone?' he says, walking back to his chair.

'What?'

'Deserve to be happy.'

'I don't know the answer to that . . .'

Ned takes it all in: this sweet green light. The woodsmoke curling gently. And he knows he is about to say it; say the thing he has never said. Never out loud. Never to another human being, never given voice to this truth, carved within himself, like water slowly dripping over rock, carving out a cavern in his heart. 'You're like me, lad,' he says.

'What's that?'

'Hopelessly in love with a Brooke girl,' says Ned. And when he has said it, he can feel his body fizzing like a teenager's. His heart banging away like he's just sprinted four hundred yards. All these new leaves on him, opening in the spring sun. He watches his words take space in the air, watches Jack absorb them.

'They're not girls, Ned,' says Jack. 'And I'm not in love with anyone.'

'If you say so.'

'I do . . . What about you, anyway? If you're so in love yourself? What are you going to do about it?'

'I don't know. There's a time for telling secrets. Maybe the time for that is gone. Maybe the time for that was fifty years ago. Maybe I missed it.'

'Well. That's cheerful.'

'Wasn't meant to be cheerful. Here. Pass that back.'

'Did you hear about Clara?' says Jack, bringing the spliff back over to Ned. 'The one who is over from the States, who was supposed to be Philip's kid?'

'What about her?'

'She's not his. She's black. And her mother was white so . . . not Philip's.'

Ned chuckles. 'Well, that's a turn-up for the books . . . Why's she here then?'

'That I can't answer.'

'Grace will be pleased,' says Ned softly.

Jack grows quiet, then: 'Maybe you're a coward, Ned.'

'Maybe you're a little shit.'

'Maybe,' says Jack.

'Anyway, I've got my plans,' says Ned. 'Time for higher ground.'

'I know what you're up to up there,' says Jack. 'Don't think I haven't seen. Frannie knows. They all know . . . you need to open your eyes, Ned.'

'And what's that supposed to mean?'

Jack shakes his head.

'Go on, lad. If you've got something else to say – say it.'

'There's some financial fuck-up. Frannie needs money, and she's doing some sort of deal with Milo and Luca for this wood.'

'Luca?'

'Yeah.'

'In this wood?'

'Yeah.'

'What sort of a deal? For what? To do what?'

'To build a clinic. A retreat centre. For psilocybin therapy.'

Ned laughs. 'That so?'

'They want to give rich fuckers the whole experience. I've seen the plans. Milo left them on Frannie's desk. They've even nicked your designs for the treehouses for the Teddy Bears' Picnic. But they want to charge people a fortune to come and stay in them. Fifteen grand for a weekend. That level of bullshit. Messed-up rich fuckwits.'

'And how did she seem, when she said it? Frannie?'

'She wasn't too happy. But she seemed to think there was no

other way. Otherwise, she would have to sell the cottage, and she couldn't do that to Grace.'

'And Grace? Does she know about it?'

'I don't think so, no. I think they're trying to protect her.' His face creases into a frown. 'When it happened with my dad, when Frannie booted him out of the cottage, I sort of understood, you know? He'd handed in his resignation, and the cottage came with the job, so he had to give it up. But this . . . this just feels . . . wrong.'

Ned smokes. He lets the news find its place, the weight of it settle in the pit of him. Everything has its own gravity. Its own logic. Everything its own time.

They smoke the spliff to the end. The sun on their heads. No rush. Never any rush. When the spliff is well and truly finished Ned pushes the roach into the ashtray, lifts his stick and gets to his feet. Jack goes over to the record player and takes the needle off the vinyl.

'Come on then,' he says, as Jack comes back across the glade towards him. 'Let's bury the old fucker.'

The two men leave the glade and walk out into the sun.

Isa stands in front of a mirror. She turns one way, then the other, while her husband watches her from the edge of the bed.

The dress is a new one. She saw it in a shop window on the walk home from work. A deep v-neck. An open diamond at the back.

It was way more than she's ever spent on a dress.

'Not too much?' she asks Hari.

'In what way?'

'I don't know. Trying too hard?'

'What are the others wearing?'

'I have no idea. No mourning clothes, that's all Frannie said.'

'I mean. You look . . . sensational,' says her husband.

'Can you zip me up?'

Hari gets to his feet and comes to stand behind her. A moment of pause, and then he gently pushes himself against her. 'How long has it been?' he says, into her neck.

She moves away. His hands release their hold.

How long has it been? Ten months? A year?

'Are you ready?' she says.

'Almost. I just need to put on a tie.'

She goes over to the window, looks out. The smoke has long gone. The deer will be almost cooked, surely, by now? She is itching for a cigarette. Has she ever smoked in front of her husband? Not since she was a student. She turns back. Hari is knotting his tie at his chin. 'Why are you wearing a tie?' she says, irritated.

'Because it's a funeral.'

'Yeah, but it's Philip's funeral. I never saw him wear a tie in his life.'

'It's respect.'

'He wouldn't have appreciated it.'

'Oh. Right.' Her husband looks stung. 'Okay.'

'I mean. You know what he was like.' She presses down her dress with her hands. She puts her hand to her wedding ring, twists it. 'Just – do what you want, but . . . don't bother on his account – okay?'

'Okay.' Hari shrugs. He reaches up, pulls the knot free. Pulls the tie away from his collar.

She stands there, drumming her fingers against the chest of drawers, watching as he rolls the tie slowly, carefully into a round, and stows it back inside his case. He is so careful, her husband – so kind. So good.

She wants to scream. She could actually scream. Right here. Right now.

'Is everything okay?' he says.

'In what way?'

'You've been super edgy since we got here.'

'It's my father's funeral,' she says.

He looks at her. A question in him. Then, 'Okay,' he says, letting it go.

'Ready then?' she says, lifting her shawl from the end of the bed.

⟡

'Do you know what autolysis means?' says Rowan to Seb.

Seb shakes his head slowly.

'It means self-digestion. Your body *eats itself*. Cells begin eating themselves from the inside out.'

'Wow,' says Seb.

'Then it's rigor mortis. Then it's bloat. That's when all the gases build up and up and the body can double in size and organs turn to liquid and you can explode.'

'Ugh,' says Rani, from where she lies on the bed. 'Stop. I feel sick.'

'Do you want me to stop?' says Rowan, quietly, to Seb.

'No,' he says. 'Will he be bloating,' he whispers, 'in the coffin? Will he be massive by now?'

'Not yet,' says Rowan. ''Cos he's just come out of the fridge. But it'll start to happen not long after he goes into the ground. His hole is only four feet deep.'

'Why?'

'Because it's a green burial. He should be closer to the surface so he can decompose more quickly.'

'Urgh,' says Rani. She puts her hands over her ears.

'. . . there's more oxygen at four feet deep. More bacteria, more carrion beetles –'

'Stop it,' says Rani. 'I mean it, Rowan.'

'The first parts to turn to liquid are the organs. The eyes first. Then the brain and the stomach and the liver. Bloody foam will come out of his nose. It'll happen faster cos it's going into summertime.'

'Urgh,' says Rani again.

'It's just death,' says Rowan.

She hadn't meant to say it like that, like death is the most normal thing ever. Like it's almost boring, it's so easy to understand, but now she has said it she likes the way it feels. *It's just death,*' she says again, turning to Rani. 'What? Are you scared?'

Rani scrunches up her nose. 'I'm not *scared*,' she says. 'But I don't really want to think about death.'

'Are *you* scared?' says Rowan to Seb.

Seb shakes his head.

'I'm going,' says Rani. 'I need to warm up.'

Rowan watches as Rani unwinds her legs from the bed.

'Thanks, Rowan,' she says, as she goes past. 'Now all I'll be thinking about while I'm singing for Grandpa is bloody foam and insects.'

She slams the door, and after a minute they can hear her in the next room, doing her singing exercises.

Seb rolls his eyes. 'Go on,' he says, his eyes wide, 'what happens next?'

In her room down the corridor, Clara is standing before the table, the box in front of her, open on the mass of white cowries. She has been trying to work out their weight. She figures there are about two kilos of cowries here, give or take. So perhaps two and a half thousand shells.

Standing here, facing them, they evoke a sort of nausea, a seasickness. It is like looking at a crime scene: this box, with its ship and its name – *Albion* – so daintily and so carefully painted on the wood.

She reaches forward, selects a shell from the pile, holds it in her palm, touches first the round smoothness of one side, then the toothed edge of the other. She thinks of its first, creaturely life, in warm, translucent South Indian water, its harvest, being lifted from the element that birthed it, that held it, the creature that it was dying, leaving only this white shell behind.

What hands did it touch as it made its way from those translucent seas to Oliver Brooke's London offices, to his Sussex desk? What transactions did it partake in, what deals? What further voyages, what hands upon hands upon hands, before it ended being sieved through the fingers of a young girl, seven generations later, playing in the Sussex sun, by an ancient oak, in the centre of a thousand acres of her family's land? If the shell could speak, through these parted, serrated lips, what stories could it tell of what it has seen? Of how it is woven with the story of this house, this family, with Clara herself – and with this beautiful view that lies beyond her window now?

She looks up and out at the green upon green, at the vista, created two hundred and forty years before, when this land was bought, when this estate was emparked. *To empark*: an ancient verb – but one that was common in the eighteenth century. This vista in itself could be the grounds of a PhD: so seemingly benign, so neutral, and yet so loaded, so layered with meaning; meaning, it seems, which has entirely escaped the inhabitants of the house.

They are not bad people – far from it, Frannie is quite clearly, by one set of metrics, very good: frank and bold and moral, a woman who has pledged her life to change. One whose gaze is set to the long future. But all that rhetoric about living *beyond politics*? As though one can look only to the future, free from the claims of the past. About one child in a thousand acres, growing up to *shelter in the shade of the oaks I planted. And her children and her children's children.* As though the natural world can exist in a category free from the messy realm of the human.

What Frannie does not seem to understand is that she is an actor, walking about on a stage set, playing her part. What makes her scary is that she has come to internalize the stage as real – as the grounds of her being, as the place from which her politics and world view, her very soul, are informed. Frannie, thinks Clara, is a woman who cannot see that her politics or lack thereof are a direct extrapolation from gazing every day at this view.

And where does that leave her, Clara? How to reckon with her own enmeshment in this deep dream of green?

She puts the shell gently back, where it nestles into place amongst its companions – in this box that has presumably been their home for the last two hundred and forty years. She hesitates, then lifts the single shell away again and stows it in her pocket, before she closes the lid. She feels a great urge to liberate the others from the box. To take them to those high white cliffs she saw from the plane and toss them over, handful after handful, back into the sea.

❧

The family walk out of the house, down the steps, making their way towards where Ned stands, the coffin beside him on a wooden bier.

There has been a sharp shower, and although the sky is clearing now and warmth is returning, the air is clean-feeling, cooler than it has been.

He watches as they move towards him: none are dressed in black, no mourning clothes, Frannie in orange and Rowan in red, hand in hand, the colours of their clothes stronger for the recent rain. Isabella and her family close behind. Then Milo and Luca. Walking with Milo the young woman who has caused such consternation. So this is Clara then: slim, relatively slight, her hair cropped close to her head, a poised, serious air. He is impatient though, looking beyond Clara to the house until he sees her.

Grace stands at the top of the steps, her arms full of flowers. She is wearing a long navy dress. Heavy linen. Not his dress, not his yellow dress with the mirrors and the bell-like sleeves. Not the dress she wore fifty years ago. Foolish, foolish man. Did he imagine she might? Still, the sight of her like this, coming down these steps with her arms full of flowers, twists in him. He rests on the rough wooden handle of the bier, steadying himself, as she moves through the knot of her family towards where he

235

stands. When she reaches him, she bends and places the flowers on the lid of the coffin: a willow band threaded with wild grasses, with cuckoo flower and bluebell and cow parsley, with ox-eye daisy and celandine. She kneels and ties them while the family stand, watching, her thin fingers threading wire through the willow he wove; the warp and the weft of it all that lies between her and the dead body of her husband, whom she will touch no more.

When the flowers are secure, she stands, comes to join him where he waits.

'Ned,' she says. Just one syllable. Just his name.

He sees where she grazed her face yesterday, her lower lip slightly swollen.

He nods to her. 'Grace,' he says.

Remember, he says, with his eyes, *I will hold you up.*

The family follow the coffin cart in silent procession, two abreast, down the hill. Only the slow creak of the wheels of the cart on the track. Only the sounds of the birds, filling the air around them, their steps measured, keeping time. No one is rushing – not even the children. No one is unsure. It seems to Ned that they follow an ancient rhythm, a dance to which everyone suddenly knows the metre, the measure, the rhyme; they know the steps even if they have never been taught them – even if they have never had a father die before, they know what to do. They walk beside the river, take the old grassy track slightly uphill to the ancient church, and arrive at the wooden lychgate where the vicar stands, waiting to receive them. Ned halts. 'You go ahead now, Gracey,' he says to her. 'You lead them all inside.'

For a moment, Grace looks bewildered, then Frannie comes forward to take her arm. 'Come, Mum, we go inside the church now, the men will carry the coffin in when we are all in place.'

At the church door Grace pauses, looking up at the carved angel above the porch.

She remembers staring at this angel on her wedding day, as she waited to enter. Her father stiff beside her in his finest suit: this porch the Rubicon, the point of no return. She remembers the excitement, the sense of a life bifurcating – another Grace sheering off into mediocrity, into golf club dinners and stuffy rooms, while this Grace, chosen on a morning of mist and birdsong, stood waiting here, ready to cross into the cool ancient church, ready to be married with her destiny.

She remembers her father's arm, tense in hers, the way she could hardly see through the lace of her veil; the only things she could see clearly were the tiles on the ground, and the edge of her dress, which she had taken in and hemmed herself.

Something old.

Something new.

Something borrowed.

Something blue.

'Alright, Mum? Ready?'

'Yes.'

She and her daughter cross the porch, just as she and her father crossed it almost fifty years before. Everything felt hallowed to her that morning. Everything drenched with meaning. What must they have thought? Her parents? Were they cowed, awed, afraid?

She herself remembers only excitement, only hope, Philip a tall dark shape waiting beyond the scratchy lace of her veil, as her father, her mild father, led her down the aisle towards the man who would be her husband.

But this morning there is no husband waiting – he is outside in his coffin, and Frannie is here by her side, and her young granddaughter is singing – so beautifully – the song Philip requested, the John Dowland song. Her voice so clear, so pure.

Grace takes her place in the first of the pews, closest to the aisle.

★

In the pew across the aisle, Clara slides into her seat.

She steals a look at Grace – her elegance, her straight back, the hair which hangs to her shoulders, cut straight. No make-up. A simple navy dress. So, this was the woman that Philip left for her mother. Such different women: Natasha crackled with life – to be near her was often like being close to a fire that was in danger of raging out of control, whereas Grace is like a cool still pool.

It is cool here in the church too, in this thick-walled, white-washed interior, which smells of time and wood and lack of use. How long has it stood for, this lonely, lovely church with its village all gone?

The last time she sat in a church it was a morning in the Caribbean, ten years ago. Christmas in St Kitts, in the village her father had been born in; she was staying in the house of her uncle and aunt. On Christmas morning they went to the tiny local church for the service, which was held at five a.m. She sat on a bench in the earth-floored church, with its roof of corrugated iron, as people gathered for worship in the darkness. She remembers the chill of the early hour, the sense of quiet reverence around her, the soft sounds of the feet of the congregation against the sandy ground. When she asked her aunt why the service was held so early, she told her:

When our people worked the plantations, we would worship early on Christmas Day, so we could get back, prepare the house and the food for the family.

We remember like this.

Like this, we give thanks for our freedom.

It was Carnival time, and in the bright light of day the colour and the noise spilled out everywhere, but later that Christmas Day, when she sat on the heat of the beach, the palm forest behind her, part of her was still in the chill of that early-morning church.

Outside in the churchyard, Jack hangs back. It is not yet time to lift the coffin, and he does not wish to stand too close to Isa and her family. There she is, with her back to him, standing with Hari and her son. That dress she is wearing, her skin framed within the diamond, is not something he can look at with any sort of ease. The dress is like a question to which he knows the answer, but the answer disturbs him, profoundly. Is this it? Is this the sad fact of it all? Was Ned right? Is he hopelessly in love with this woman? He cannot gauge it, has no metrics to understand his feelings, which are unloosed, untethered. It disturbs him to see her with her husband and her children. Hari, this tidy, elegant man. Does he have any idea what his wife said to him this morning? Does she herself have any idea of what she said? Or does she just say things? Is he just her plaything, to take out when she is here in the park, in the wood? He thought he knew what he wanted, where he was going – and she has come and shaken him, and he cannot find the ground beneath him, cannot see the path ahead. Just then, as though she has heard his thoughts, Isa lifts her head and turns to him. Catches his gaze, returns it. Then her husband steps in, says something in her ear, puts his hand on her back, steers her away, guides them into the church.

Jack turns and takes a few steps in the opposite direction, kneels to his own mother's grave. Jeannie Kyd. The flowers he brought last week are wilted now. He takes them from the block of foam. And as he stands there, helpless somehow – these wilted flowers in his hands – there is a call from the church. It is Ned, telling him it is time. He turns and places the flowers in the crook of the trunk of the yew and comes to join the other men.

'Can we just have a moment here,' says Milo. 'Bring it in, brothers. Please.'

They come together, Jack, Hari, Ned, and he puts his arms around them all. 'Legends,' he says. 'Thank you. Thank you all for this.'

'You okay, Milo?' says Hari.

'I'm good,' he says. 'Yeah. I'm actually really fucking good.'

Hari puts a hand on his back. 'Alright. Well. We're here for you, man.'

'Thank you.'

'And for Philip.'

Their steadiness, their strength: they are all good men.

'I'll go at the front with Hari,' says Ned. 'You and Jack at the back.'

'Are you going to be okay?' says Hari to Ned. 'Without a stick?'

'I'll be fine – we just need to keep steady. The coffin itself is light, and Philip doesn't weigh so much, but balance is the key. Just make sure not to go too high at the back. And don't go too fast. I'll set the pace.'

They move to either side of the bier, take the woven wicker handles.

'On my three,' says Ned. 'One . . . two . . . three.'

The men jostle to get the coffin onto their shoulders.

For Milo, beside Jack, it feels – what? Surprisingly possible – not easy, exactly, but possible, this carrying of his father into the church – and just as his father feels surprisingly light, as though what was dense in him has been lifted, has been given to the air, so he himself feels light too: this morning he went into the kitchen, and he opened one of the bottles of the ten per cent wine. The natural stuff. The glou-glou. Luca was right, it was Ribena, hardly alcoholic at all.

So, he took the bottle up to his room and had a couple of gentle glasses while getting dressed, and now, he finds, he has exactly the right amount of alcohol in his blood for the task at hand.

This, he thinks, as he enters the church, was always it; this was what he struggled with – just reaching the right level, so the sharp edges of the world are gentled, without tipping over into drunkenness. All he needed was better, more natural booze. It all, always, has only ever been a question of degree.

The woven wicker presses into his cheek. A smell, slightly earthy: the willow, the calico of the coffin, the scent of the wildflowers resting on its lid. And behind it, perhaps only imagined, the corporeal tang of his father. His father's great leonine head. Close to his.

· There will be no more roaring from him now.

And they are inside the church and there is music – his niece is singing – dear God! What a voice! His – what? – twelve-year-old niece, filling this ancient church with this ancient song. His heart. His skin all gooseflesh now and tears already studding his eyes. And these men who are beside him, ahead of him, he is filled with such gratitude for them, for Ned and Jack and Hari as they walk the aisle, as their feet sound on the tiles. They reach the front, and they lower the coffin into position, and then he turns to find his place between his sisters on the first pew.

Rani stops singing and there is silence, and in the silence Milo speaks.

'Wow,' he says. 'Fucking hell, Isa. You never told me she could sing like that.'

Isa colours. 'Shh,' she says, as Rani comes to take her seat beside her.

And now the vicar is there (the vicar from the church up in the village at the top of the hill, Milo remembers him from childhood, though the man was younger then, and now he is old), standing at the lectern, saying a few words, something about John Dowland, something about that being one of Philip's favourite songs, but Milo doesn't really hear him, because he knows he is up next, and his pulse is racing. And when was the last time he drank water, actually? He should have brought a bottle. He is sweating from the exertion of carrying his father into the church, and he looks up and down the pew, but no one seems to be carrying water, and there is none up there by the lectern, and now the vicar is beckoning him to stand, to come and stand by the coffin and speak, saying Milo will read from one of Philip's favourite writers.

And so Milo, feeling woozy now, rises and walks the several paces across the floor. The sweat pricking on his back, at his temples, at his hairline. He holds on to the heavy wooden lectern and gathers his breath. He looks out at the crowd before him, searching their faces, filled with the sudden jolting sense that someone is missing. That they should not start – not yet, because someone important is not here. And he feels a hot red panic begin to engulf him – until he understands it is his father. His father who is absent. And his throat constricts as he grips the sides of the lectern and forces himself to breathe. 'Sorry,' he says. 'I just – sorry . . . one moment please.'

He looks over to the coffin – takes it in. Understands his father is here after all.

'Philip Ignatius Brooke,' he says. 'Pa. You know, until yesterday, I never knew what the Ignatius meant. So I googled it. And guess what, it means fiery. Fiery one.

'Never was a name more aptly given. You burned, Pa. You burned.

'And I know you wanted your pyre to go out on; I know you wanted to burn right up to the end. But here we are, to honour you nonetheless.

'I have a reading here,' he says, 'from Richard Jefferies, the Victorian naturalist, one of Pa's favourite writers.' He takes the book from his jacket pocket, opens the pages before him. The text is swimming before his eyes. He squints, and the letters resolve themselves into sense. Is he crying? He can no longer quite tell.

'The meadow is bare,' he begins, 'but in a little while the heart-shaped celandine leaves will come in their accustomed place. On the pollard willows the long wands are yellow-ruddy in the passing gleam of sunshine, the first colour of spring appears in their bark. The delicious wind rushes among them and they bow and rise . . . it lifts and swings the arching trail of bramble . . .

'I wonder to myself how they can all get on without me – how they manage, bird and flower, without me to keep the calendar for them. For I noted it so carefully and lovingly, day by day, the seed-leaves on the mounds in the sheltered places that come so early, the pushing up of the young grass, the succulent dandelion . . . Day by day a change; always a note to make. The moss drying on the tree trunks, dog's-mercury stirring under the ash-poles, bird's-claw buds of beech lengthening – books upon books to be filled with these things. I cannot think how they manage without me . . .'

In her place on the pew Frannie shifts in her seat. Milo is doing better now, she thinks, after a shaky start.

She was awake in the library until the dawn, trying to find the right words, and exhaustion and adrenaline are competing within her now, as Milo's reading draws to a close, as her brother climbs down from the lectern, as the vicar says something about her, about Frannie, the first female of her line to inherit, and it is her turn now, and so she rises, makes her way to the lectern, opens her notes. She lifts her head, reminds herself to breathe.

'Anyone who has spent any time near me in the last week,' she says, 'will know that I've been struggling with this. There were so many ways to begin. So many paths by which one might approach our father.

'Should I talk about the height of him? The way he stood, like an immutable fact of nature. So huge you could not get past him?

'I think of those glades we made, he and I – ten years ago, when we felled trees – trees that should never have been planted, forty-year-old conifers. I think of the moment when we opened the ground to the sky. How it was brutal at first. How I doubted. How Pa never did: he knew new life would come. And it did: birch and thorn and oak, new, tangled, messy, complex, beautiful life.

'I think he was like those glades. A tangled, complex, messy, but beautiful man.

'I think of how often I would look up from my desk to see his stooped frame stalking over the long grass. Knocking on the door of my office to show me a butterfly or report a bird he had seen.

I think of the phenology books that he and Rowan created together, the care and the beauty that is in those drawings he made. The child in him who lived again through this place.

'I think of his final days. The binoculars he kept beside him on the bed, even when they were almost too heavy to hold, so he might see his beloved birds.

'He saw the chiffchaffs come back, the week before he died.

'He did not hear the nightingale though. The nightingale I heard on Thursday morning. The nightingale that chose those glades, those tangled messy complex thorn bushes, for its safety – a safe place to rear its young.

'I think of the fact that, for many years, Pa must not have felt safe. Because people who feel safe do not hurt others. Or inflict harm.

'I think of the pain of his parents' early death. What must that have been like? To inherit all of this at the age of eighteen?

'And I think, perhaps, that all the damage he caused was the behaviour of a child who did not feel safe. A young man who had never been given limits.

'We know he left. Again and again. And we know that his leaving hurt us all, in ways seen and unseen, in ways that continue to echo today.

'But I want to talk today of the father who stayed. The part of him that understood the need for roots. To be rooted. The man who, once he had let those roots reach down into his native soil, and learned to live with them, through them, to draw sustenance from them, was able to be good. I think, in the last years of his life, he felt that safety he longed for. And he was able to love this patch of land of his. Able, in the deepest way, to come home.

'But here's the thing . . . it was no narrow vision of home. It was a home which reached out, which acknowledged the deepest facts of our interconnection with the non-human realm, with the animals and the plants and the trees and the soil.

'He was a great oak of a man, and like an oak, he harboured

new life in his dying wood: his last great project was the vision of joining with other landowners to form a nature corridor across Sussex to the sea. He understood that nature cannot thrive in pockets, that if we are to have any chance of getting out of this terrible mess, then we must join together.

'I take hope from this vision. I take heart.

'Pa, you gave us dreams like acorns – and we will tend them. We will take your acorns and we will think like oaks.'

Grace listens as Frannie speaks. She is proud of her, so proud! The way she stands here, so steadfast, so true. She and Philip did something right, she thinks, after all, to have borne her; all that was crooked in him and all that was thwarted and stunted in herself transformed somehow – made upright in their eldest daughter.

And as Frannie finishes, as Grace stands to take her place at the lectern, as she passes the coffin, she is filled with something strange, something unexpected, for the man inside – not love, not that, never that again, but something close to gratitude. And as she passes her daughter, she grasps her arm, 'Beautiful,' she says to her. 'You spoke beautifully.' And then she takes her own place before the ranged faces of her family and begins to read.

Rowan watches Granny Grace. She is reading a poem about a thrush, about the last thrush singing in the evening, and her face looks shining, there are tears there, but they don't look like sad tears, and she is not crying, not really, it is more like the tears are making her shine. And when Granny Grace has finished, the vicar speaks, tells them they must stand again now, and the men lift the coffin again, and they all follow it outside, taking an earth path past bluebells and cowslips, past gravestones all rubbled and lichen-grown, until they reach the plot at the edge of the churchyard: a hole dug four feet deep into the earth.

Rowan stands beside her mother and her grandmother at the

edge of the grave. As the coffin is lowered down, the air feels very thin and very thick at the same time.

First her grandma steps forward with her handful of soil. As she moves to the grave edge, Granny Grace looks up, and Rowan sees Ned, standing on the other side, looking back at her. And Granny Grace looks back at him. Then she throws the earth onto the lid of the coffin, where it lands with a low thwuck. She whispers something Rowan can't hear to the coffin at the bottom of the shallow hole. Or perhaps she is not whispering, not making a sound at all, only moving her lips like a prayer and her face looks peaceful and soft.

Then her mother steps forward, bends for her handful and throws. It's like a full stop, Rowan thinks, this low sound of the earth: the last full stop at the end of Grandpa Philip's life above the ground. There will be nothing more now of his life above the soil. But underground, she thinks, the conversation is just beginning. She bends to take her own handful of earth and feels dizzy suddenly, thinking of all of the life in even a handful like this: the springtails, the mites and the symphylans, the mycelia and bacteria, hundreds of millions of life forms all getting ready to do their work and turn Grandpa Philip into something else; into soil himself.

She looks up, across the grave, and sees Rani and Seb standing on either side of Aunty Isa. She said she wasn't scared – that it was just death – but her breathing's going all funny and she feels as though she might fall into the hole. Or like a big hand might reach out and push her down. And then – she can't explain it, but it's like she can hear him, her grandpa, like he's close by and speaking to her.

Do it for me, Ro-Ro. Please.

She throws her earth.

Once she has done it, it's like lightning bolts are travelling down her arms and legs, telling her to run, to move, to jump. And it is hard, almost impossible, to wait, her hand twitching in her mother's while the others throw their soil, this need to move is so strong – once they are out of the gate, at the top of the field, she turns to her mother. 'Can I run, Mum?'

'Go on,' says Frannie, smiling. 'Run if you need to.'

And so she runs, and Seb breaks away too and both of them are racing now, up the hill, towards the field kitchen, raw-lunged, glad to be free, glad to leave the family way behind.

The table stands, perched on the lip of the hill. It is dressed in a heavy embroidered linen, and along the surface of the cloth the food is set out on platters, between which stand small jugs of flowers and herbs, rosemary and flowering mint and elderflower, their scents delicate on the afternoon air.

And now, thinks Isa, it is done. As she takes her place between her son and her daughter, she is full of relief, relief that it has been simple, that it can be simple after all, to lay a body to rest. That it can be peaceful, and tranquil. That the world has resolved into this simplicity – into a family, sharing food on an afternoon in May.

From where she sits, she cannot see Jack. And she is relieved at that too. She can almost, in fact, imagine that he is not here.

And it was fine not to speak. In the end, she did not regret it, did not feel small or less. Those who spoke did well; they were generous, but honest. And she is proud of her daughter – so proud – she who sang so beautifully. Her daughter who sits beside her now. Her son. She puts her arms around them both, pulls them close, kisses their cheeks in turn; this family, this life – these beautiful tender lives that they have made.

On the other side of their son's head Hari is aware, acutely so, of a disturbance, of something coming into focus – something that he has kept at bay. Something that is troubling him profoundly – something about Jack, the man who sits diagonally

247

opposite him now. Something about his wife. Something about the colour of Jack's suit that echoes the colour of his wife's dress, his blue the echo of her blue, both at the periphery of his field of vision.

He saw the way Jack looked towards his wife earlier, in the churchyard. His face was unguarded then, naked, but now is studiously blank. Hari dredges his mind for what he knows of him, for what Isa has told him.

He thinks of the back of his wife's dress, of that exposed diamond of flesh.

Frannie stays standing, Wren waiting beside her, while the others take their seats.

'Wren has cooked for us today,' says Frannie, 'and worked exceptionally hard to pull together these plates, so I'll hand over to her, and she can take us through the food.'

'So . . .' Wren says, 'starting at the top, we have crayfish from the lake with a tempura batter, then marrow and courgette tempura with a wild garlic mayonnaise. In the centre we have earth-oven venison, cooked on the bone, with a venison garum on the side. The deer was a two-year-old buck, shot and hung and cooked by Jack in a specially dug pit.

'Moving down, we have Sussex chorizo from our Tamworth pigs . . . kale from the vegetable garden. A tomato salsa. Roasted heritage beetroot and carrots. Smoky grilled leeks with a sheep's milk curd. Then borage flowers with dill and greens.'

When she has spoken there is a small flutter of applause.

'Oh,' says Wren, 'and thanks to Luca for the natural wine. We swapped in some of the bottles with the red. We thought Philip would approve: the orange wine pairs very well with the venison, and the Pet Nat is great with the fish.'

'Can I serve you?' says the man on Clara's left.

She turns to him. The friend of Milo. Early forties. Handsome, if you like that sort of thing. Everything about him so studiedly neutral that it signals a sort of low-level serious wealth. 'Thanks,' she says. 'It's fine. I can serve myself.'

She reaches for a spoonful of carrots.

'What about some venison?'

'No, thank you. I don't eat meat.'

'If you were to, then this would be as close as you could get to cruelty-free. A good life. A wild life.'

'I'll bear that in mind.'

'You should try the garum,' he says. 'Even if you don't like flesh.'

'I'm not so familiar with garum.'

'Oh, really? They used it all over the ancient world before the fall of Rome. The juices in the gut leak, it takes a couple of months of fermenting and straining, and then you have this strong, salty liquid, terrifically pure. It's taking the whole snout-to-tail thing to a whole other level.'

'I'm good for garum,' she says. 'Thanks.'

He smiles. '*Tant pis*,' he says.

She feels his eyes rake her; he has not finished with her yet. Interesting, she thinks, how he obviously feels no need to disguise the fact of his looking. Of the small-scale violation of his gaze. She has met men like him before. They have a sort of laser focus, able to turn the whole force of their personality onto you – to make you malleable, amenable to their will. She took the decision a long time ago not to be amenable to anybody's will. She turns to him. His eyes are amber, flecked with green. 'I'm Luca,' he says.

'I'm Clara.'

'I know.'

He is, what? Not dangerous, not exactly, but something adjacent to it.

'So, you're the not-half-sister?' he says.

'Yes. And you're the friend of Milo?'

'Milo and I have been friends since we were kids.'

She nods. 'So you know this place well then?'

'I do,' he says. 'I started visiting when I was fifteen. I've always loved it here.'

'It's beautiful.'

'Isn't it? And this place . . . speaking as a foreigner, at least partially . . . my mother was English,' he says in an intimate, confiding tone, 'but my father is Italian . . . this place has always spoken of the finest qualities of English soulhood.'

'Oh?' she says. 'And what would you say they are?'

He sweeps his eyes out over the park. 'I think . . . I'm going to say . . . attention to the importance of tradition, coupled with an irreverence, an eccentricity. An appetite for risk.' He smiles. 'The whole family are disruptors on one level, and caretakers on another. I knew Frannie when she was living in a tree. And Philip . . . well, he was a legend. The Teddy Bears' Picnic will live on in history. But I'm forgetting – you knew him. Of course.'

She inclines her head.

'And I've seen some places,' he continues, 'I have never been someone who has shied away from beauty, but – just look at that house. It's unreal.'

She follows his outstretched hand, to where the house sits beneath them, the sandstone glowing in the afternoon light, beyond it the glint of the river, the calm blue surface of the lake. Unreal, she thinks. Yes. Unreal this table. Unreal this food strewn for the feast. This is the high art of extravagant simplicity: this cornucopia of beauty, lying here as though no human labour were involved. Like one of those pastoral poems where the deer stretches its neck to the blade, where the crayfish leap from the lake and the sheep offer their swollen udders meekly to be milked.

Unreal this tablecloth, with its delicate green thread, its embroidered horns of plenty, scattered in repeating patterns of abundance – forever spilling their grapes and their apples and their acorns: the kind of object that is freighted with a certain kind of nostalgia even in the act of its utility. Everything speaks, everything whispers its siren song: *life could be like this, life could be this good.*

She took a class one semester as an undergraduate: the Socio-Political Context of the English Pastoral. She was the only black person in the room – the professor one of those men who lives in aspirational tweed and blazers. When he handed back their term papers he stared at her as if to say – *you? The black girl gets the A? The black girl writes like this on Virgil? On Sidney and Jonson and Carew?*

'Have some wine,' says Luca, 'at least. Do you like your natural wines?'

'I guess,' she says. 'I haven't had them much.'

He lifts the bottle and pours her a glass. 'This is a great place to start. It's a Bacchus. The vineyard's not far from here. Close to the coast. An old friend bought it a few years ago. He's doing great things. They've started ageing their wines in Qvevri.'

'Qvevri?'

'Clay vases. Shaped like large eggs.' He cups his hands together, holds them like that. 'They originated in Georgia. They press the grapes, then put the juice, skins, stalks, pips, everything in there. Then they bury it in the ground and let it ferment – five, six months. Winemaking is holy there.

'Here.' He brings his hands to his glass, moves it with the slightest of circular motions; the orange liquid responds with languorous, glossy loops. 'I'm thinking of investing.' His voice is low, intimate again. 'Climate change. English wines. The big champagne producers are buying up vast hectares of Kent.'

'Are they?'

'But that way of making wines . . . I think it's over, don't you? It's far too obvious. This is the future: just a little fizz. Everything in moderation, right? No one likes ostentation anymore. Taste it . . . please . . . I'd love to know what you think.'

She lifts her glass. Inhales. Tastes. The wine is slightly funky, fermented. Surprising. 'I like it,' she says. 'It's good.'

'Well,' he says, and smiles; easy, tranquil. 'That makes me happy. Thank you, Clara.' He lifts his glass to hers. 'I think you might have just got me over the line.'

She takes another sip of wine then puts the glass down on the beautiful, embroidered tablecloth. Her food waits on her plate: the sauces bleeding into each other – scarlet tomato turning pink against a yellow slick of mayonnaise.

She knows she cannot let the food pass her lips – that if she does, she will be taken, like one of those stories where people must stay in the land of faery and never come back. And that which was taut is slackening, she can see; the family have become a tableau of benevolence: well fed, well drunk. The afternoon is ripening, the light mellowing, almost five o'clock and the sun is in the west, starting its descent. She sees them as though they are posed at this table for a portrait: the house below, the park stretching all around. A scene where the whole natural world gentles and bends itself to the will of this family as they sit, arboured amid the hum of the bees and the scent of the flowers. Soon, she knows, they will raise their glasses, they will begin to toast, and that which is already blurring will only dissipate.

She bends to her bag beside her chair, and pulls out her notes. Holds them in her lap, where they are hidden by the tablecloth.

She thinks of the box of shells in her bedroom. The delicate painting of a ship in sail. The name, *Albion*, on its lid.

'Are you alright?'

Luca is looking at her. Her pulse is racing. Sweat pricks her upper lip. She pushes her plate away, places her notes on the tablecloth before her, puts her hands against the side of the table and stands. A sort of rushing sound, as of a far-off waterfall, fills her ears. She is aware of the chair she sat on a second before, rocking behind her. Aware of Luca grabbing it, steadying it, of the family, their faces turned towards her in bemusement and surprise. And she would not have chosen this moment, but it seems this moment is choosing her.

'I'd like to say a few words,' she says. 'If I may?'

Frannie looks up as Clara stands.

She feels only exhaustion at this interruption. Surely all of the words have been spoken by now? But here Clara is, with some papers arranged before her, clearly with something to say. And here her family are, all looking towards her, because Clara's question – *If I may?* – was directed to her, and she knows that it falls to her, as head of the family now, to reply. To speak for them all. And so, despite the fact that she feels this interruption is a tug on the fabric of a day she has woven so carefully, so exhaustively, a day that, for all its portents, has passed well – despite this, and because Clara has flown here, all this way, alone, to pay her respects to Philip, and because she knows it would be the greatest discourtesy to refuse, Frannie nods. 'Of course,' she says to Clara, pushing her plate away, finding a smile. 'Please do.'

'I –' Clara falters, she looks out at the faces ranged around the table – all staring at her, expectant, quiet, benign. 'I want to start by saying how grateful I am for this opportunity to join you all. And to thank you all for how you've welcomed me here today, on this day which is all about Philip.

'Frannie asked me yesterday what I remembered of him – I think I said something like *he was so tall!*'

The family smile, they laugh and nod.

'I know that – as you said in church, Frannie – he was a deeply complex man, but so much of my life has been touched by an act of his generosity that I would like to honour it today.' She takes a breath.

'Twenty-seven years ago, when Philip and my mother Natasha were first together, Philip bought a gallery in downtown Manhattan and an apartment for them both to live in. In order

253

to make this possible, I know he sold a property in London that had been in your family for generations. A few years later he made the gallery hers. She had means for the first time in her life – which meant that in time she was able to pay for my education.'

A smatter of applause ripples around the table, like small rain from the clear blue sky. Clara is taken by surprise, and she hesitates, reaching for her water. Across the table from her, Milo gets to his feet. 'Can I speak?' he says. 'Just briefly.' He is holding his wine glass out, his hand flailing for the bottle before him.

Something in the gesture makes Frannie fearful, activates a small flutter of alarm: Milo has been drinking.

Milo is drinking.

She tries to catch his eye, to signal to him – *slow down*. But he is over on the far side of the table, lifting the bottle and pouring himself another glass.

'I think,' says Milo, 'if I may, Clara – that we have all been used to thinking of our father as someone whose secrets were toxic. Hidden. But here, in you, Clara, in your evident grace and intelligence, is proof that he was a man who could do private good. This makes me happy,' he says. 'And it makes me proud. Of you and of him. I'm sure I speak for everyone here, in saying that we are glad you're here amongst us today.'

A murmur of assent rises from around the table.

'To Pa,' says Milo, lifting his glass, 'and to Clara.'

Frannie looks to her mother for any sign of distress, but even Grace is lifting her glass, her face calm, inscrutable, and so Frannie reaches for her own wine, raises it, and joins the toast.

'Thank you,' says Clara, with a swift smile. 'And I hope it doesn't seem too ungrateful to say that it wasn't that I had forgotten where the money for my education came from, but after so many years I no longer thought much about the man whose generosity had allowed it: he was a part of my past, and my mother's past, and as the years went by, we talked of him less and less. When my mother died there were no longer any shared memories of Philip . . . until Isabella's letter arrived.

'When I replied and Isabella emailed me to tell me of Philip's death, I put his name in a search engine and found the website of the project. I followed the link to the magazine article – the photograph of the family in front of an oak tree – and I remembered a book that Philip had left in the apartment; one I had loved to look at when I was a child: a small hardbound volume of Joshua Reynolds paintings.

'I stared at the picture that used to enchant me when I was a kid: a family posed against the trunk of an oak on a beautiful spring day, and I understood something in that moment, that I am ashamed to say I had not considered before; we were connected, Oliver Brooke and me. It was *his* fortune, passed down through the generations, that had allowed my education; a thread connected us over almost two hundred and forty years. And I understood too, my education almost completed – that thread was one that I had to follow.

'Everything I have to say today, all of the clues I am about to give you, are a matter for the historical record, accessible through public libraries, through short searches on internet sites – for many of the relevant documents it would be necessary to have an academic login, but not for all. The story is by no means complete, pointing the way, as it does, to many other stories. Many other histories.'

She takes a breath, steadies herself. 'I realized I had been incurious,' she says, 'about the origins of my financial ease, and since I had been so, I guess I'm wondering if . . . you all have been incurious too.'

Frannie's pulse is jumping, and her body is flaring a warning – there is danger here now, she can sense it. She lifts her hand. 'Clara,' she says, and she is careful to make her tone calm, conciliatory. 'I think, with all respect, this is not the time for this. But let's make some time for whatever it is you've found, whatever it is you'd like to share. As a family. Let's do that before you go. This is important, and I want to hear it, but please – not now. Not today. I think I can speak for everyone here when I say today is a day for family, for thinking about Philip.' She lightens her voice, finds a smile. 'We can make time for the ancestral line before you go.'

There is a silence in the wake of Frannie's words, into which nobody raises their voice to support her, to soften the silence or turn it into something else.

Isa is the first of the family to speak. 'No,' she says, her voice carrying in the still air. 'You can't, Frannie. You cannot speak for me.'

Frannie turns to her sister.

'I'm sorry, Frannie,' says Isa. 'But I think we need to hear this.'

'Isa is right, Fran,' says Milo. 'Let Clara speak.'

A stinging flush comes over Frannie, burning her from within. She looks to Grace, beseeching, but her mother's face is the usual mask of dignity. And she feels a sudden fury with this dignity of her mother's – the ways in which that very dignity might have shaped her, contorted her, as she strove so hard to emulate it. Did her mother never want to rip off that mask?

'Go on, Clara,' says Grace, with a small, elegant gesture of the hand. 'We are listening.'

And it's true, thinks Frannie, they are. Milo with a puppyish wide-eyed gaze of masochistic delight. Isabella with grim resolution in her eyes. Isa's children are staring down at their plates. No one moves, only Rowan, shifting in her seat to turn her eyes towards Frannie's. 'Mum,' she whispers. 'What's wrong?'

Frannie imagines another self – one less schooled in dignity perhaps – getting up from the table and taking Rowan with her. Simply taking her by the hand and walking away. Shielding her from whatever is about to come. Driving somewhere. Or just lying in bed, side by side, and letting themselves be taken by sleep.

'Nothing, darling,' she says, pulling her daughter's hand into her lap. 'Nothing at all.'

Clara reaches for her water and Frannie sees that she is quite still and calm – the gravity of the afternoon has settled with her. There will be no more interrupting her now. She watches as Clara reaches into her pocket and brings out a single cowrie shell, which she places onto the table before her, then looks up and out. Frannie feels Rowan's hand grow tense in hers. 'It's alright, Ro,' she says, as she strokes her daughter's knuckles with her thumb.

'Your ancestor Oliver Brooke,' Clara says, 'was a very successful man. As you mentioned yesterday, Frannie, marine insurance was his primary trade, but he also had a varied portfolio with a wide range of interests – from lending money to underwriting to dealing in goods. At the time of building this house he was forty-eight. He had lived in London for twenty years. His offices were on Philpot Lane, right in the heart of the City: if you put the address into a map, you can see there's a skyscraper there now, with a Sky Garden at the top. It promises the best views in London from its restaurant on the top floor.

'Oliver Brooke was an independent underwriter, one of seventy-nine founder members of New Lloyd's. New Lloyd's was a coffee house, but it was also a marketplace – somewhere men could gather, trade information – a crucial hub of the shipping industry, and by extension, the mercantile activity of the British Empire. In the course of the 1770s and 1780s Oliver Brooke built close working relationships with shipowners and merchants there. The strongest of these seems to have been with a man called Richard Davenport, operating out of Liverpool. Davenport invested in over one hundred voyages to Africa between 1760 and 1790. From the correspondence I was able to find, Oliver Brooke made himself indispensable to Davenport. In 1775 he approached him and asked to act as his agent in the City, *to transact your business with regard to shells*. The shells in question were money cowries. As their name suggests, these money cowries were used widely as currency.

'By 1775, Brooke was already well established as a bead and shell trader with connections in both the British and French East India companies and with bead manufacturers in Europe. In a letter from early 1775, he writes to Davenport of his success in obtaining low-priced cowries for him, *owing to my coolness with the sellers*. He must have been pretty cool with those sellers, because between 1776 and 1780, Oliver Brooke provided thirty-nine thousand pounds' worth of beads for Davenport alone.

'I think it's important,' Clara looks up from her notes, 'to think of what that amount would mean today: there are many ways in which academics can express old money in today's currency, but the two most obvious are calculating through price inflation, which gives us a multiple of a hundred times – so that thirty-nine thousand becomes the equivalent of almost four million pounds – or calculating through wage inflation, which is a multiple of a thousand times, and gives us forty million pounds.'

Frannie's heartbeat is low and fast.

'This larger figure may seem excessive – maybe even beyond the bounds of belief, especially when we consider the size of this tiny white shell . . .'

Clara lifts the shell from the table before her and places it in her palm, holds her arm outstretched.

'I'm wondering whether,' she says, 'for the sake of argument we could agree to land somewhere in between those two figures – say twenty million pounds over four years – which makes a turnover of five million pounds a year from cowrie shells alone?'

Clara pauses. And slowly, Frannie realizes she wishes them to respond, to agree. And they do so: yes, they nod; Isa and Milo and Grace – yes, *five million from cowrie shells alone*. And Frannie – though it feels absurd to her, stagey almost – knows she must add her own assent, and she does so, acceding with a small tilt of the head.

Clara nods. 'Thank you.' She looks down again at her notes. 'At the same time as he was dealing in cowries, Oliver Brooke was insuring the voyages of Davenport and others. To give you a clearer idea of how this worked: let's imagine him walking the short distance from his offices on Philpot Lane to New Lloyd's in the Royal Exchange, drinking his morning coffee while reading the New Lloyd's list, meeting brokers, taking the temperature of the times. Insurance, as we know, is the business of managing risk: a broker looking to insure a voyage would have approached Brooke alongside perhaps ten others, and Brooke would have written lines of five hundred pounds or so per voyage alongside the other underwriters, taking a share of the risk and the premium.

'In this way Oliver Brooke underwrote ships which travelled from the quays of London and Liverpool, replete with enough cowries to buy the lives and liberties of enough bodies to fill the hulls of the ships which he insured: first they sailed to the coast of West Africa, then to the Caribbean or to America – the middle passage – returning filled with slave-grown produce. He also insured what was known then as West Indiamen: larger cargo ships which travelled exclusively between Britain and the Caribbean, carrying sugar and other slave-grown commodities.

'So . . . if we were feeling generous, we might call Oliver Brooke's dealings slave trade *adjacent*: he was no plantation owner. The names of his heirs do not appear in the databases of those who received compensation for their human "property" at the time of abolition. He only underwrote them as they became that "property", as their humanity was stripped from them. Because somewhere during their voyage across the Atlantic, those people *became* commodities, they entered the capitalist system, they became figures in a ledger in an office in London, thereafter to be known only by their physical condition. By their weight. By their names in captivity.'

Clara pauses.

Please, thinks Frannie. *Please stop. You can stop now. Please.*

'In 1788,' says Clara, 'something unexpected happened. The year of the buying and enclosing of this land, the year before he would be painted by Sir Joshua Reynolds, Oliver Brooke called in a debt from Richard Davenport. For a reason which is not clear from the records, Davenport did not or could not pay for the last three shipments of cowries. In exchange, Brooke took whatever assets Davenport could give him. One of those was the cargo of a ship that was already at sea – a ship carrying a full hold of enslaved Africans on their way to Grenada.'

Frannie reaches for Rowan, pulls her closer, her arms over her chest. She lets her gaze rest on the pink tip of her daughter's ear. The red edge of the cotton of Rowan's dress.

'What was a *full hold of enslaved Africans*?' says Clara. 'With respect to this voyage, the specific details of which are accessible by typing a simple search term into the Trans-Atlantic Slave Trade Database, we can learn that the ship carried four hundred and twenty-five souls.

'We can read, with a few clicks of a mouse, that they were purchased at Bassa. That there was an insurrection at the port before they set sail. That when they finally sailed they landed sixty-six days later in Grenada. That of those four hundred and twenty-five souls, forty-five died on the middle passage to the Caribbean. We can learn the name of the captain, John Muir, and the name of the vessel's owner, Richard Davenport. We can learn that eleven per cent of the enslaved – approximately forty-four souls – were children.'

Rowan moves a little in her seat, wriggling herself free from Frannie's grip, and Frannie becomes aware she has been holding her daughter far too tightly.

Go, she wants to say to her.
Go and run.
Run now. Take Seb.

But Rowan does not run, does not even turn back to Frannie, only sits, very still, back straight, listening.

'On arrival in Grenada,' says Clara, 'Oliver Brooke, the new owner of the ship and of its human cargo, requested for the enslaved to be sold at the dockside market, *for the best price and prices and most money that can or may be had or gotten.*'

Clara reaches for her water, drinks, swallows. 'I wonder if any of you know,' she says, 'the name of the ship that Oliver Brooke inherited?'

Her gaze comes to rest on Frannie, who shakes her head once. 'The ship was called the *Albion.*'

The word seems to hover in the still air, gathering density, gathering weight. There is a small aspiration – a gasp from the other side of the table. Grace perhaps? Isa? Frannie is not sure.

Frannie closes her eyes, feels the thud of blood in her ears. She can feel a low dark tide, something coming towards her, something travelling fast.

Clara's words are reaching her from a distance now.

'We can only surmise the deal was a good one, because several months later Brooke bought and emparked this land, and commissioned a young, as then unknown architect to start work on a house: a young architect who had just returned from his Grand Tour, whose mind was on fire with Greek temples, and who designed a house for Brooke that would embody symmetry, order; the ideals of a revolutionary age; the rationality of the Greeks.

'He commissioned a landscape designer who stood here, at the top of this hill, beside this tree, and sketched the village below out of the way: the cottages and the children and the trees they climbed, erasing them forever, for they had no place in the grand design, in the vista of this gracious house, these Enlightenment ideals, these rational Doric columns uniting heaven and earth.

'And Oliver Brooke retired from marine insurance and mercantile activity, and became a landowner, interested in legacy, in security, in stability. There is no mention anywhere on the

Trans-Atlantic Slave Trade Database of Oliver Brooke, and yet he is woven with the story of this ship, just as we are all woven with the sixty-six days the *Albion* took to cross the Atlantic, with the forty-five souls who would have been thrown from its deck into the sea.

'You see, your ancestor, my sometime benefactor, this bean counter, this cowrie trader, was, in fact, an alchemist: this solid, stolid man knew well how shells were turned into bodies, and those bodies entered a system in which they turned into abstraction, in which they became money, which turned into land, into golden Sussex sandstone, which transformed in the hands of artisans into columns and pilasters, into mahogany desks and billiard tables and the sweetness of pineapples brought to maturity beneath myriad panes of glass, of landscape designers creating vistas of green as far as the eye can see.

'These bodies – their terror and displacement, their hopes for liberty, their pain and their distress, their lives and their deaths – were turned into a thousand acres of good English soil, preserved for all the seven generations to come. And for the seven generations after that.'

And Clara's gaze comes to rest on Rowan.

'This morning I found a seven-year-old girl playing with shells in the sunshine. I asked if I might borrow them.' Her voice softens. 'Rowan, thank you for lending them to me. And I'm sorry, I know I promised to put them back. I will do so later today.' She looks up and out again. 'This morning, searching for the value of cowries in the West African slave trade, I managed to find the following online: *Exact numbers are impossible to calculate, but at a possible rate of around 6 kg of cowries (5000–6000 shells) for one slave, the São Bento cache could have been used to purchase three slaves.*

'Using this calculus, I want to suggest that two kilos of shells, the weight of this box, a third of the weight paid for one adult slave, would have been enough – there or thereabouts – to purchase a child.

'I am struck,' says Clara, 'by the strangeness of finding a seven-year-old girl playing with a box of shells on a beautiful morning in May. A young girl who stands to inherit one thousand acres of English soil.'

There is a silence. A small breeze rises and falls away. Pollen drifts lazily through the air.

Milo begins to clap, slowly at first then faster. Then he stands, clumsily. 'Fucking hell,' he says. 'I just want to say . . . that was . . .' He leans in and lifts his glass. 'To the truth,' he says. 'To the mother-fucking *truth*.'

'Thank you, Clara,' says Isa.

Frannie looks to her sister in fury.

Oh, Isa, this is all on you.

You who brought her here. Dragging us all into your wound of unmet need.

Rowan twists to Frannie. 'Mum,' she says and her eyes are wide. 'What does she mean?'

'Don't worry, Ro,' says Frannie. 'Just – give me a moment.' She rises to face Clara. 'Thank you, Clara,' she manages. She is shaking, and it is hard to find her voice. 'You have spoken and we have listened, and now, as I'm sure you'll appreciate, we need some time alone, as a family, to reflect. Can you please leave us to do that?'

'Of course.' Clara gathers her papers. Folds them slowly.

Luca stands, he moves Clara's chair for her, and she leaves the table, and she walks, a solitary figure, across the park.

'Rani,' says Aunty Isa. 'Can you take the kids back to the house? Why don't you go and put a film on for Rowan and Seb? And then we will all come back to the house in a little bit. When we've had a chance to chat together?'

'Sure,' says Rani. 'Come on then, kids. What do you guys want to watch?'

'Mum,' says Rowan to Frannie again. 'What did she mean?'

'Listen, Ro.' Her mum gets down in front of her and holds her arms. 'We will talk about all of this. I promise. Just not yet.'

'But why? Why was she talking about me?'

Frannie reaches out and touches Rowan's face. 'I absolutely promise I will come and find you soon. But for now, please, sweetheart, just go with Rani and Seb.'

Frannie kisses Rowan fiercely. Her mum's breath smells sweet, a bit sickly, like it always does when she has been drinking wine.

Rani sets off for the house, Seb beside her, his hand in his big sister's. Rowan drags behind. She can see that life is still normal for them, and that they have each other – but nothing feels ordinary or normal for her. Her body feels funny, as though she is inside and outside it at the same time. She doesn't want to watch anything. She wants to understand what is happening, and if whatever is happening is about her too, then why is she not allowed to know what is going on?

Two kilos of shells, the weight of this box, would have been enough to purchase a child.

Struck by the strangeness of finding a seven-year-old girl playing with a box of shells . . .

She knows Clara meant her, Rowan: *she* was the girl playing with the shells. Is this all her fault then – all of the ways in which today turned strange and frightening – because she took the shell box from the desk? Because Clara found her with it?

And how can a box of shells be the same weight as a seven-year-old girl? Sometimes she and the other girls try to lift each other in the playground, and she knows that seven-year-olds are way heavier than that box of shells.

It doesn't make sense.

And she knows she won't be able to think about it properly in that house, up in Rani's room, watching a film; she needs to be alone to untangle all the hot thoughts inside her head.

She turns and looks up the hill to where the table is, at the edge of the field kitchen, but no one is looking her way. Rowan looks back towards Rani and Seb. 'Rani?' she calls. Everything feels very still and very warm. A dragonfly buzzes past her ear, its body bright turquoise and black.

'Mm?' says Rani, looking over her shoulder. 'Are you okay, Ro?' she says.

'I just need to do something. I'll come and meet you in your bedroom in a minute.'

Rani frowns. 'I'm supposed to be looking after you though.'

'I'll be quick.'

'Okay,' says Rani. 'C'mon, Seb. See you up there, Ro.'

Rowan watches them go up the stairs, then disappear beneath the glass of the cupola. She turns and makes her way back along the park, running, so she can't be seen by those who stand at the table, whose raised voices she can hear on the afternoon air. If she can just lie in her old bed for a bit and unravel her thoughts, then maybe everything will right itself and come back to normal again.

The front door of the cottage is locked, so she goes through the side gate, the one they always used to use. The garden looks different – bigger; her trampoline has gone and the trike and the pushbike she had when she was little, they are all stacked up in a pile by the shed. The swing is still there, hanging from the rowan tree – the tree which still has the last of its white flowers. She thinks about swinging on it, but decides against it, goes instead to try the back door, which is unlocked. She pushes it open gratefully. It is dark in here, after the light of the afternoon, and cool, like the moment when you slide into water on a warm day, but it smells different: it smells of paint. The room stretches before her, it's an odd colour, a sort of grey that makes it feel darker and sad. It was bright white before and covered in her drawings, as her mum always just let her write on the wall, but all her wall-drawings have gone: the drawing she did of a wolf on a ledge, howling at the moon, and all the places where she drew around her hands and coloured them with different patterns. The stickers she stuck on the light switches one Hallowe'en and her mum never took off. And all the photos her mum printed out and stuck on the walls, the ones she knew by heart – not framed photos, not like up at the house in silver frames, just photos stuck on the walls with Blu-Tack that always came off.

She feels that tightness in her stomach again as she goes out of the kitchen, down the corridor. When she goes into her old bedroom, she sees immediately that the measuring wall has gone – you can just about see the felt-tip that her mum used one year, when she was four and a half, glowing ghostly orange through the new grey.

The skin on her arms raises in goosebumps.

All of her things have gone. Everything that made it hers has gone.

It's like she has been rubbed out.

Why? Why did her mum agree to give their home away?

And she understands something, standing here, in her old room – it is all her mum's fault. She could have told Granny Grace no. She could have said they weren't going to move into that house made of bodies and blood.

She thought it would feel good, being here, but it feels worse than awful, and she knows she cannot stay. She makes her way back out through the kitchen, into the garden, past the rowan tree, along the front path and back out into the park, where she walks along the treeline until she is close to the big house. She doesn't want to go up to the room which is supposed to be her new bedroom, doesn't want to go to where Rani and Seb are. Doesn't want to watch a film and wait until her mum is ready to come and find her. She makes her way instead along the colonnade to the library doors, pulls them open and steps inside: she wants to look at Oliver Brooke.

His pale face looms in the cool dark light of the room. He doesn't look bad, doesn't look like all those things that Clara said he was, standing there with his wife in her pink dress and his son and their dog and the oak tree behind him. But then, it is impossible to tell. People's insides do not look like their outsides.

She thinks of her mother's outsides. How often they seem closed to her. How often she doesn't listen. How busy she always is. And she feels all her hot anger in her again. She opens the drawer to Grandpa Philip's desk and takes out the old letter knife, then she leans over the leather of the desk and starts to carve. It takes her a long time to write what she wants to say, because the leather is quite thick and the knife is not very sharp, but all of her feelings are pouring into the desk as she carves, and when she has finished her heart is going bam bam bam bam and her palms are all greasy with sweat and she feels burning and scared and excited all at once, and she climbs down from the desk and walks to the terrace, where she opens the door and runs across the park.

Only one person sees Rowan go. He is walking slowly back to the house, having left the family up at the field kitchen. And so it happens that he is walking through the park alone, just in time to see this little girl in her red dress running through the grasses, her face a picture of distress and fierce intent, her dark hair streaming behind her, and as he watches her run, he feels his heart contract.

How has she been left alone like this – to bear the weight of the afternoon?

He understands he has no choice but to follow where she goes. And he does so, at a distance. Watching her run up the path towards the old oak, where she seems to disappear. Where she seems to turn into a tree.

Somehow, she is not quite sure how, Frannie finds herself at the table with Milo and Isa. Grace has gone, Luca has gone. Jack and Ned have gone. Hari has gone. It is just her and her siblings.

Albion,
Albion,
Albion.
The vessel's name was Albion.

'Are you okay, Frannie?' says Isa.

'Did you know?' She is shaking. 'What she was going to say? Did you set me up? Both of you? Is that what this is?'

Milo shakes his head. 'Jesus, Fran, give us some credit . . . Besides,' he says, 'this is not all about you.'

Isa holds up her hands. 'Milo,' she says warningly, then she comes to where Frannie sits, putting her hand on her arm. 'Of course not. Of course we didn't, Fran.'

'I need to be alone,' says Frannie, snatching her arm away. 'I hope that's okay. I'm going to go and find Rowan and lie down.'

'Of course,' says Isa.

She rises and leaves the table. As she walks back down the hill her feet feel heavier and heavier – it is almost impossible to move. All she wants, all she longs for, is to lie beside her daughter, to hold her close, and to sleep. She climbs the steps to the house, goes in under the cupola, mounts the stairs to the landing, walks slowly down the corridor to the room next to Isa's, where she knocks on the door.

Rani lies on the bed, Seb beside her. Seb has his headphones on, watching the screen of his iPad; Rani is frowning at her phone.

'Where's Rowan?' says Frannie.

'She went to do something,' says Rani. 'She said she'd be back.'

'When was that?'

'Um . . . when we were coming up to the house?'

'That was a little while ago now.'

Rani sits up, casts her phone aside. 'Sorry, Frannie,' she says.

'Don't worry,' says Frannie. 'She likes to wander around the estate.'

'Do you need me to help find her?' says Rani.

'No, you're okay . . . I think . . . I'm just going to go and lie down,' she says. 'When she comes back, can you tell her I'm in my bedroom? To come and find me there?'

Frannie goes into her room, lies on her bed, kicks off her shoes and curls around herself. It is only moments before sleep comes, swelling, rising; she can feel it at her back, towering, ready to take her down.

Rowan sits in the cool darkness inside the oak, her arms clasped around her knees. She's got her chocolate here beside her on the ground, but she doesn't feel like eating it. She feels too angry and upset for that. Usually, when she is away from people, her thoughts have a chance to order themselves, to calm and to settle, but today they are spiky and red as though there were small fires lit beneath each one.

There are footsteps on the other side of the trunk.

She knows it will be her mother, come to find her, come to tell her off, and she feels suddenly afraid of what she has done – and all the anger seems to drain from her, but when a face appears in the oval of wood above her head, it is not her mother. It is Luca, Uncle Milo's friend.

'Hello,' he says. 'This is a good hiding place.'

'Yes.'

'Are you playing Sardines?'

'What's sardines?'

'You don't know Sardines?'

'No.'

'It's a game, where one person hides, and everyone has to find them. The first person that finds them hides with them, and then each person that comes has to hide too, until everyone is hiding.'

She thinks about this for a moment. 'It only works,' she says, 'if the others know that we are playing too.'

'Well, even if they don't, they will definitely want to come and find you, won't they? Tell you what,' says Luca. 'How about I sit here, on this side of the trunk? So we're sort of hiding together but you're in there on your own.'

'Okay,' says Rowan. He puts his back to the tree, and she can't see him anymore really, only a little bit of his shoulder and face, and hear him, which is okay.

They are quiet for a bit, then: 'How old do you think it is,' he says, 'this tree?'

'Four hundred,' she says, 'or five hundred years old. It was here before the house. But we can't count the rings anymore because it's hollow.'

'How did it become hollow? I've always wondered that about an old tree. Do animals eat it?'

'Not animals, fungi. They eat the deadwood, not the living wood.'

'Gosh. That's clever,' he says.

'The fungi eat all the minerals that have been stored in the centre of the trunk.'

'Poor tree, though.'

'Not really,' she says. 'Hollow trees are better in storms. They don't get knocked over by winds. And lots of things live inside. Bats and birds. Hedgehogs. Bugs. The temperature always stays the same inside.'

'Wow,' he says. 'You know lots about trees.'

'Yes,' she says. 'I do.'

'I don't know much about them,' he says. He sounds a bit sad when he says this.

'Why not?'

'I don't know, really. I suppose I've never had to learn. I've got some lovely trees at my house. And I like looking at them. But I don't really know much about how they live.'

'But they're the most important thing we have,' she says. 'My name is the name of a tree.'

'Ah. Yes, I knew that, I think. Tell me about your tree,' he says. 'Tell me about the rowan.'

'Well . . . it can live a long time. Not as long as this tree. Not as long as an oak. But . . . a hundred years. Two hundred years.'

'Blimey. Would you like to live that long?'

'Maybe till a hundred,' she says. 'Would you?'

'Oh. Yes. I think so,' he says. 'I intend to. To live to be a hundred at least . . . Go on.'

'Well . . . it has white flowers. They're out now. The rowan blossoms. And they'll turn into red berries. And when the birds eat the berries, their poo turns purple. You get purple splats everywhere under the trees in the autumn.'

'Do you now?' His voice sounds like he's smiling.

'You can use the wood to stir milk to keep it from curdling. And it protects you. Against bad magic. Against spells. And you can make jam. Ned makes rowan jam. He makes it every autumn and I help.'

'Ned sounds pretty cool.'

'He is. And when my mum was going to have her baby that was me, she held on to a rowan tree in the garden when her contractions were really bad. And she knew she was going to call me Rowan.'

'That's a lovely story. It must be nice to have such a cool name.'

'It is.'

He moves a little, so she can see his face again. 'How're you doing in there?' he says. 'Can I get you anything? Are you thirsty?'

'No.'

'Are you ready to come out now?'

'Not yet.'

'Why not?'

She takes a deep breath, shifts on her cushions. 'I hate that house. I don't want to live there anymore. It's made of blood. And my mum made me move there. So I don't want to see her either.'

'Ah,' says Luca. 'That's a lot to be thinking about. I can see why you might want to stay in here to do all that thinking.'

They grow quiet again, then: 'We didn't get any pudding,' she says. 'At Grandpa's lunch. After Clara talked.'

'Oh no, we didn't. I didn't think about that.'

'I've got some chocolate,' she says. 'If you'd like to share?'

When Frannie wakes she has no idea of the time. How long has she slept for? One hour? Two?

For a moment, her mind feels drained – deeply empty – and then she remembers, and she sits straight up, goes quickly down the hall to collect Rowan from Rani's room. But there, on the bed, are only Hari and his children, watching a film together on a laptop.

'Where's Rowan?' says Frannie.

Hari looks up, frowning. 'I thought she was with you. Rani said you'd gone for a sleep.'

'She's not with me. She didn't come to find me.'

She is aware of a small ticking clock of fear in the far corner of her consciousness.

'Are you okay?' Hari says. 'Can I help?'

'It's fine,' she says quickly. 'Stay here. Stay with your kids.'

She goes out onto the landing. Then she goes to Isa's room and knocks on the door, pushes it open. Isa is outside the open window, sitting on the flat roof of the floor below, smoking a cigarette.

'Isa,' she calls, stepping into the room. 'Have you seen Rowan?'

'Rowan? I thought she was with you?'

'She's not with me.'

'How long has it been since you've seen her?'

'I don't know. A couple of hours.'

'Fuck.' Isa puts out her cigarette, clambers back inside the room.

'It's okay,' says Frannie. 'She does this. She wanders.'

'For this long?'

'No. Never before.' Frannie feels sick.

'Is there anyone we can call? Where does she like to go?'

'Ned,' says Frannie. 'She goes to see Ned sometimes, on her

own. He will have her.' She pulls her phone from her pocket, fumbles, drops it onto the carpet. Bends to pick it up.

'Hey,' says Isa, putting a hand out to still Frannie. 'She'll be fine. She won't have gone far.'

Frannie calls Ned, but his phone rings and rings.

'Wren?' says Isa. 'She looks after her sometimes, doesn't she?'

'Yeah, but she wouldn't be up there, I don't think.'

'Just – call her.'

Frannie does so, but there is no answer there either.

Hari comes out onto the landing. 'Can I do anything?' he says. 'She's been gone for a while, right?'

Frannie nods. The fear is everywhere now, her jaw, her tongue.

'Let's be systematic,' says Hari. 'Frannie, why don't you and I take the rooms on this floor, and Isa, you look downstairs?'

'Okay,' says Frannie, gratefully. 'Yes. Thanks.'

First, she goes into the bedroom that was intended for Rowan, that Rowan has not yet properly slept in. Her things are here, the suitcases of clothes, the desultory attempts to unpack. Her baskets of toys. She looks underneath the bed. Inside the wardrobe. Behind the curtains. She stands in the middle of the floor and calls. 'Rowan,' she says. 'Ro?'

Next she goes back inside the bedroom that she and Rowan share, where the bed is unruly, unmade. Frannie jerks the duvet as though Rowan might be hiding beneath. 'Ro?' she calls.

She goes out onto the landing. 'Ro-wan!' she calls. 'Come out! Please.'

There is no response.

And she knows it is irrational, she knows it is her tiredness. But she is filled with the fear that something has happened to her daughter, that something has been loosed by Clara's words – a rent in the fabric of history. She rests her hand on the cool wood of the banister rail. Stares at the chequerboard tiles of the hall far below. How many children on the voyage? How many children thrown overboard?

Four? Five?

Her knees buckle slightly and she grips the rail.

She hears Isa calling her.

She hurries downstairs, where the door to the library is ajar; she pushes it open to see her sister standing behind the desk. 'Come and look at this.'

'What am I looking at?' says Frannie, coming to join Isa where she stands.

Isa gestures to where the letter knife lies on its side and the leather of the desk is cut, scored, letters carved into it. At first they are a jumble, until they resolve themselves –

Fuk of Mum.

Frannie's spine quickens.

Isa looks up. 'Fran – was she angry with you? Did she have a reason to run away?'

They have nearly finished the bar of chocolate when there comes the sound of shouting. It's Frannie. It's her mum, calling her name.

'Shall we answer?' says Luca to Rowan.

'No. Not yet. I don't want to see her yet.'

'I think we must. I think your mum is going to be very worried. She sounds very worried indeed,' he says. 'I'm going to stand up and tell her where we are. I hope you won't be too cross.'

'Rowan's here.' Luca stands up, walks around the front of the tree. Calls out. 'She's here. She's safe.'

Rowan hears running footsteps. Harsh breathing. Her name being called. Then a tussle, as though they are fighting – her mum and Luca. And it's frightening. Her mother's voice, hissing. 'No. Not you.'

Then her mum's face appears at the hole in the tree, twisted in anger; she reaches in, grabs her wrist, and pulls her outside. Rowan starts to cry.

Luca is standing close by, Frannie screaming at him – screaming all sorts of terrible things at him. Telling him to *leave my daughter alone.*

And it seems to Rowan that her mother is wild. Like a wild animal. She looks as though she could kill Luca. As though her ordinary skin has been ripped off and you can see the animal beneath; a vicious, killing animal, with very bloody insides.

❧

The field kitchen is abandoned. The table sits in the evening sun – the sun which is setting on the plates and the deer and the bottles of wine and the wine glasses. The people are all gone. The animals watch the table. They watch the plates.

The first to breach the invisible line are the birds, making quick forays, quick swooping dips, coming away with morsels of food and spiriting it back to their young. Blackbirds come, and thrushes. Goldfinch hunt in packs: bolder for their numbers, raiding for minutes at a time – some keep watch while the others feed – taking it in turns, then returning to their chicks in their deep-cupped nests, high in the forks of tree branches; nests whose mossy bases are woven from grass and from spider silk, packed inside with wool and with feathers. Bringing their hungry chicks scraps of venison fat. Or carrot. Or pea.

When the corvids come, they sit on the table: the crows and the jays. They sit right beside the deer, and they tear into it, pulling at the flesh which clings still to the ribs.

❧

Late evening, shadows lengthening across the park. Isa stands at the window, looking out at the wide sky beyond the glass – the way the sun is setting, throwing its light up to the clouds.

Something makes her family laugh, and she turns to look at them, hunkered together, Hari in the middle, Rani and Seb on either side. The laptop playing on the duvet in front of them; an old movie they love, that they know all the words to.

She can see that her kids are okay, grounded again after this strangest of days, by this silly film, in their father's love, his arms heavy and steady around them. She has chosen a man who makes his children feel safe. Ordinary miracle.

She would like to climb into the middle and insert herself between them – have her husband father her too. But there is no real room for her on the bed. And besides, her eyes keep getting pulled back outside – to the parkland, to the clouds, which have lifted, and the sky, which is a high thin beautiful dome streaked with gold and pink.

Hari looks up, sees her agitation, her indecision. She watches him extract himself from their children, clambering over Rani's long legs to come to join her. 'Hey.' He stands before her, his hands on her upper arms. 'You okay, Is?'

'I'm not sure.'

'What do you need?'

What do I need?

'Some air, I think. Some perspective . . . What did you think? About it all?'

'Lots of things,' he says. 'And I think we should talk about it properly when we get home. Not yet. Not tonight.'

'Doesn't it make you appalled?'

'Of course it does, but I don't think me having an opinion about anything is the most useful thing right now.'

'How are you so reasonable?' She doesn't mean it to, but it comes out as an accusation, and he looks stung.

'I mean, we can go into it,' he says, 'if you want? I've got plenty to say if you really want to hear it now?'

'I'm sorry,' she says. 'I didn't mean it to sound that way. I just – it's a shock.'

'It is,' he says, and he is gentle again. 'And when there's shock you can't think properly. You can't respond from a place that makes sense. You've just got to do the basics. Drink water. Keep warm. Eat food if you're hungry. Are you hungry?'

'No. Not at all.'

'Are you warm?'

'I am,' she says. 'In fact, I need air, I think. I need to walk. Is that okay?'

'Of course. I'll stay here with the kids. Take your time.'

She goes downstairs slowly, makes her way beneath the cupola, and out through the park, where the birdsong is thickening. Ahead of her a small group of ponies crosses from the treeline to the lake – she stops to watch them move, their small sturdy bodies lit by the setting sun, they bend their necks to the water and lift them again, their breath steaming into the evening air. Her dress snags on a bramble and she looks down, surprised. It is only now she realizes she is still wearing it, that in amongst all the turmoil she has forgotten to change.

She skirts the lake, crosses the stream, takes the path past the bend until she is at the treehouse in the old beech tree.

She calls: the answering call comes, as though they were animals, calling to each other in the evening light. As though the last twenty years were nothing at all.

She climbs the ladder slowly, finds him sitting in the semi-darkness, amidst a dark green castle of leaves. He is wrapped in a blanket and his face is shadowed as she comes to sit opposite him on the boards. 'You're here,' she says.

'Yeah,' says Jack. 'I went home after the meal, I wanted to be alone. But then I wanted to be outside again . . . Besides,' he says, 'it's my last night. I wanted to spend it here.'

She leans her weight against the trunk of the beech, can feel its smooth bark against the exposed skin of her back.

'How's everything,' says Jack, 'up at the house?'

The air is cool, fresh with the new leaves and the wood of the beech and the silver scent of the river.

'Rowan disappeared,' says Isa. 'For quite a long time. A couple of hours. Frannie was distressed.'

'Is Rowan okay?'

'She ran away. She was hiding in the old hollow tree. She was with Luca. But she was safe.'

Jack nods, listening. 'That was a lot for her to hear.'

'Yes,' she says. 'It was.'

'And are your kids okay?'

'Yeah, they are. They're fine, I think.'

'That's good . . . and how's Frannie?'

'Okay. No. Not okay. I don't think any of us are okay, really. Do you?'

'What do you mean?'

She exhales. 'I think we're poisoned. I think we're poison . . . And when Clara spoke,' she says, 'it made sense. Like she was uncovering a curse.'

He regards her steadily. 'No,' he says. 'You're not. You're not poisoned, Isa. Go far back and every family has done terrible things.'

'Have they though? Do you really believe that?'

In answer he doesn't speak, only moves towards her across the wooden boards. When he is close, an arm's length away, he takes her hand and lifts the palm to his cheek. Then he puts his other palm flat against her hand. His eyes are closed. She grazes her thumb against his closed eyelid, over his lips. The curve of his cheek. She puts her forehead to his.

'What are you doing?' he says.

'Remembering you.'

They stay like that, her breath mingling with his. This is how it was, she thinks; this is how it always was when they were together. Anything felt possible here, beneath this net of leaves.

There is a sheet of sound, and they are beneath it: the sounds of the birds and of the water, all of them making this song of the evening, continuous, liquid, and the green is like a tent and the birdsong is like its fabric.

'You saved me,' she says.

She speaks to the line of his cheek, to the pulse at his throat.

She speaks to the net of leaves and to the water.

'I am sorry,' she says. 'For any hurt I caused you.'

And the green fuse is speaking through her now – it is in her tongue, which can speak it still, can still be fluent in this language of green.

Day Four

In the billiard room, in the almost-dark, Milo is getting drunk – drunk with a practised steady dedication he had forgotten he possessed.

Last night, once everyone had dispersed, he came into the kitchen and carried on with the wine. There were several bottles of the natural stuff that no one apart from himself seemed interested in. And then, when everyone else had gone to bed, he came in here and started on the whisky. And it's the whisky that has really done the trick.

He's been playing with the billiard ball, chucking it across the table and seeing how many cushions it can hit before it comes to a stop. It's childish and stupid but it's kept him going for hours now.

Throw, ricochet, catch. Throw, ricochet, catch.

The birds are doing their thing outside. Whatever it is they sing about, or sing *of*. Of joy and aliveness and spunk and territory and life life fucking *life*.

How do they feel about this place? This place that they live in. All the blackbirds and the blackcaps and the robins and the ravens and the rest – this place where they build their nests and raise their young? Generation after generation? Singing and fucking and fighting and living their blameless, conscience-free lives.

Oh, to be a bird.

He has been thinking about conscience. About consciences. About morality. He's been looking at the pictures on the wall: his great-grandfather, a captain in the Sussex Yeomanry, a photograph taken of him in uniform on his wedding day, a year before he was blasted to pieces on the Somme.

And then his grandfather, also in uniform, at the end of the Second World War – sent to fight in Jerusalem with Allenby; killed in a car crash alongside his wife in 1965, leaving Milo's father alone in the world.

Is it any wonder his father turned out like he did?

He's been remembering when he was younger, when he and Luca would come down from school for the weekend. It must have been sixth form. Exeats. Or the holidays. Whatever. They'd go down to Ned's and score some weed and then they'd come in here and raid the booze and get slaughtered while Grace was upstairs.

Sometimes, not often, his pa was around – and there was that one time, he and Luca must have been about sixteen, when Philip came down and joined them here. He drank with them, smoked with them, quizzed them on their sexual exploits (almost zero, really, in Milo's case; not so with Luca). Philip got out his best whisky, and rolled his best joints, as he told them stories about what he got up to when he was in London.

That night his father basically admitted to his son and his son's best friend that he was a sexual predator, with a predilection for very young women.

He remembers though, that night, with the whisky and the expert joints his dad rolled, how proud he was that Luca was here to see this, to hear this, how, as the night wore on, he felt this strange sense of – what? Pleasure, closeness, initiation? – yes, that. Like he was ready to hear it now that he was sixteen, ready to receive it, to open his throat and have the poison poured right down his neck. It was as though Philip had opened the door to a room. A room within this one, this billiard room, but situated somewhere else. Somewhere deep in the psyche. Somewhere deep in the basement of his ancestral psyche he had opened the door to his son, and showed him what was inside: inside were monsters. Waiting in the dark.

But instead of standing there, saying, *nah, Pa, you're alright* – instead of turning back to sunlight and daylight – Milo walked right in. He lived in that room for years and years. Maybe he's never got out.

He knows now that in that basement were Philip's own ghosts: his father and his grandfather and back and back and back and back, to Oliver Brooke and beyond – all the lack of love and the loneliness and the violence of the twisted fucking creed and brutality of the ruling class. Like somewhere, somehow, something had come and severed them all from their hearts, cauterized them from the neck up – and that injury was so great they felt the need to inflict it forever more. On their sons first, always on their sons first; then on the rest of the world. Or were they just psychopaths, the lot of them – psychopaths all the way down?

Whatever. It was after that night that Milo began visiting the drinks cabinet as a matter of course. Not just when Luca was down with him, but whenever he was in the house. He would come in here and take a dram of something, usually whisky, which would help immoderately with whatever was on his mind.

Where was his mother? Sleeping? Not sleeping, upstairs.

Had she known what her son was up to? Had she cared?

It was here, in this billiard room, that he drank the whisky and took the pills and stumbled down to the lake to try to row to the island.

If it was a cry for help, then the only one who heard it was Ned.

Throw, ricochet, catch. Throw, ricochet, catch.

What was it Clara said? Shells turning into bodies, into stone, into columns and pineapples and mahogany and ivory billiard balls.

He lifts one of the balls. These ivory balls.

Eight pairs of elephant tusks to make a set of balls. He remembers Philip telling him that when he was a child: eight pairs of elephant tusks.

Throw, ricochet, catch. Throw, ricochet, catch.

Eight dead elephants.

It's pretty twisted if you think about it. Strange he never has – balls made from actual tusks, pressed into service for a game.

He dredges his brain for what he knows about elephants. They used to be his favourite animal as a child. He loved to watch them when he was taken to the zoo.

Memory. Their memory. They have graveyards – they walk miles, don't they, to visit the skeletons of their loved ones?

Imagine, a herd of elephants, trampling their way through the park. They would certainly do a good job of churning the earth. Better even than the Tamworth pigs and the Longhorns. They should get them down. Call them in. Call in the ancestral elephants to visit the billiard balls and come and trample the sward. It makes him smile, just a little bit.

Throw, ricochet, catch.

The door opens quietly, and a figure enters into the half-light. Milo covers one eye and the figure resolves.

'Luca, mate.'

'Hey, Milo.'

'I've been playing against myself.' Milo throws the ball against the pocket – it misses, bounces off the table and rolls across the floor.

'Who's winning?' says Luca.

'No one. Me.'

Luca bends, picks up the ivory ball, places it back onto the baize and gives it a little roll. It comes to rest on the opposite side, just by where Milo is standing. 'I came to say goodbye,' says Luca. 'I've got some meetings to get to in town this morning.'

'Oh,' says Milo. 'Sure. Okay. Shit.'

'Are you okay? You don't seem all that great.'

'Yeah. I think, I'm . . . pretty pissed.'

'I can see that. What are you drinking?'

'Whisky. You want one?'

'No, thanks,' says Luca.

'Delayed grief,' says Milo, waving a hand. 'All that.'

'Mate,' says Luca. 'You'll get no judgement from me.'

'Sure. I just – you know – needed to let off a bit of steam, I guess. Bit of a blindside yesterday.'

'It certainly was.'

'I've been remembering though. The old days. You and me, coming down here. Getting wasted on Dad's booze.'

'Good times.'

'Yeah,' says Milo. 'They weren't though, were they. Not really.'

'Hey,' says Luca, softly. 'I'm not proud of a lot of what we did. But neither am I going to waste time being ashamed. We were different people. We were kids, Milo.'

'Sure.' Milo steadies himself against the billiard table. 'Fuck,' he says. 'Sorry, mate. I'm really fucking pissed.'

'Have you got water?' Luca says. 'Maybe switch to water.'

'There's water in the decanter I think.'

Luca makes his way over to the low drinks table, pours a glass of water into a tumbler, and brings it to him. 'Drink this. And then drink a couple of pints more,' he says. 'And it's a beautiful morning out there. Maybe you need a bit of light on the situation.' He goes over to the shutters, opens the door to the terrace, and the morning spills into the room.

Milo wavers across the room to the open doors, where he looks out to where the dew-soaked grass is smoking in the early sun.

'Fuck. I've been in a hole here. Thanks, man. Look at that. You're right. It's a beautiful day.'

'I've got to get going' – Luca rests a hand on his shoulder – 'but we'll talk in the week.'

'Sure, mate. Thanks for coming.'

'No problem. It's been quite the weekend.'

They hug, and Milo feels the weight of Luca in his arms – his oldest friend.

He pulls out of the hug – 'Hey, Luca, mate, I love you,' he says. 'You know that.'

'I love you too, mate.'

'We don't tell each other that shit enough, do we? Men? Us. But I'm here for it. For the transformation. I'm here for the work. For the love. And you know what – you're right. They were different times. What matters is the future, right? The next bit. We've all carried poison in our veins. It's what we do with it that matters. How we *alchemize* the shit, right? We're going to heal the shit out of this place. Out of this land.'

He looks across at Luca, who has taken a couple of steps away.

'I'm sorry, Milo,' he says. 'That's not going to happen. At least not with me. Or with Clarity.'

'What? What do you mean?'

'In light of yesterday – the revelations about the estate. This is exactly the sort of thing that people don't want to touch. You know that, right? When something like this rises to the surface it smears itself over everything. Everything starts to stink.'

'You're serious?'

'I am I'm afraid.'

'C'mon, Luca. That's insane.'

'I'm sorry, Milo. I know what this meant to you. There will be something else to collaborate on. I'm sure.'

'No,' he says. 'No no no. Hang on – this will happen. I assure you. I fucking *assure* you, Luca.'

'If your father had given you the land in the will, there would have been a chance we could have separated the clinic from the estate. A new start. A separate entity from the Albion Project. As it is, it feels murky.'

'Murky?'

'Can I give you some advice, Milo?'

'I have a feeling you're going to give it anyway.'

'Only if you're ready to hear it.'

'Sure. Go on. Hit me. Lather me with your advice, Luca. Bathe me in it.'

'Don't be a victim. Drink water. Sleep. We'll speak in the week.'

The room starts to revolve, starts to spin, slowly, slowly.

'There's Grace,' says Luca.

In the far distance, a figure is moving, walking towards the house. The two men watch her approach in silence.

'You know what I have always admired about your mother?' says Luca. 'She's a supremely elegant woman. Whatever she may or may not have had going on, she rose above it. That's how you rise above the shit, Milo. You float on top of it – you style it out.'

And just like that Luca is gone – out to meet his mother, to greet her on this morning grass. Milo cannot hear what words are exchanged between them, sees only the kiss on the cheek, Luca speaking to her in low and serious tones. A small hug. And then Luca has taken his leave, walking briskly away. And his mother is coming towards him, crossing the grass to the terrace, coming into the house.

'Mother, Mother, Mother. Good morning. What are you doing up?'

'I went for a walk,' she says. 'How are you, Milo?'

'Drunk.'

'I can see that. Don't you think you ought to stop drinking?'

'Probably.'

'Well,' says Grace. 'I'll leave you to it then.'

'Don't go. Sit down. Join me. Have a whisky.'

'Thank you, but no.' But Grace does not leave, instead she stays there, half in, half out of the door. The morning light haloing her. It snags on his heart, the sight of her.

'You look well, Mum. What have you been up to?'

'I went to take some small things down to the cottage.'

'Ah.' He makes his way back towards the whisky bottle. Waves it at her. 'Sure?'

'I'm sure.'

He pours, drinks, turns back. 'Not many nights more in this house now, eh?'

'No.'

'When do you move?'

'Tomorrow.'

'You must be very relieved.'

She inclines her head.

'How have you been? Since yesterday? I haven't seen you.'

'I didn't feel much like speaking to anyone. After everything. I needed to rest.'

'Not shocked then?'

'Not shocked, no.'

'Not surprised?'

'No.'

'Me neither. Poor Frannie though, eh? Saddled with this shitheap. Maybe it's not even a shitheap. A boneyard.' He laughs suddenly. 'I mean . . . imagine naming your rewilding project after a fucking *slave ship*. Jesus fucking Christ.'

'Have you seen her this morning? Your sister? I'd like to know how she is.'

He shakes his head.

'And what about Clara?'

'No,' he says. 'Only Luca. I've just been here alone mostly . . . remembering.'

'What have you been remembering?'

'Oh,' he waves his glass in the air, 'all sorts of things . . . Dad and poison and . . . I need to ask you something. Can I ask you something? All this time, and I never asked you why.'

'Why what?'

'Why you let it happen. Why you let him send me away. I mean, it's the central fucking question I've been circling for more than thirty years; it's the central fucking question of my life. And I've never had the courage to ask you why.'

'You know why, Milo,' she says.

'Tell me. I want to hear it.'

'Because your father had decided. His mind was made up. There was nothing I could do.'

'But don't you see how that's just not good enough?'

'I do see. Yes . . . Perhaps I've never told you how desperately hard that was for me too.'

'So *why*? Why did you let it happen? Do you know how frightened I was in that place?'

'I didn't, no. Not at the time. Your letters were always cheerful, Milo. I had no idea.'

'They *read* them. They read our fucking *letters*, Mum. It was like living with the Stasi.'

'I tried, Milo.'

'Did you? Did you really try, Mum? How? You *left* me there. You left me in a place without love . . . It would have been easier you know, so much easier, if you'd been like Dad. If you'd never fucking cared. But you loved me. And then you stopped.'

'No. No, Milo, I never stopped loving you.'

'You did – when I came home you couldn't touch me. I remember it. All I wanted was for you to hold me. And you couldn't do it. I was *eight years old*.'

'It was you, Milo. You who pulled back. You who wouldn't touch me. You wouldn't let me hug you, or –'

'They told us it was *weakness*. They told us it would be better if we didn't hug our mothers. If we shook our fucking father's *hands*. They taught us to believe that love wasn't real. To mistrust everything and everyone. *You'd* sent me away. You are my *mother*. It was *your* job. Your job to push harder. To break through. Why didn't you?'

'Milo, please – don't you think I was punished too?'

'How? How were you punished?'

She takes a breath. 'You didn't want me near you. I couldn't reach you. I loved you more than anything and it was as though you were behind a pane of glass.'

'I was. I *was*, Mum. It was filthy as fuck. And you'd put me there.'

'I'm sorry, Milo.' She takes two steps towards him. 'I'm so sorry.'

He stands, daring her to cross the line, to move first, to be the first to touch him, to hold him. 'Even after I took the pills,' he says, 'you couldn't touch me.'

'Because I thought you hated me,' she says. 'Because I thought that was why you did it.'

'I did.'

'Oh.' She bends over herself as though he has punched her. 'Oh,' she says again. 'Please,' she says in a small winded voice. 'Please believe me, Milo. If I could go back I would do it differently. I would fight for you. I would keep you with me. I would never let you be sent away again.'

She lifts her head, reaches out her hand, and he takes it – their fingers enlaced. And then he is stumbling forward, into her embrace. Her arms are around him. And he is here, in his mother's arms, in this moment that he has longed for, and his mother is holding him, but it is not how he imagined, and he is drunk – so fucking drunk. He pushes himself back, holding her at arm's length, trying to focus on her face.

She looks old, he thinks, in this cruel sideways light from the French doors, her face mangled with tears and with pain. He doesn't want his mother to be old. All those years, all that time, when she was young and beautiful and she could have held him, and they could have been close to each other, and now she is old and they have lost them all – all of those years: gone. And he feels dizzy now, and sick, and full of a revulsion so strong it threatens to capsize him. 'Too late,' he says, pushing her away. 'You're too fucking late.'

He turns, and grabs hold of the billiard table to steady himself. Ahead of him, the balls swim on the baize. He reaches for one of them, plucks it and then, with a twist of the wrist, throws it at the panes of the French doors, where glass shatters in thin, brittle shards.

'Woah,' he says, and he starts to laugh. 'That's really very fucking satisfying.'

'Here.' He turns back to the table, holds out a ball to his mother. 'Do you want to have a throw?'

Grace's arms are clasped across her chest, and her head is bowed. Her body shaking with her weeping.

He turns, sends a second ball into the glass – splintering it, letting it shatter. And he can almost hear the elephants cheering him on, trumpeting their pleasure: *Take it down. Take it all downnnnnn.*

His mother does not move. She simply stands there, head bowed, as though waiting to be pierced, as the glass shards and shatters at their feet.

❧

As Isabella approaches the back of the house, she sees her daughter in the distance. Rani is leaning against the car, phone in hand. There is something in her posture though, something troubling, something troubled.

She sees Hari come outside. He is carrying a suitcase. He says something to Rani that Isa cannot hear. Then comes Seb, barrelling out of the house. 'I can't find her,' he is calling. 'Where is she? Where's Mum?'

'I'm here,' she calls.

Rani looks up – at first her expression is open, bathed in relief, almost smiling, she lifts her hand in a wave and Isa waves back. But then her face becomes clouded and dark.

'Mum's here,' she hears Rani say, dully, to her father. And Hari looks up, looks towards where she stands now, a little way from her family – because it's strange, but something, some invisible force, is preventing her from moving any closer.

Only Seb seems to have the power to break it, to cross the line. He runs straight for her. Flings his arms around her. 'Mummy!' He presses his face against her stomach. 'Where have you been? You smell of outside. Did you sleep outside?'

'Seb,' says Hari. 'Let's leave Mum. She needs some time alone. We need to get to Grandma's.'

'What's happening?' says Isa.

'We woke up,' her husband says, 'and you weren't there. So we figured we would get ready to leave. My mum's expecting us for lunch.'

Seb lifts his head. He looks from his father to his mother and back again. She sees him, frantically trying to decipher the nature of whatever is moving between them. She holds him tighter. 'Where were you, Mumma?' he says to her. 'Where have you been?'

'Come on, Seb.' Hari steps forward and pulls their son away from her. 'We need to go.'

'No,' says Isa. 'Not yet. Just – wait. Hari, please. Just give me five minutes. To explain.'

'Where have you been, Mum?' says Rani. 'Why are you still wearing that dress? You have grass in your hair. It's everywhere. It's all over you. You're soaked.'

'I slept outside,' she says. And she sees something cross her husband's face – disgust. Pain. 'But Hari – wait. This is not what you think.'

'Get into the car, Rani,' says her husband.

Rani complies, but Seb stands between his parents, head whipping one way and then the other, until Hari takes him, grasping for his wrist roughly with one hand as he wrenches open the back door of the car with the other. 'Get in, Seb,' he says. And his voice is sharp. 'Now.'

'Mum?' says her son, his voice rising to a wail.

Hari bends down, wrestling Seb's seat belt across him.

'Hari,' she says. 'Wait –'

Hari slams the door.

'Just give me two minutes. *Please.*'

Hari stands, his back blocking the car window so she cannot see her son.

'Fine,' he says. 'Go on. Lie. See how much lying you can manage in two minutes. Go on. Tell me you weren't with him.'

She says nothing.

'Tell me you didn't spend the night with him, Isa.'

'I did,' she says. 'But nothing happened. I promise. It wasn't like that.'

'What was it like, Isa? *You spent the night with him.* Go on. Tell me – what was it like?'

'We talked. Or I talked. He listened.'

'Okay. Right.' He gives a brief, bitter laugh. 'Did he listen more than me? Is that what you need? Someone to listen. Have I not listened enough? Jesus Christ, Isa, have I not *listened enough*? Listened for years to you?'

'I promise you, Hari. I didn't do anything last night.'

'I trusted you.'

'You *can* trust me.'

'Can I? Can I trust you to tell the truth?'

'Yes. Yes you can.'

'Okay. Then tell me the truth. Have you been faithful to me, Isa?'

'Nothing happened. I promise. Hari – please.'

'It's a really simple question, Isa. There's a yes or no answer. Have you been faithful to me?'

She is silent. 'No,' she says. 'But not last night. Last night we just – I understood something. About myself. About who I am. It's not about him. About Jack. It's about me.'

'Of course it is. Of course it's about you, Isa. It's always about you. It's always only ever been about you . . . You know what your problem is?'

'Tell me.'

'You say you hate your father. You say that he was a narcissist. But do you know who you are most like in this world?'

She shakes her head.

'Philip,' he spits. 'You're his daughter through and through. You're a liar, Isa.'

'I'm not. Not now.'

'Oh – so when? When were you unfaithful?'

'It was years ago, Hari.'

'How many? How many years?'

'It was when his mother died. When I came down for her funeral.'

'Ah. Oh. Okay. Okay – I get it. So, it's just a funeral thing? Just a twisted funeral thing you two have got going on?'

'Please, Hari. I didn't. Not last night. Because I love you. All of you. Too much.'

'I'm sorry, Isa. Forgive me, please, if I never believe anything you ever say again.'

He goes around to the driver's side. She sees her son, his face. He must have heard it. All of it. She presses her hands flat against the glass of the car window. One hand for her daughter, one for her son, as her husband climbs into the car and slams the door. As the engine starts, she steps back, lifts her hand, but Rani is not looking, she is bent, hunched, her hair over her face, phone in hand.

Hari reverses, turns, drives through the gates, up the lane, and is gone.

⚘

Jack is making his way along the river and through the wood. He is dressed for the plane; showered and ready. His bag is packed.

He is thinking about endings, as he treads this familiar path – about his mum, his dad, about leaving them here in the earth. Thinking of Isa. Of how it was to be with her again. Of how much he wanted her, how much he has wanted her, longed for her and loved her; but how right it was last night that they did not do more than lie like that, holding each other, and how he is full, somehow, of that holding, full in a way that means he can leave without regret. How grateful he feels for that.

He is thinking that when he told her, when he was angry, that whatever was between them was in the past, he wasn't speaking the truth – it is only now, he thinks, that he can truly let it go.

And he can feel himself lighten, as though whatever gravitational force has held him here for so long is lifting, and though he is going to a place he does not know, the not-knowing is no bad thing. It is time, he thinks, for a change. He has said this often, but he has not truly believed it. Now he does.

And rounding the corner of this bend in the stream, he hears music. He stops. Listens. Dylan. 'Visions of Johanna'. Ned's favourite. He loves this song too: the all-night girls and their escapades out on the D-train.

The beauty of things not needing to make sense to be right.

When will he come back here? Will he ever in his life round this corner of this stream, pause here, and listen for Ned's music again? Not for a long time. And when he next walks this path, what will have changed? Will Ned be alive when he returns – if he ever returns? Will he see him again? All the old ones are dying now.

And then it will be his turn.

Will he return here then? To the earth where his father lies, his mother lies? To lie himself down in the Sussex clay? What sort of clay will it be the day they bury him? Clodgy? Gawm? Slab? Pug? Stodge?

Strange thought for such a beautiful morning as this.

As he enters the glade, he sees Ned busy with something in his workshop.

He takes a mental photograph: Ned working while Dylan blasts into the green.

The fire.

The battered kettle on its tripod.

The way the light strikes through the young oak leaves.

He will get this picture out, he knows, in times of loneliness – revisit it in his mind. He calls and Ned answers, beckoning him over with a raised arm.

Jack puts the bag he is carrying down on the ground; he bends to it, unzips it, takes out a parcel, wrapped in cloth. 'Here,' he says, crossing the glade to where Ned stands. 'I made this for you.'

Ned unwraps the cloth and lifts out a knife, its handle carved from a single piece of antler. Jack watches as he turns it in his hands, the blade sharp and gleaming in the sunlight.

He knows it is perfectly weighted. Perfectly made. He spent hours getting it just right.

'Thanks, lad,' says Ned, when his inspection is done. 'I'll cherish this.'

'I'm sorry,' says Jack. 'For that stuff I said yesterday. The stuff about you being a coward.'

Ned waves it away with his hand. 'You're probably right.'

'And . . . I just wanted to say . . . I think you should. Maybe. Tell her. How you feel. You deserve happiness, Ned. You do.'

Ned smiles. 'Have you got time for a spliff?'

'I can't.' Jack picks up the rucksack, zips it up again. 'I've got a plane to catch.'

'Blimey,' says Ned. 'Things really are changing round here.'

Jack leans in and they hug. He can feel the rough wool of Ned's sweater. He inhales deeply: woodsmoke, sweat. Dope.

'Go well, lad,' says Ned. 'Send word. When you're settled.'

'I will.'

❦

In the library, Frannie paces. She takes out her phone and tries Simon, but the call goes straight to answerphone – so he wasn't lying when he said he was out beyond Wi-Fi signal. But she needs him. She needs him now. What would he say if he were here?

Just hold tight, Fran. We don't know what this is yet – what it means. Stay strong and I'll be back soon.

But she is anything but strong, here in this place that has always meant strength to her: the library, her father's desk – carved, now, with her daughter's words:

Fuk of Mum.

It would be funny if it weren't so awful.

She has hardly slept, her nervous system alive to every creak and shudder of the house, full of the sense that something lurked in the shadows, something that might come to take her daughter, to snatch her when she turned her back – something she has not tended to, not turned towards.

And she knows full well what it is.

The box is here, lying on the desk before her. Clara must have put it back last night. The ship painted on the front, its three masts in full sail, the blue sea beneath it crested with white waves: *Albion*.

She opens it slowly, staring down at the tumbled mass of shells. *Twenty million pounds' turnover from shells alone.* Clara is right – it is almost unimaginable.

She remembers the fury and horror she felt yesterday when Clara introduced Rowan into the story of these shells, *two kilos of shells . . . enough to purchase a child.* And yet she knows too that Clara had tried to speak to her, the evening before. Is it her own fault then, that Rowan heard what she heard? That Clara spoke in the way that she did?

She takes a breath, brings her computer towards her, opens it and types into the search engine. A website comes up immediately with a banner of teal blue – *Trans-Atlantic Slave Trade Database* – very official, very accessible. She hovers her cursor over the options, finds 'Ship, nation, owner', and clicks on it. A search page comes up, asking for 'Vessel name' or 'Vessel owner'. She types *Albion* into the search box, clicks Apply.

It takes all of five seconds, and there they all are. She counts, nine of them: nine *Albions*, nine ships, their voyages ranging from 1699 to 1849. Heart quickening, she clicks onto the voyage that took place in 1788, where she reads the name of the vessel owner, Richard Davenport – the flag of the vessel, Great Britain. Where she reads that the ship was constructed in 1783 in Liverpool; that it weighed two hundred and twenty tonnes. That it carried four guns. That it began its voyage in Liverpool, before purchasing captives in Bassa. That four hundred and twenty-five enslaved humans embarked there. That there was an insurrection at the port of Bassa before departure. That three hundred and eighty people disembarked in Grenada sixty-six days later. That forty-five people lost their lives on the voyage. That eleven per cent of the enslaved were children.

It is all there, in the chilling precision of legalese: the language of administrators, of those, like her ancestor, who wrote columns in ledgers – of the men who compiled the records that are referenced at the bottom of the page, the *Lloyd's Register of Shipping*, the British National Archives Kew, the *New Lloyd's List*.

Particular outcome of voyage: Voyage completed as intended.
Outcome of voyage for captives: Slaves disembarked in Americas.

She calls to her mind what she knows of those voyages; of the middle passage, of the captives chained together below decks, the shit and the filth and the fear. The rape. The death. She knows that those who died on the passage were thrown overboard. She knows sharks followed the ships. Five children then, thrown overboard. A man defaulting on a payment for shells. Another man, her ancestor, becoming the owner of three hundred and eighty souls at sea.

Voyage completed as intended.

Oliver Brooke selling those people as swiftly as possible, taking the profits, buying this land a year later, and building this house.

She turns to where he hangs, implacable, on the wall behind her, with his serene wife and his tousled-haired son on his endless spring day, where the blossoms are always fresh, and the oak leaves young and green. *Who are you?* he seems to say. *To look at me like this? Who do you think I did it all for?*

You

You

You.

And who is she – this land's inheritor – in the light of this new knowledge? Who does it make her? Where, on the scales of just-ice, does she now stand?

She does not know.

This is what she knows, this is what she knew: that Oliver Brooke insured ships in the eighteenth century, that there was a box of cowrie shells beside a globe on his mahogany desk. That it was on this box her father looked one afternoon, when they were together in the library, trying to find a name for their project. Albion, he said.

Yes, she said. Yes! Of course. *Albion* – because it was a word big and bold enough to hold a vision inside. She made a world within it, but the world was built on something foul: the soil is quicksand and beneath it is a swamp.

She remembers the feel of the eyes on her yesterday, when she tried to intervene at the meal, when she tried to stop Clara from speaking.

When she tried to stop Clara from speaking.

And why? Because somewhere, she knew. Not this – not the history of these shells, or this ship – but *something*: a shadow, reaching forward in time. She wants to steady herself against the desk, but the mahogany is itself traitorous, she knows – implicating her further in tangled webs of suffering. What was it Clara said? *Mahogany desks and billiard tables and pineapples* . . . it is as though, since yesterday, everything that was solid is liquefying, shape-shifting, everything is in the process of becoming something else.

Who is she, then, that she did not look further, dig further?

She could say: *It was a different time.*

She could say with her hand laid firmly on her heart: *I care for the future. I have never been a person much concerned with the past.*

She pushes herself to her feet, goes over to the French doors, and opens them onto the terrace. The morning is warm, remark-ably so – warmer even than yesterday. She steps out onto the sunlit park, away from the shade of the colonnade. Ahead of her the hills look more blue than green this morning – the rise of the ridges etched clearly against the sky. The lake, too, is blue, and closer in, above the ragged outlines of thorn bushes, swallows dip and rise in the insect-thick air. Life – everywhere she looks. She stands, drenched in the simple, blunt fact of her love for it all: this land, this life, all around her; life which knows nothing of history, which wants only to have the chance to thrive.

And if she had discovered what Clara has discovered, if she had put in the hours of diligent research in libraries, and found what Clara has found, then what would have followed from that? She would likely never have moved back here, would have turned away, let life take her elsewhere, away from this land – her land. And if she had never moved back here, then what? The estate would have stayed as it was, managed for game, for shooting parties, the conifers would have stayed standing, the feed hoppers would have remained in place. The pheasants would have fattened, and the men would have come down from London and from Gatwick in their rented Land Rovers and their rented clothes and they would have paid their money to shoot their birds and the rapeseed would have grown and the river would have stagnated and sickened, and there would be no little grebe or kingfisher. No spotted flycatchers in the wisteria. No water voles. No lampreys. No nightingale. And her father would have died, as men must, and the financial picture would have been such that they would have had to sell. All of it. To what then? A hotel?

No.

No.

She pulls her phone from her pocket, calls Luca, who answers immediately and agrees to meet her in the library. Then she goes back inside, eyes adjusting to the dimness, and sits at the desk. She takes out paper, places it over the leather where her daughter carved her missive, and begins to make notes. When the knock comes at the door, she lifts her head. 'Luca,' she says, standing to welcome him, 'thanks for coming.'

'It's fine,' he says. 'I'm heading out in a minute, but I always have time for you, Fran.'

'I wanted to apologize,' she says. 'For yesterday. The way I was. I was tired and stressed, and terribly worried; Rowan had been missing for a long time. But I shouldn't have behaved like that.'

'It's alright,' he says. 'There was a lot going on for you, I get that. I tried several times to persuade Rowan to come out, to come home. But she was . . . reluctant. So I stayed with her. I thought it was best.'

She nods. 'Thank you,' she says. 'I'm glad then, that she had company.'

'How are you doing today?' says Luca.

'I'm feeling . . . like I need to take stock.'

'Of course. You all need time as a family. Don't worry.' He holds up his hands, a small smile. 'I'm out of here.'

'Although . . . before you do go, Luca. I just want to make sure you know that, as far as I am concerned, we are still in conversation. Nothing has been stopped here – just paused. I'd love to put in a time to circle back to this when the dust has settled a little, when I have had a chance to check in with Simon. What do you say?'

'I'm really sorry, Frannie,' he says, 'but I'm afraid I can't commit to this collaboration. When this comes out, the brand will be tainted, I'm afraid.'

'The brand?'

'The Albion Project. There are a lot of eyes on me and on this fund. I can't afford a misstep.'

'A *misstep*?'

'I can't afford to be seen to invest in anything that looks like trouble. The external optics would not be good.'

'Listen,' she says. 'I'm not saying anything about the bigger picture here. I don't think I'm qualified to say anything, yet. We need to take time, as I said, to reflect. To respond. But as far as the future of the estate is concerned, we can contain this – while we take some time to process. There are only a very few people who know about this right now. Simon will be back tomorrow. Let's just wait until then. Speak then.'

Luca's face is calm, gentle even. 'I'm a little surprised you'd take that stance, Frannie.'

'I'm not taking any stance, Luca,' she says. 'I'm just asking you to wait before making any big decisions about investment while we all take stock.'

'I'm afraid that's just not going to be possible.'

'And why not?'

'I have to pull out. It's the moral thing to do.'

'Seriously?'

'Seriously, yes.'

'I cannot believe you, of all people, are lecturing me on morality.'

'I'm not lecturing you, Frannie, I'm letting you in on my reaction. How you choose to react is your business. Although . . . a word to the wise . . .'

'And what's that?'

'The history of the transatlantic slave trade is no longer a personal matter.'

'Jesus Christ.' She shakes her head.

'I'm sorry, Frannie, these are the times we're in.'

'Well thank you, Luca, for pointing out the blindingly obvious. Let me be clear, once again: I'm not saying I'm not going to address this horror. All I'm asking for is a little time, the day after I bury my father, to take stock.'

'Of course,' he says. 'And I hope you don't think I'm judging you. I'm just giving you my counsel. For what it's worth.'

'I understand. Thank you.'

He holds up his hands. 'I didn't mean to trigger you, I'm sorry.'

'You didn't *trigger* me,' she says. 'Don't worry, Luca. I think we're done here, don't you?'

But he doesn't move. 'Fran,' he says. He takes a step towards her, a shift in him she cannot read. 'How's Rowan?'

'Rowan's fine. She's with Grace, watching a film.'

'I'd like to see her, before I go. If possible. Might that be possible, do you think?'

The hairs lift on her arms. 'Why would you want to see my daughter before you go?'

'Because I enjoyed meeting her this weekend. Very much. She's a great kid. And I'd like to see her again . . . If you agree.'

'Now, why would I agree to that?'

'C'mon,' he says. 'Really? It was here, Fran . . . this desk. It was right here. Did you think I'd forgotten? Did you think I can't do simple maths?'

She presses her hands down. The torn and carved leather.

'Fathers have rights,' he says.

'That may be so,' she says, lifting her eyes and meeting his gaze, 'but you have no rights, Luca, because you're not her father.'

'Well, I think I am. In fact, I'm convinced of it. And if you won't acknowledge it, then I'd like to find out properly. I'd like to do a test. Have it confirmed.'

'No. Never.'

'I can help you,' he says, his voice low.

'Help me? How??'

'I can see how you're struggling. Look at you. You're ragged.'

'I'm not ragged, and I'm not struggling.'

'She doesn't seem happy, Frannie.'

'Don't –'

'I would say, in fact, that Rowan seems troubled . . . especially in her relationship with you.'

'Don't you *dare* –'

'I was with her for several hours yesterday.'

'Several *hours*?' Frannie starts to laugh. 'You're kidding me, right?'

'I heard a lot in that time.'

'Forgive me – sorry, Luca – you spent several hours with my daughter and now you're an expert on her inner life?'

'*Our* daughter. And – I'm sorry. I can see what a good mother you are. But I can also see that you're ragged, and exhausted, and she's . . . wonderful. And she's my *daughter*, Frannie.' His eyes are unguarded, an expression there she has never seen before. 'I'm offering to help. If you acknowledge me, if you let me into her life, I can help.'

'Help how?'

'Well, first things first. What do you need? What does the estate need to feel secure? So you can feel secure? What do you need to lose the stress? Tell me . . . Three million? Five? An anonymous donation. No one would ever have to know.'

'Are you serious? After everything you've just told me?'

'There are ways,' he says, softly. 'The key is to be discreet. The key is always to be discreet.'

'You're venal, Luca, and however you dress it up, that will never change.'

'Venal how? Because I make money? Come on. Seriously? Please don't take the moral high ground, Frannie. I think you'll find it's no longer available. Besides – if you think so little of me, why did you let me in, that night? What was it you wanted of me?'

She is silent. Her body flaring. 'Leave,' she says.

'Please,' he says, and his tone is coaxing, pleading almost. 'Let me into Rowan's life.'

'Just – leave,' she says.

'Okay,' says Luca. He takes a breath. 'But – just be sure. Okay? I want you to be very sure what you are saying no to.'

'And I would like you to be very, very sure that you're not welcome here. Discreet or not, I don't want your money. I want you to leave my home. Right now.'

He reaches into his wallet and puts a card down onto the desk between them. 'That's my number. And beneath it is the number of my lawyer. You can call either of us anytime. And if I don't hear from you, I'll be in touch.'

He goes. Shuts the door quietly. She stays standing at the desk. In the distance she hears car tyres on gravel.

And then, from far away, she feels a great wave travelling towards her, a wave which is silent for now, but which is gathering power, gathering certainty, gathering speed.

She will lose the estate.

Her first act as inheritor. They will come and take it from her. Cut up the land into little pieces. Erect fences and barbed wire. Sell off the farm machinery, auction the furniture, the shame of her failure and bankruptcy laid out on the parkland for everyone to see.

She moves away from the desk and walks over to the doors that lead to the terrace, goes back outside, where the day is well advanced and the sun is high.

It is hot. And this day, that minutes ago was so beautiful, has curdled: she knows that this morning, for all its beauty, is too warm. And she feels the clench in her jaw; the old, deep, physical dread, chest tightening, the wave travelling faster, faster. She takes the path up the hill, walking as quickly as she is able, then half running, half stumbling, pulling air into her body, up towards the sentinel oak, heading towards its outline on the ridge, its old bole, its shrunken crown, and when she reaches the tree, she reaches out and puts her hands to it.

Tell me, she thinks.

Speak to me. Please. What is being asked of me now?

But she hears nothing back. And she feels only fear now, only the low deep tug of dread. The terror of uncharted territory. Fear for Rowan, who she has taught to love and trust this land, to love and name the creatures here – this place of oaks and water, of newts and slow-worms and nightingales. She wanted to make her daughter safe, the oldest want in the book – wished for her to grow rooted in love of place, straight and true and wild.

And what will Rowan look upon when – if – she reaches the age that Frannie is now? When – if – she stands here, by this oak, by this tree?

Her father got out at the right time. His, the generation that inherited the earth, whether they were the owners of a thousand acres or not. Whereas she has been chosen, hers chosen to be the generation that watches everything break down: a future which is accelerating, a fabric which is unravelling, fast, faster than any models can keep pace with. And the temperatures will rise and rise. Unloosed. And time will whip and spit like an angry snake, no longer circular, no longer the ouroboros, no longer the great unchanging rhythm of the seasons, of renewal and return, only an acceleration, a hastening, an unravelling, a great terrible linear unravelling until the end times have come.

Her daughter will not shelter in the cool green shade of oaks but stand in a land of fire beneath an orange-red sky. And she herself has been like the boy in that story, standing with her thumb in the dam. The future is here – she cannot stand in its way, it has found her, sought her out. Dragged her down, just as it will find and fell them all. All of the accounts are being settled now. All the debts called in. And her daughter will have her ringside seat for the end times – it was booked as soon as she was born.

It is hard to breathe – there is this pain in her heart, this terrible pain, and she is struggling for breath. She plucks at her throat, at her chest. Perhaps she is dying. Perhaps this is what dying feels like: perhaps this is the day she dies.

She kneels on the ground and grinds her forehead into the rough bark of the oak, and then she does it again, and again, because she wants to match this pain inside her – she wants to break her skin. She slides her forehead against its gnarled and knotted and ancient wood, then she puts her hands on its roots and scrapes them too, and as she does so she makes a sound, a deep animal sound.

She hears more sounds, and knows they are hers, but knows

they are beyond her. At a certain point she understands she is weeping, and that this, finally, is grief.

◆

Clara packs her small bag, her clothes, laptop, phone – still out of battery.

No one came to check on her last night; no knock at her door, no food offered. No connection sought. She stayed in her room, did not even go out to use the bathroom – peeing in the sink. Frightened of what, exactly, she could not say. The vengeful spirits of the house?

At a certain point she heard a commotion – there were voices calling for Rowan, and then she herself grew afraid, until she saw the little girl had been found safe. She watched the procession through her window: Frannie, Rowan, Luca, Isabella, Isabella's husband, returning to the house; Rowan weeping, clearly distressed.

She remembered Rowan's face – the way the little girl was listening so fiercely while she spoke. She knows she brought horror to her door and she is not proud of that. Why did she do it then? Why speak in that way in front of them all? Was it her own ego's need for the centre of the stage? But she had tried, hadn't she, in the library, to speak privately to Frannie? And she had been dismissed.

She finally slept when the sky was growing light. She has no idea how long she slept for – four hours? Five? The sun is high now and she is weak with hunger and fatigue, and a frayed, unfinished feeling. She does not know what she imagined but she knows she did not wish for it to end like this – in discord and pain. What did she hope for? Some sort of dialogue? Some sort of reckoning, of settling? She sees now how insane that was.

And if she had not spoken. If she had let them sit there, beneath the tree, in peace and plenty, would that have been better, after all?

What would her mother say?

Was it worth it, honey? Are you sure?

She puts the last of her things into her backpack, clips it tight.

Her flight is not until the next morning, but she will find somewhere in the village to stay tonight. All she wants is to get the hell out, but she knows she needs to at least find Frannie before she leaves. She shoulders her bag, opens the door to the landing, walks past bedrooms whose beds have been stripped of their coverings, their occupants gone – late last night perhaps, or early this morning. One door is shut, the sounds of a movie coming from behind it – Rowan's room, she guesses. Part of her wants to knock, to say something to the little girl. But what can she possibly say?

She hesitates – then moves on, heading downstairs.

The kitchen is deserted. Someone has been here and cleaned – yesterday's plates stacked neatly on the table; the tablecloth folded beside them. She fills her water bottle at the tap and thinks of yesterday's food – that beautiful food – there must be leftovers here, in the fridge, in cupboards, but hungry as she is she knows she could not stomach it. She'll find something to eat elsewhere.

She goes back out to the corridor, into the hall, moves to the library, pushes open the door slightly. The room is dark; Oliver Brooke and his family are dark. The door to the terrace is open, but Frannie and the rest of the family seem to have gone to ground. Should she leave a note then? On the desk?

No.

She will write to Frannie when she is home. When she has slept. When she can think clearly again. She steps back into the hall, pulls the library door closed.

She heads down the back corridor, steps outside into the sunshine, meets no one as she walks across the gravel car park, taking the high track so she can't be seen by the house. She stops and shades her eyes, wondering where to go. If she heads down the treeline, staying close to the trees, she can get to the stream – that should take her through the wood, to the outer road below. She can either walk back into the village from there, call a cab, or keep walking. Hitch a ride.

So she dips down, leaving the path, walking through thorn-scrub and grasses until she reaches the ancient oak tree, but as she rounds its trunk, she sees someone lying face down on the ground. It is Frannie, in a twisted posture, her back moving in great shuddering breaths.

Clara imagines that whatever has occurred, or is occurring, Frannie will not want to be witnessed in her pain, but perhaps she is injured, perhaps she needs help – and so she hovers, uncertain what to do, until Frannie turns onto her back and groans. Her hands are pulpy. She has cut her forehead; a large ugly gash and the gash is bleeding. 'Shit,' says Clara. 'What happened?' She takes a step closer. 'Can I help?'

Frannie slides herself so she is sitting with her back against the trunk of the tree.

'You should get that seen to,' says Clara. 'Cleaned up. I think you need a bandage. I can go back to the house if you like?'

Frannie looks down at her gouged palms as though they are not her own.

'Do you want water? Here.' Clara puts her backpack on the ground and brings out her bottle. 'I can pour it if you like?'

Mutely, Frannie puts out her hands and Clara kneels beside her, pouring water over them, cleaning them as best she can, before handing her the bottle. Frannie drinks, then winces. 'Thank you,' she says, handing the bottle back, and her voice when she speaks is scraped and raw.

'What happened to you, Frannie? How did you hurt yourself?'

'I'm going to lose the estate,' says Frannie, her eyes coming to rest on Clara's.

'I don't understand. Why?'

'In part because of your speech yesterday.'

'What? That doesn't make any sense.'

'We were hollow inside,' Frannie says, in that hoarse, ragged voice. 'You just came and kicked us over.'

'But . . . I don't understand. I had no idea things were so precarious. It was never my intention to destroy anything here.'

'What was your intention then?'

'I –' Clara shakes her head. 'At first, to share what I'd found, over the last three weeks, and my implication with it. But then, I guess . . . when I found Rowan with the shells . . . with the box. With the painting of the ship . . .'

'When you found those, what?'

'Then I knew I had to speak.'

Frannie moves stiffly, bringing her injured hands palm up on her knees.

'I tried to speak to you, Frannie,' says Clara. 'Do you remember? That first evening in the library? I tried to tell you what I'd found.'

Frannie looks at her for a long moment, then she nods slowly. 'I do remember,' she says. 'And you did. And I know I didn't have time to listen. And now I have listened. And I am listening, but I want to say this . . . because if I don't, then I will regret it. I want to tell you, with all of my heart, that whatever horrors Oliver Brooke may have been responsible for, I can think of no better use for a thousand acres of land than the use to which I am putting it. Have chosen to put it for the last ten years. I will lay my life on the line for that truth.'

Clara goes to speak, but Frannie holds up her hands to stop her and her hands are shaking. 'No,' she says. 'Please, just – hear me out. Do you know how out of time we are? How *utterly* fucked we are as a species? Everything, every *single thing* I have done has been for the future. For the generations to come. To try to mitigate the disaster that's coming for them. That they have had no part in creating.'

Clara can feel Frannie's anger – a lit torch, flaring in the air between them.

'My fealty is to the living world, to all of this.' Frannie raises her head towards the land laid out before her. 'Surely our human dramas have taken the stage long enough?'

'Long enough?' says Clara in a low voice. 'Really, Frannie? You think we have spent long enough talking about land like this and slavery? Land like this and enclosure? What about the villagers who were displaced to make way for these acres? What about their stories?'

'What would you do, Clara? If you were me? Chop it up? Find out who the descendants of those displaced villagers are – go up to the Green Man at closing time and give everyone three acres and a cow?'

'There are better ways.'

'Name them. Name them and I will consider them.'

'Do you know what, Frannie?' says Clara, rising from the ground. 'It's not my job to name those ways. Or not my job alone. All I know is this: they want to be a part of the story. Those people who were sold on the docks; they would have wanted their bodies and their souls and their hearts and their dreams for their children to be a part of the story of this place. This isn't about blame, Frannie. Or shame. It's about acknowledgement. It's about story.'

'There are no stories at the end of the world.'

'Really? I'm not sure that's true. I think people have told stories of the ending of worlds from the beginning of time. I think people will continue to tell stories about the ending of worlds and the beginnings of new ones . . .'

And she is furious, now, finally, with this woman, with her obstinacy, her willing blindness – even this blood, these injuries feel performative.

'You speak about the end of the world, Frannie, but *whose world*? Yours? Rowan's? Whose worlds had to end to build this? To create all of this beauty? To make it all *yours*? It's all connected – can't you see? Those children, sold on those docks by Oliver Brooke. The carbon in the air. Until you look at those children, you can't face the future. That's all I know.

'I want to tell you this,' Clara says, 'because I respect you, and because I think you're a good person, but . . . Frannie, you're not the centre of this story, however it might feel right now. This is not about you – or about what you may or may not have to give up. We're all going to have to relinquish a hell of a lot if we're going to fit together into a future where we can thrive. And maybe we don't get to decide what those things are. And maybe we don't get to decide the timelines.'

She reaches for her backpack, shoulders it. 'I'm going to go now,' she says. 'And I wish you well.' She turns to go, then hesitates – turns back. 'You know, if you ever want to talk to me, about what's next – I'm here for it.'

Clara turns away from Frannie, from where she leans, slumped against the oak, and walks along the treeline. Her pace quickens, and she is walking fast, full now only of the desire to get away. As she crosses the stream she dips beneath an old battered wooden sign, the faded outlines of cartoon characters painted on it. *Teddy Bears' Picnic* it says, in just-decipherable letters. After a while of following the water, she arrives at a clearing in the wood. In the centre of the clearing is a fire, and by the fire sits a man, the man who pulled the coffin yesterday. Behind him is a huge old school bus. Rounded front. Beautiful lines. He is busy with something in the fire, but when he hears her, he looks up and raises a hand in greeting.

'Hey,' she says.

He stands with difficulty, manoeuvring himself upright with his stick. 'I don't think we've been properly introduced,' he says, coming towards her. 'I'm Ned.'

She shifts her backpack on her back. 'Clara.'

His eyes are gentle as he extends his hand. His palm is callused and rough. 'How are you doing today, Clara?'

'I'm leaving,' she says. 'Just heading to the road. Going to find somewhere to stay for the night. My flight's tomorrow morning.'

'Right. Well. Can I offer you a cuppa before you go?'

'A cuppa?'

'Tea.' He smiles. 'Can I offer you a cup of tea?'

'Oh, yeah. Right.' She shifts her weight. 'I mean. Okay. Thank you. Have you got coffee though?'

'Sure I do. Have a seat.'

She looks around. A person lies asleep on the sofa, a heavy blanket laid over him. Milo.

'Don't worry about him,' says Ned, following her gaze. 'He won't wake for a while.'

She takes her bag off her back.

'Here.' Ned gestures to a wooden stump close to the fire, roughly carved. 'Have this one. I'll get the coffee going.' As she sits, he makes his way over to a lean-to, beneath which is a wooden sideboard whose shelves are filled with glass bottles and jars.

'How did you hurt your leg?' she says, as he spoons coffee into an old metal contraption.

'Quad bike,' he says. 'Last year.'

'That looks pretty bad.'

'Bad enough.'

He comes towards the fire, where he places the coffee maker onto a grill plate, which is slung beneath a battered tripod. Then he goes back to the lean-to, gets two mugs and a tin of milk, and places them on a small table beside him. He draws up a camping chair. 'Do you know where you're heading then?'

'Anywhere. In the village? Nearer to Gatwick? Are there any Airbnbs close by? There must be, right?'

'I imagine so. I wouldn't be the one to know, though, not really.'

'My phone's dead, so I can't check. Oh,' she says. 'Do you have a charger? I left mine on the plane.'

'Of course. Hand it over.'

She unzips her bag and brings out her phone. 'You could just tell me where it is, then you don't have to get up.'

'Sure.' He gestures towards the bus with his hand. 'It's by the bed. Little solar thing: just plug in your phone on the USB.'

She gets to her feet and crosses the glade to the bus, climbs the three steps and goes inside: a neatly made bed covered with an embroidered bedspread, a bookshelf filled with books, their spines creased with reading, and on the bedside table, a charger. All along the back of the bus are some pretty healthy-looking plants. The whole place is infused with the heady aroma of woodsmoke and coffee grounds and dope. She plugs in her phone, waits while it comes to life, then makes her way back outside into the mellow afternoon light. 'It'll take about forty minutes,' she says. 'For the phone to charge.'

'I've got all the time in the world,' he says. 'Are you hungry? I've got some potatoes cooking in the fire. They'll be ready soon. You can break bread with me. Or eat a baked potato, at least.'

'I don't know,' she says, taking her seat again. 'Maybe.'

'Well, first things first,' he says. 'I'm going to have a little smoke with my coffee. You're welcome to join me.' He reaches for a tray with a tin of tobacco and starts to assemble a joint. 'Do you smoke?'

'I vape weed.' She shrugs. 'Sometimes.'

'You kids,' he says, shaking his head. 'With all your vaping.'

'I don't vape nicotine. It's bullshit. But I do vape weed.'

'I can make this without tobacco if you like.'

'I'm fine, thanks. You go for it.'

Over on the hotplate the coffee begins to boil and spit.

'Can I get that?' says Clara.

'Sure. All the necessaries are there.' He nods to the table. 'Just make sure you use the glove for the coffee maker. The handle gets hot.'

She goes to the fire. Using the big, blackened glove, she lifts the pot over to the table and pours thick black coffee into the mugs.

'I'll have a splash of milk in mine,' he says.

'Is this the milk?' She lifts a small, red-lettered tin.

'That's the one. You should try it,' he says. 'Condensed milk. It's about the most English thing you can get.'

She pours milk from the tin, hands him his mug. 'It's okay,' she says. 'I take it black.' She walks back to her seat with her coffee. 'It's a cool set-up you've got.'

'Thank you.'

'How long have you been here for?'

'Fifty years, give or take.'

'That's a long time.'

'Long enough.' He smiles.

'So, there was a big party here, right? Back in the day?' She sips her coffee. It is viciously strong and extremely hot.

'The biggest,' he says. 'Well, at least, the best.'

'I saw the sign,' she says. 'The Teddy Bears' Picnic, right?'

'Right.'

'And you were here for it?'

'Oh yes, I was here for it all.'

'What was it like?'

'The Teddy Bears' Picnic?' He grins. 'It was fucking magic,' he says. 'Tell you what. Why don't we have a bit of music?'

She shrugs. 'Sure.'

'Why don't you choose?'

'My phone's not charged yet.'

'We don't listen to phones down here,' he tuts. 'We listen to vinyl. Go ahead and have a look. Choose something.'

'Where are your records then?'

'Over there.' He gestures with a tilt of his head to where several large black flight cases stand beneath the lean-to. 'There's quite a few,' he says. 'But they're alphabetical.'

She goes over to the lean-to, where she lifts the lid of the first flight case. 'Wow.' There must be several thousand records there.

He chuckles. 'Go on, see what you can find.'

She runs her fingers along them, flicks through and through and through, her mind blank for a long while. Eventually she sees a sleeve she recognizes, lifts it: hot pink. An oil sketch of a woman's upturned face. 'Where's your deck?' she says.

'Just behind you.'

She finds the deck on a specially built and fitted shelf, lifts the lid, puts the vinyl on the turntable, hovers the needle, lets it fall.

> *Lilac wine . . .*
> *Put my heart in its recipe . . .*

'Beautiful,' says Ned. 'Crank it up.'

She goes to the stereo and turns the huge volume dial. Nina's voice fills the wood.

'My mom loved Nina Simone,' she says, as she comes back to her seat. 'She had this album on vinyl too. I think it was a gift from my dad. He had written his name on the sleeve.'

'Who was your dad then?'

'He was a photographer,' she says, 'from the island of St Kitts. I didn't know him. He died at thirty-three.'

'I'm very sorry to hear that. What was his name?'

Clara hesitates. 'Allan,' she says. 'Allan Nelson.'

It feels good, she thinks, to speak his name out loud.

'That's a name to conjure with,' says Ned. 'Nelson.'

'Yeah,' she says.

'That your name too?'

'Yeah,' she says. 'Clara Nelson.'

Ned nods. 'You seen his column then? Nelson? In Trafalgar Square?'

'No,' says Clara. 'But I know there's a black soldier on it. On the carving at the bottom.'

'Is there now? I did not know that.'

'He spent time in St Kitts – Nelson. He married a woman from Nevis. I guess somewhere along the line we got close to that story.' She takes another sip of her coffee. 'For the longest time I felt like in my name was everything painful about empire – my father, descended from enslaved people, carrying this name that didn't speak to his ancestry at all – but now I am proud of it. I'm proud of my father and I'm proud of my name.'

Ned nods. 'So you should be. That was quite the speech yesterday . . . How are you faring? In its wake?'

'I mean,' she gives a shrug, 'I've been better. I just saw Frannie.'

'And?'

'And . . . she's pretty broken. She's hurt herself quite badly.'

'Really?' He looks troubled. 'You think she needs help?'

'Maybe. I tried to offer but she wouldn't accept.'

Ned nods. 'That sounds like Frannie . . . Well, it'll take some time, I reckon,' he says, 'for her to come around.'

'You think she'll ever come around?'

'Oh, I imagine so. In her way.'

She feels the anger rise in her again. 'Don't you think we've all been waiting long enough for people like her to come around? I mean – I'm tired of waiting, and I'm twenty-four. Surely you're tired? Surely people like you have been waiting for people like them to come around for millennia?'

'That's true enough,' he says, with a half-grin. 'Do you know,' he says, 'I've never really minded waiting for things.'

'No?'

'But you know. That's just me. I think everything has its time.'

'Sure. Nice. Well, you just sit here in your wood with your dope and your records and wait for the long arc of history to bend towards justice.'

'I didn't say justice.'

'What then?'

'It's not a word. It's a feeling.'

'Feelings aren't going to turn this ship around.'

He finishes rolling the spliff and lights up. 'So what do you want then?' He looks up at her, regards her through the smoke. 'Revolution? Heads on pikes? The world turned upside down?'

'Not the violence. But I wouldn't mind the world upside down . . . or inside out.'

'You're not going to go all Pol Pot on me? Year Zero?'

'No. Jesus. Of course not. But it's such a tired trope.'

'What is?'

'You invoke the worst excesses of a certain strain of a certain idea – like, maybe the idea that land shouldn't be in private ownership. And you use those excesses, those failed experiments, to justify the ongoing depredations of landowner capitalism.'

'Fair enough.'

'You know,' she sips her coffee, 'there's this quote. From James Connolly? Have you heard of him? He was one of the Irish martyrs from 1916?'

'Sure. I've heard of him,' He grins. 'My grandmother was Irish. She loved a bit of Republican ire.'

'Really? Okay, well, I saw it online the other day . . . and since I've been here, I can't stop thinking about it: it was like 1910 and George the Fifth was visiting Ireland, and Connolly wrote this article for a newspaper, and I guess everyone expected him to say, you know, no – he's not welcome. Bullshit. Fuck you, George. But actually he said, yeah sure, let him come – but then he said this other thing – *we will not blame him for the crimes of his ancestors if he relinquishes the royal rights of his ancestors; but as long as he claims their rights, by virtue of descent, then, by virtue of descent, he must shoulder the responsibility for their crimes.*'

Ned nods, listening.

'I mean,' says Clara. 'That's it. Right there. Isn't it? This family are here, still drawing to themselves all the privilege of these thousand acres. However complex, however precarious, however stressful that might be, Frannie is still claiming the rights of her ancestors – and so, it seems to me, she must shoulder the responsibility for their crimes.'

'That sounds about right,' says Ned softly. 'I'm not going to argue with that.'

'And me too, right?' she says. 'The part of me that has benefited from Oliver Brooke's money. The part of me that is implicated too. I want to be honest about that. I want to turn towards it. Understand it. Live my life in relationship to it somehow.'

'How are you going to do that then?'

'Well, coming here was a start. But you know. I fucked that up. So.'

He smiles, gets to his feet, leans in and pokes at the fire, where a log opens, spits embers. He places another on top, straightens up, leaning on his stick, staring into the flames. 'My ancestors were Irish,' he says to the fire. 'A hundred years after yours were being sent across the Atlantic in slave ships, mine were being packed in coffin boats. Forced thousands of miles from their villages, their homes. Millions of them too.'

'And aren't you angry about that?'

'Not really,' he says.

'Why not?'

'I'm seventy-six. Anger is fuel for the young, not the old.'

'Well, I'm angry. I'm fucking angry. And I'm not going to be ashamed of that.'

'Nor should you be.'

'Thank you. I don't need you to legitimize it either.'

He falls silent. 'I'm sorry.'

'It's okay. I just –' She shakes her head. 'Why are we still having to have this conversation?'

'What do you mean?'

'How are these lands still in the hands of the families who took them? Who stole them? Hundreds of years ago?'

He turns to her, regards her steadily, then: 'Tell you what, I think these fellas are ready.' He gestures to the potatoes in the fire. 'How about you get me some wild garlic and we can put it in the butter?'

'Wild garlic?'

'It's growing everywhere,' he says. 'Just a little way up the path. The green leaves with the little white flowers. If you get a handful of that and chop it up that would be lovely. You'll find a knife on the counter there.'

She stands, walks a little way away from the clearing until she can see it: great low clusters of long fleshy-green leaves topped by delicate white flowers. She bends to it and plucks a fistful, brings it to her nose and inhales, then she carries it back to the lean-to, where she finds a knife and chops it on the wooden board.

'That's the one,' he says, from the fire, where he is pulling potatoes from the embers with a long metal fork. 'Once you know what it is, you can do all sorts with it. Make a nice pesto. Lovely soup. Bring it over with some butter and a couple of plates. Knives and forks over there. Salt and pepper.'

She gathers the cutlery, finds the butter on the side, a bright yellow slab in a chipped dish, a couple of plates on the drying rack near the sink, brings them all over to where Ned waits. He unwraps a couple of potatoes for each plate, slices into their blackened skins, slathers their steaming insides, mushes the wild garlic into the rapidly melting butter, then loads each one with salt and pepper and passes her a plate.

They don't talk while they eat. She eats slowly and steadily, and she cannot remember ever tasting anything as good in her life.

When the food is finished, warm in her belly, she feels immediately tired, as though she could curl up, wrap herself in a blanket like Milo and sleep by the fire.

Ned gathers up his plate, comes for hers, takes them both back over to the lean-to, where he flips the record over to the other side.

'What's he doing down here?' says Clara, gesturing to Milo, as Ned comes back to the fire.

'He needed a break, I think, from the house. He was drunk. And he needed to sleep. He's always come here in times of need. They all have.'

'And how is that for you?'

'Well, they have let me live here for fifty years, rent-free. So, I've always seen it as the least I could do.'

'*Let* you?'

'Well . . . yes.'

'You know they displaced a village? The village that belonged with the church and the land. This would likely have been common land. He enclosed it. Oliver Brooke. There would have been hundreds of people living here.'

Ned sits again, settles himself in his chair. 'I know,' he says. 'I've felt them.'

'Who?'

'The villagers.'

She laughs. 'What do you mean?'

'Some nights,' he says, 'this would be when I was younger – when I'd walk more – I'd be down there where the old village was, on the other side of the river, late nights, or early mornings, when the light was flickering – and I'd catch a glimpse. I'd hear them. Especially down where the barn was. It does all sorts of funny things, the light over there.'

She leans forward, breath caught. Astonishingly, he appears to be telling the truth. 'And where is that?'

'What? The old village? On the other side of the church.'

'Where exactly?'

'Come out of the wood,' he says, 'and follow the river to the lake. When you come out at the lake you cross back over and you'll get to the church; go through the churchyard into the first field, there's a double-trunked ash tree, beneath it you can find some tumbled stones. The ground is flatter there. That was the barn, you can see it on the old parish maps. Philip used to have them, up at the house. Medieval. Or older. I'd go down there sometimes. It's a peaceful place. I'd like to think of the dancing they would have done in there: arm in arm. Flattening out the earth floor. And then, when I'd been going down there long enough, I'd start to hear them.'

'You're serious?'

'It's like tuning a radio,' he says, getting to his feet and going over to his workshop. 'Sometimes you get just the right frequency. These help.' He points to a mason jar on his shelves.

'What are those?'

'Mushrooms. Psilocybin. I used to take a fistful, but no more. Now just a couple. It's enough. The land gets inside you. Tunes your vision – your hearing. You can hear a lot with these fellas. Hear a lot without them too. But they can help.'

'Can I see?'

'Of course.'

He brings the jar over to where she sits, hands it to her. She opens the catch and the lid and peers in. Inside is a tangled heap of small, dried mushrooms, a slight golden sheen to their tips. A funky earthy smell. Not unpleasant. 'They grow all over here in the autumn,' he says.

'All over this land?'

'Yes, all over this land.'

She closes the jar, pushes it down on the ground beside her.

'He's planning on setting up a clinic,' he says, nodding towards Milo.

'What sort of a clinic?'

'Psilocybin.'

'Where?'

'Here.'

'What – right here? In this wood?'

'So I hear.'

'So where are you going to go?' she says.

'That's a good question,' he says. 'Where would you go if you were me?'

'Nowhere,' she says. 'This is perfect . . .' She takes in the soft afternoon light, Nina singing. The smoke rising in the air. 'I'm sorry,' she says, 'but I truly don't understand. How can you have him here, around your fire, to know he can just turn around and . . . throw you off – like that.' She clicks her fingers. 'How does that make you feel?'

'I don't know, is the honest answer. Lots of things make me feel lots of things.'

'Like what?'

'Right now?'

'Sure.'

'Well . . . right now . . . I feel touched,' he says, 'by the music. By the rest of this album. I'd forgotten how good it is. Forgotten how much I love Nina. Her voice. How much pain she can hold in that voice without it breaking. I feel the food in my belly. And I'm grateful for it. I feel the pain in my leg from the accident. How I have been holding the pain in my body. How that pain is a part of me now.

'I feel the beauty of those flowers over there – the hawthorn, the wood anemone. They don't tell you this, Clara, not when you're young, but it all becomes more beautiful, stranger and more mysterious and inviting, the older you get. You love the world more and more as you're getting ready to leave it.

'I feel there's disturbance in the wood – the alarm call of a blackbird which means there's a predator near. Maybe their eggs have gone. Stolen from their nests? Who knows? I'm feeling the sun on my skin. And the fire,' he says. 'Always the fire. The fire telling me where it wants feeding. Where it wants the log on next. Exactly where. It speaks to me so clearly. I'm feeling how grateful I am for its companionship. How it's kept me company for so many years. It's been my greatest friend, my confidant. The things I've told this fire.'

The vinyl crackles. A new song begins.

'Oh,' says Ned. 'This one. I'm feeling that I love this song.'

He closes his eyes, listening.

> *Love me, love me, love me, love me, say you do*
> *Let me fly away with you . . .*

She watches him, where he sits. He is somewhere else, somewhere deep and private that the music has taken him.

'I'm feeling that I need to be braver,' he says eventually, opening his eyes. 'That I'm going to be brave. And I'm feeling you: how brave I think you are.'

There's a stirring from the sofa. Milo groans, sits up. The music builds, reaches its crescendo and dies away.

'Fuuuuck,' he says.

Ned chuckles. 'How're you doing, lad? You look like shit.'

'I feel like shit. Oh,' he says, as he sees Clara. 'Hey.' He lifts a rueful hand in her direction.

'Hey,' she says.

Ned gets to his feet, goes over to the lean-to, selects one of the jewel-bright bottles from the shelves, pours a long measure into a shot glass and brings it back out to the glade. 'Here,' says Ned to Milo. 'Drink this.'

Milo inches upwards, takes it, downs it. Winces and shivers. 'Fuck,' he says. 'That's rank.'

'It's your insides that are rank, not the herbs. How are you doing?'

'Ask me in an hour.'

'Me and Clara were just about to have another cuppa,' says Ned. 'Would you like one?'

Milo grimaces, shudders, shrugs.

'I'll take that as a yes.' Ned picks up the kettle, fills it at the water butt, brings it back over to the fire. 'Tell you what,' he says, when he has hung it on the tripod. 'I'm going to tell you both what we're going to do. I don't think Clara's been given the hospitality she deserves, what do you think? Clara, you can stay the night here in the bus. I've got clean sheets and everything.'

'Where will you sleep?'

'On the sofa.' He puts up his hand as she starts to protest. 'It's more than comfy enough. I like to sleep outside at this time of year. Don't know how many more dawns I'll see. They're precious. You'd be doing me a favour.'

'Thank you,' she says. And she feels it land in her body: relief – the possibility of rest.

'You're welcome,' he says. 'And now, before any of us do anything else, we're all going to have a couple of these fellas.' He reaches for his jar of mushrooms. 'Not too many. Nothing to scare the horses. Just a couple. Just to get this land inside us. What do you say?'

Day Five

It is night, or it is morning. It is the place between. Milo and Clara are walking, each wrapped in one of Ned's blankets. They have emerged from the wood, and are following the river path, single-file, Milo leading, and the moonlight is stronger here, now they are away from the thick canopy of trees.

'Hey,' says Clara.

'What's that?' Milo stops, turns around, his torchlight swings into her face.

'How would it be,' she says, putting her hand up to shield her eyes, 'if you switched off your torch?'

'If I switch off my torch, then we won't see a thing.'

'Yes we will. Look, the moon is almost full. And we're following the river, right?

'So?'

'So, we can navigate by the sound of the water. When we come to the lake then we take the bridge over to the island. And then the field's on the other side. And anyway, Ned gave us that bilberry tincture, didn't he? Isn't it meant to help us see better? In the dark?'

'I'm not sure,' he says. He feels the prickings of an old familiar fear.

I can't. I'm afraid of the dark.

'Just – switch it off,' she says. 'Please. C'mon. Let's see if we can see.'

'Okay,' he says. 'Hang on.' He switches off the torch. For a moment all is blackness, then shapes appear. The moon is high and casting great cloud shadows over the park. 'Oh,' he says, feeling his breath settle. 'Yeah. That's actually okay.'

'See? Let's go.'

They walk on in silence, only the sounds of the soles of their shoes against the dry path. He can feel his other senses start to rise, can smell the river in the darkness, a fresh green dankness. The sound of the water silvering over rocks. Whatever foul potion Ned gave him earlier has worked, his headache has quite gone, and he feels strangely okay. And it's good to walk like this, in the dark.

A sound ahead stops him short. Loud rasping breathing. 'What the fuck is that?' he says. His heart is pounding now, cortisol spiking in his blood.

'I don't know.' Clara comes up behind him. 'Don't you know?'

'How should I *know?*'

'This is your place. This is where you grew up.'

'It doesn't mean I know what the fuck that was.'

'Did you never come out at night before?'

'Sometimes. But if I did, then I went straight down to Ned's fire. And then back again. I never . . . roamed. Besides, there's a lot more wildlife around here nowadays.'

'It sounds like an animal.'

'No shit.'

'A big one . . . You said the cows were safe though, right?'

'That was in daylight.'

'What else have you got around here then?'

'God knows. Horses. Pigs. Roaming herbivores . . . dinosaurs. Who the hell knows . . . I'm not sure we should go this way.'

'Aren't we almost at the lake?'

'Yeah.'

'Come on then,' she says. 'I'll go first. If I get eaten, you can write my obituary.'

'Nice,' he says. 'I mean . . . I don't know you at all, but sure.'

'You can make it up.'

'Great. Go for it.'

They walk on, slowly, until ahead of him, Clara stops. 'Wait,' she whispers.

'What is it?'

'Something huge. I nearly fell over it.'

A large animal blocks the path in front. Its hindquarters towards them. The smell of dung and grass. He brings out his phone, switches his torch back on, hands it to her. 'It's a cow,' she says. 'It's asleep. Oh – wait. Oh my God . . . look. It's got its calf with it. Oh,' she whispers. 'Come and see.'

She angles the torchlight away from the animals, and he can see them, a mother and her baby, curled around each other in a patch of flattened grass. The calf's skin is matted, and the mother is licking it rhythmically.

'Oh,' breathes Clara. 'Oh wow.'

They stand there amid the sweet warm smell of the grass and a deeper smell, blood and urine and minerals and earth, and the animals and the peaceful sound of their breathing. 'How old do you reckon the baby is?' she says.

'I have no idea,' he says. 'Very, very new? I know Frannie was on the hunt for a female that was about to give birth. This must be her.'

'Wow. They're beautiful.'

'They are. But can we get past?'

'Yes, I think so. We can skirt this way.'

He follows her as she makes a wide circle around the mother and her calf and then switches off his torch again, handing him back the phone as they walk on. Soon they reach the lake.

'I recognize this,' says Clara, coming to stand at the edge of the jetty. 'I swam here, two days ago. It was beautiful.'

'Really?' He comes to stand beside her. Low moonlight lies on the water. The island in the middle of the lake is swathed in mist. There is the quiet suck and pull of the small waves beneath the planks below their feet. 'This place always unnerves me.'

'Why?'

'Because I came down here to kill myself once.'

She turns to him, her face close to his in the darkness, her eyes steady, waiting. 'When?'

'I was twenty-two.'

'Why?'

'I just couldn't imagine going on.'

'What happened?'

'I had done something which I felt was unforgivable. Which I felt I could never live in the wake of. So I came down here with some pills and a bottle of whisky. Classic.'

She doesn't say anything; she is listening, waiting for him to go on.

'I ate a few of the pills – not many, I was too drunk by then. I had planned to take the boat to the island, so that no one could find me, but I was so drunk that I collapsed here instead. Ned found me a few hours later. I was in a bit of a state, I think. All sorts of . . . leakage. He brought me to his fire, cleaned me, wrapped me up. He put me to bed in his bus and he looked after me for a few days.'

'Fuck.'

'Yeah.'

'I'm sorry, that sounds really rough.'

'Yeah. Well.' He pulls his blanket tighter around him. 'It's strange to think Philip was with your mother while that was going on.'

'I'm sorry,' she says again.

'It's not your fault. It was just – all the time I kept expecting him to appear. To come back from America to see if I was alright. But he never did.'

He can feel it again, bottomless – despair with no end.

'I'm so sorry,' she says.

'I spent years wondering why he didn't come home. It was only when I was a lot older that I understood that my mum hadn't told him anything about it.'

'Jesus. Why not?'

'He was sort of dead to her, I suppose, until he was resurrected. Until he came back.'

'Didn't she tell him then?'

'I suppose she must have. But a lot of damage had been done.'

'Wow. What a mess.'

'Yep. And after that, I guess I just sort of . . . doubled down on everything. Booze, drugs. Women. Work. All fairly predictable really. I mean, by one set of metrics I was doing okay. By another, I was totally fucked. Hated my job. Hated myself.'

He takes a deep breath. It tastes of night air and the tang of lake water.

'And then one day I woke up in a toilet somewhere near Liverpool Street station. I'd been on a bender. I was covered in my own shit. It was the second time in my life that had happened. So I called Luca and he told me to go to this clinic in Amsterdam.'

'And?'

'And it changed my life. I really thought I'd nailed it. Until I came home for the funeral and hung out with my family for the weekend.'

She laughs. So does he. It feels good.

'Yeah,' says Clara. 'I heard this thing once, this Buddhist teacher I like. She said, you know Ram Dass or someone said, if you ever get smug and think you're getting close to enlightenment, just go and spend some time with your family.'

'That's true enough.'

'You okay?' she says, after a while.

'Yeah,' he says. 'I'm good. Come on, what's the mission then?'

'We have to head up past the old church.'

They skirt the churchyard, and on the other side, they start to walk through the field. The grass is chest-high in places, damp with the dew. Clara is leading and he is happy to walk in her wake. 'Wait,' she says. 'Over there, can you see? The double-trunked tree?'

He follows where she points, and they move more quickly now, towards the tree, until they reach a place where the ground levels. 'Here!' she says. 'This must be it.'

A tumble of stones – all smooth and covered in lichen and mosses. Just a few, but enough to see that there was once a building here.

'So this is where it was then?' he says. 'The barn?'

'I think it must be.' She walks out into the middle of the flattened area and lies on the ground.

'What are you doing?' he calls.

'I want to lie down,' she says. 'I want to lie where they would have danced.'

'Isn't it damp?'

'A little. It's fine. The blanket's great.'

'Hang on.' He rewraps his blanket around him and comes to lie on the earth beside her. He can feel the chill of the ground beneath him, but he is warm here, close to Clara, wrapped in Ned's blanket in the dark.

'How long did he say a barn was here for?' she says.

'Eight hundred years. Since Domesday. Before that.'

'That's a lot of time . . . Eight hundred years is a lot of dancing.'

'Yeah,' he says. 'And incest. And domestic violence. And other violence. And plague. Black Death. Infant mortality. Bad teeth. But sure, dancing too . . .'

She gives a small low laugh – then, for a long time neither speaks, they just lie there, in a companiable quiet, with the stars and the satellites and the sky above.

'Are you feeling anything?' she says. 'From the mushrooms.'

'I don't know. A little, maybe. It's all rather phenomenal though, isn't it?'

'Yes. It is.'

'It's crazy,' he says, after a long while. 'To think there is all this magnificence happening every night. All of this . . . *sky*. And we're all just . . . huddled inside on our screens. Like – what would shift if we were living in relationship to all of this?'

'Yeah,' she says. 'You're right.'

'I think I've always been afraid of the dark,' he says.

'Really?'

'Yeah. When I was a kid, I'd have nightmares. And at school they didn't let us have nightlights. And that just made it worse. I still sleep with the light on.'

'That seems like a shame . . . The dark's not really dark, is it?' she says. 'When you look at it? When you give it a chance to be seen.'

'No,' he admits. 'It's not.'

'Do you think Ned meant it?' she says, propping herself up on her elbows. 'About hearing them. The dancers?'

'He doesn't lie,' says Milo. 'At least, not that I know. Sometimes he stretches the truth . . . but only so you can see starlight through it.'

'I like that,' she says, and he can hear the smile in her voice. 'Can I keep it?'

'My pleasure,' he says. 'Of course.'

They fall silent again then. 'What are you going to do?' she asks him.

'What? Next?'

'Yeah.'

'Who knows?' he says. 'But I don't envy Frannie, navigating the next stage. I don't know . . . there's a weird sort of liberation in it all; I meant what I said after the funeral, even if I was drunk. It was a relief to hear the truth of what you'd found out. Like someone had come along and lanced a wound that people had forgotten was there . . . had thought was some sort of . . . architectural feature . . . When actually it was a boneyard.'

'Well, thanks,' she says. 'Though I'm not sure your sister feels the same. I think Frannie thinks I'm one of the four horsemen.'

'What do you mean?'

'She basically implied that I was bringing apocalypse to her door by pointing to the foundations of Oliver Brooke's wealth.'

'Well. I mean. It was a strong moment. I mean, I loved it, as you know. But I have less skin in the game than Fran. And that's starting to seem like more of an advantage than it did a few days ago.'

And it's funny, he thinks, but he does feel lighter. It might be the mushrooms, or whatever tincture Ned gave him, or just lying here with someone in the dark and not feeling afraid, but he's feeling better than he has felt for a long, long time.

'Look,' he says, turning his head to Clara. 'The thing about Fran is . . . she's a very particular sort of person. She's at one and the same time totally brilliant and *insanely* controlling. She's more moral than anyone I've ever met – except, perhaps, for you. I think Frannie has more of a grasp on how colossally fucked humanity is than the vast majority of people I know. And because she understands it, because she stares it in the face, then she gets very overwhelmed. I mean – I massively shove my head in the sand. Distract myself with anything to hand, always have: dopamine dopamine dopamine, just – give me the dopamine and I'll be fine. Whereas Frannie has the courage to stare it all in the face. But Frannie's also suffering from the delusion that's she's going to have to fix it single-handed. So I think she feels pretty isolated. And pretty stressed. Which is clearly unsustainable in the long run. She can be flexible. But never straight away. This is going to be hard for her. She takes time to come round. But you know, she's going to have to.'

'You sound like you really know her.' Clara turns her face towards his. 'And love her.'

'Well, yes,' he says. 'I suppose I do. Thanks for pointing that out . . . So, what are you going to do, Clara? When you go back home? Finish your PhD? Be a doctor? Write a book?'

'I don't know,' she says.

'Seriously? You seem like someone who knows rather a lot about where they're headed.'

'Yeah, well. Not true. I'm failing my PhD. I'm way behind. I'm in trouble.'

'I'd never have guessed.'

'It started a while ago. The doubts about what I'm doing. I think it happens a lot, like so many people give up doctorates, right?'

'I'll have to take your word for it . . .'

She brings herself up to sitting, her hands clasped around her knees. 'And then I guess, the last three weeks – what I uncovered. All the truths about Oliver Brooke. I hadn't understood how entangled in the stories of this place I was. And then those shells. The weight of them. In every way, you know?'

He nods. 'I think I'm starting to, yes.'

'And then, I mean, I love my work, but I'm moving on rails that were laid out by others, not for me. And that's not about Philip or Joshua Reynolds or Oliver Brooke – it's about the fact that I can strive and achieve as I always have and slay the competition and . . . ascend. But at what cost? And where to? Towards a room where I am only ever going to be a guest? Like, what if I become a professor, and get tenure and still have that feeling? What if it never goes away? There's this part of me, a big part, a part that's getting bigger every day, that's wondering if perhaps the most radical thing I can do with my life is to just – give up. Do you know what I mean?'

'I'm not sure, no . . . Give up what?'

'Well, what would it mean to get out of the straightjacket of academic prose? To stop achieving the shit out of my life? Proving myself again and again? And then the other part of me goes – no. Fuck that. We need more black professors. We need black professors and PhDs *everywhere*. To give up would be a travesty. I *need* to excel. But what if excelling itself is part of the programme? Like – am I still in the master's house?'

'What do you mean?'

'You don't know the quote?'

339

'No.'

'*The master's tools will never dismantle the master's house.* Audre Lorde.'

'Oh,' he says. 'Gosh. Yes. I can see, I think. What you're getting at.'

'So I guess, the question I have is – how do I move towards my own liberation?' She grows quiet again, her gaze returning to the vastness of the sky above them.

'That's a very fucking good question,' says Milo. 'And one I am not unfamiliar with myself.'

'Please don't tell me I need to take a load of mushrooms to get there.'

'I wasn't going to. But isn't that exactly what we've done tonight?'

'Oh.' She gives a low laugh. 'Shit. I forgot all about that. Yeah. Well. Not loads, right?'

'Not loads,' he says softly. 'No.'

'Whatever else I know,' she says. 'I know that I am not free. Not yet. I mean, I decided a long time ago I wasn't going to be amenable to anyone; to smile and make myself agreeable. But after a time that starts to feel . . . constricted. Like. How could I be that would not in some way be a reaction to whiteness? And what does it mean to be free? It may be messy. And loud. It may be angry, and very fucking far from okay. And kind, and wild, and graceful as all hell. And it may not look like anything I can imagine right now. The future might not look like anything *any* of us can imagine right now.'

'Well . . .' says Milo. 'I wish you well.'

'You too.'

'Thank you.'

They lie there for a long time. And it is pleasant to lie like this, thinks Milo, with the sounds of the night all around them. With her warm body close by. Letting her words settle in him. After a while he props himself up on his elbow. 'Clara,' he says.

'Yeah?'

'Will you be my half-sister?'

She gives a low laugh. 'Your half-sister?'

'I mean it. I need to practise having platonic relationships with women. And I like you a lot. I mean. You're remarkable.'

'Sure,' she says. 'I reckon I could be up for that.'

'Will you be my pen pal?'

'Your pen pal?' She laughs. 'Yeah, okay. I've never had a pen pal.'

'That's because you're a poor orphaned child of the digital age.'

'Yeah, well. I'm definitely an orphan,' she says.

'Shit. I'm sorry, I didn't mean that. Sorry.'

'S'okay. Don't worry . . . I know. Hey – maybe I can send you postcards,' she says. 'From time to time. I always wanted to send a postcard.'

'Postcards would be great,' he says. 'I'd love that. Send me postcards of your path to liberation.'

'Nice,' she says. 'Okay. I will.'

She is smiling, he can hear it in her voice.

'Oh, hey. What time is it?' she says.

He brings out his phone. The screen is garish, ridiculous. 'It's four,' he says. 'What time is your flight?'

'Eleven. I guess I need to be at the airport by eight? Nine? I should go,' she says. 'If I'm walking to the village. I should try to find a cab or something.'

'Don't be silly,' he says. 'I'll take you. We can go back via Ned's, pick up your bag, and I can drive you. It's only half an hour at most. We'll have time for a cuppa before we go.'

'Really? Are you sure?'

'Totally. I'm not going to go back to the house. Not for a while. I've got my car keys on me, I'm ready to leave anyway. I'm going to head back to London, get some sleep . . . be somewhere my family are not for a while.'

'Okay. Great. Thank you. Oh . . . wait . . .' She sits up, leans forward, reaching into her backpack. 'I almost forgot. Ned gave me this.' She brings out the bottle of dandelion wine. 'He told me I should libate with it.'

'Excellent.' Milo brings himself up to sit beside her. 'I do love a bit of libating.'

'Does he always do that?' she asks. 'Ned, I mean?'

'Do what? Libate? I should imagine so . . .'

'No, I mean, just, give you a shot of something?'

'Oh yeah. For as long as I can remember. He has tinctures for everything. He will always ask you how you are and give you something for whatever ails you.'

'That's beautiful.'

'It is,' says Milo. 'I never stopped to consider it. It's just what he's always done.'

She turns to him, the bottle of wine between them. He can see her more clearly now, in the lifting light. 'You know,' she says, 'when I was younger, seventeen, I went to St Kitts. I went to find my father's family. Those that were left.'

'How was that?'

'It was . . . seismic. I went to the village my dad had been born in. Met my great-aunts, great-uncles – those that had stayed, those that had come back home.'

He waits for her to continue.

'I went with my uncle, and had drinks at this hotel, this old plantation hotel – Ottley's – and we sat in the garden, and it was all perfectly manicured, like . . . *perfect*. Like – how the hell could you get grass so perfect in the tropics?

'And around the house and behind the house there was this road, this perfect road. All these bricks, laid perfectly, no weeds anywhere, leading into the interior of the island.

'And we signed up for a tour of the rainforest behind the plantation, and I walked this road, and as I did, I thought about my ancestors, and how they might have built this very road, and if not this one, then one like it, brick by perfect brick, and then this perfect road stopped and you were just there, in the rainforest, and there were these huge ravines and the hugest trees – you would never have known, from the crust of the island, what it was like. It was so . . . sobering. Understanding what my ancestors had been asked to clear. How hard it would have been to clear that land to grow sugar on it. How brutal and how beautiful that rainforest was. And we had this guide, for the tour, this Rasta guy, and he showed us around, showed us all the plants the Caribs would have used . . . and all I could think was what it would have been to land there. To not know the plants, to not know your pharmacopoeia. Like. What would that be like? You have to feed yourselves. With what? It's like going back to the Stone Age. To be so far away from what you knew. To not know what you can eat. What's poisonous. What might kill you. What might cure.' She grows quiet again, then: 'They smuggled seeds, did you know that?'

'Who?'

'The enslaved. They smuggled seeds from their villages, from their homes, in their hair. In their children's hair. So they might plant them wherever they were going.'

'Fuck,' he says.

'I know.'

'I'm sorry,' he says.

She is silent for a long time, then she reaches for the bottle.

'Anyway. I have this wine. And I'm going to offer it to the earth now, and I'd love for you to join me.'

He sits up. She is kneeling now, beside him in the dark.

'There's this tradition,' she says, 'in the States, of Land Acknowledgement. Often, before an event, we will name the original inhabitants of that land. And it's a way of honouring those people who lived on that land and tended that land and loved that land before the settlers came. It's a way of honouring the complexity of our history. Speaking it out loud.'

'Okayyyy. Is that what we're going to do?'

'Yes.'

'Go on then. You go first.'

'Okay. So.' She takes a breath, 'My name is Clara Nelson. My ancestors are the Nelsons of St Kitts on my father's side, and on my mother's side I have Irish, Russian and German blood. And I'm here to offer this dandelion wine to you.' She turns to him. 'Wait – who are the people who would have lived here? On this land? Did it have a name? The village that was moved to make room for this park?'

He winces. 'I am afraid to say I don't know.'

'Well, maybe you should find out. There will be parish registers. You can look in the graveyard, you could find some names.'

'I guess I could.'

'I think you should. Then maybe one day you can come out here and speak those names . . . Okay, go on,' she says, handing him the bottle, 'your turn.'

'Seriously?' he says.

'Do your best. Just – try.'

'Okay.' He takes a big breath – lets it out. 'My name is Milo Ignatius Brooke . . .' He stops. 'I feel silly.'

'Sure you do. You gotta ride it. Go on . . .'

'My ancestors have lived here for seven generations. And I want to – apologize.' He looks towards her. 'What am I even saying here?'

'Go on. You're doing great.'

'I want to apologize for the moving of your village. This place where you lived, and ate, and worked, and played and . . . danced. I'm sorry for what was done to you, for what my ancestor did.'

It is getting easier to speak.

'Your ancestors lived here before mine,' he says, 'for hundreds and hundreds of years before mine. And what my ancestor did was wrong. And I'm sorry. And . . . this is for you.' He pours a little of the wine on the ground, then hands the bottle back to Clara.

'How do you feel?' she says.

'Good, you know. Actually . . . that felt pretty good.'

She gets to her feet, begins to pour the rest of the wine out onto the ground, moving in a long, slow circle. 'For you,' she says. 'For you all.'

'What are you doing?'

'Come on,' she says, coming over to him, holding out her hand for him to take. He stands up, comes to join her in the middle of the circle of wine.

'You're crazy,' he says.

'Am I?' She turns to him, grinning in the moonlight.

❧

When Rowan wakes, the first thing that she notices is the sun, which is already bold and bright at the window. The second thing is that her mum is in bed beside her. She is lying on her back and sort of snoring: her mother is asleep.

Rowan stares down at Frannie, astonished. Her face looks like someone has taken the stuffing out of it. Her forehead has a bandage over it where she hurt it yesterday, and her hands are bandaged too, but the most extraordinary thing of all, she thinks, is that she has never, ever, as far as she can remember, seen her mother asleep.

She wonders if she should wake her, because surely she will be missing something important by sleeping? Something must not have worked properly, like her alarm or her phone or something, and any minute now she will probably wake up and be cross that Rowan didn't wake her sooner and rush about and shout and maybe swear.

And it must be time to get ready for school – from the look of the light they might already be late. So, should she be getting herself dressed? Her mother usually lays her uniform out for her on a chair at the end of the bed, but there is nothing there this morning, only the clothes they were wearing yesterday in an untidy heap.

But then she thinks – what if her mum *needs* to sleep? After hurting herself, and after the funeral, and after everything else that has happened?

So, instead of waking her, Rowan slides back down under the covers where she reaches out a foot, and her foot touches her mum's calf. And Frannie stirs slightly, but still, she does not wake.

It is warm beneath the blankets. It smells of her and her mum – a warm smell, like straw. It is comforting, like being an animal in a den.

After a long while of lying like this, Rowan can feel her mum stirring, can feel that part of her which is a long way away, or that is far far underwater, slowly start to come to the surface. Rowan watches, fascinated, as Frannie rises into herself, until she opens her eyes and blinks. 'Oh,' she says. 'Hello, Ro. Morning.'

'Hello,' says Rowan. 'You were asleep.'

'Yes,' says Frannie. 'I was.' She reaches out a hand to touch Rowan, but the hand is bandaged. 'Ow,' she says.

'You hurt yourself,' says Rowan. 'Remember? When you fell on the tree. Aunty Isa bandaged you.'

'Yes. So I did.' Her mum puts her hands over her face, feeling it. 'Is it still sore?'

'It's okay,' says Frannie. 'It'll be okay.' Then she sits up slowly and rubs her eyes. The air in the room is cool with the morning, but beneath the covers it is still warm. 'I had a strange dream,' she says.

'What was it?'

'I'm just remembering,' says Frannie, and then her mother is silent for a long time.

While she is quiet, Rowan watches her. The light in the room is yellow. The sun lies in a fierce oblong on the bedcover. Everything seems very clear and still, as though the world were telling her to notice it.

'What day is it?' says Frannie eventually.

'Monday.'

346

'Is it? Gosh. It must be a school day then. Are we late?'

Rowan can feel a falling feeling inside her, like slipping down a small slope. 'Maybe,' she says. 'I think so. Probably. Yes.'

'Tell you what,' says Frannie, lying on her back. 'How about you don't go to school today?'

'Really?' says Rowan. 'In real life?'

'In real life, yes.' Her mother reaches out, and gently touches her cheek. 'Let's spend the day together, shall we? Let's have a day out of time.'

'A day out of time?'

'Yes.'

'What will we do,' says Rowan, 'instead of being in time?'

'I don't know . . . We'll have to wait and see.'

They walk side by side through the park, and Rowan slips her hand into her mother's. And it is not just the rough bandage Frannie has over her palm – she feels different. So does everything – the same but different. She cannot say why. She cannot say what. It is inside her mother and outside too, and inside her and outside too: the world feels fizzing, like a birthday, but not a birthday. It is part of the same feeling she had in the bedroom earlier, like something is going to happen. Like the world is asking her to notice it: the bluebells, for instance, which are at their most blue. She knows they will grow less blue soon, that soon they will grow crispy and die, but for now they are at their very bluest – so blue she can feel it in her body. As they cross the stream, under the sign for the Teddy Bears' Picnic, they hear music, voices, occasional laughter. Still, they don't speak. Still there is this sharp, fizzing feeling, as the path widens into Ned's clearing. There are three people sitting around the fire: Uncle Milo, Ned and Clara. They are all wrapped in blankets and drinking tea. Rowan has the sense of something having been finished. Or something just beginning. The smoke goes straight up into the morning sky. The sun pours through the trees and makes shapes on the ground, it lands on the jewel colours of the liquids in Ned's jars.

It is very peaceful in the clearing. There is music playing softly. They look like they are all friends – like something has happened between them, something good, and they are here in the after-wards of this good thing.

They stand facing the fire, hand in hand, Rowan and Frannie, waiting to approach.

'Hello, ladies,' says Ned when he sees them. 'To what do I owe this pleasure?'

To what do I owe this pleasure?

He speaks like a character in a book.

Frannie does not answer; instead, still hand in hand with Rowan, she comes to stand opposite Ned. Without speaking, as though someone or something has told them what to do without words, Milo stands too, and Clara. Last to stand is Ned, who takes his stick, and gets himself slowly to his feet.

Once he is standing, he straightens himself out. He passes his hands over his hair. Something in the way he stands shows that he, too, knows that something important is happening.

'Do you have a knife?' her mum asks Ned.

'I do, as it happens. I have one right here. Milo,' he says, 'would you mind passing that bundle over to me?'

Uncle Milo does as he asks, passing a cloth-wrapped bundle to Ned. Ned slowly unwraps it and Rowan sees a beautiful knife inside, its handle made from the antler of a deer.

'Here,' says Ned.

Her mother comes around the circle of the fire and takes the knife from him. Rowan watches her weigh it in her hand. She knows what it is: the knife made from the antlers of the deer that was killed for Philip. And she knows who made it for Ned: Jack.

She thinks about Jack. She knows he will be away from here by now. Maybe in Scotland already. She thinks about the deer dying. And what Jack said about honouring it. About the way he looked, with the deer on his back, half man, half deer; about things turning into other things: the deer into the knife, her grandfather into the soil. These thoughts have a tug to them, a low pull of sadness and excitement: thoughts she wants to unpack, to unroll, and spend time with. But for now, there is this startling moment happening in front of her, this blade flashing in the sunlight: Jack in the knife and the deer in the knife, both of them here too in the middle of this moment, in the middle of this glade.

Her mother gets down on one knee and kneels on the earth. She puts her palm flat against it and holds it there for a long time. As she does so, the air seems to grow still, as though the animals were listening, the animals and the trees, and all the creatures in the trees, above and below and seen and unseen, and her mother looks like a knight, Rowan thinks, in a fairy tale. Something from an ancient story.

The light is around her as her mother lifts the knife in her bandaged hand, and using the tip of its blade, traces a square into the earth, and then cuts deep into that square. She cuts out a clod and then she stands, holding the earth in her outstretched hands.

Rowan can see the layers in it: the crumbly mud at the top, the damp clotted mud beneath.

'It's yours,' says her mother to Ned. She speaks quietly, but her voice is strong. 'This wood is yours. All fifteen acres of it. It's been yours for fifty years. It's taken me till now to see it. I'll make it yours in deed and in trust. But for now: here.' She holds the earth in her two outstretched hands. And then, with a great leap of her heart, Rowan understands what her mother is doing: it is like the moment in the Puck book when Puck hands the clod of earth to the children in the field, and all the magic begins. 'It's taking seizin!' she says. 'Like in the book! The Puck book!'

Ned steps forward. He bends his head, and he takes the earth from Frannie. 'Thank you,' he says. Then Frannie bends to Rowan. 'Will you sit with Ned a moment,' she says. 'Stay by the fire,

349

I won't be long.' And so Rowan sits by the fire, while her mother goes to speak to Clara.

She watches them walk a little way from the glade, her mother speaking low and Clara listening, then Clara speaking and her mother listening. After a while, not too long, just as her mother said, they stop speaking. They reach out their hands to each other; Clara's hand is in her mother's, both of Frannie's bandaged hands clasped around it. Then her mother says something else and Clara nods quickly. Rowan cannot hear what is said. After a moment Uncle Milo goes over to join them too, he holds out his arms for her mother, and they hug. And all the while Rowan is sitting beside Ned, and neither of them is speaking, and she is thinking about how this is Ned's wood now, properly, now the taking seizin has happened: but how it never, as far as she can remember, was ever anything but.

They walk on together, Frannie and Rowan, to the edge of Ned's wood, and as they emerge, they see the house before them in the sunlight. Aunty Isa is standing at the top of the steps. When she sees them, she comes down to join them.

'Hello,' she says. 'What are you two up to?'

'We're having a day out of time,' says Rowan.

'Are you? That sounds good,' says Isa. 'Can I join you?'

Frannie looks down at Rowan. 'What do you think, Ro? Shall it be just us or shall we walk with Isa too?'

Rowan thinks about it. 'You can come for a bit,' she says.

Isa smiles. 'Thanks, Ro,' she says. 'I'd love that.'

The three of them walk together then, through the park, up towards the sentinel oak, and then further, to where the conifers used to be, taking the path into the wide glades, where there is no canopy and the sunlight falls in great pools, not dappled like in Ned's wood, but great warm pools of sun, and the young birch and the bracken and the oak saplings drink it up.

They walk slowly, side by side, not speaking, each of them

absorbed in their thoughts, in the flickering life and lives around them. Rowan sees the bluebells like a blue mist hanging over the forest floor. The fungus on the dead tree root that is so strange and yellow it looks like the skull of an animal, the bronze coppery heads of the unfolding bracken. She puts her finger to them; they are so alive-feeling, the life all coiled up in the spirals at their tips. Soon they will be so high that this path will be invisible.

All of these things take her attention, all of these things call her to them, and time moves differently, and she is in it and out of it at the same time.

Grace stands before the window, wrapped in her dressing gown. She has packed the very last of her things: her washbag, her handbag. The last small case of her clothes stands waiting by the door.

All that remains is to get dressed, to walk out of this room, down the stairs, and cross the park to her new home. But now the moment has arrived, she feels unmoored.

She has spent so long believing she deserves it – this final act – but does she, really?

Perhaps there are only a few more years left for her; perhaps she should stay, not disrupt, not insist on her own desires, instead let her daughter keep her cottage, her granddaughter keep her home?

She has made such a mess of it all: her marriage, her children, each of them in their own way unhappy. Perhaps there was never any other way it could have been, in this place so founded in cruelty. But it makes her terribly sad. That she failed them. That she wasn't stronger. That she didn't have the courage, all those years ago, to spirit her children and herself away.

She pulls the dressing gown around her. A figure is jogging across the park towards the house – Milo. And she feels the old, familiar catch of fear that something is wrong, that something is awry with her troubled son – he is moving so quickly, another figure following him. She comes closer to the glass, sees it is Ned, moving much more slowly, pulling something behind him; it looks like the wooden bier that carried Philip's coffin, and it seems to have something balanced on it. It is all quite the strangest of sights, and alarm rings in her blood.

Milo disappears beneath the portico, and soon she hears footsteps running up the stairs. There is a knock at her door. She moves away from the window as her son bursts into the room. 'Good morning, Ma.' He is breathless, his cheeks flushed, eyes bright. A smear of mud on his cheek.

She crosses the room towards him. 'Milo, what's happened? Is everything alright?'

'Good, Ma, it's good. I'm driving back to London,' he says. 'I'm taking Clara to the airport on the way. I only have a minute. I just wanted to come and say goodbye . . . And that I'm sorry . . . truly . . . for yesterday. I was drunk and stupid. And you didn't deserve it.'

'Well . . .' she says, taken aback. 'Thank you, Milo.'

Then he leans in and holds her, holds her properly, and there is no smell of alcohol on his breath, he smells only of outside, of woodsmoke and earth.

'And,' he says, releasing her, stepping back, 'I also came to deliver a message from Ned.'

'Oh?'

'He says to tell you he's by the oak. He's waiting.' Milo stands before her, clasps her hands in his. 'He's waiting for you.' He smiles, reaches out and touches her cheek, tenderly. 'I have to run,' he says. 'Clara has a plane to catch. See you soon?'

'Wait.' She reaches out – touches him on the arm. 'Wish Clara well from me.'

He smiles. 'Thanks, Ma. I will.'

And he is gone, running down the stairs, the sound of his footsteps reminding her of when he was a child, when he used to run like this, when he would throw himself around the house, fling open doors with his readiness for life. It is as though the child he was is running across her heart, has never stopped running across her heart. Her heart which is jumping now, feeling wayward, as she makes her way back over the uneven floorboards to the window, opens it and leans out. And Ned is there. He is standing by the sentinel oak, just as Milo said he would be.

He is looking towards her. It is hard to see properly, but it looks as though he has moved his stereo out into the park: his record player, his battery, all of them on the wooden bier. So that's what he was dragging up the hill.

And then, as if her appearance at the window is the cue, he lifts his hands in salute, and bends to the record player.

And it may be the stillness of the day, but the music is loud, louder perhaps than it has ever been – gentle piano chords, then a woman singing, low and plaintive:

Love me, love me, love me, say you do
Let me fly away with you . . .

She brings herself inside. Her skin feels taut, electric. She tells herself to breathe. She knows what she needs to do, but still her fingers are clumsy, as she goes to the small case and unzips it. There it is – yellow, the colour of the sun. The bib is heavy, crusted with embroidery, there are mirrors on the yoke, mirrors on the sleeves. Kneeling on the floor, Grace holds the dress to her, inhaling its deep scent of time and of earth and of faraway places: slightly sour but not so much. She stands, places the dress on the edge of the tapestried bed. She slips off her dressing gown, and pulls the dress over her head. The bodice and the sleeves are heavy but the skirt below is free, moving around her, against her, and the voice of the woman still sings outside her window, as she walks out of the bedroom, down the stairs, her bare feet stepping from cold stone to damp earth.

I am alive, she thinks.

As she walks it is as though the last poisoned parts of a spell or a curse or a dream are lifting. She is alive, simple miracle: alive and walking towards Ned. All of her life here, she understands, for fifty years now, a part of her has been walking down towards this man who has been waiting for her. Who waits for her. And her whole body is alive with the truth of him and the promise of him.

When she nears him, she stops.

And because there is music, she thinks, there should be dancing.

She is dancing. She is wearing a yellow dress. There are mirrors on the dress which catch the light – this morning light which seems to emanate from her – to shard itself against the green leaves of the oak. And it is here, he knows, the moment: it is now, it is then, it is here, and it is there. He can dip his hand in the current, in the river of time, and anoint himself with it. Fifty years is nothing – when this song has finished, he knows he must be brave. He needs to risk it all for a kiss, a kiss that never was, a kiss that might yet be.

But for now, he is simply watching her, watching her spiral, watching her arms reach to the sky.

After a while they go and sit in one of the big pools of sunlight. Frannie leans against the stump of an old conifer tree, and Rowan sits between her legs. Isa lies on the ground beside them, her eyes closed.

Rowan leans back, lets her weight settle against her mother's chest, her belly. She can feel that her mother does not want to go anywhere else or be anywhere else. There is no tugging inside her. No threads pulling her elsewhere. They are out of time, and they are together in this out-of-time place.

'It was good, Mumma,' she says to her. 'Giving the land to Ned. The taking seizin. It was the right thing to do.'

'Thanks, Ro.'

'What did you say to Clara?' says Rowan.

Aunty Isa opens her eyes, listening.

'Oh,' says Frannie. 'I said that I'd like to talk to her again, if she would let me. That I'd like her advice.'

Rowan listens. She can feel her mother's heart, behind hers. The steady strong beat of it. Just then, a bird flies past them, a flash of blue in its tail.

'What's that?' says Isa, sitting up.

'It's a jay,' says Rowan. 'Jays plant oak trees. Didn't you know?'

'No,' says Isa. 'Tell me.'

'They take acorns in the autumn, and they bury them, thousands of acorns to eat in the winter and the spring. But they bury so many they forget, and the ones they forget become trees. And so the jays plant the oak woods. They will have planted most of these saplings.'

They look around them – some of the oaks are knee-height, some are taller, their leaves almost but not quite unfurled. Rowan sees a flickering, a butterfly. A pearl-bordered fritillary or a tortoiseshell. It has landed on a bluebell and so she scrambles to her feet, and walks through the sunlight to see.

Frannie, her back against the stump, the sun on her skin, watches her daughter go.

One day, she knows, like her father before her, she will be gone. And when it is her own turn to go, to leave her daughter on this earth without her, she will tell her to look for her here, to come here, early on a morning in May, or at dusk, or on a morning like this. If she ever feels alone on the earth, and for as long as this glade stands, she will tell her to find her here; for it is here she is woven most deeply; woven with bracken and birdsong, with jay and with thrush.

'Fran,' says her sister, sitting beside her.

Frannie turns to Isa. She looks different, she thinks. She cannot say exactly how. And she is filled with sudden love for Isa – for her fierce little sister. 'Yes?'

'Have you thought about what you're going to do?'

Frannie is silent for a long while. 'I don't know,' she says. 'Not properly. Not yet. The estate is still desperately insecure, but . . . I think I'm going to sell the Reynolds. We may not qualify as a heritage property without it, but we will still have a chance.'

'Seriously?'

Frannie nods. 'There's a buyer. Simon thinks so. I don't know if they'll still want it, after what we know now, but I think they might.'

'And what will you do?' says Isa. 'If you do get the money from the sale?'

'I want the project to carry on. So much. But . . . I don't know. Do I even have the right to want that?'

'I think you do. You have the right to want it, Fran. But I'm not sure any of us have the right to assume it will.'

Frannie nods. 'But then, if there is any money, if we don't lose the house, I can start a fund. It's not really ours, is it? The money. It never really was.' She turns to her sister, holds out her hands. 'I need help,' she says. 'I need you. Will you help me, Isa? Please?'

Rowan is bending to the bluebell – to the butterfly perched on the frilled edges of the flower. It is not a fritillary after all, it's a tortoiseshell – more common, but no less lovely. She bends, watching, as it opens its wings; behind her she can hear the grown-ups, talking in their low voices. The warm current of feeling between them.

She turns her head to where they sit, turned to face each other, her mother's hands on top of Isa's, their foreheads resting on each other's.

They seem happy, she thinks. She can't remember when she

last felt this, her mother and her mother's sister happy together. And then this thought slides to the back of her consciousness, like the sounds of the voices, because most of her is taken up with looking at the wings of this creature – the grey-blue spots on the edges, the deep orange, its antennae moving gently as it tastes the sun.

Above her comes the small high drone of a plane. Rowan looks up, sees the sun flashing silver on its belly. She knows Clara will be flying in a plane soon too. And Rowan imagines her, up there, looking down at the estate, where they will all be so small to her, and then the land between here and the sea, all the green, strange, beautiful land beneath her flight.

Acknowledgements

My heartfelt thanks to the following people:

For helping to advise on aspects of the novel: Nicholas Draper, John Dwyer, Eliza Ecclestone, Tom Forward, Corin Stuart and especially Charlotte and Alex.

To my incredible agent and first and most trusted reader, Caroline Wood, and all the team at Felicity Bryan Associates.

To Helen Garnons-Williams for her editorial brilliance and integrity, and to Ella Harold and the team at Penguin General.

To Anna Stein at CAA.

To Edie Astley and the team at HarperCollins US.

Although I read many books both before and during the writing of *Albion*, Corinne Fowler's *Green Unpleasant Land: Creative Responses to Rural England's Colonial Connections* (Peepal Tree Press, 2020) and *Slavery and the British Country House* edited by Madge Dresser and Andrew Hann – available as a free download from English Heritage: https://historicengland.org.uk/images-books/publications/slavery-and-british-country-house/slavery-british-country-house-web/ – were invaluable as I began my research.